# BEYOND

At the center of Crassmor's world lay the Singularity, ruled by mysterious, never-aging King Ironwicca. It had been created by the Circle of Onn and was somehow guarded by the prophecies of the Tapestry.

Outside that lay the Beyonds, touching all the Realities, from which any manner of strays might wander. One day it might be Bill, who had been a god. The next it might be Little John and his band of not-so-merry men. And there were monsters and armies bent on conquest, to be met and overcome by the unfortunate knights who patrolled those changing, flux-haunted lands of the Beyonds.

But those dangers were expected. The real problem Sir Crassmor had to face lay in the very heart of the Singularity, and within the core of his own family. And nobody would listen to him or trust him!

**Also by Brian Daley**
*Published by Ballantine Books*


**THE DOOMFARERS OF CORAMONDE**
**THE STARFOLLOWERS OF CORAMONDE**


**HAN SOLO AT STARS' END**
**HAN SOLO AND THE LOST LEGACY**
**HAN SOLO'S REVENGE**


**TRON**

# A Tapestry of Magics
# Brian Daley

A Del Rey Book

BALLANTINE BOOKS • NEW YORK

For Chris—and
an unslain dragon

# — ACKNOWLEDGMENTS —

Thanks to Alice Marriott and her wonderful *Saynday's People* for an introduction to the Trickster. And to Jeff Pagano for tolerance and friendship. My gratitude to Hilton Berger, soldier and scholar, connoisseur of old liquor and young women, for his interest, advice, and friendship.

# — CONTENTS —

## PART I
## IN ALL PROBABILITIES . . .

## PART II
## "BY WHAT ETERNAL STREAMS . . ."

## PART III
## AS FATE WOULD HAVE IT . . .

*"And all my days are trances,*
*And all my nightly dreams*
*Are where thy grey eye glances,*
*And where thy footstep gleams—*
*In what ethereal dances,*
*By what eternal streams."*

TO ONE IN PARADISE
Edgar Allan Poe

# — PART I —

# IN ALL PROBABILITIES . . .

# Chapter 1

## AT HAZARD

**The dead man** lay face down in a patch of plants that looked like masses of translucent bulbs, one of the lizard riders' two-pronged steel darts standing out from his back. Like all the others in his army, he wore a uniform bearing the strange insignia:

卐

*A supremely unsatisfactory way to spend eternity*, Crassmor thought, stepping around him. *To be a corpse is to be nothing more than an addition to the general clutter.*

This one had lost helmet and field pack; his rifle, with fixed bayonet, rested near him. Crassmor saw no other corpses in the immediate area and concluded that the man had wandered away from his unit or been chased and harried by the lizard riders, who dearly loved such sport. The soldier had been dead for some time; tiny scavengers—multilegged mites—swarmed over him like a black, moving skin. A number of small, scuttling reptiles were feasting too.

Crassmor was relieved to see that the claw tracks of the savages' lizards were old. He wasn't far from the huge main camp, and it was absolutely imperative that he not be discovered. The aspirant knight led two horses, making his way around a thorn hill. He was very careful to keep well clear of the impenetrable tangle of thick, purple vines with their foot-long, poisonous spikes. The thorn hills harbored creatures of their own strange subworld, prey and predators alike, who'd adapted to the deadly thickets for shelter and sustenance. A swarm of little animals shaped like living airscrews flew by overhead.

Crassmor left the two mounts, Kort and Bordhall, to wait for him while he sought to edge around the thorn hill and look down at the enemy camp. Kort, the stallion, and his dam, Bordhall, extremely intelligent and perfectly trained, would wait there for him or come if he summoned them. They lowered their heads now to crop at the coarse, sparse clumps of red-yellow grass which grew intermittently all across the landscape. Crassmor had been grateful that the horses could forage here; the supply of feed he'd brought into the Beyonds was exhausted.

He lowered himself onto his stomach, the moss and grass rubbing against his haubergeon, his sword bumping against his back. He drew himself just around the edge of the looming thorn hill.

The barbarians seemed to be celebrating, judging from sounds of revelry drifting up from the enormous camp. *As well they might,* he thought to himself. From all signs, they were doing well in their war against the broken-cross soldiers and controlled most of the alien wilderness which now occupied this entire area of the Beyonds. The wilderness was part of the barbarians' home Reality, having come into existence in the Beyonds when they'd entered it. The lizard riders' shaman had opened a way from their home Reality into the Beyonds as an avenue of invasion. Their avowed purpose was to make their way through the Beyonds in order to conquer the Singularity, Crassmor's home.

Now the aspirant knight watched smoke curl up from victory fires and heard savage lizard riders roaring, singing, laughing, and shouting boisterously. He tried without success to spot his brother Sandur, the Outrider, among the warriors. Crassmor was not surprised; the camp stretched away toward the horizon, teaming with tens of thousands of men and their vicious reptilian mounts. He gnawed his lower lip and worried. He'd been staying as close to the camp as possible for days now, against the moment when his brother might need help in escaping. The previous evening, though, Crassmor had found himself with no choice but to withdraw into nearby hills and hide, as patrol activity around the camp was stepped up. More contingents had entered and left the place, apparently in connection with some major battle.

In his pouch was a small red bead of crystal, mate to one carried by Sandur. The crystals had been prepared by Daldoor, one of the Singularity's best artificers. The crystals had, when near enough to one another, the property of empathy. If one were shattered, Daldoor had assured them, the other would fall to dust. That was to be the signal from Sandur that he'd been forced to try to flee, or from Crassmor that the lizard riders had discovered him. Crassmor had checked his crystal only a short time before, finding it whole, but feared that in withdrawing he'd gone beyond the limits of the crystals' communion. The thought that Sandur's signal might have gone unregistered by Crassmor's crystal tormented the younger brother.

He crept backward now and stood up when he was safely out of sight of the camp. He was tall and slender, not quite nineteen years old. His movements were limber, but not as assertive as those of most Knights of Onn. His hair was a pale red, fine and thin, shaping him a high, white brow, making him look older than he was. His eyes were a watery blue and his face asthetic, not as strong of jaw as Sandur's. His facial hair was sparse; he followed the custom of shaving it, but did not have to do so often.

He had on a light haubergeon of woven mesh; the hilt of his sword, *Shhing*, a heavy cavalry rapier whose scabbard was held to his back by a broad leather baldric, extended up over his left shoulder. He wore a light blouse, durable buckskin jerkin and trousers, and knee-high boots. He'd removed his sallet helm with his House Tarrant device of a phoenix on its crest and left it fastened to his saddle on Kort. Now he put a hand on the pommel of his baskethilted parrying dagger and thought.

He dared go no closer to the camp. To be captured or even sighted would mean ruin. The thought of stealing into the enemy camp was dismissed at once. Crassmor had no reliable way to insure the well-being of Kort and Bordhall while he was gone, and the horses would be absolutely necessary if he and the Outrider were required to make a run for their lives. Crassmor was racked by the thought that he might have missed the signal of the crystals and that Sandur might be dead or undergoing the cruel treatments dispensed by the lizard riders to their captives.

Despairing, Crassmor found a moment in which to regret that some more capable, decisive man hadn't been chosen to accompany Sandur into the Beyonds. It was a pointless regret; there were only three people who could handle Kort and Bordhall adequately: Combard, their father, whose vested powers and affinities kept him tied closely to the Singularity; Sandur, who'd trained the horses under his father's watchful eye; and Crassmor, who'd been at Sandur's side through most of that training and had the horses grow used to his hand.

Crassmor dipped into the pouch at his belt, drawing out a tiny, padded bag. He loosened the carefully knotted drawstring and made to pour the crystal out onto his palm, as he had so often since Sandur had entered the camp. A stream of pulverized red powder flowed from the bag, some of it collecting on his leather-gloved palm, the rest carried away by the wind. Crassmor gaped at it in numb horror.

Then he broke his paralysis with a wordless cry. He threw himself onto his belly once more, peering down at the camp. He saw a figure dashing away from it at desperate speed. It didn't occur to him to doubt; he knew it was Sandur. Without quite realizing how he'd gotten there, Crassmor was in Kort's saddle, taking up his lance and long, triangular shield. He seized Bordhall's rein—though he little doubted that she would follow just as faithfully if he didn't—and was off.

It was no lizard rider sprinting full out from the camp of the barbarian hordes. They were easy to identify by their odd, wildly varied trappings and exotic weapons. The man running for his life across the gritty soil was dressed in the uniform Crassmor remembered, taken from one of the broken-cross soldiers captured by Singularity scouts. It was the black dress uniform of jodhpurs and tunic, high boots and red armband, of the—what had the captive called them?—Blackshirts. The fleeing man had lost, or left behind, his black cap. Loose soil sprayed into the air behind his flying heels. Now men came running from the tent lines of the lizard riders' camp, waving greatswords and two-pronged lances, seeking his life.

Sandur had a good start, though. Leading Bordhall downslope to rescue his brother, Crassmor saw that he was running in good form and seemed to be unharmed. The Outrider was tall, long-limbed, and brawny. The looks of Combard of Tarrant were more strongly evident in him than in Crassmor. Sandur's gritted teeth showed through a beard like new copper; his red mane flew behind him. He skirted a clump of strange shrubbery that resembled green glass fiddleheads, then hurdled a squat, needle-guarded, rock-hard water plant.

Sandur had a good lead on those who were chasing him and had never lost a footrace since coming of age. The barbarians yelled wild war cries; Sandur lengthened the distance between himself and them. Crassmor charged down at the gallop, leading Bordhall.

A new element entered the deadly race. A mounted lizard rider was pressing through the running mass of his fellows, making good headway. From the distance another barbarian bore in, a sentry. Whoops of encouragement went up from the running savages, urging their comrades on. The one coming through the pack brandished his lance, calling out threats to Sandur, narrowing the distance between them. With his other hand, he played on his control whistle, sending his mount into a battle frenzy. The whistle was pitched above human hearing, though its vibrations could be felt. Sandur could also hear the rider's mocking whoops and the hiss of his mount.

The Outrider whirled, dropping to one knee, yanking from its holster the weapon that went with the captive's uniform. Sandur had been forced to go into the camp armed with only the captive's pistol and dress dagger; bearing his own cut-and-thrust broadsword would have betrayed the masquerade. Sandur—and Crassmor—had disliked that part of the plan as much as any other; weapons and devices from other Realities had a way of malfunctioning or otherwise failing those not used to them.

Now Sandur held up the pistol, aiming at the lizard rider with little skill. The weapon cracked and cracked, its reports sounding flat in the open country. Beast and rider were so close that Sandur could scarcely miss. The beast threw its head back and shrilled as two bullets found its chest, another its pinkish underbelly as it reared. Its rider threw his head up too, the black plaits of his beard whipping, his horned headpiece flying loose, dropping his lance as a lucky shot hit him. Crassmor saw his brother turn and spy the other mounted barbarian.

Sandur brought the pistol around, making to fire, but no shots came. He worked the weapon's toggle once or twice. Giving up on the jammed weapon, he cast it aside and began running again. The lizard rider, this one wearing a fantastic animal mask, bore in at him. The lizards could move very quickly in straight dashes, but were less adept at turns. Sandur dodged to one side and the reptile pounded past, the lance missing him by inches.˙ The barbarian laughed and jeered, coming around for another attack.

Sandur had been so preoccupied with his flight that he hadn't seen his brother approaching, nor had the barbarian. Crassmor, steeling himself, rode in on an oblique course, dropping Bordhall's rein, knowing the mare would follow her training and use good sense.

The lizard rider saw Crassmor and tried to bring his lance around. The barbarian dropped his control whistle in his haste to snatch up a gleaming, polychrome lizard-hide shield from his saddlebow. The lance had two heads, long and bright and wavy-bladed in the fashion Crassmor had heard called flamboyant. Crassmor crouched, gripping his own sturdy lance, shield braced, clutching with his knees and leaning in to strike at what he prayed to be the right moment. He did it all with a feeling of unreality, pushed to this sudden, madly determined attack by danger to Sandur. Both lances missed, but the barbarian, taken by surprise, nearly lost his saddle in the effort to avoid Crassmor's blow. Like all of his kind that Crassmor had seen, the man was dark-haired and light-skinned, somewhat shorter than Crassmor, but powerfully built.

The man jerked hard on his lizard's nose reins, whirling the beast around painfully. Crassmor could smell the grease and sweat on him, see every detail of body harness, bracelets, and armbands, and smell the reek from his mount's femoral pores. The lizard was a big, scarred brute with keeled, pointed scales, gleaming black and brown on its back and sides, green on its underbelly. It snapped at the horse. Kort reared, nimbly avoiding the bite, striking out with sharp-shod hooves, opening a long gash in the great prefrontal scales on the lizard's snout. The creature shied back; Crassmor withdrew.

Sandur was ahorse now. He snatched up his shield, which Crassmor had fastened to Bordhall's saddle. Sandur had no lance, though, since it would have made awkward carrying for Bordhall. Crassmor reined around, preparing to gallop for it. Sandur blocked his way, yelling, "Give me your lance!"

The lizard rider had drawn back for a moment, taken by surprise at Crassmor's appearance, unsure if this were some ambush. The barbarian would see the truth of it in a moment, though, and there were now other sentries converging on them, more lizard riders streaming from the camp. Crassmor shouted, "Sandur, you can't—"

*"Lance!"* he roared. His eyes, darker than Crassmor's, flashed. He guided Bordhall with his knees, holding out his free hand. Crassmor had seen this look on his brother's face before. The Outrider had been mocked and nearly killed by an alien savage; he would not stand for that. Used to obeying, Crassmor passed the weapon over. Sandur heeled Bordhall's sides. She launched herself at the barbarian, who in turn came at the knight. Crassmor divided his attention between the impromptu joust and the oncoming reinforcements, agonizing.

Knight and lizard rider came together with a crash. The shaft of the two-pronged lance splintered. Sandur's spear drove through the barbarian's guard, lifting him back out of his saddle, his sandaled feet driven from his tasseled stirrups. The lance head punched through an ornamental pauldron made from insect carapace, passing through the barbarian's shoulder and lodging there. Falling, the lizard rider pulled the lance from Sandur's grip. The reptilian mount hunkered away from Bordhall, its blood still flowing from the wound Kort had given it.

There was no time to recover the lance. At Sandur's subtle command, Bordhall reared, turning away, leaving the bleeding enemy and his wounded mount where they were.

The other lizard riders were closing in, already casting their darts. Crassmor could feel the silent birring of their control whistles as they urged their animals to battle frenzy. "Come!" Sandur bade as he raced past.

He needn't have worried. Crassmor was already digging heels into Kort. The pair fled up the long rise with precious little lead. Kort and Bordhall were fresh, though; faster than the reptiles. Crassmor was thankful that the horses had seen good use and were in trim, and that the coarse grass hadn't put any weight on them. There wouldn't be much opportunity to stop and tighten saddle girths, not for some time to come. They topped the rise to find the way open; their lead over the vengeful savages increased.

*All of which would be wonderful,* Crassmor realized in dismay, *if we weren't headed in the wrong direction!*

They rode hard through the long afternoon, sometimes over bare ground which would hold their tracks, sometimes over thick, springy, tough plants or hard soil which wouldn't. This part of the Beyonds was lit, as was the lizard riders' home Reality, by a purple-white sun.

They broke their trail many times on stone and on shifting sand meadows. They made for hillier, broken country where they would be more difficult for pursuers to spy. They hid twice in folds in the land, deep washes from the brief rainy season, as large enemy units rode in the direction of the main camp, not looking for Singularity fugitives.

Toward evening they came to a place Crassmor had found previously, a clearing like a little inlet in the middle of one of the thorn hills, reachable through a narrow passage. Working carefully with sword and gauntlets, Crassmor had managed to put together a sort of screen to block the entrance. There they stopped.

Crassmor had brought along a change of clothes for Sandur, and his sword and shield and bow. Sandur retained the boots and jodhpurs of the Blackshirt officer. He threw aside the black leather belt-and-shoulder-strap harness and began unbuttoning his tunic. Crassmor eyed the discarded harness. Both holster and sheath were empty. "When you fired that weapon I was surprised, brother. I didn't think the savages would let you keep the thing."

Sandur grinned, tossed the tunic aside, and began pulling at his black necktie. "They didn't. The dagger named *Solingen* they left me, accounting it no great danger. The pistol the shaman took. He'd seen those devices before."

Crassmor was puzzled. "Where, then, is the *Solingen?*"

Sandur had cast aside the tie, following it with the brown shirt. He was ducking into a quilted gambeson. "In the shaman, last I saw. There was much going on when I killed him; I didn't have time to recover it." He was lacing the gambeson, settling it comfortably with great care. A wrinkle or fold could become extremely irritating under armor. Sandur grimaced. "I recovered that *Luger* thing, though, and it let me down. A lesson: alien weapons are not for the likes of us, not if we can avoid them. It's not the first time I almost got killed using one. I mislike them."

"But the shaman?"

Sandur was grim. "Smelled me out. He was the First shaman, their best, the one who opened the way from their home Reality into the Beyonds. He suspected me all along. He'd asked me more than once about the red crystal I carried, Daldoor's. I said it was only a lucky piece; the Warlord accepted that."

Sandur was shrugging into the mail shirt now and adjusting his gorget. "But the shaman must have divined something about the crystal. He was canny enough; almost kept the lizard riders from making war on the broken cross."

But war there had been, Crassmor knew. He'd seen furious

engagements fought all across this alien terrain, overwhelming hordes of lizard riders against the destructive power of the broken-cross weapons. The army of the broken cross had wandered into the Beyonds by accident; much of it was mechanized, though much of it was horse-drawn. Its arrogant commanders had shown nothing but hostility for the envoys of the Singularity. The lizard riders had come into the Beyonds purposely to conquer the Singularity.

The Singularity had become aware of both forces groping their way through the uncertain environs of the Beyonds. It had been Sandur's plan to set them at each other's throats, to eliminate them both before they reached that stable island at the center of the Beyonds, the Singularity.

It had been the Outrider, with a force of the King's Borderers, who'd captured a small peace party of broken-cross soldiers on their way to the camp of the lizard riders, a miraculous stroke of luck. Instead of the real emissaries, Sandur had gone in, posing as a turncoat. He'd warned that the broken cross meant to war on the barbarians and asked sanctuary and rewards, pretending disaffection with his "own" side. With what he'd managed to learn from his captives, he'd made his claims seem true.

It had been a good plan, perhaps the only way to save the Singularity. By guile and force of personality and prowess at arms, Sandur had won the tentative trust of the invaders' fearsome Warlord.

"The shaman asked to see the crystal for a moment; I dared not refuse," Sandur explained. His cut-and-thrust broadsword was buckled around his hips now, along with his parrying dagger. He was pulling on elbow-length gauntlets banded and reinforced with metal lames. "He knew it was something mystic; he smashed it. He'd foxed me. We were alone, his only mistake." He set his sallet helm on his head, leaving its visor up. "I knew that would bring you running, so I had no time to spare."

Crassmor felt pride in his brother's confidence in him, but a twinge of guilt too at how close he'd come to letting Sandur down when he'd withdrawn into the hills. Before he could admit to that, though, Sandur went on.

"So I left *Solingen* in the shaman and could lay hands on no other weapon but the pistol."

The rest Crassmor knew. "Will the broken cross now make common cause with the barbarians?"

Sandur shook his head. "There has been too much killing on both sides, too many deaths among the hordes of the barbarians, which their clansmen won't let go unavenged. There is no trust left between those two armies." He remounted.

"Who will win?" Crassmor wanted to know, as he followed suit.

Sandur reached out with his sword to flick aside the thorn screen. "If we are lucky, neither. I think, though, that we could handle the broken cross more easily than the savages." He seemed distant, concerned for a moment. Crassmor hadn't seen misgiving on his brother's face very often; this afternoon it had been there many times.

"We are in exactly the wrong place," Sandur went on. "This war sprawls in all directions. It's sudden and fast-moving; I've never seen anything quite like it." He almost smiled then, realizing what he'd said. "But then, you already know that."

Indeed. Crassmor had done much dodging and hiding during his wait for his brother. There would be a great deal more of it before they could make their way back through the shifting Beyonds to the Singularity. Too, it would be across the barbarians' type of country. Crassmor looked up at what seemed a green cloud, caught by the lowering sun, and saw that it was actually a long, cohesive drift of spores, like smoke.

"I'm in exactly the wrong place," he seconded his brother sourly, having no taste for heroics.

Sandur laughed. "Not to my way of thinking. Or at least, not earlier this afternoon."

That gave Crassmor a warm feeling. They'd managed to break with their pursuers, at least for the time being. Traveling at night, they might evade watching eyes, and the lizards were inclined to be less active after dark.

\*     \*     \*

Crassmor pulled his scarf tighter around his face to keep out choking, windblown sand and the stench of burning vehicles and flesh. He and Sandur looked around them at the dozens of broken-cross bodies littering the battlefield.

It wasn't the first scene of pitched combat that they'd seen. The fight here had been particularly fierce, though. *And to the winners?* Crassmor mulled. *A few acres of alien wilderness in the Beyonds, which they promptly vacated in order to search for more enemies.* He wondered if these broken-cross soldiers had even had any idea what the conflict was about.

He gave Kort a touch of his spurs to catch up with Sandur. The lathered horse quickened just as Sandur drew rein at the crest of a little hillock and stood up in his stirrups to peer through swirling sand for signs of pursuit. Crassmor pulled his scarf aside to yell over the wind, "Is there sign of them?" He reached right hand over left shoulder nervously to assure himself of *Shhing* at his back. His stiffened haubergeon, clogged with windblown grit, hampered him.

Sandur, squinting into the wind, shook his head, then pulled up his own scarf. "But that means nothing; this storm is little better than night."

Crassmor nodded unhappily. The wind had kicked up all the loose sand in this part of the Beyonds; visibility varied unpredictably from near-normal to end-of-the-nose. "Still, that is not without its redeeming aspects," Sandur finished.

"Forgive me if I'm less than cheery about it," Crassmor grumbled.

Sandur added, "Those riding lizards lack the stamina of horses, most especially of these two beneath us. Still, Bordhall and Kort have seen hard service. Would that we had time to rest them."

"Would that I had a more sedentary brother!" Crassmor hollered back. The Outrider guffawed.

Crassmor surveyed the scene. Metal vehicles, some of them ranging up in size to that of a small cottage, had been gathered in a hasty circle at whose center the pair had paused. Some of the machines were already partially buried by sand; smoke wafted from the interiors of several, to be pulled away quickly by the wind. Everywhere were signs of the furious hand-to-hand combat that had ended the engagement as it had the others the brothers had come across.

The lizard riders, victorious, had borne away their slain, of course. The soldiers who wore the broken cross lay on all sides, their blood blackening the sand. Various scavengers were at work; a flock of four-winged creatures had taken to the air at the Tarrants' approach. The bodies had been stripped of jewelry and the odd decoration; the barbarians had no use for the machines or equipment of their beaten foemen.

"The same thing happened here," Sandur concluded, sweeping his gauntleted hand at the slaughter. "The broken-cross men had their way of it—at first." Witness to that, the ground was littered with the shining metal cylinders, large and small, from the spent rounds of the weapons of the slain. The mechanized soldiers' equipment had finally failed, their weapons silent for lack of ammunition, their vehicles halted for want of fuel. Their supply lines had, of course, been severed when they'd wandered from their own Reality into the Beyonds. Eventually, through sheer weight of numbers and unflagging hatred, and with weapons that never needed reloading, the barbarians had annihilated them.

Sandur's face held somber despair; Crassmor knew a current of sympathy. The Outrider wasn't mourning the fallen, who'd had their own dreams of conquest, but rather the failure of his plan. By every sign the pair had seen over the last two days as they'd evaded elements of both armies and tried desperately to work their way back to the Singularity, the lizard riders' host was still enormous. The barbarians were regrouping, after their extermination of the broken cross, to conquer the Singularity.

Crassmor's troubled preoccupations with what that meant for the Home Plane was broken by his brother's voice. "It's clearing."

A pale nimbus in the sky was their first hint of sunlight that day. They could see little more than a mile across the shifting wasteland. There was no sign of the invaders.

*Invaders,* Crassmor thought. Wanderers into the Beyonds were almost always alone or in small groups, bewildered and disoriented. It took them time to apprehend where they were—or rather, were not. And while those who couldn't or didn't wish to find their way home again often made their way to Dreambourn, the Singularity's capital, it usually took some time. The stern, well-organized lizard riders, though, promised to lose no time invading the Charmed Realm, the Home Plane—the Singularity. They warred without quarter, their numbers were vast, and they considered attrition their ally.

The way to the Singularity now lay open before them. For the hundredth time, Crassmor wondered why the diverse warriors of the Singularity hadn't already come forth to do battle. Surely King Ironwicca must know by now that Sandur's strategem had failed?

"Best to rest the horses," Sandur decided. He dismounted tiredly; they'd been in the saddle long before the uncertain daylight had come. Neither of them was certain just how long ago that had been; the passage of a day, here in the fluxes of the Beyonds, was subject to change and distortion.

Crassmor took his lower lip between his teeth, tasting grit. He was not yet an appointed knight and had taken on this duty because no one else could have done what was needed. "Do you think we've gotten clear, then?" he asked. "Is it safe?"

Sandur, gathering saliva only with effort, spat sand. "No, but neither is it any more dangerous. Even Kort and Bordhall must rest."

True enough; the horses had already saved the brothers' lives three times. When Sandur had first entered the barbarians' camp, it had been with the knowledge that the lizard riders and their animals had developed a fondness for eating horseflesh. The practice also lessened a captive's chances of escape, since the invaders' riding beasts responded only to their strange control whistles. Thus, Crassmor's role in things. Sandur's poor saddle horse, the one on which he'd entered the camp, had been served up at a feast by the Warlord. In a way, that had been beneficial. Convinced that

Sandur had no means of escape, the Warlord had been that much more inclined to believe him.

Now Crassmor felt his face flush, hoping it didn't show under the caked sand. "I didn't mean—"

Sandur, securing his horse's rein at the gun carriage of a silent eighty-eight-millimeter fieldpiece, interrupted. "If you're not disturbed at the prospect of encountering those wild men, you damned well ought to be." He set hands at the small of his back and arched his spine. "I know *I* am."

Crassmor knew his brother was being kind. He sniffed. "I am altogether disinclined to closer acquaintance with them, never doubt it!"

Sandur barked a quick laugh as Crassmor dismounted. "Father will be proud of you; no Knight of Onn would be slow to boast this deed." Crassmor half-smiled in embarrassment; that pride was something he very much desired.

The warmth he felt for his brother seemed to Crassmor a strange thing here in this laager of the dead. He wondered again who these men had been, whence they'd come, what their Reality had been like. The wind broke his thoughts with its susurrus, the sand with its hiss. His gaze went back to the open stretch they'd put behind them. Cold compressed his middle.

He spoke as calmly as he could, determined that the Outrider would hear no quaver in his voice. "There; they come."

# Chapter 2

# IN FLIGHT

**Sandur whirled where** he stood, having been studying the terrain ahead. A sizable war party was racing directly toward them. The barbarians themselves were difficult to discern well at this distance, but the darting gait of the big riding lizards was unmistakable. "Those beasts probably have our scent by now," he told his brother.

"That's all of us they're going to get." Crassmor frowned, less confident than he sounded. Kort and Bordhall were possessed of remarkable strength bred into them by Combard of Tarrant; on the other hand, the lizard cavalry looked fresh.

Sandur slapped Crassmor's back and vaulted into the saddle. "Come! This will take a bit of doing. We'd best be at it." Bordhall, sensing what was to come, made a little caracole.

Crassmor resumed his saddle with less animation, aware that he was not as confident or bold, that he wasn't the Outrider. A last look back told him that the lizard riders were looming larger already. Their mounts' squat legs carried them along at good speed, the clawed feet throwing up sand. With tongue clicks, spurs, and reins, the brothers quickly got their horses moving.

*My first deed of errantry,* Crassmor mused, *and my last as well? This derring-do is even less appealing than I'd thought.* If he'd said it aloud, he knew, Sandur would have instructed him sharply to keep his mind on his riding. This he did anyway.

Bordhall and Kort galloped hard, necks straining, performing as no other horses could have after the exertions of the past two days. Crassmor bent low over Kort's neck, his stomach hard against the saddle's high pommel, and stayed well up behind his brother. Thoughts came to him unbidden.

Combard had been absolutely opposed to Sandur's plan and had spoken harsh words against Crassmor's proposed participation. That had to do with the old man's lack of faith in his younger son's martial spirit. Too, there had been Crassmor's adolescent irresponsibility, with a period of fairly frequent peccadilloes and predisposition toward sins of the flesh. Combard hadn't forgiven those or been prepared to recognize that Crassmor's devotion to Sandur outweighed all else. In the end, it had been Combard's deep love for his first-born son that had changed the old man's mind. That Sandur would try his plan, entering the barbarian camp, was certain; Ironwicca, the King, had set him the task when Sandur had proposed it.

And, should the Outrider's life depend on the endurance and speed of a contingency horse, it wouldn't do, in Combard's mind, for that horse to be any but Kort or Bordhall. Reluctantly, Combard accepted; Crassmor had gone into the Beyonds.

Bit by bit, after Sandur's escape, the two had worked their way around the huge clash of savages and mechanized army, to discover that the plan had failed. The lizard riders had slaughtered the broken-cross soldiers and were ready to advance once more.

The sand had closed in again. The brothers pounded along, listening to their horses blow for breath. They came to the top of a long, gradual slope. Sandur drew rein, scanning, squinting. "That way!" His muffled voice came as he pointed off to the right.

Crassmor never questioned his brother's decisions, least of all in matters of action. Anyone native to the Singularity had a certain sense for access routes to it and its location relative to the Beyonds. The Outrider's was more acute than most, though, his ties to their homeland more reliable. The horses blew foam from their lips. "Wish you'd stayed home?" Sandur asked.

"Wish the lizard riders had!" Crassmor countered. His

reward was Sandur's full laugh behind the scarf; it was enough. They set off again.

Without warning the turbulent sand parted before them. They were confronted with lizard hide, with exotic barbarian ornamentation and riding tack, with glittering reptilian fangs, and most of all with bright, wavy-bladed weapons. It seemed to Crassmor that the world was suddenly filled with bloodthirsty, heavily armed savages.

There were, in reality, only three men in the patrol that had happened across them. Before the barbarians, who were as startled as the two brothers, could react, Sandur had swept out his broadsword and ridden in at them, whirling the blade, whooping through the scarf.

*There! There is the difference between us, nothing I'll ever change,* Crassmor thought. Teeth on edge, scalp prickling, he wished there were some other way out. No use looking for a line of least resistance, though, he saw; Sandur was already in the thick of things. Crassmor reached his right hand up over his left shoulder, drew *Shhing,* and went in after.

The first barbarian wore an amber gem clipped to each nostril, a choker made of fangs, and a helm of enameled leather and ivory. He was bringing his lance into line while his red and gray mount hissed and showed a red, forked tongue. The lance was studded with glass beads and decorated with colorful plumes which the wind tugged. Twin prongs glittered cruelly as Sandur set on the man. The barbarian's face still held a look of surprise.

The broadsword chopped; the two-pronged lance head went flying, severed from its shaft. Sandur turned the same slash into a backhand and hacked with that amazing strength that had seen him through so many duels. The lizard rider yelped, parried—barely—with the remainder of his lance, then threw himself back for his life. The slash only opened a line of wound across his chest, parting a strap of his bejeweled war harness. He was all but unmounted.

Sandur laughed his wildest laugh, then batted his opponent with the flat of his blade, a kind of generosity in the heat of battle that was characteristic of him and always astounded Crassmor. The barbarian howled as he was thwacked in the helm, bits of ivory flying from it; he tumbled out of his lizard-hide saddle as if hit by lightning.

Horses and lizards hissed, kicked, snapped, and feinted. The two species hated one another even more than did their respective riders. The other two barbarians were closing on Sandur, having overcome their surprise. He turned to engage the closest, mindful to keep that one between himself and the next. The fighting had begun so suddenly that the barbarians had lacked any time to pipe their mounts into suitable battle frenzy with their control whistles. Now that the two brothers were upon them, the lizard riders had no thought for anything but combat, compelled to direct their mounts with spurs and lip reins alone.

With the second lizard rider, there was no question of cleaving a lance shaft. Sandur charged, trusting to his own prowess for timing. The barbarian wore a headpiece shaped like a bird of prey and his face was a swirl of tattoos. The lance head eluded Sandur's shield, but the knight's broadsword hilt came up between its needle-sharp tines. It was an awkward parry for the horseman; the lizard rider could exert considerably more leverage.

Sandur's knees clenched hard to the barrel of his horse. The powerful Bordhall dug in as she'd been trained, transmitting force to her rider. The lizard shrilled, its great weight conveyed to its rider via its high-cantled saddle. Weapons trembled against one another, but the Outrider's renowned strength saw him through. Though both men were in danger of being unhorsed it was the barbarian who broke contact first, reining his mount away.

Sandur snagged the lance head with a twist of his blade; with the threat of the broadsword before him, the barbarian let go of the weapon to draw a wavy-bladed sword from his saddle scabbard. He and Sandur collided again, their blades striking sparks. The lizard missed a bite at Bordhall; her hooves battered at its plated head.

Crassmor had perforce reined up at his brother's first impact so as not to slam into Bordhall's croup. That saved his life. The third enemy, coming at him obliquely, missed with his lance, surprised by the pause. The savage drew back to thrust. By that time Crassmor had thrown up his shield, taking the stroke in safety. Fear clamored in him; he thought, *Would that I had time to entertain a full-blown panic!*

The lizard's forked tongue and its master's lance made a weird symmetry. The man wore a gorget of steel lozenges and a helm adorned with long, insectile antennae. His plumed lance and his beast's blue and red hide filled Crassmor's eye for an instant. Then training took over. Crassmor got in at close quarters, ending the barbarian's advantage of lance length. The reptile's rank scent was thick in his nostrils. He managed to grab the lance shaft with his gauntleted shield hand. The lizard rider had no choice but to release the weapon, barely eluding *Shhing*'s edge. Then the barbarian pulled forth a sicklelike shortsword and swung.

Crassmor turned the sickle's first blow handily with his shield, launching a counter slash. *Shhing*'s greater weight carried the curved blade back, though that gave Crassmor no great confidence. He had an unshakable faith in misfortune.

His caution was justified. With his left hand, the lizard rider snatched a steel dart from the bandolier of them hanging from the big, gem-set horn of his saddle. He tossed the twin-tined dart underhand, intending to take the other in the throat as he leaned forward for a sword stroke. Crassmor's extreme wariness had him alert; he saw the palmed dart and ducked aside to hear it zip past his neck. On his recovery he turned *Shhing* edge on. The heavy, cup-hilted cavalry rapier caught the barbarian at the crook of his elbow, just above a vambrace of stiffened lizard hide and bronze bossing and below the thick armlet banding his bicep.

The barbarian screamed as his blood flowed. He swung madly at his foe to keep Crassmor from following up on the hit. The lizard backed away in response to its master's spurrings, hissing its anger, making Crassmor miss his next cut. Kort went after the lizard once more at Crassmor's urging. Crassmor parried the barbarian's wild swing, then went for the opening in his guard.

Only the lizard rider's frantic effort to throw himself aside saved him. *Shhing* sliced through more plummage and accouterment than flesh. The lizard rider lost his seat; the reptilian mount paused for a moment, uncertain what its master wanted of it. Crassmor leaned, as much from nervousness as from enthusiasm, with a vigorous thrust. He only managed to prick the barbarian lightly as the man tumbled from his beast.

Sandur rained blow after blow on the other enemy, parrying the blows that came in answer. Crassmor hewed at the man he'd just unhorsed. The two riderless reptiles were racing off across the sand, injured, not heeding the control whistle being piped by the man on foot. That barbarian evaded a final swing by Crassmor to run off after his beast. Crassmor turned to help his brother.

Just then Sandur penetrated the last enemy's guard to strike home. The man dropped his weapon, clutching at the wound in his chest. Dark blood coursed between his fingers and down his harness of red leather and hammered brass. The scaly mount bolted away, aware that its rider no longer directed it. The barbarian slid from his saddle to land in an unmoving heap.

The dust settled as Crassmor watched one lizard rider running off after his mount. The second lay stunned, the third dead or dying. Sandur's face was set as he clashed sword back into scabbard. Crassmor slowly emulated him. The younger brother was about to essay some remark when there came from a distance the war whoops of the larger party, still in pursuit. The sand squall was clearing; the lizard riders had drawn frighteningly close.

"Ride for your life!" Sandur called. They raced off side by side, coaxing last bursts of energy from Bordhall and Kort. Crassmor, bent low over Kort's neck, risked a look backward under his armpit. The war party was gaining; the freshness of its lizards outbalanced the horses' natural advantage of speed.

The older brother led the way into a broken area of chasms and ravines. Crassmor wanted to protest, alarmed at the possibility of the barbarians' trapping them with their backs to some wall or cliff. He held his tongue, though, trusting in his brother. The sounds of pursuit reached them even over the drumming of hooves, their own panting, and that of their horses. Sandur yelled something that Crassmor couldn't catch, something that seemed to hold a note of increased alarm.

Sandur veered suddenly; Crassmor kept up close behind. The Outrider reined in hard and his brother did the same, Bordhall and Kort skidding to a stop with hooves chopping and plowing the sandy soil at the very brink of a chasm.

There was no seeing the bottom of it in the reduced light; it was umber dusk down there. The rim stretched away right and left as far as they could see. The far side was better than five paces away, Crassmor saw, though it was somewhat lower than the one on which they'd stopped. They'd come to the narrowest point in the chasm; Crassmor decided that Sandur must have spotted it from the high ground back at the dead men's laager. Then Crassmor realized his brother's plan with abrupt dread.

"Names of assorted gods' vitals!" Crassmor screamed at his brother. " 'Rider, even Kort and Bordhall can't—we'll be killed if we try this jump!"

"And nothing less than that if we don't," Sandur pointed out calmly. "Did you not hear the battle pipes? That's *him* back there, their Warlord himself. We won't elude him any other way; those lizards aren't much as jumpers."

"And our horses hold no great promise as birds!" Crassmor spat.

Sandur was peering back at the rapidly growing figures of the war party, wearing an expression of doubt. Crassmor sensed in his brother a misgiving he'd never thought to see there, one raised by the Warlord. It shocked the younger brother; he would have sworn that Sandur feared no man alive, not even Ironwicca the King.

Sandur reached out to seize his brother's arm with a grip that hurt. "No time for quibbling! We must!" His tone softened. "Trust me."

Crassmor assented to that, adding ruefully, "Here's what errantry gains me!"

Sandur was turning his horse with a reckless laugh. "Pray it's all you get!" Then he was heading back toward the lizard riders, who, not far off, had broken into a ragged charge. Crassmor followed, seeing that Kort and Bordhall would need a long start for the jump.

It was terrifying in every degree to charge straight at the oncoming barbarians, watching the distance close as panic mounted. Sandur reined in as dual-tined darts began ranging on them. The lizard riders could be seen blowing their intricate, silvery control whistles.

The Tarrant brothers brought their mounts around and galloped back the way they'd just come as darts fell all around them. They could hear the mad trills of the war party; yowls of triumph signaled the lizard riders' certainty that they were about to take their prey. Crassmor and Sandur roweled their horses: Bordhall and Kort, true to their bloodlines and training, surged forward with all their speed and power.

The chasm came up all at once. Bordhall carried Sandur into the air. Crassmor had to force himself not to hesitate or draw rein at the last instant, but he'd taken the Outrider as his exemplar. Kort used the muscles of his great neck and shoulders to aid in the jump, as those of his back and loins gathered. Crassmor, up in his stirrups, seconded the horse's extension of neck with his own arms and chest. Kort bore him after his brother, and they were over empty space.

Bordhall landed fairly well; she'd done less carrying than Kort on this sally into the Beyonds. Kort's back, convex when he'd made the jump, now became concave under Crassmor. The stallion's forequarters absorbed the first shock of landing; he barely made the opposite edge. Kort teetered for a moment, whinnying, eyes rolling in fear, rear hooves digging for purchase, sending bits of gravel and soft sand spilling into the abyss. More darts fell around Crassmor. The second or two during which his horse flailed on the edge of eternity seemed a century. Crassmor dared not return to his saddle; he crouched in his stirrups, feeling a peculiar emptiness in his middle.

Then hooves found good purchase; Kort thrust himself onto solid footing. Several more darts dug into the ground where he'd been. Crassmor cantered to the right, where the chasm widened sharply, holding his shield aloft. The lizard riders, when they reached the brink of the chasm, waved weapons and cursed at the brothers; none cared to attempt the crossing on their bulky, truculent animals. The pursuers set off to parallel their quarry, who now followed the chasm's rim at a prudent remove. The barbarians continued blowing their control whistles, keeping their beasts in blood-thirsty arousal. The range being long for their darts, the barbarians' fire gradually stopped, as they tired of losing their missiles to the chasm.

A birring of battle pipes made the horsemen pause. On the opposite rim, the barbarians drew aside in haste, making way for their Warlord. It was the first time Crassmor had seen the man. He then understood Sandur's worry and wariness.

The Warlord was astride a crimson and black lizard of unusual size, its hide inset with flashing sequins and precious stones, its saddle horn carved from a single piece of agate in the form of a serpent reared to strike. He wore a bib of ruby pendants, a headband of twisted gold, and a corselet of silver lamés and green lizard skin. He towered above his men, but was thickset for all of that, with a scarred, broken-nosed face and brows that were a single black curve. What parts of him were uncovered by oddments of armor, harness, ornaments, and trappings were thick with muscle. His hair was dark but streaked with gray, bound with clips of bone and shell. He carried a lance longer than those of the men around him, handling it as if its weight meant nothing.

It was the look on his face, a fury that blasted across the gap at Sandur, like a physical force, that brought home with greatest impact the sheer danger of the man. His words, when they came, seemed to rattle the very air. Yes; an enemy to raise misgivings even in the Outrider.

"You! Sandur! Traitor!" The Warlord's lance shook in his hand; its war streamers and pennons snapped and swayed. "This is no escape, it is *reprieve!* Do you hear me?"

Sandur sat his horse as a statue might. "I hear you, Ravager."

"Yes, Ravager! It is Ravager! Bringer of slaughter! Emptier of Lodges! I am the Blight Who Ends Life!"

Crassmor shivered at the anger in that voice, believing all that the Warlord said. "Look for no safety in your Singularity," Ravager went on. "Word has come to me; one of my hordes has already thrown down your best fighters, the flower of your armies!"

The Warlord spat in the sand and laughed harshly, without joy; the men around him muttered their malign satisfaction with that. The Warlord's riding lizard shifted its weight and flickered forth its forked red tongue, still stirred for killing by the control whistles, looking about it for a victim. Ravager said, "The broken-cross soldiers are all dead now. I still have the Horde of D'nith and the Horde of Rong, the Militia of Kek and the Corps of Booth the Mighty, the Five Armies of Chula and all the others who ride to my command! Your lords of the Singularity will be under my heels in days, you *twice traitor!*"

Sandur's face tensed when he heard the accusation again. Ravager's mount stirred; the Warlord quieted it with an angry jab of his prick spurs. Such was his strength that the beast squealed in pain and then became still.

"Come back and fight me!" Ravager challenged. Sandur only stared at him.

Crassmor wondered what was going through his brother's mind; no one had ever used that word on the heir of House Tarrant. "My, such odium," Crassmor murmured, but Sandur gave no sign of having heard.

The Bringer of Slaughter wasn't through. "You are so eager to protect your home, coward? Come, strike down Ravager, and your Singularity is safe! Well? Liar! Coward! Come back and fight!"

The Warlord took from the arming belt at his middle a small rod, whittled from some dun-colored wood, intricate and inset in a manner that Crassmor couldn't quite make out, banded with beaded cord. His eyes held Sandur's like a hawk's.

"Here: my medicine wand, safe passage for you! Accept it and no hand can be raised against you but mine." He held it high, where his men could see it too. "Come, craven; ply swords with me, for your own life and your homeland's!"

All the lines of Sandur's face were pulled taut; his hand was now at the hilt of the cut-and-thrust broadsword. His lips began to shape a reply; his chest swelled to hurl it. That it would be acceptance, Crassmor doubted not at all.

" 'Rider!" he barked, a sharper tone than he'd ever used with Sandur in his life. "You're on the King's commision; you are Cup Bearer, the Outrider, Knight of the Order of the Circle of Onn. You have your report to make!"

Sandur's gaze shifted to his brother, then back across the chasm. The Warlord still held up the medicine wand, waiting, but everyone there sensed that a moment had passed. Sandur's duty was as clear as Crassmor had said; it included nothing of personal duels. The Outrider gave a grudging nod, but his face was flushed with unutterable anger. He tugged irresolutely at Bordhall's reins.

Now that the brothers had made it this far, they stood every chance of returning to the Singularity safely. They rode off slowly, sparing their horses. The lizard riders called jeering insults and crowed laughter. Ravager's barbs followed them for a long time. Sandur rode with shoulders slumped, as if in a downpour.

"Pay no mind," Crassmor encouraged, trying to sound lighthearted. "You did what you were sent to do. Sandur, at least we're alive; give over."

"Escaping with our lives is not the same as success," the other said, so quietly that it could barely be heard.

"Well, brother, neither is getting killed," Crassmor reasoned.

# Chapter 3

# IN THE CHARMED REALM

The Beyonds, Crassmor and the Outrider discovered as they made their way homeward, now pressed their instability in close upon the Singularity, a depressing omen.

A fixed sphere amid the fluxes and flows of the infinite Realities, the Singularity was buffered from them by the indefinite zone of mutability and access, the Beyonds. In the Beyonds, people and other things passed into and out of the Realities. If the opening were of the right sort, whole regions along with their populations might come into existence in the Beyonds, or leave them.

Sometimes those who traveled between Realities found their way home again; sometimes they perished, or became lost and strayed into a Reality not their own. Sometimes they arrived at the Singularity or simply found themselves a place, for a long stay or a short one, in the Beyonds.

Those not born in the Singularity who wished to leave it had merely to venture out once more. If they again survived the Beyonds, they were likely to find their way, eventually, into some other Reality. It was seldom a simple matter, though, to reach a chosen destination. It was a consistent phenomenon, on the other hand, that those native to the Singularity often encountered difficulties in seeking to leave it for good. Events had a habit of bringing them back in curiously ineluctable fashion.

There were areas of relative stability in the Beyonds, particularly those close to that intangible boundary demarking the Singularity. But now, with the coming of Ravager and his hordes and their powerful influence in opening a way from their Reality to the Beyonds, things had shifted. The huge amounts of human quanta released

by the barbarians had altered formerly stable areas. The
wilderness which had its origins in the lizard riders' home
Reality had extended itself to the very borders of the
Charmed Realm. It had simply replaced what had been
there before, provinces and inhabitants that had been virtually a part of the Singularity.

Crassmor, riding, considered the great lake-canal system
of Gaftower, which had now departed the Beyonds. In
the same manner the brooding forest of Chevord, a stretch
of the Appian Way, the fertile plains of Jatahr, and the
sudden crags of Webtissia had yielded up their places. It
was an event with only a handful of precedents in the
recorded history of the Home Plane.

To their surprise, the brothers encountered none of the
Royal Borderers when they crossed into the Singularity.
They'd expected to see at least some of Ironwicca's hand-
picked watchmen keeping roving surveillance. It happened that the brothers re-entered the Charmed Realm at
a point touching on their vast ancestral lands, those of
House Tarrant. That had them more worried than ever;
this was the closest point, along the Singularity's circum-
ference, to Dreambourn, putting Ravager and his warriors within striking distance of both the capital and their
home.

The two entered an area of quiet woodland and virgin
timber where they'd both roamed and hunted as children.
They saw no one still, and passed across the hills above the
vineyards of Tolbur, then down through Blue Dell's mists.
Only a few workers moved in the fields far below, most
of them women. Sandur concluded that the men were being
mobilized for defense. Crassmor knew that stopping now
was out of the question, but he longed nonetheless to
pause at the family stronghold, clean himself up, and
sluice the dust from his gullet with one of the vintages
from his father's capacious cellars. *And just perhaps,* it
occurred to him, *there would be time to make the acquaintance of that comely little handmaiden whom Aunt Byborra has taken on.* He wished ardently for the days when
there was nothing more pressing or perilous to do than tag
along with Sandur for an evening at the Malamute Café.

They were drawing up on an outlying farmhold, a thriving but ramshackle place, when there came to their ears an uproar. Men, women, and children were shouting at some unseen threat and yelling conflicting exhortations to one another. Chickens, geese, pigs, and hounds raised a din. The brothers reined in as they saw a small buff form come leaping over a tumbled-down fence. Crassmor could see a hoe-swinging farmhand give up pursuit afoot.

The brothers thought it a farm dog at first; then they saw that it was one of the little wild dog-wolves found in certain parts of the Beyonds, a coyote. This one held in its jaws a weakly struggling hen, leaving a trail of gyrating gray and brown feathers behind it.

"Here's luck!" Sandur proclaimed. Crassmor saw that he was gathering himself up for the chase, ready to spur.

Crassmor overcame his surprise in time to protest, "It's only a chicken he's got, Sandur! You're on Ironwicca's business!"

"You're forgetting whom the coyote raised," Sandur returned. "We could use that kind of help in this war!" With that he was off, Bordhall taking up a smooth gallop, her muscles rolling.

Crassmor came after, realizing now what his brother had meant. It might be that this was some simple animal, drifted in from the Beyonds and hungry enough to invade the haunts of men during the day against its habit. But it might also be that this was Coyote, embodiment of its tribe. The tribe of Coyote had raised one of the most formidable heroes.

Across the open country they went, over terrain that didn't favor their quarry, which looked fatigued. The riders bore down a meadow after the creature, their horses' hooves showering clots of turf and grass. The brown-yellow predator hurtled between the rotting, ivy-grown rails of an old fence that should have been replaced long since. Sandur took the fence cleanly; Crassmor kept himself from balking, and Kort carried him well. They were closing the distance, but Sandur made no move to pull forth his bow. The coyote sought to dodge this way and that, but the horsemen veered to either side, driving it on. The land in that area had been cleared long before; there was little cover for the thief. Crassmor heard his brother bellowing to the beast to surrender.

A broad, deep river cut across the bottom of the meadow. The coyote, running with near-exhaustion, darted to the right, following the bank; the horses could ford far more quickly than he. Sandur, knowing the lay of the land, gave a shout of triumph. Stone slopes, low but sheer, marched along the river in that direction, leaving only a narrow apron of overgrown riverbank between themselves and the water. The horsemen raced over young weeds, driftwood, rocks, sand, and stagnant pools.

A quarter of a mile farther along, the cliffs closed down to meet the river. A deep backwater eddied there. The brothers drew up to see the coyote trotting back and forth at bay, hesitant to try to dodge back past them, the pitiful hen hanging, nearly formless, in its jaws. The thief's weary movements told of its spent strength. Sandur stopped while they were some way off, signaling Crassmor to do the same. Crassmor asked, "What—?"

Sandur, dismounting, replied, "I want to treat with him, not slay him. The way is narrow here; ride back and forth a little, so that he knows you stand prepared to block it." With that he walked forward.

The coyote had stopped to watch now, feet spread, head hung low. Sandur paused a dozen paces away, empty hands wide apart. The beast looked him over with what Crassmor thought to be intelligent assessment. "You are a long way from your home, plains child!" Sandur began.

The coyote suddenly sat back on its haunches and dropped the unmoving hen, setting one forepaw on her almost daintily, and studied the knight. It panted, its red tongue lolling, its nostrils flared wide, eyes slitted, quite the most devious-looking creature Crassmor could recall having seen. It licked white fangs with a dripping tongue and waited.

"I have met your folk before," Sandur continued, "in the Beyonds. And I have met as well the man-child who was raised by your tribe. I thought that, if you were about, he might be. We sorely need his—"

Sandur stopped, peering more closely at the coyote, who in turn watched him with head canted to one side. Crassmor paused in the slow pacing of his horse. Sandur threw his head back and laughed, the first time he'd done so since his exchange with Ravager. His parley formality fell away. He pointed at the little buff-colored thief.

"Abandon that shape! Show yourself!" He was trying not to dissolve into belly laughter. "Prankster! Lazy, careless Saynday! You've given yourself away once more!"

Making a more careful examination of the creature, Crassmor saw now that it had a very odd-looking mustache, resembling that of no dog or wolf, hanging down from its muzzle. The coyote gave its snout a waggle, trying to look at it cross-eyed. Then it snorted a sort of embarrassed chortle and somehow looked sheepish. In another moment it began to change shape.

Crassmor had a hard time following the procedure. The beast's outlines flowed and elongated. Its pelt changed to red-brown skin and its muzzle retreated into its face. In moments Crassmor, dumbfounded, was staring at a most peculiar man. Sandur, hands on hips, was shaking his head in exasperation, but chuckling.

The man was gangling, almost emaciated, but his biceps and the other muscles of his limbs ballooned, to draw in tight and skinny once more at his joints. His eyes showed a vast guilelessness which, Crassmor suspected, camouflaged a shrewd turn of mind. A straggling wisp of mustache drooped down around his mouth, his error in disguise. When it came, his voice was high and nasal, plaintive and cracked.

"Well, Sandur, you still ride pretty good," Saynday admitted.

Sandur turned and instructed Crassmor wryly, "When Saynday gives you a compliment, brother, look to your horse, look to your woman, look to your tent, and look to your purse!"

Saynday erupted in a string of shrill, nasal laughs. "Thou Trickster," Sandur went on, not without affection, "few ride as well as you run. Tired you must be, to come to bay so easily." Saynday shrugged; Crassmor noticed that he was covered with sweat. "What brings you here?" Sandur finished.

Saynday rose from where he'd been squatting on his haunches. He wore low shoes of soft-tanned skins, soled with rawhide, and a much-worn breechclout with tattered beading. He kept one toe on the hen as he grinned amiably at the knight. "Things were pretty quiet, back where I come from—"

"And where there is no mischief, Saynday will go looking for some," Sandur said. "Plainly, your hunting has been poor."

"Well, I've been fuller," the gangling man admitted, rubbing a shrunken stomach. "This place isn't much like the plains, you know. But I was comin' along, to see what was goin' on in your Singularity. And then I got too hungry when I smelled those chickens." He conspicuously avoided looking at the deceased hen.

"Lucky were you that *real* dogs didn't pull you apart!" Crassmor called, intrigued and amused.

Saynday returned the scrutiny. He shook a little bead bag, decorated with feathers and porcupine quills, thonged to his breechclout. "You don't blame yourself for seein' a Coyote, do you? So don't blame the dogs for smellin' Bear, Wolf, and Mountain Lion." He suddenly issued the high giggles again. "Those dogs won't follow without plenty of men with 'em."

Sandur said, "I'd hoped I'd come across Coyote himself. The Singularity is in great danger, and all help is needed. I'd hoped that Pecos could be contacted."

Saynday fingered his chin. "Well, he's White Man's son; Coyote was just lookin' after him. But he won't be comin', Sandur—not if what I smell on you two is war. Bill fights his own fights and does his own deeds; no armies. He's a fierce one, is Bill, but not one of your soldiers."

Sandur looked at the Trickster for a moment, then nodded and reached for his rein, Crassmor having brought Bordhall up during the conversation. "It's best you were gone, Saynday," Sandur warned as he mounted. "No prank will keep you from danger here." Then he was in his saddle, settling his sword.

Saynday inclined his head, accepting that. "And keep the chicken," Crassmor added on impulse. "We've no time to return it anyway."

The Trickster made a mocking imitation of a courtly bow, a burlesque from one who'd never bent knee in earnest. Crassmor frowned and Sandur chuckled. "Looks like I owe you for the warnin'," Saynday told the knight. And to Crassmor he added, "And, maybe, a little somethin' for the chicken."

Crassmor stopped in the act of reining around. "And how are you to be found?"

Saynday's eyes danced. "Just bring along the meat I love best." He stooped and gathered up the chicken.

Crassmor would have asked on, but Sandur gestured; they'd already lost precious time. The two cantered back toward the ford in the river.

They stopped at the granary at Lateroo and, giving Bordhall and Kort a respite they'd more than earned, commandeered two remounts from the Tarrant factotum there.

There too they heard grave tidings. The King had called up volunteers and levies along with members of most of the martial groups, combining them with a contingent from his small standing army. Apparently a large force of barbarians had moved closer to the Singularity, and battle had been likely. This had been several days before; no later word had come to this outlying place since the departure of the troops.

Sandur and Crassmor looked at each other, thinking of the Warlord's boast that he'd already bested the arms of the Singularity. The two made no mention of that to the people there. Sandur, though, under his own authority, instructed the factotum to curtail operations as soon as possible and move his people to the nearest Tarrant stronghold and to send out word for others to do the same.

Exertion and exhaustion had caused the journey to take on an unreality. Crassmor dully followed his brother across the uplands of Daske, passing among the flocks and herds. They descended through the flowered meadows of Hurnalle,

which usually resounded with the axes and saws of lumber-
men in the surrounding hills but were now silent except for
caroling songbirds. Above them soared gorgeous butterflies
with wingspreads of a pace and more. The Tarrant holdings prospered as ever; Combard's mystic ties to the land
were still in effect. Stalks were heavy with yield; herds
and flocks were swollen with outsize, meat-heavy animals;
trees in the orchards bent under the weight of their fruit.
The grass was lush, the timber sound, the weather tem-
perate.

They rode the border of the lands of House Comullo,
the Tarrants' nearest neighbors, then swung back across
tended fields as the sun went down. The brothers followed
old, straight roads lit by the brilliant night sky of the
Singularity. Wolfing a meal at a roadhouse there, they vol-
unteered no information to host or guests except to advise
against straying into the Beyonds. They slept on bedrolls
flung down on truckle beds on a floor of cut bracken and
resumed their way early.

They were on main roads now, passing strolling players,
postal riders, itinerant workers and artisans, clergy of every
sort, pilgrims, and wanderers. There were quacks and
healers, minstrels, footloose students, soothsayers, drug
sellers and herbalists, beggars, and a number of fellows
whom Crassmor suspected of being highwaymen. There
were, ominously, none of the mercenaries or swords-for-
hire who were usually to be seen, save for those employed
by traders or the wealthy. The roads were wet from recent
rain, deep with muck compounded of mud and the droppings of horse, mule, cow, sheep, and fowl. Those afoot
were befouled to their knees with it; the muck spattered
the horses' legs and encrusted their bellies.

They saw Dreambourn in the dawn and reached it in
early light. By far the Singularity's largest city, it probed
the sky with a bewildering assortment of fortified towers,
elfin spires, lacy minarets, and sleek steeples. Many of
these were crowned with observatories. Dreambourn's architecture was a multiform blend of the many influences it had
felt. There were crystal manses next to delicate, carven

villas; steel cupolas hard by marble forums; geodesic domes and wooden longhouses. Smaller cottages, tents, yurts, huts, and shacks were tucked into whatever space was available. Overhead, Crassmor saw a flock of brilliantly plumed parrots; far off, a pterodactyl glided.

The city was surrounded by miles of hundred-foot-high walls of tightly joined stone, with ramparts so wide that ten horsemen could ride abreast on patrol. The fortifications made the brothers feel no better; the lizard riders in their staggering numbers wouldn't be stopped by mere walls. At the entrance to the capital, Sandur motioned to the guard detachment keeping watch in full armor with bows and pikes. It was undermanned, stripped for the King's expedition.

Through the main gates of Dreambourn, which rose fifty feet and were arched with white marble, moved the river of traffic which seemed never to stop, day or night. Some of the travelers were residents of the Singularity, but many were those who'd filtered in from the Beyonds. Tinkers bent under heavy packs, and traders tugged at mules, horses, and other less conventional beasts of burden. A dignified gentleman dressed in a tailcoat and homburg hat churned past on a high-wheeled velocipede. Noblemen and ladies made their way along in carriages, or ahorse. Heady perfume wafted to Crassmor from a carefully curtained sedan chair carried by four brawny bearers. Farmers, craftsmen, sly-looking men with weapons and an eye out for opportunity, milkmaids and dancing girls, all passed through there.

Only a few powered vehicles—a Trevithick steam carriage; an articulated, doughnut-tired rover—were navigating along slowly and carefully. Complicated machinery frequently came to grief in the Singularity.

Off to one side, Crassmor noticed, were a young man and woman with a nervous, red-haired dog beside them. They were taking it all in with amazement, obvious wanderers-in. They wore similar clothes, faded denim trousers and heavy, checkered flannel shirts under puffy down vests. Their footgear was sturdy hiking boots; each bore a backpack framed with metal tubing.

The man saw that Crassmor was inspecting him. He called, "Look, could you help us? We were on the Appalachian Trail—"

Crassmor felt pity, but had no moment to spare, and gave what brief advice he could. "You're no longer in your own Reality, but you'll be safer inside Dreambourn than out!" Then he had to catch up with Sandur, who, preoccupied, had not even noticed the exchange.

Sandur moved through the throngs with uncharacteristic curtness, making others give way. Many there recognized him, the Outrider, King's Cup Bearer, renowned champion even among the revered Knights of Onn. Those who didn't yielded way just the same to the forbidding warrior whose red hair streamed behind him now that he was unhelmeted, his armor and trappings marked by recent combat.

A group of Glitchen, the little troll folk who so loved abstruse mischief, hastened to drag their sledge out of the way. They were dressed in elaborate outfits of silk and pearl, with curling points on the toes of their shoes and long, drooping ones on the tips of their colorful hats. After Sandur passed them, they resumed pushing and pulling their sledge, whose runners slid with mysterious ease over the cobbles. The Glitchen's haunts were the caverns and deep places; they must, Crassmor knew, be in Dreambourn to see about expediting their cargo to another Reality, which required costly and expert help. Curious, he read the stenciling on the crates with which the sledge was loaded:

SILICA THERMAL TILES
SPACE SHUTTLE PROGRAM
N.A.S.A.

The two brothers went on up the capital's main thoroughfare, Fey Passage. They ignored temples, taverns, counting houses, bazaars, and the noble edifices and primitive encampments along the way, although there was much that was new. The Charmed Realm was above all a place of change. The scent of fires assailed them with smells of hardwood, dung, coal, and resin. The cobbles were carpeted with droppings, slops, mud, and puddles of brackish water. People moved by in their fantastic variety. Crassmor usually reveled in the city; now he could only think of the danger to it.

The palace of Ironwicca was known as the Anvil, a squat, dark, adamantine subcity in its own right, a formidable assemblage of creneled turrets, hornwork, battlements, and moats. An equerry came forward to take their reins when they entered the courtyard. Members of the Household Guard, tall, redoubtable men in shining mail, armed with swords and polearms and bows, were stationed all through the place. None challenged the two brothers; all knew the King's Cup Bearer. Sandur was ungauntleted now; the golden heir's ring of House Tarrant glittered on his finger, an exacting duplicate of the Circle of Onn.

Sandur walked the long, polished mosaic floors of the palace with wide, urgent strides. A chamberlain bustled up as the two approached the throne room, though, to say that court was not to be held that day. The King was, instead, to be found on the palace roof. A detour up flight after flight of broad stairs took them to the summit of the Anvil.

On an uppermost tower stood a construction shaped for the King years before by a master craftsman, a worker in metal and clockwork who'd employed more than a little arcane magic in his arts. Fashioned in the form of an egret, it was erect on gleaming gilt legs, eighty feet and more in height, its plummage dazzling with gems and bright filigree, the metal of it iridescent in the sun. A gong, a disk of opal, was set near the sturdy anchoring of one glittering foot; Sandur struck it softly with the padded mallet that hung there. A moment later the bird tower began to move with a smooth working of joints and gears, its head descending. Down and down it came, bearing with it Ironwicca, King of the Singularity.

# Chapter 4

# BACK

**The resplendent egret** head stopped only a foot or two from the surface of the roof. It was an observation platform of some size; the King stood there with three others. The brothers were only slightly surprised to see those other three.

Combard of Tarrant considered his sons, his eyes grave and intent beneath bushy brows. Age had changed his red hair with an even mixture of gray, and the thick beard and brows had followed suit. Though Combard's shoulders had begun to stoop and his midsection to expand, fine garments and martial bearing hid most of that. His fists were on his hips as he regarded them. On his finger was the lord's ring of House Tarrant. Like the heir's ring, it re-created the Circle of Onn, but in stone rather than in some precious metal. Combard's sword's worn, jewel-capped hilt protruded from his long cloak.

Next to him was Teerse, Lord of House Comullo. Of an age with Combard, lifelong friend and neighbor to him, Teerse was slight, nearly skinny, but erect and dignified in an open, warm way. Most of his hair was gone; mustache and beard were trimmed down to narrow, carefully kept rows. Teerse's eyes were, as always, pouched with care despite his easy smile. He was of a gentler nature than his doughty neighbor and friend, a much-consulted counselor of the King. His trousers and cape, still elegant, had seen some mending. As Combard's hereditary powers were bound up in the land, Teerse's were embodied in the Tapestry that the heirs of his family had been weaving over the generations, forming slowly under the Jade Dome at House Comullo, reflecting events in the Singularity.

At Teerse's elbow was his daughter Willow, sole heir to
his name and the duties of the weaver, promised in marriage to Sandur at her birth. Crassmor had spent considerable time trying to isolate just what made her so attractive.
Certainly the brown-green eyes, wide and direct, contributed. Her brows and lashes were fair, though, and
Willow took no pains to darken or alter them, as other
women might. Her hair was glossy and soft but usually,
as now, pulled back into a smooth brown cap and wound
into a tight braid, and so not conspicuous. Her nose, now;
a bit too long, a perfectionist might have said, with a hint
of ridge at the middle, yet Crassmor thought it fine. Her
mouth was wide; an engratiating portraitist had once tried
to alter it in his rendering. Willow had put her foot down,
making him paint her as she was.

She was so slender that she appeared taller than she was
—chin-high to Sandur. The planes of her face, while not
startling or arresting, were prominent and pleasant to the
eye. She was no lady from a poem; nevertheless, Crassmor
knew few people who didn't relish Willow's company and
wit and prize her friendship highly. She wore a long gown
of pearly macramé and a thick, blue-white fur pulled
around her against the morning chill.

Behind those three stood Ironwicca. His features, set
and calm, still betrayed the elemental power of the man.
A long-fingered hand clenched the railing of the egret-head
balcony, the musculature along the forearm in high relief.
It occurred to Crassmor with some surprise, as it always
did, that the King hadn't changed since Crassmor had
first seen him as a boy. Ironwicca still looked like a man
in his robust forties, his face formed in intent, high-cheekboned lines, black hair tumbling in thick ringlets around
his shoulders, dark brown eyes showing glints of gold.
Those eyes were keen and penetrating, prone to miss nothing, with a gaze that was difficult to meet for long. The
King's cheek was seamed by an ancient scar; his lips were
full, his mouth broad, his forehead high but heavy-
browed. His nose was a hawk's bill. Dense curls of beard
sprang from a square jaw. Ironwicca's body, even within
ceremonial vestments, implied might and speed; no jungle

cat demonstrated more lethal grace in repose. His brown
skin had been made even darker by the sun.

Ironwicca had been King of the Singularity for a time
outreaching the memory of anyone else alive, or anyone
who'd spoken to a living soul. It had been Ironwicca who,
wandering in from the Beyonds as so many had before
and after him, had championed the Singularity out of constant warfare and strife, forging a kingdom. Some of that
he'd done with statecraft, but the majority with sword law.
His origins were unknown; prying into his past was best left
uncontemplated. No one knew the secret of his long life.
He'd proved himself a canny ruler, utterly ferocious, devoted to his subjects, a man of elaborate guile and animal
patience.

The brothers saw that the four people on the egret balcony were unsmiling; both wondered how bad the news
was. Ironwicca leaned forward, brushing the back of a
sinewy hand up through the black rings of his beard,
thumb and forefinger parting to pass around his wide jaw
as he studied his Cup Bearer. Crassmor held his sallet
nervously in the crook of his left arm, staying behind and
to the right of his brother.

Sandur took a step nearer the egret's head. Without
qualifier, he reported, "I failed."

Combard's face went from shock to outrage. He burst
out, "Your Majesty!" to deny this admission from the son
of his heart. Crassmor too had it on the tip of his tongue
to cry out *No!* in violation of every polite form. He was
subdued by the presence of the King.

Ironwicca held up an open palm without taking his eyes
from the Outrider; the others all held their peace. He
touched some control and a panel in the egret's head swung
away, a small ladder unfolding. Sandur took it as tacit
invitation, mounting the marvelous bird tower. The King
beckoned with a finger; Crassmor, who'd been in a dither
as to what was expected of him, hurried after.

There was ample room for all. Combard gave Sandur
the traditional welcoming embrace, pressing him close.
Crassmor he took into his arms too. Crassmor moved to

Willow's side, in part because he'd always enjoyed her company, but in greater part to make himself less conspicuous. Ironwicca turned aside and spoke some word none of them quite heard. The ladder refolded itself and the panel swung shut; the egret began straightening once more, lifting its head high. Crassmor gripped a golden, intricately wrought handrail as firmly and unobtrusively as he could. The huge construct moved smoothly, though. In moments it was again upright.

They gazed out over the Anvil, Dreambourn, and the surrounding countryside. Crassmor found that he could see House Tarrant itself and beyond. It made him dizzy. Off in the other direction, the River Deal flowed toward the Sea of Endeavor, also called the Sea of Strife, which glistened and twinkled. He thought he could spy the island, out to sea, where the Storm Priestess contended with the powers of weather, stirring that great Singularity treasure, the cauldron of the winds. The air up in this high place was chilly, stinging more than that below. Crassmor understood, though, why the egret tower was one of the King's favorite places. Ironwicca spent much time up here, meditating upon and looking out over his realm.

Sandur had been gazing about as well. He cried, "See!" and pointed. Crassmor followed the pointing finger and saw that a long winding column of people on horses and people afoot was joining with the stream bound for Dreambourn's main gates. As he watched, other traffic was moved aside to give the column way. It could only be a military corps, Ironwicca's expeditionary force. Crassmor could discern many different elements in it. The column moved slowly, with many stragglers and in poor order, a bad sign.

"Yes," Teerse said as they watched the first of the troops reach the gates. "We've had some few dispatches from them already; the word is not good." He sounded tired unto death; Willow looked at her father's tragic eyes and turned away. Crassmor realized that he and Sandur, arriving from another direction, had just missed meeting up with the expeditionary force at the gates.

The King tore his gaze away from his troops, his expression a question to Sandur, who answered. "I turned the barbarians against the broken-cross soldiers, but the lizard riders slaughtered them all and are still in numbers uncountable." He looked down to the gates of Dreambourn, through which troops now poured, then back to the King. "They'll be there, at the gates, as soon as they can re-form."

Crassmor dared a look aside to see how Willow took this. For once, her face was closed; Teerse was as noncommittal. Combard was only barely restraining himself.

The King's response was pitched low, holding amusement and rebuke. "I'd thought better of the Outrider's grasp of strategy."

That put surprise on Sandur's face. Ironwicca went on. "Turning aside the barbarians for a time, that was no achievement? Reducing their numbers by the thousands upon thousands, at no cost to our own ranks, that was not an accomplishment? Eliminating the broken-cross soldiers was failure?"

The King's mouth tugged now, but not in a smile. "You have decided, have you, Sandur, that even partial success is all failure?" His tone was edged like a razor. "Save this roundabout pride for others! It wins you no esteem from me!"

The tension hanging in the air in the wake of that was difficult for Crassmor to bear. Combard seemed about to explode. Sandur's jaw muscles jumped; Crassmor thought for a moment that his headstrong brother was about to have hard words with the King, a dangerous—if not fatal —undertaking.

Ironwicca smiled through his black beard first. "But your deeds do. Perhaps I shall put you in your place with some reward, punish you with accolades."

Sandur's expression nearly formed for laughter then; Crassmor silently let his breath out. The King fell serious again, but not as perilously so as before. "That will have to await another day, though. Now, tell me all, in detail."

Crassmor saw that his father's mien had softened. Combard was nodding to himself; the old man's world was right again, with this bit of moral instruction. Sandur obeyed,

telling of the mission into the Beyonds but, Crassmor
noticed, omitting the insults and challenges hurled across
the chasm at him by Ravager. Those had plainly burned
hot against his pride and were, in his estimate, matters of
no consequence otherwise. Something in the recounting,
though, or in the King's knowledge of men, set Ironwicca
to gazing at Sandur with doubt. "And you fled from the
chasm and the Warlord instanter, to carry word to me?
With no backward glance?"

"That was my duty," Sandur parried without inflection.
Crassmor thought his brother dangerously close to dissembling, but it never occurred to him to comment, not
in this company.

Combard, thinking he'd heard some criticism of his son,
was quick to defend. "So it was, and well carried out!
Your Majesty, I shall be candid: it is no easier for Sandur
to fly before the enemy than it is, with profound respect,
for you yourself. Where is the man who doubts your Cup
Bearer's sword arm? He has struck down mightier men
than this lizard lord!"

The King saw that the conversation had turned from its
intended course with Combard's misunderstanding that
courage, and not accuracy was in question there. Ironwicca
left the subject of the Warlord for the time being and bade
the report continue. Sandur finished the little that remained,
mentioning the news he'd had of the Singularity's arms
riding forth by way of a question, looking aside again at
the returning troops.

The King was inclined to respond. "Did you think I had
all my plans a-dangle from one hook? I had other scouts
out while you were playing trick-and-slip with the barbarians. That Warlord had sufficient strength to send a probe
around the zone of battle with the broken-cross soldiers
for a feeling-out of our mettle."

He turned and spoke that low word again, or another
much like it. The egret began to descend once more. "It
may be that we were fated to meet these invaders squarely
from the first."

Crassmor, drinking in the last of the scene below, watching the ragged expeditionary force's return, with a mind's

eye view of the limitless encampment of the lizard riders, found himself blurting, "But they are without number!" before he recalled his whereabouts.

Aghast, he saw the King glancing at him strangely. Sandur and Teerse and Willow pretended not to have noticed. Combard glared wrathfully at his younger son. *He thinks it's the whine of a craven,* Crassmor saw. *But it's truth!*

"They *have* a number," Ironwicca replied with equanimity. Crassmor heaved an inner sigh, that he'd been spared a royal reprimand. The egret came to a halt, the panel opening once more. The Singularity's monarch went on as he stepped down the short ladder. "If it is too much in excess of our own, we shall find some other method of dealing with them than straightforward battle."

Another figure appeared on the roof of the palace, a man flanked by distressed servitors who were tensed to catch him should he fall. He limped with pain and walked unsteadily but gave no sign of wanting assistance. The servitors, knowing the reputation of the Red Branch knights, kept their hands to themselves.

The knight's scarlet cloak was torn; pendants were missing from it, as was its brooch. Blood stained his white tunic. His kilt and greaves were spattered with mud. Though his helmet was gone, he held his notched sword in his hand.

Ironwicca waited impassively. The newcomer stopped before the King, swaying slightly. His long blond hair fell across his face, the circlet having been lost from his brow. He knew the King cared nothing for protocol when serious matters were at hand. He spoke with a flourish of his sword.

"The lizard riders broke our formations and drove us back off the Heights of Meridion," he told Ironwicca. "We held them through six attacks, having the better position. Their leader has no concern for the squandering of lives."

Crassmor heard a little intake of breath from Willow and saw Sandur's mouth tighten. The Red Branch knight drew a hand across his face and went on.

"How many of them we killed I cannot say, but it was many, your Majesty; many. The lizard riders now hold the

Heights and control the plains of Ruall as well. Our commanders organized rearguard—a number of the men and women of the Sodality of the Sword, men of the Red Branch, some of Oishi Kuranosuke's stern fighters . . ."

He winced in anguish, clutching his side, and began to fall. The King crossed the space to him in a single leap, caught him, and bellowed for a litter. Teerse, practiced in arts of healing, knelt to examine the wounded man, whose eyes fluttered open. "It will not be many days before they reach Dreambourn, Highness."

When the Red Branch knight had been taken away to the attentions of Ironwicca's personal healers, the King resumed the long walk to see his visitors off. "The barbarians' first probing force," he mused, "a vanguard." Yet they'd managed to throw back some of the best warriors in the Singularity. Though the King's voice was controlled, something in him that usually smoldered was now close to flame. "They care nothing for their losses, Sandur?"

Sandur considered that as their steps resounded in the halls. "They come of a dying world, Majejsty, where death is common, a world exhausted. The lizard riders are an elite, each supported by the labors and hardship of a score of wretched serfs. They are born to die in war. This Warlord has united them as no one has ever done in their fractious history. What he commands, they will do. They've nothing to lose, and must conquer new domains or see their way of life pass away. That, or perish."

The King was silent until they came to the great entrance doors, then said, "So first strategies have been unsuccessful. This is not the end of it." He felt of his beard. "What numbers they must have! Yet not infinite, eh, young Crassmor?"

Combard's younger son swallowed hard. "No, Highness."

Ironwicca growled a laugh. "This takes more thought, however. Teerse, remain behind, if you will. You others have my thanks for your aid, thoughts, and deeds."

Willow, Combard, and the two brothers descended the long flight of steps to the courtyard. Pressed by his father for details, Sandur made much of Crassmor's steadfastness in staying near the barbarian camp despite adversity and

danger. Combard admitted gruffly that Crassmor had ac-
quitted himself well; the aspirant knight embraced it as
high praise, trying not to think how close he'd come to
failing.

A group of Tarrant armsmen, Combard's escort, were
awaiting their liege. They were all known to the brothers;
they waved swords and clashed shields in greeting. With
them was Bint, Crassmor and Sandur's matrilineal cousin,
two years younger than Crassmor and also in knightly
training. Bint, orphaned years before, was a member of the
Tarrant household and had come to regard his cousins and
uncle highly. Sandur was Bint's idol, though; today the
boy spared little attention for anyone else. When the Outrider greeted him and clasped hands, Bint's face appeared
to shine from within.

Another Tarrant hurried up, Combard's younger brother
Furd, abbot of the Klybesian monks. Overfleshed, over-
hearty, sanctimonious Furd had always made life rather
trying for Crassmor. Furd and Combard embraced warmly
—they'd come through a difficult childhood together—
and Furd made signs of the Klybesian benediction for one
and all. He wore a red kirtle worked with some of the many
mystic symbols important to the Klybesians, his stout belly
wound in a sash of black velvet, a square-brimmed, high-
crowned, gray silken hat on his balding head.

"I heard this grievous news of defeat," Furd explained,
heavy jowls flopping as he shook his head. "I rushed here
to offer prayers of consolation with the King."

Sandur told him, "I doubt the King is inclined to prayer
just now, uncle. He's trying to divine new ways of killing
lizard riders before they kill us."

Furd drew himself up. "Times of peril are not times to
ignore religion, m'boy!"

"Nor the sword," the Outrider pointed out.

Furd shrugged with what Crassmor thought to be ill
humor. "No doubt, no doubt. Still, your safe return is joyous news indeed." He waggled a finger at Crassmor. "As
is yours, youngster. A new leaf for the wastrel, eh? It's
gratifying to see that your old uncle's preaching is finally
taking root!"

Crassmor found himself thinking about the time when Furd—it could only have been by following Crassmor— had discovered his fondness for sneaking off to watch the lusty sports of the centaurs. The abbot had boxed the ear of the eight-year-old boy and hauled him away, though the centaurs themselves had protested that they had no objections to Crassmor's presence. Furd had told Combard, of course, just one of many impieties that Furd had considered himself duty-bound to report.

Sandur was about to reply to Furd, angry at the abbot for trying to take a share of Crassmor's merit, but the Klybesian was hurrying on his errand. The horses had been brought. Willow and the Tarrants rode forth from the Anvil together with the armsmen behind. As they came onto Fey Passage they saw a sad procession.

The remnants of the expeditionary force went by. There were Paladins of Ur-Had-Bon, Kassa and his Masterless Swords, Knights of Onn, the Thieves' Troop, gladiators of Mu, a company of Bow Maids, and more. Many bore a wounded comrade; more than one had carried home the body of a close friend rather than leave it to the carrion eaters.

Combard watched them all solemnly but without comment, deeming no other reaction worthy of a lord of one of the Singularity's Elder Houses. Sandur kept rein over his emotions with some effort. Bint was too shocked and frightened to react. Willow, hating what she saw there, turned her head away. Her gaze fell on Crassmor. With each passing moment the younger Tarrant son grew more appalled.

A ranger of the Woodsmen of Lyrr fell from his saddle as he drew even with the group. He hit the ground and lay still, dead. Others of his band wearily stopped to drape his body over his horse and continue. A cry escaped Crassmor, at the sorrow of it. Combard turned a scathing glare on him, disapproving any show of weakness when all strength would soon be needed. Crassmor fought to keep emotion from his face. This, only because he wished before all else not to displease his father, not from any shame.

Then Crassmor marked someone he recognized, watching the dire parade from the other side of Fey Passage. The man was tall, gaunt, black-skinned, and had a haunted look. He wore whiteface makeup and was dressed for mourning in black silk top hat, frock coat, and dark glasses. His chin was bound closed with linen as if he were a corpse. He was Baron Samedi, *Loa* of graveyards and burials. Crassmor had seen him before, on the night the younger Tarrant had danced the *banda,* one of the many indiscretions that had earned Crassmor Combard's displeasure. The baron was a perfect example of personages in the Singularity better left undisturbed. His powers might have been of great help in the coming war, but such creatures cared little about mortal conflicts. So great was the danger posed by the likes of Baron Samedi that Ironwicca and the other Singularity leaders chose to let them go their own way as long as they caused no harm in the Charmed Realm.

Combard broke the silence. "Enough; there is much to do if this grievous review is not to be repeated." He put a hand to Sandur's mailed shoulder. "I shall ride directly to raise up men in our southern grants, among the sworn of Gwall and our liegemen in the lands all around. You go through the uplands. Call up the levies of Hinn and all the others in those provinces who owe me fealty; they know you and will flock to your banner."

He turned to Crassmor, who waited eagerly for a man's task. "And you, young man: see the Lady Willow safely home, then get you to House Tarrant and assist in getting things prepared against our absence. Help put all things in readiness."

Crassmor was crestfallen, understanding the implication. Though he was well known and welcome throughout the Tarrant holdings and much of the Singularity, it was as a singer of songs, harper, boisterous if modest drinker, and, if a wastrel, then an open-handed one. Combard was as much as saying that he doubted that fighting men would rally to Crassmor.

The old man turned to Willow with a kinder look; he loved her as he would his own, in great part because of her own wisdom, humor, and spirit, but in as large a measure for the fact that she was betrothed to Sandur. Combard held her especial for the love he perceived between the two.

His voice held an unaccustomedly husky note. "I am sorry that this preparation must be for war instead of for that grand day when you two will be one," he declared. "Yet that day will come, I swear it. We'll see to that, your father and I."

Sandur started guiltily, shaken out of his preoccupation with the defeated troops. He and Willow shared a look that Combard presumed to be the sadness of delay in their marriage; the old man courteously looked the other way. Crassmor knew differently. This was the sort of tragedy seldom treated in the sagas and great dramas. Good friends, admiring and liking one another, Sandur and Willow simply didn't love each other and never had.

Combard was blind to that. He was about to say on, with the sort of promises he'd taken to making lately, of a wedding without compare, lavish gifts, and grants for the newlyweds and the offspring he presumed them to want as much as he. Sandur, long grown uneasy with such talk, almost tormented by it, shifted the subject.

"In the Beyonds, Crassmor comported himself well. He was shield brother to me. He's earned a good place among us, sir."

It was as close as he'd ever come to questioning his father. Combard made a sour face as the topic changed from a most favored one to a least. He pursed his mouth, gazing at his younger son, then nodded. "That is no less than true. Wait at House Tarrant as I have instructed, Crassmor. When I go to the settlements at Kurn, your standard will be next to mine." He sketched a smile. "Let these traits continue, son. Do what is right; do what is brave. You'll win high honor."

Crassmor lowered his head in a modest bow, as was expected. His heart leaped, however reluctantly this compliment had been given to him, and with what qualifiers. "Thank you; I shall try, father."

The old man grunted, eyes sliding away from his

younger son. He touched Crassmor's shoulder in salute, not the comradely grip he'd given Sandur, but his hand lingered there for a moment and squeezed gently a time or two.

The moment ended; the hand fell away. "To work!" Combard commanded. "Our paths divide here; we reunite at House Tarrant in two days' time. Good fortune, all!"

Then he was off at the gallop, Bint and his armsmen clattering behind. The Lord of House Tarrant was erect in his saddle despite his years. He looked no more upon the defeated men and women he passed. The other three did, though, long after Combard had vanished from sight. There seemed no end to them, the beaten and wounded and dying who came with no hope in their faces.

Sandur said in a grating, low voice, "If I were granted one wish, it would be to stop all this." He looked to Crassmor. "If I had only taken the medicine wand! I would trade off this bloodshed for single combat, gladly!" The moment's fervor faded from him. "But I failed in that as well; I let the opportunity pass."

"You did what you had to do," Crassmor told him with complete conviction. "You did what it was your oath to do." Willow was watching them, not understanding the details but sensing the nature of the exchange.

"I let the opportunity pass," the Outrider repeated sadly. "I'll regret it all my life." The words were a physical blow to Crassmor.

Sandur leaned to Willow and kissed her cheek, then her hand. She reciprocated, then told him, "Good fortune, Sandur."

His regret yielded to a brief, bittersweet smile. He traded forearm grips with Crassmor, making the younger man feel as much an ally as a brother. Spurring his horse, Sandur departed. Crassmor's attention went back to the ruined army. The moment's elation had ebbed. The scene drove everything but despair from him.

A hand covered his, at his pommel. Willow didn't attempt false bravery or affected cheer. "It does no good to stay here," she chided him gently. "Our tasks are set now. No one can stave off this war."

He didn't look away from the suffering before him. "One man might," he said, "given the chance." *Do what is right,* his father had said. *Do what is brave.*

He ignored her questions. All at once he'd brought his horse around and was galloping back along Fey Passage without another word. Soon he was lost to her sight.

## Chapter 5

# FORTH

**The lizard riders'** new bivouac was much closer to the Charmed Realm. Crassmor began encountering their patrols almost as soon as he'd left the Singularity.

The barbarians were confident, though, and by nature not much given to diligent scouting or careful route riding. They were even less so now, flushed with double victories over the broken cross and the King's first expedition. More, Crassmor had stopped and retrieved Kort from the granary at Lateroo; the horse's splendid speed and endurance were major factors in his penetration of the invader's lines.

The encampment was even larger than before, swelled by the warriors who'd been off fighting during Sandur's stay. To make himself go on wasn't as difficult as Crassmor had feared it would be. It was, in a curious way, easy; when he remembered Sandur's expression back on Fey Passage, Crassmor found himself with few doubts or second thoughts. For Sandur to have come back out here without the safe-passage guarantee of the Warlord's medicine wand might have been tantamount to suicide. Ravager would not be bound by an offer already refused, nor would he be obliged to renew it. The Warlord would be free to have the knight cut down on the spot or remanded to his torturers.

But if Crassmor, who considered himself of no consequence to Ravager, were to present himself and offer to serve as courier, the Warlord, from Sandur's stories of him, might very well repeat the challenge and send forth the wand. Ravager's reasons, as Crassmor calculated them, would be twofold: he hated Sandur and wished personal revenge; and he'd already made the challenge before his men. Crassmor did his best not to think about what would happen if the Emptier of Lodges did not happen to see things the same way.

The thought of obtaining the medicine wand did nothing to cheer Crassmor, though; he knew anguish over the peril in which the duel would put Sandur. There again, a number of factors came into play. First was Sandur's own declaration that it was his desire to take up the challenge. Second was the likelihood that, given the barbarians' staggering numbers, their eventual victory seemed assured; there would come the day, in any event, when the Outrider would face the Warlord. Fought later, that contest would be little more than a closing note to the war, and the Singularity would not be saved. Fought now, it might mean salvation. The last was an unspoken matter; Crassmor suspected from Sandur's words that he was mulling over the idea of returning into the Beyonds on his own. Crassmor meant to see that, if and when that happened, Sandur would at least have the protection of the medicine wand.

That the Outrider would win such a duel Crassmor never permitted himself to doubt. Sandur had never been beaten on field of practice or field of war. As Cup Bearer and the Outrider, he was counted among the best fighters in the Singularity. And in the end, the decision whether to meet the Warlord or not, once Crassmor had brought the wand home, would be Sandur's.

Flamboyant prongs of the lance lay against Crassmor's breast. The lizard mount stood directly in his way; *Shhing* was still in its scabbard. The barbarian picket, should he so chose, could hardly fail to kill Crassmor.

"You are too big to throw into the cooking pots and too young to fight," the lizard rider scoffed, though he himself looked no older than Crassmor. The fluttering clan pennons and feathered war fetishes on the lance shifted in the breeze. As the lizard stirred, the barbarian's ancestral pendants swung lazily; light flashed from his armbands and the beaten-gold mascles of his harness. "What shall I do with you, eh?"

Striving to hide his trembling, Crassmor held his chin high, replying, "Since I am here to see your Warlord, you may either get out of my way or escort me to him." He pointed to the camp, Ravager's colossal ziggurat-shaped tent rearing at its center.

The picket looked around warily but failed to detect any other enemy. "How have you come here?" he demanded. "Where is the rest of your war party?"

Crassmor showed irritation he half-felt. "A man rides into your camp alone, arms sheathed, with no attempt to hide. Are you lizard lovers so simpleminded that you can't recognize a parley rider when you blunder across one?"

The young barbarian snarled; the needle-sharp tines dug at Crassmor's mesh armor shirt. Sweat from fear trickled from the young Tarrant's helmet brim, joining that already produced by the heat of the day. Other pickets and sentries were already converging on them, though. Their battle pipes were sounding, signaling an enemy. The decision to kill Crassmor or not had passed from the barbarian's hand, and he knew it. With another deadly look, he drew back the lance head by a hairsbreadth.

The rest encircled him, horse and lizards eyeing one another with no more liking than their riders. There was a dispute among the naturally cantankerous warriors; more than one favored the idea of skewering Crassmor and taking him to their Warlord at the apex of a half-dozen lances.

One said, "You have no love of life; you will not have yours for long."

"I am here to make a representation for Sandur," Crassmor answered loudly. The lizard riders murmured among themselves in surprise. *The tale has gone abroad among the hordes,* Crassmor saw. That, at least, boded well.

*"Sandur,"* he shouted this time, "sends word to Ravager, the Bringer of Slaughter. If you'd prefer to do battle with

one lone envoy, have at me. Luckily, I brought no companion, else it would require an entire clan to threaten me." In the back of his mind he was saying prayers.

One rider backed his balky, tail-thrashing mount out of the way, returning the butt of his lance to its rest. Another did the same, then two more. In a moment they'd fallen in around Crassmor and he was on his way into the war camp of the lizard riders.

The enormous camp was under an odorous pall of strange foods, fires fueled by the odd plants and trees of this alien wilderness, latrines, incense, and human and reptilian stenches. There were no women or children to be seen, nor any other camp followers. The lizard riders slept in small tents or under fantastically embroidered awnings, in groups ranging between two and a dozen or so, which Sandur had said were family groups. There didn't seem to be much booty in sight, though all the warriors were well armed and well equipped. Crassmor could see no herds or flocks. Here and there he spied empty boxes, bags, and containers of the kind used by the broken-cross soldiers.

*A hungry army,* he thought, *from a used-up, hungry world. A dangerous enemy.*

Their lances were sharp, though; their weapons bright. Their lizards split the air with piercing shrieks, as the barbarians blew on their silvery control whistles, the unheard sounds sending shivers through Crassmor. The reptiles, scenting Kort, straining to fight or prey on him, had to be restrained sharply, both with whistles and with the sharp lizard prods many of the invaders carried. This close, Crassmor could see that many of the riding lizards were afflicted with tiny parasites, like multicolored barnacles, clinging tenaciously to the joints of their keeled scales.

Barbarians turned out of their tents to line the way, which was hard-packed by the passage of many feet and claws. Shouts and curses and insults rose up; weapons were waved. Though there were no other domestic animals to be seen, the camp was populated by flying creatures the size of small birds or large insects, each having four green, translucent wings. As Crassmor watched, one of them left its perch on a tent pole, settling in a blur of wings onto the back of a stakedout lizard. The beast made no complaint as the flying thing began picking and prying at the tiny parasites among its scales.

The group came at last to the ziggurat tent. Sandur's name was again invoked. Crassmor was ordered down off his mount. He left Kort, with a warning that nothing had better happen to him. The barbarians seemed unimpressed. The horse was rolling his eyes nervously, showing much the same emotion that Crassmor felt as he entered the tent.

The stuff of the tent, not beige silk but something very like it, admitted a great deal of the outside light; still, it was dim within. At ground level the interior had been partitioned off with hangings, awnings, and tapestries depicting scenes of battle, hunting, and celebration with surprising skill. Overhead yawned the upper reaches of the tent, undivided, supported by cleverly joined tentposts and taut guy lines.

Crassmor and his escort passed through several spaces that held nothing but armed, waiting, glowering men, some seated cross-legged on the rich carpets or among thick cushions, others standing. They thumbed their weapons when they caught sight of him, but held their tongues. A last drapery was drawn aside. Beyond it was the innermost chamber of the tent, a spacious place within gently wafting hangings. There were standards and totems of the lizard riders on their upright poles, and a number of the battle flags and gonfalons of the broken-cross soldiers as well.

Crassmor found himself in the presence of the Warlord. Ravager sat before a brazier with dozens of his men, all of them arrayed in magnificent trappings and ornaments. All around the chamber their lizards crouched, reclined, or stood, tearing at dripping chunks of meat, hissing among themselves. Many of them were staked out with chains.

The Warlord looked up. His face contorted in fury when he saw Crassmor; Crassmor trembled. Then Ravager laughed.

"The little one!" he roared, slapping a thick thigh with his massive hand. "You hid like a sandmite, then stole

Sandur from under my hand, you with your sudden appearance and spare horse!" He motioned to one of his conferees. "Bank the fires and heat iron for this foolish boy. There will be meat for our mounts tonight, tender and rare!"

Crassmor hoped that his quaking knees weren't too obvious. "Would you care to hear Sandur's words first?"

Ravager spat; the spittle popped and steamed among the coals of the brazier. "I will have them out of you anyway, once you're roasting. You will tell me all I wish to know, not so?"

Crassmor considered replying with some brave defiance, but could think of none. The crackle of the ill-smelling fire and some streak of honesty made him answer, "Unquestionably." The Warlord's brows lifted a little at that candor. "But it will do you no good to hear my message when I'm basting."

The Emptier of Lodges rose, crossed the carpet between them in three long steps, and stood peering down into Crassmor's eyes with fists on hips. Close up, Crassmor saw that the Bringer of Slaughter had chosen to wear, as a token of victory, one of the decorations of his fallen enemies, a metallic cross enameled in black. The lord of the invaders was bigger than Crassmor had thought, bigger than Sandur, or even Ironwicca. He spoke in a calm tone. "Tell, me, then, frightened mite on your drastic mission, what is your message?"

"Sworn oath kept Sandur from taking up your offer of combat at the chasm. I am come to see if you still offer battle and the medicine wand."

That somehow aroused Ravager's suspicions. "Does Sandur know you're here, foolish boy?"

Again the impulse to lie; again the sudden decision to attempt no dissembling before this man. Crassmor stared up at the hard, broken-nosed face. "No. And my name is Crassmor of Tarrant, my lord. I will carry your wand to Sandur the Outrider if you'll send it, but I doubt he'll take it any other way. He is my brother."

The Warlord's smirk showed his teeth and twisted the scars on his face. "Now that he knows I can win in war,

Sandur the Traitor has rethought the challenge, eh? Nothing to lose, is that it?"

Crassmor saw with sinking heart that he'd made Sandur sound the coward. His brows knit; he countered, "And what would *you* do, Oh Ravager?"

The lizard riders muttered angrily at that, but, after a moment's surprise, the Warlord threw his head back and exploded in brief laughter. He thumped Crassmor's chest with the back of his great fist, not unkindly. Crassmor was obliged to take a half-step backward to retain his balance.

"Just the same thing!" the Warlord proclaimed with a sly nod. Then the humor left his face and Crassmor suddenly found the medicine wand thrust at him.

He took it in wonderment. It was as he recalled, whittled of dun-colored wood in unintelligible symbols and esoteric, curling script and glyphs, inlaid with precious stones and lizard ivory, beaded and corded. It was rudely polished and smudged by much handling, not quite the length of his forearm. He knew from Sandur that each lizard rider created his own medicine wand with much thought, painstaking ritual, and soul swearing. Here was an object of great power.

Now the Warlord scowled; Crassmor found his mouth dry. "Guard it well, young Crassmor," Ravager warned. "I trusted him, Sandur, even liked him, and he betrayed me. I want him here. It may be that I would have done the same thing in his place, but I was not in his place. Your Singularity will be mine in short order, but I won't have your brother dying in battle and cheating me of my revenge. See to it that—"

A furor had risen during his speech, coming from without the ziggurat tent. Now there were screams and yells of rage, the brief clash of steel, a cry of pain, and the unmistakable pounding of a horse's hooves. The curtains flew apart and Sandur plunged into view astride the war horse Bordhall, an appropriated lance in one hand, his broadsword in the other. A guard clung to his saddle, trying to pull him down.

Ravager and all the other barbarians in the place howled,

reaching for swords, lances, and darts. Sandur leaned aside as a two-tined dart passed over his head. He struck the clinging lizard rider with the butt of his lance; the man fell away, clutching a bleeding scalp.

Lances came up. The Outrider had to rein in Bordhall cruelly to avert a death on the thicket of wicked points. Men were hauling back their arms to hurl more darts. Crassmor was pulling *Shhing*, shouting to Sandur in words he himself didn't understand. A half-dozen barbarians threw themselves on the younger Tarrant, dragging him down and holding him immobile, only prevented from slaying him by the medicine wand he bore.

Ravager drowned out his men with a gigantic shout of command. The lizard riders spared a glance aside, then refrained from the hurling of darts and the thrusting of lances. They made a ring around the knight, though, primed to slay. The Warlord bellowed for silence in a voice that hurt Crassmor's eardrums. A quiet settled over the tent, except for the panting for breath that came in the wake of the action, Bordhall's snorting and stamping, and the lizards' hateful noises.

An almost nonchalant gesture from Ravager made the lances fall away, the barbarians drawing aside to let him pass. There were now many weapons ready to fly at any provocation. The Warlord paced across the rich carpet and fixed his enemy with narrowed eyes.

"So Sandur the Traitor is returned." The knight's face twitched at the insult. "Could you not await your pitiful herald? Are you so eager to die?"

*Shhing* had been wrenched from Crassmor's hand, his parrying dagger taken from its sheath. He saw a man rearing back to cast, expecting the Warlord's order. He shrieked, "No! I have the medicine wand! I have the wand!" He held it up as far as clutching hands would let him, showing it to all sides. "It is Sandur's safe-conduct!"

"Release my brother," Sandur ordered Ravager in a low voice, gesturing with his sword, bringing Bordhall around by the pressure of his knees. "You have me here now; your fight is with me." Lance heads came up again to hem him in.

The Warlord went to look down at Crassmor in thought. "My fight is with whosoever bears arms for the Singularity," he said over his shoulder to the knight. Crassmor was held up before him. Ravager snatched the wand from Crassmor's hand; the younger Tarrant abandoned all hope then and there. The Warlord thrust the medicine wand into Crassmor's belt, motioned to his men, and stepped back. Crassmor was pulled out of the way, but then unhanded.

Ravager went to where he'd been sitting, to draw a short heavy, hilted yataghan from its place at his arming belt, which also carried his control whistle, battle pipe, and belt knife. He thrust the yataghan through the carpet, buckled on his belt, and took up the weapon again. He carried no darts. "Come down off that horse, traitor, coward!"

Sandur carelessly tossed aside the lance, limberly pulling one leg up over his pommel. He slid down, alighting with sure agility, sword ready. His only armor was a light haubergeon, about the same protection as the Warlord wore. He went to Crassmor; Ravager didn't object. At Sandur's peremptory glance, the barbarians near his brother drew back a pace or two.

"I'm all right," Crassmor assured him. "How come you're here?"

"Word of the marshaling had already gone abroad," was the reply. "Most of my work had been done for me. It chanced that I passed Lateroo, to hear that you'd been there and taken Kort into the Beyonds. Thinking back on things that passed between us, I found the rest not so hard to piece together." Sandur shook his head sorrowfully. "I should have kept my own counsel. I tried to catch you, to stop you short of the camp. I only arrived in time to see you being led in."

"I await you, Sandur," the Warlord reminded him.

It had all gone wrong. Crassmor began, "Sandur, I never meant for——" He couldn't finish.

"This duel is welcome, brother," the knight told him. "It's as I would have wished it. You did no wrong."

*"Turn and fight!"* Ravager commanded. Sandur gripped his brother's shoulder once, then turned his attention to his foeman, shaking his red mane back out of his way.

"This is a challenge-in-arms of the hordes," the Warlord declared, striding toward the knight. "You know our rules, which is to say: none. Any weapon may be used that comes to hand."

Nor was there any formal signal to begin. Ravager launched himself at Sandur, yataghan held high. They clashed for a moment; the barbarian showed a surprising nimbleness for a man of such bulk. He demonstrated all the power of wrist that his size implied. But he made no inroads against the knight. After a moment's defense, Sandur brought his length of blade into play, driving the other back.

Both Sandur and Crassmor had been surprised that the Warlord had allowed himself such a disadvantage in weapons. But the first conversation of blades had only been a preamble; a moment later, Ravager broke off the match for a moment, stepped back, and casually pulled a sword out of the hand of one of his men. The lizard riders were all grinning maliciously. Crassmor realized that every weapon in the tent except for Sandur's own was, in effect, the Warlord's. Sandur snatched out his long, heavy parrying dagger to even the match.

Swords crossed, to be intersected by parrying blades, the metal rasping and ringing. The two held the pose for a moment, trying their brawn. Neither man gave as weapons strained hilt and hilt. If Ravager was surprised at that, he gave no sign; from Sandur's red beard came the flash of his grin, as ferocious as any barbarian's.

All at once the static scene became a whirl of motion, cut and parry, thrust and block. Blades circled and hacked and stabbed; any stroke could have ended the duel with a beheading or disembowelment. The two attacked and withdrew in split-second campaigns. Soon the combat moved back and forth over a wider area. The onlookers had to be quick to keep out of the combatants' way. Even the pampered riding lizards, sibilating their displeasure, moved aside or were tugged or prodded by their masters, whose cheeks bulged at the control whistles, their fingers racing across the stops and keys. A flock of the parasite-eating bird things rose from the agitated reptiles with a racket of tiny wings.

The Warlord circled a mound of cushions, then bounded over it to attack unexpectedly. Sandur evaded, locking blades in a *corps-à-corps,* and held his ground. Then he assailed Ravager in a flurry of strokes, driving him from one carpet to the next. Baying lizard riders—Crassmor, now forgotten, among them—swarmed to follow the action at a cautious distance.

The Warlord, drawing on weight and thews and speed, stopped the knight's advance with a determined counterattack. They stood hacking at each other's defenses. Men roared; Bordhall, shrilling and kicking, retreated to a corner of the tent, where she kept the savages at a distance with teeth and hooves.

The barbarians howled encouragements to their lord; Crassmor did the same for the Outrider. Few of the lizard riders noticed him; none tried to silence him. Overhead, side, and backhand came the blows. Parries made the blades sing.

A sudden thrust from Sandur's parrying dagger nearly passed through Ravager's abdomen. The Warlord was forced back a step, but took advantage of an opening in the knight's guard. Sandur parried the counterstroke, stepping backward, nearly tripping over a ceremonial gong. The Warlord thought to pounce on him; Sandur avoided it with a tremendous leap backward, clearing the fallen gong.

The ziggurat tent was a madhouse of snarling lizards, wailing, cheering barbarians, and flickering blades. A sweep of the Warlord's sword carried Sandur back. On his recovery, the knight disengaged his dagger from the savage's yataghan, to open a deep slash in his forearm between thick bracelets. At the same time the Warlord reached with the yataghan and, parting the light mail, laid open the flesh of the knight's shoulder.

All four blades engaged once more. The hilts of Ravager's sword were oddly curled and curved; now he used them in a secondary office. Entwining one around Sandur's parrying dagger, he brought his sword around with all his might. The reinforced hilt gave him purchase on the knight's trapped dagger; with a much-practiced twist, the Warlord sent the dagger flying from Sandur's grip, in among the crowd, lost.

Sandur backed off, taking his broadsword in both hands, defending himself with a succession of frenzied strokes. The Warlord advanced, meeting the blows with two weapons, able now both to parry and to attack while his enemy must choose between the two. Sandur dodged; Ravager's sword point opened a vertical rent in the tent wall behind him. The knight leaped, and a slash missed his legs. He nearly opened the Warlord's skull then, the barbarian having become impetuous. Ravager parried with the yataghan. Sandur had to retreat once more.

Crassmor, choking back sobs, thought to throw his own sword or dagger to his brother, then remembered he'd been disarmed. Tears of futility blurred his vision. Then something different from mere bravery seized him, something more substantial, undeniable.

Plucking up the mallet that had fallen along with the gong, he threw himself at the nearest lizard rider, swinging once, twice, and a third time, even as the man went down. Crassmor was instantly upon him, tugging at the weapons at his belt. Tentative cries went up as the bystanders took notice. Crassmor and the barbarian were a tangle of limbs, but the Tarrant son had yanked a long, stout hunting knife from the other's sheath.

He flailed himself free, hacking at those about him to keep them back. He somehow eluded their grasp, uncaring of the cries of pain he drew. The clangor of the duel came to him clearly.

" 'Rider!" he yelled, voice breaking, as hands reached for him and weapons began to appear. He saw his brother's head turn as Sandur skipped back to keep clear of the Warlord for the split second it took to risk a glance. Crassmor could say no more; fists and clawing fingers and blades were near. He lofted the knife into the air. He didn't care when he was pulled back, pummeled, and kicked. He had no sense of pain as he went down, having seen Sandur jump high and catch the knife by its handle.

Crassmor was pinned to the carpet with two-pronged lances jammed down over his arms and legs. Rough-soled boots and sandals were set on his neck and back. Sandur went at the Warlord again, the knife equalizing them, the barbarian yielding ground to the knight's white-hot anger. Then Sandur spun and sprang at the lizard riders who were preparing to carve into his brother.

They wavered and yipped in alarm at the red-haired demon charging at them with blades gleaming and nothing short of murder in his eyes. Their lances came up.

Again that tremendous bellow went up from Ravager; a relative quiet returned to the tent. Sandur, panting, paused and glanced from those holding his brother back to the Warlord. At an angry gesture from their Warlord, all but those men pinning Crassmor drew back.

Ravager's words resounded through his tent. *"Let the man who would not help a brother kill that boy for doing so!"* The look on his face told what would happen to such a man in the tent of Ravager. Everyone stood absolutely motionless. There was only the shifting and spitting of the lizards, Bordhall's nervous tramplings, and the slow billowing of the walls. It was a moment in which Crassmor was amazed to feel no fear.

Sandur, satisfied, broke the tableau. With sword and knife, he sped back across the tent. The duel resumed at an even more savage pitch. Ravager didn't bother to attempt his disarming trick again; Sandur wouldn't fall prey to it twice. The knight drove hard. The Warlord gave way, waiting for this prodigal waste of energy to run its course, confident that he would finish the other as soon as it did. The retreat carried them to where the Warlord's lizard and those of his generals had been staked out with chains chased in silver. The animals squirmed nervously as the duelists struggled in their midst.

Sandur's advance faltered; the Warlord judged that his moment had come. In attacking, though, he opened his guard. The knight instantly sought to take advantage; the falter had been a ploy on Sandur's part. With a titanic swing, he struck Ravager's sword from his grip, gambling everything on that one blow. The Warlord lost his footing and fell, avoiding a second slash, as lizards snapped and filled the air with their stridence. They showed forked tongues, crowding against one another, some moving away from the Warlord, coming Sandur's way.

Ravager lay with only the hilted yataghan against the knight's broadsword and knife. Crassmor, straining to see from where he lay transfixed, tried to croak a war cry for House Tarrant: *"No end but victory!"*

But Ravager plucked from his belt his silvery control whistle. He blew desperately, fingers flying on the stops and keys. The lizards heard; the command was to kill.

As suddenly as that, Sandur found himself surrounded by maddened reptiles avid to sink long fangs into the first thing they could reach, enraged to slay. Plated heads snaked and darted around him; jaws gaped and snapped. Tails thrashed; red eyes glared. Sandur whisked his broadsword's edge around; a scaly head flew, spattering blood. He laid open the ventrals on the throat of a second with his backhand stroke; it fell back to die. A third he impaled through the chin shields under its jaw as it sought to rip his left arm off, then he ducked past it. Men with lizard prods were trying to hold the creatures at bay, playing calming notes on their whistles, but several of them had already been mauled. Crassmor, not in immediate danger, was held where he was.

Ravager didn't retreat to let the lizards do his work, or call for another weapon. He was in among them, chancing death, waiting. Sandur, concentrating on steel-trap jaws, drew close, not hearing Crassmor's torn wail of warning. The Warlord came at him from the side, before the knight was aware. There was a split second of struggle, the beginning of a defense on the Outrider's part.

Ravager drove the yataghan through mail, into Sandur's side, gripping him close. Blood gushed across them both. Sandur's head lolled back; the weapons fell from his hands. Crassmor closed his eyes and said his brother's name in immeasurable grief. Ravager let loose his hold and the knight's body slid to the carpet.

Lizards were being beaten and prodded and whistled

back by handlers. The Warlord turned from the body of his enemy, heaving for breath, wounds flowing, near the end of his own limits. He came back to himself, spying Crassmor as if for the first time. Ravager stepped near, snapped his fingers once or twice, and the younger Tarrant was released.

Crassmor picked himself up, sobbing, gazing at Sandur and then at the Warlord in a daze. He was groggily pondering the correct course of action now, as if it were some lesson he'd forgotten. Surely it was his duty to die attempting revenge? He knew with great fear that he was about to give up his life. Crying, nose running, he looked around for some weapon. Finding none, he concluded that his only alternative was to attack with bare hands; his brother's blood was still on the yataghan.

Ravager had read his thoughts. Shaking his head, the Warlord indicated Sandur's body. "It's not for you to die today, boy," he told Crassmor quietly, as lizards bickered and men began to restore calm. "Your obligation is to bear your brother home, and not leave his funeral to his enemies. Keep my medicine wand for now; my war parties will recognize it, and you will go unhindered. The Singularity's greatest champion is slain; no other man of the Charmed Realm will stand against me if he wishes to live."

He let fall the yataghan tiredly. "Bear your brother home, Crassmor. And tell them Ravager comes."

## Chapter 6

# BROTHERLESS

**He remembered** few things about the ride back to the Singularity. Before he'd properly apprehended the stark fact of Sandur's death, the body had been lashed across Bordhall's saddle, Kort fetched, and his own and his brother's weapons turned over to him.

There had been none of the gloating and glorying he would have expected from the barbarians, perhaps because their Warlord demonstrated none, or perhaps in deference to the Outrider. The mob had dispersed quickly, though many eyes had followed him out of the camp. Ravager had spoken no other word to him.

Crassmor wasn't stopped or challenged by any patrols. He never knew if that was chance or if the word had gone out in some manner. He didn't touch the food they'd tied to his saddle, and drank only sips from his waterskin. He paused for no rest, riding numbly, following that instinct common to those born in the Singularity, going home. Had it not been for the task of seeing Sandur's body back to House Tarrant, he would have dismounted, sat down in the middle of that otherworldly wilderness, and never risen again.

In the descent from the hills overlooking the vineyards of Tolbur, he passed into Blue Dell, whose five waterfalls cascaded to fill the place with the perennial mist which gave it its name. There he encountered his father.

Combard galloped up into Blue Dell like an avenging spirit, his dark cloak flapping behind, at the head of several hundred men-at-arms, assorted archers, swordsmen, knights, and lancers. Crassmor, who had dreaded this moment above any, now found himself inexplicably empty.

Combard registered shock at seeing Crassmor, even as his gnarled hand flew up to halt the fighting men at his back. He reined his own mount to a sliding stop-on-haunches in the slick grass. The Lord of House Tarrant took in Crassmor's devastated expression, the numbness of it, and the ominous burden draped across Bordhall. Then his face assumed an aspect Crassmor could hardly credit: wide-eyed, white-faced, unbelieving, as if the world had come apart.

The old man was shaking as he drew nearer to Crassmor while the others held to their places. Breath seemed to come to Combard with difficulty; he stopped before his younger son.

"What have you done?" Combard whispered, scarcely to be heard over the splashing waterfalls. He moved closer. They were side by side, facing each other.

"The Warlord had offered Sandur single combat, offered his medicine wand as safe-conduct," Crassmor said in a monotone. "Sandur refused, came home to make his report instead. The King's command . . ."

He could meet his father's burning stare for only a second or two at a time, dropping his eyes to his own hands, clenched on his reins. "After he heard of the defeat, Sandur wanted to accept the challenge. The medicine wand would at least protect him until he reached the camp of the lizard riders. So I—went to fetch it." He touched fingertips to it now, still tucked through his belt. "But Sandur found out; he followed me—"

Combard's hand flashed, cracking Crassmor's cheek, snapping his head around. The blow brought tears, but did him neither harm nor good. He went on. "Sandur fought the Warlord and lost, lost."

Combard threw his head back then, eyes screwed shut and fists pressed to his temples, throating a keening sound resembling nothing Crassmor had ever heard from the man. Hastily, as if to disprove what he had cried, Combard struggled down off his horse. He moved as if palsied staggering to Bordhall, dragging his footsteps in the dewy grass. Crassmor dismounted and went after.

Combard's quaking fingers slipped the careful knots, threw back the corner of the wrapping. Sandur's head hung down there, face gray in death, hair still aflame. The old man sank to his knees, cradling his heir's head with heaving sobs, tears laving his cracked cheeks in the mist. "What . . . have . . . you . . . *done?"*

Crassmor, coming up slowly behind, thought the question was meant for him. "What I thought would help him, father; what I could to keep him safe." He moved his hands aimlessly.

Combard came back to himself, releasing the Outrider unwillingly, and stood. He signaled to his troops; Bint came forward alone. Crassmor was surprised to see that the boy rode fully armed, then realized that Combard, on discovering Crassmor's and Sandur's absence, had gathered up every available man, even the untried Bint, and set out at once. Had Combard crossed into the Beyonds, it would have been the first time that he, with his special ties to the land and waters of the Singularity, had departed it since his coming of age.

Combard held out Bordhall's rein; Bint took it hesitantly. "Get you all back to House Tarrant," was the order. "Await me there."

*Not "Await us,"* Crassmor noticed dully. An icy node of fear was born in his middle. No matter; banishment or disownment meant nothing against the tragedy of Sandur's death.

As Bint took the rein, Combard's grief changed to reproach, which he turned on Crassmor. Bint led Bordhall out of Blue Dell with the rest at his back. Hooves drummed; in moments father and son were alone in the mist. Crassmor made a last effort to explain. "It was— when Sandur reported to the King of the Warlord's—"

Combard, erupting in rage, swept out his longsword, his heart a wasteland. His strong, aged hands gripped it tightly, so that the blade quavered a little. He lifted the weapon.

*A life for a life,* a part of Crassmor intoned, citing the justice in which his father believed. Stunned, feeling himself as culpable as his father did, he made no move to defend himself or withdraw.

"No word spoken before the King was spoken to *you*," Combard grated. The last word bore such a weighted despisal that Crassmor's anger flared. His resignation fell away; his voice filled Blue Dell.

"If you didn't mean the words, *why did you say them?* How could I ever know that my father's words and his intent were two different things? *When did you ever teach me that, Combard?*"

The longsword poised in the air, lifted for a headsman's stroke. Crassmor turned his jaw aside, presenting an unprotected neck, but held eye-lock with his father.

Combard's strong, stooped frame vibrated; the sword point made erratic debate overhead. Then the Lord of House Tarrant let his blade fall to the misted grass, turning away with face buried in hands. The shuddering of his shoulders and back tore at Crassmor's heart even more than had Combard's wail of lamentation. Crassmor stared dumbly, arms hanging uselessly at his sides.

Combard, presenting his back to Crassmor, said at last, "Tell me, please, how my—how your brother died."

Crassmor did, haltingly, in simplest terms, as Combard seemed to shrink in on himself. At the end, the old man stared off into the mist for long minutes. As Crassmor was about to speak again, Combard retrieved his sword, wiped the dew from it slowly, and returned it to its scabbard. The old man gathered his horse's reins, then went to his surviving son. Combard embraced him with a free arm, an embrace that was heartfelt, yet lacked all vigor. But with that, Crassmor found that he no longer wished to die.

"When you have made your report to the King," Combard bade him, "then come you home to your mother and me."

He mounted tiredly for the ride back to House Tarrant and the funeral of the son of his heart.

Ironwicca was in his throne room this time. He was the only one there. Crassmor covered the floor that was more vast than a drill field and ascended flights of broad steps leading to the dais, crossing landings where whole companies of courtiers and luminaries kept their places at other times. He listened to his own footfalls come back from the sculptured ceiling; he went the whole way under the King's watchful eyes. Crassmor knew from his instant ushering-in by servitors that Ironwicca expected him; he wondered just what the monarch's hidden sources of information were.

The King waited out Crassmor's approach in silence, drawing long fingers through the ringlets of his beard. Next to the monolithic throne was the King's heroic, curled drinking horn, laquered in red and blue, heavily gilt, rimmed in weighty, twisted silver. The horn had been torn, it was said, from the skull of its original owner by the King himself. It was in its stand of platinum-leafed teak, half the height of Ironwicca himself.

The King indicated it as Crassmor topped the last step to stand before him. "Empty. And I've no Cup Bearer to fill it, have I?"

Crassmor's mouth worked. Though Ironwicca usually drank from ordinary vessels, it had been Sandur's honor as Outrider to fill and fetch the great horn on occasions of highest importance. "You have not," Crassmor confessed at last, eyes sliding from the King's.

"Then you fill it," Ironwicca commanded harshly.

Crassmor saw a keg nearby, set on a rack to one side. He ascended the dais and, with a final look to assure himself of the King's permission, lifted up the drinking horn. It was heavy, as Sandur had said it was, and clumsy to handle.

"You know the protocol, of course," Ironwicca said with particular emphasis; Crassmor's "yes" was less steady than he'd have wished. They both knew why Crassmor was familiar with the process; he'd seen Sandur discharge this duty scores of times.

So each step covered many that the Outrider had taken. Every gesture was a haunting; the filling of the horn resurrected Sandur. *He should be doing this, not me! Outrider, I'd have died in your place if I could!*

His brother's casual comments on the ritual came back to him. There was a trick to charging the horn, turning it at first so as not to trap air in its pointed tip. By the time he presented the brimming horn to Ironwicca with the prescribed bow, laboring a bit under its weight, Sandur was all around him. Nothing could have been more evocative of his brother's death than this.

The King's hand took the horn's handle; muscle jumped as Ironwicca lifted it. The sound of the keg had told Crassmor that the King had already done prodigious drinking, but he showed no sign of it. Nor had Ironwicca ever, even on nights of revelry that had left wooden-legged drinkers under the tables.

The King drank deeply, then looked at Crassmor. "I have no Cup Bearer."

"No, Majesty." Crassmor's voice had nearly broken.

"And *now*," Ironwicca declared in a tone more alive, one that stood the Tarrant son straight up and riveted his attention, driving out remembrance. "Now that you've walked his steps and felt his absence, you have been punished as much as you deserve. That is my decree. And the punishment isn't for Sandur's death; it's for your presumption in thinking to shoulder guilt that only fate may bear. Be warned, or you'll be of no use to me, Crassmor; the next time it may be a capital offense, and the verdict handed down by a practical world. Keep Sandur in your heart, but only punish yourself the more if you care to dispute *my* judgment."

He drank again. Crassmor stared at the toes of his own boots, throat working, then nodded.

"Enough," Ironwicca boomed, setting aside the horn in its stand. "I have the bare facts already. Tell me now the whole of it. Mind you omit no detail."

Crassmor obeyed, though he found it hard to put some things into words. Mention of the medicine wand brought questions from the King and explanations from Crassmor, since Sandur hadn't spoken of it or of Ravager's challenge and insults. When that had been clarified, Ironwicca growled, "Your brother's report was incomplete that morning in the egret tower. Why didn't you speak up then?"

Crassmor gulped. "Majesty, whoever invited my comment, or gave me leave to make it?"

The monarch reclined in his throne, stroking his beard. "Fair enough," he admitted at length. "Go on."

Crassmor complied, telling of the sad parade along Fey Passage, Sandur's words, his own foray into the Beyonds, and what had come after. When his voice choked with emotion from time to time, the King chose to ignore it, drinking contemplatively from the great horn until Crassmor regained his composure.

The story finished, Ironwicca gazed off into the reaches of his throne room for long moments. Then he said with finality, "It's changed." Remembering Crassmor, who was afraid to ask what that had meant, he went on. "And that is the medicine wand there in your belt? The safe-conduct talisman?"

Crassmor affirmed it and held out the wand. "It's linked to the aura of him who shaped it, Ravager himself. Part of the peace that binds his hordes and prevents blood feuding is the exchange of these rods and the soul oaths that are sworn by them."

Ironwicca took and examined it, asking, "Would you say that the Warlord's challenge still stands?"

"His safe conduct does, at any rate," Crassmor judged. "And so, by implication, does his challenge. What's more, he boasted in loud words before his men. I doubt he would refuse single combat."

The King rose up from his throne in thought, to pace the dais with the tread of a feline. "No, he cannot," the King decided at last, hands tensed on the wand. Crassmor almost gathered the temerity to warn against Ravager's prowess, but it came to him that Ironwicca, who'd known Sandur well, would appreciate the danger posed by the man who'd killed him.

"It would please my father to have Sandur's death avenged," he told the King.

"It will please him even more, then," Ironwicca returned, "when you describe it to him. You'll be there to see it."

Crassmor stuttered, shocked that events still included him, not unterrified at the idea of returning to the encampment. "That is, thank you, Highness. You do my House, uh, good honor. But why—"

"To chastise you, in some part," Ironwicca replied. "To exonerate you as well, for your role in all this. And to have at my side a companion who knows the lay of the land and is familiar with the barbarians. Before all else, though, your being at my side when I ride into that camp will let every man there know why I've come. You took forth Ravager's challenge and Sandur's body; you return with me. Ravager won't be able to change his mind, even if he should wish to."

Remembering Combard's last instruction, Crassmor ventured, "But my father—"

*"Serves me!"* the King thundered, and Crassmor could not bow quickly or deeply enough. "By oath of fealty, as does your entire family," Ironwicca finished. That settled the issue.

"Majesty." Crassmor quaked.

The King stared down at him, hands clasped behind his back. "Do you know what it is that your father fears in you?"

No question could have astonished Crassmor more. *"Fears,* sire?"

"The blood of Lewan-the-Rake Tarrant," the King told him, watching to see what effect that would have. The name was little more than words to Crassmor, the name of Combard's father, a face gazing down from old busts and portraits. It evinced features in common with Crassmor's own, granted, but the resemblance had never sparked much curiosity.

Lewan's lordship over House Tarrant hadn't been one of great repute, though the land and water had been kind. It had only been with Combard's ascendancy that House Tarrant had regained its reputation for deeds of arms, along with a weightier influence in matters of politics and additional grants of lands and holdings.

"Your servant doesn't have the least idea what your Majesty means," Crassmor confessed.

"There are resemblances, at least in Combard's mind.

Lewan-the-Rake had your love of parties and feasts. He had a roving eye for women as well, and enjoyed a good jape more than anything."

Crassmor had heard approximately these same things, in more condemnatory phrases, from Combard. The long-lived Ironwicca's speaking this way, though, from personal knowledge, gave Crassmor fresh insight into his grandfather.

The King continued. "Lewan's arranged marriage gave him a spouse who had none of those things in common with him. She took refuge in raising her sons, Combard and Furd, keeping apart from Lewan as much as she could. He made no objection. I would be surprised if she did not speak against him to them. Your grandmother died embittered and young. It is understandable that her sons felt that she'd been driven to an early grave."

Of his grandmother Crassmor had heard much; she'd been sainted by his father and uncle. Not focused on the King, the polished artistry of the throne, or the opulence all around him, he listened closely.

"Combard of Tarrant saw his own image in Sandur," Ironwicca said. "He took comfort that his heir was a kindred soul."

Crassmor couldn't keep his lips from turning up at the corners. "Then I came along." It was rueful.

"Yes, Crassmor, with some symptoms of becoming another Lewan-the-Rake. Or so thinks Combard."

Crassmor made no answer. The King went on. "Has your father ever condemned himself for having a second son, have you wondered? For not being content with Sandur?"

Crassmor had, but right now he wondered another thing. "Why do you tell me this?"

Ironwicca ignored the lapse in protocol; his face betrayed nothing. "For now, simply lay it to the fact that you've rendered service in fetching that medicine wand, and will do another in returning to the Beyonds. How else am I to reward you? What would a bauble or sword or another parcel of land matter to a scion of House Tarrant? A piece of yourself is what I give you. Do with it as you see fit. My own advice is to keep it to yourself, at least for the time being."

He rang for servitors. "You'll rest here while preparations for our journey are made. I'll dispatch word to your father. Come the dawn, we set forth."

Crassmor warned, "My father will certainly remind your Highness that I am no appointed knight."

"Easily attended to," Ironwicca drawled. His sword came forth from its scabbard all in an instant, a plain, long, heavy, well-used weapon that left a wicked chiming in the air. The King approached him. Crassmor stood rooted for a moment, then hurriedly dropped to one knee.

The sword touched his shoulders, the King setting aside solemn rituals and days-long ceremony, saying the words that made Crassmor a knight of the Singularity. Crassmor stammered his fealty in all things and his promise to uphold the King's laws, and was bidden rise as a knight. It was done before he'd overcome his shock.

"Take that as an object lesson," Ironwicca advised matter-of-factly. He sheathed his blade with a sound like cymbal and drum. "There's no technicality or huggermugger that is indispensable. Substance is all; form, nothing."

For a moment his eyes ranged around the acres-square glory of his throne room. He shrugged. "I was a serving warrior a long, long time before anybody's sword rested on *my* shoulders."

# Chapter 7

# A RETINUE OF ONE

**The presence of** Ironwicca made for a much more respectful escort into the midst of the lizard riders. The King was in black silken shirt and breeches, with a sleeveless shirt of ring-mail and a purple cape streaming back from his shoulders. He wore no crown, only an iron cap with a crouching lion on its crest. His serviceable sword was belted to his side with a broad band of leather and heavy metal plaques.

The new knight rode beside his liege. Crassmor held high the Warlord's medicine wand. The two entered the camp with a hundred barbarians on every side, but none too close.

The invaders' encampment was now a chain of extensive bivouacs paralleling the Singularity's border. Everywhere there was preparation for the first great strike into the Charmed Realm. The parasite-eating birds clouded the sun. Tents filled the high places and the low, not clustered any longer, but packed tightly, separated only by narrow byways and makeshift lizard pens, ranged out as far as could be seen. The rank smell of reptiles and fires and slit trenches clogged the air. Off to one side, on an open stretch of plain, a reviewing area had been measured off. A contingent of thousands upon thousands now wheeled and maneuvered there. It was toward this parade ground and not the ziggurat tent that the lizard riders guided Ironwicca and Crassmor.

The camp was even more of a wonder to the neophyte knight than before. He had no idea how someone could keep such an awesome force supplied. Apparently, Ravager had the trick of it, though, if only barely. As they crossed the unending camp they saw wide, rutted roads, feeder arteries to the barbarians. Lines of lizard-drawn sledges moved along them, bearing provisions for men and animals alike. Although enormous amounts of provender were arriving constantly, Crassmor saw, they were being doled out meticulously, in modest portions, to clamoring men. Numbers this great, he saw, could impoverish even the best logistical organization—and the lizard riders were not used to this sort of thing.

*Sandur said that their home Reality is dying and barren,* he recalled. *Who, where, is making such fearful sacrifices, that this army might eat? This spells starvation for someone.*

As he and the King rode along, Crassmor heard lizard riders both mounted and afoot call their customary curses and provocations while they wolfed miserly rations. Crassmor thought, however, that the savages, noting Ironwicca, moderated their shouting considerably. The King and the knight came to the place where the Warlord reviewed his troops from a platform fashioned from yellow wood in the semblance of a riding lizard.

Ravager was dressed in full battle harness, luminous gems, and glittering trappings. His weapons were the same that Crassmor had seen before, with a sword as well.

The many units had assumed their formations, spread out across the field. Closer in, a group of some thousand or so had dismounted, leaving their lizards in close ranks. These warriors stood in files before their Warlord, each man's lance planted butt-down in the sand to one side, his longsword thrust point-first into the ground on the other.

Seeing Ravager rekindled Crassmor's misgivings, but the sight of his massed hordes drove home the reasoning behind the King's decision to make a duel of it, regardless of risk. Single combat held the only prayer for the Singularity's survival.

The knight had added reason to be nervous, having done a good deal of thinking on the way in. Both he and Ironwicca rode under the protection of the medicine wand, but, as the King had taken the trouble to point out, formalities were subject to dismissal in the name of convenience.

Too, Crassmor had come to see through the illusion of

safety that the company of the King had at first imparted. To be sure, Ironwicca was legendary for his knack of getting through every conceivable misadventure alive. Stories of his exploits included mêlées, duels, shipwrecks, quests, escapes, rescues, wanderings, and assaults by mystical forces. What worried Crassmor was that on a number of occasions the King had been a lone survivor, or lost all-too-numerous comrades-in-arms. The companionship of Ironwicca, who possessed tremendous powers of strength and endurance, was no guarantee that an ordinary mortal would also elude death. In fact, it greatly increased the likelihood of finding oneself confronted by situations quite beyond the resources of a lesser man. *Which I readily concede myself to be,* Crassmor reflected glumly.

Seeing them, the Warlord leaped down lightly from the platform, hands on the hilts of his weapons. The confidence he exuded turned to curiosity when he studied Ironwicca. Ravager must long since have had word of their coming, but he chose to examine them with feigned surprise. His broken-nosed face creased into a grin. Ignoring the King, he said to Crassmor, "So—you have managed to find another opponent for me, sandmite? Hard to credit that even the Singularity could contain two such fools."

Crassmor bridled at the reference to Sandur, barbarian hordes or no, but held his tongue. Ravager pretended an amused inspection of the King; Crassmor saw that it was in fact a sober evaluation of an enemy to be reckoned with. The Warlord gestured to the ranks of men dismounted before him with longsword and lance to either side, and to the thousands upon thousands beyond.

"Those are my clan chieftains, and these afoot here my overlords," he told the knight and the King. Crassmor wondered how many scores of warriors each one represented. "This killing will have a certain prestige for me."

Ironwicca said nothing, shedding his cloak and dismounting without demonstration. Ravager saw the disdain in that; anger showed on his face. Crassmor, remembering propriety, rushed to dismount and accept Ironwicca's reins when the King handed them aside. The King kept an open hand extended. After an instant, Crassmor realized what

Ironwicca wanted and put the wand in his palm. The Warlord was watching carefully, weighing, assessing.

The King gave Crassmor a meaningful sideways glance. With a start, it came to the knight that he was now Royal Herald. He blurted, "His Majesty, Ironwicca, sovereign of all the Singularity." The King's manifold other titles had fled his memory. Crassmor didn't elaborate, simply happy that his voice hadn't cracked.

"Your name precedes you," the Warlord told Ironwicca, "but you are known to me by some other, are you not?" He shook his head, pacing toward the King in a long spiral while Ironwicca waited. "And yet, you are no enemy I have ever met, nor any friend either."

The King held up the wand. "To that, supply your own answers. My only purpose in this miserable place lies with this." He had the wand in his left hand; his right freed his broadsword in an arc of light. "And this."

The Warlord's sword came forth too, and the yataghan. The King was about to cast down the medicine wand to free his left hand for the shortsword. Crassmor's dismay at seeing his only safeguard thrown aside got the better of his sense of decorum. He made a strangled sound that the King caught. Ironwicca raised one eyebrow, then handed his shaken herald the wand. So low that no one else might hear, he informed Crassmor, "While that may not speak highly of your confidence in your sovereign, Crassmor, it pays good praise to your prudence." His mouth pulled a quick grin.

He handed over the wand. It was scarcely in Crassmor's palm before the shortsword was out, reflecting the purple-white sun. The knight bounded backward like a startled deer as the Warlord charged his enemy, screaming a hair-raising battle cry. The King, as was his habit, joined combat without a word.

Twin streaks of silver marked where the Warlord's weapons cut the air; Crassmor couldn't follow the blades themselves. Edge sheared against edge, Ironwicca parrying with both swords. The collision, powered by Ravager's weight and speed, drove the monarch back a step, his foot skidding a bit in the gritty soil. His counterattack was instantaneous; the Warlord had to move quickly to stay alive. The blades took up an astonishing dialogue.

Weapons pealed in contention. Passage after passage of sword work rang, with neither man gaining or losing ground by more than a pace. They dueled at a rate and with an exertion that ordinary fighters could not have sustained for more than moments. The Warlord laughed, taunting the King as he fought. Ironwicca conserved attention and strength for matters of points and edges alone, yet something in him that Crassmor had never seen before had been unleashed.

It was clear from the first exchange how near-even the match was. The barbarians broke ranks, running to form a wide circle around the combatants. This time no one bothered to restrain or disarm Crassmor, who followed the duel with an eldritch feeling that he'd lived it all before, the image of a laughing Sandur in his mind's eye. The lizard riders kept a watch on the new-made knight, though; he knew that there would be no throwing of a replacement blade to the King.

Each duelist's life was in constant danger. Any second in the contest carried the possibility of being the last. The fight began to take up more and more space, swords thrusting and arcing in, parries tolling. Soon the footwork opened up. As with Sandur's combat, the barbarians had to enlarge their ring, with Crassmor keeping to the edge. Both antagonists were showing increasing determination now. Their blade work was less conservative. They ended a feeling-out phase in which most of the swordsmen known to Crassmor would have met death. The two advanced and retreated with barely a pause in between.

Cuts came more quickly; Crassmor saw that it was the Warlord who was accelerating the pace. Ironwicca obliged him with no sign of distress. The King surrendered ground, backing toward the marshaling field. With a determined attack, the Warlord drove Ironwicca among the ranked longswords and lances set there. The King nearly backed into one grounded lance despite Crassmor's yelp of warning. Ironwicca turned Ravager's attack aside at the last moment, then ducked. The Warlord's blade clipped the lance's shaft neatly in two, sending its streamers and a third of its length into the dust ten feet away. Ravager's return swing barely missed as Ironwicca sucked in his gut. The two fell to it again.

The King pressed the Warlord in his turn, raining blow after blow from every quarter, working cleverly with his shortsword. The bigger man gave way grudgingly, giving no sign that he was in trouble. Ravager counterattacked all at once, throwing all his height and bulk into it; the King, wielding his weapons brilliantly, managed to contain him. They shuffled, feinted, and lunged in among upright lances and longswords, raising dust. Crassmor and the barbarians came after, threading among the planted weapons.

Suddenly the Warlord engaged his sword's curled quillons around those of his adversary's shortsword, twisted, and whirled the weapon out of Ironwicca's hand, flinging it far, even though Crassmor had been at great pains to warn his sovereign of that trick.

The King responded instantly, with a slash that nearly found his foeman's gullet before the yataghan turned it. Ravager bellowed in triumph, but the King stretched out his arm, snatched up one of the longswords, and was two-sworded once more. Swinging them both with haste and determination, Ironwicca won himself time and room.

It was difficult to use a longsword of the lizard riders well with both hands, however, and the King could spare only one. In the fleeting respite he'd gained, he thrust his own broadsword into its scabbard and came at the barbarian with the longsword in a two-handed grip. For all the weapon's weight and length, the King moved it with amazing speed and force, and a precision that had the Warlord on the defensive, second blade or no. The longsword's mass and reach gave Ironwicca a new advantage; his sheer brute strength and feline coordination made its unwieldiness insignificant. Ravager learned that the Singularity's monarch was aware of the rules of the contest—any weapon that comes to hand.

The King made rampant advance, giving the lizard lord no time to form any defense. Both Ravager's weapons were needed to stop the longsword's stealing his life; there was no opportunity to make a stand. With a stupendous swing, Ironwicca snapped the yataghan off at its hilt.

Ravager lost no time in leaping back, casting his sword at the King—who ducked it—and plucking up a longsword of his own. Ironwicca rushed at him. They renewed their contest, moving now onto harder-packed ground where the riderless lizards were tethered. Crassmor and the other on-lookers emerged from the forest of lances, following. The knight had again remembered religion; half-forgotten prayers were on his lips.

The Warlord had backed a step in among the staked-out reptiles, waiting. Ironwicca went to meet him, disre-garding the fate of the Outrider. One lizard swung its head at him, aroused by the fighting and commotion and antag-onized by his alien smell. The King showed no concern; he struck it on the internasal plates of its head, eluding its fangs, with the flat of his blade. He thereafter ignored it as the lizard scuttled away from him.

Ironwicca threw himself at the Warlord, but this time with a one-handed stroke, clutching for his enemy's wrist with his left to wrestle the barbarian's guard aside. Ravager took his left hand from his longsword to seize Ironwicca's wrist instead. They grappled, lurching in a giant's *corps-à-corps*, spinning further in among the grouped lizards. Crass-mor feared that the King would fall prey to the stratagem that had claimed Sandur.

It was a vicious deadlock. With an explosion of effort, the two pushed apart. Then they were together again, clash-ing with swords held two-handedly. The treacherously curled hilts met, entwined, and strove against each other. Gradually, the Warlord's forced the King's downward.

The intensity of it was eloquent in the quivering blades, in the hunched shoulders and bunched muscles of the duel-ists, and in their clenched teeth. The Warlord had the ad-vantage of leverage. Ironwicca's weapon descended beneath his enemy's until both points and lengths of the two blades rested on the hard ground. The unbinding of the swords now lay completely in the lizard rider's control. The King, Crassmor saw with dismay, could either abandon his weap-on or be killed or wounded after that unbinding.

Ironwicca chose a third option. In a single motion he shifted his big, lithe body, still gripping his hilt tightly and keeping both blades firmly against the ground by dint of intertwined hilts. He raised his booted foot, to bring it down across the Warlord's blade with enormous power. The barbarian's weapon snapped across, as did the King's. Ironwicca jumped back, dropping his useless stub of a sword, tugging free his own tried broadsword. In the same moment, his left hand produced from his belt a control whistle; he blew a tremendous breath into it, fingering the keys and stops.

Lizards around the two went mad. The King's notes sent them into a bloodlust; they snapped at both men and one another. Barbarians, overcoming their astonishment and outrage, began groping for weapons, howling to one another. The Warlord ducked a fanged maw, reached for his belt, and fumbled uselessly. It came to Crassmor with a jolt that Ironwicca had stolen the Warlord's own control whistle during their *corps-à-corps*.

Men were lofting weapons and replacement blades to Ravager, shouting, seizing their own whistles to blow counterorders. The King drove their own beasts at them in all directions with blade and whistle. There was shrieking, confusion, bloodshed. One weapon, a shortsword thrown on blind chance, landed near the Warlord, who cast aside his broken blade. But the King was there first, one foot planted on it; the barbarian backed away. Ironwicca advanced. The Warlord took up the only defense left to him in the midst of the lizard's insanity, his belt knife.

The King gave vent to his whistle again, his chest expanding to pour air into it. The birring hurt Crassmor's ears. A lizard that the Warlord hadn't noticed behind him turned in instant fury, fastening its fangs into his arm, opening a terible wound. A second reptile, smelling blood, rushed at Ravager as he fought the first with nothing but his knife and bare hands. Its jaws closed on his shoulder and part of his neck. Two more lizards sidled in for the kill.

Another rushed at the King. Without ceasing his hate notes, he bent out of the way of its sinuous strike, then beheaded it. Crassmor thought, *Any weapon that comes to hand*, as he watched the beleaguered Warlord understand that he was doomed; the knight felt only a sanguinary content.

Barbarians tried to scatter their beasts and battle their way to their liege. Yowls, shrieks, and hissing deafened everyone there as weapons and lizard prods swung and flew. The air was filled with dust, making a yellow half-light in which men and animals strove. The barbarians' calming notes had little effect.

At last a path was cleared. Horde members charged in to the rescue. Crassmor came after, coughing from the dust; he fetched up against a mob of men who stood unmoving. The knight wormed his way in among them and none objected. Breaking through their circle, he found Ironwicca standing over the corpse of Ravager.

The King's sword was wet with the blood of riding lizards. The Warlord's lifeblood was seeping into the hard ground. Nearby lay the body of the lizard Ravager had killed with only a knife before the others had pulled him down. Crassmor wondered why the sight gave him no pleasure, as he went to Ironwicca's side.

There may have been some sign that the knight didn't catch. The ring of barbarians, thumbing weapons, began closing in slowly. The King weighed the plain sword in his hand, the gore dripping from it. Crassmor swallowed only after some trouble and put a hand halfway to *Shhing*'s hilt. *Too bad there isn't a minstrel within miles,* his mind jibbered. With his left hand he produced Ravager's medicine wand, pushing it high into the air.

"I came under the wand," Ironwicca's calm voice said, somehow easy to hear even over the pandemonium of the lizards and the injured. "Under *your* law, not mine. My herald and I go in that same manner. Any man here who wants to lay claim to duel vengeance will have his wish. Where is he?"

In the ensuing silence each lizard rider eyed his neighbors, waiting for one of their number to step forward. Even their foremost champions recognized that their Warlord had been the best fighter among them. The man who'd killed Ravager could easily slay any of them.

Crassmor saw one young buck of the hordes who seemed about to speak out. An older warrior who stood beside him, kinsman perhaps, put a hand on the youth's shoulder and shook his head gravely; to go against Ironwicca the King would be to waste a life.

One graying brave spoke up. "Go your way for now, O King. We have a new Warlord to select, and this one to honor. But harken: on a day soon, you will find yourself among us again."

The rest were quick to second that. Soon voices were raised in a war chant. Weapons were being beaten together in time, though no one made a move toward the King and the knight. But when Ironwicca walked toward them, the lizard riders fell back and opened a path for him. Crassmor was at the King's heels, trying to look as unhurried, holding the medicine wand conspicuously. Around him resounded the war chant, lifting from the throats of the massed lizard riders, riving the stillness of the alien wilderness.

## Chapter 8

# TAKEN IN AND CAST OUT

"But—but how could Ironwicca possibly know how to use a lizard rider's whistle?" Willow asked. "Isn't that a guarded secret among them?"

Crassmor nodded. They sat together in the untended gardens of House Comullo, the House of the Jade Dome. He was still in armor, tired and foul-smelling. She wore loose pantaloons and blouse of a lavender, feather-light material. Elsewhere in the dilapidated, once-grand place,

Ironwicca took counsel with Willow's father Teerse and with Combard.

Crassmor's mind was still fixed on the expression that had illuminated Willow's face when he'd first appeared with the King. A look compounded of several elements, it had shown joy and relief the most. There had been another thing in it also, which Crassmor had refused to let himself think about too much. A glory had suddenly transformed her face at his safe return. Willow's expression had been so fluent and compelling that he'd had to resist the impulse to turn and look behind him to see for whom it was meant. He'd felt that he happened to be standing between Willow and someone who had called forth her innermost beauty; it had been inconceivable that that radiance had been meant for him.

He'd known her all his life and always made himself keep his feelings for her in some insulated compartment locked by his love of Sandur. Seeing her that day, back from death, he'd let himself acknowledge how unique and utterly precious Willow was.

"Ironwicca knew the whistle nonetheless," he answered now. "He played it with the skill a lizard rider might have envied." He frowned for a moment and framed his next words carefully. "And it seemed—oh, seemed that they knew one another or had something in common, Ravager and the King. Ironwicca would say nothing on it, laughed when I asked. He was an eerie grim-merry all the way home, even though the barbarians are jostling right now to choose the new Warlord and carry on the invasion. Ironwicca wasn't concerned, even when he left orders to monitor the lizard riders closely."

Though the King's decision to come to House Comullo rather than go on to Dreambourn had surprised Crassmor, objection had been the farthest thing from the knight's mind. Combard had been visiting Teerse and seeking Willow's company in mourning. Though she hadn't said as much, Crassmor understood that this was a source of discomforted helplessness to Willow. Sandur's death had hurt her terribly, but Combard's grief was all-consuming, an implication that hers and Teerse's should be the same. Such boundless, debilitating sorrow wasn't in Willow's nature.

"All the arms and fighting contingents that can be raised have been," she said. "It's plain that Ironwicca feels the need for counsel now."

*But why here?* he asked himself. Certainly Willow's father was astute, calm, sparing with words yet keen and candid with those he used. Crassmor couldn't understand, though, why the King would seek that advice alone, before he consulted his generals, statesmen, and seers.

Boots sounded on cracked paving-stones, grinding the rubble of those that had fragmented over the years of neglect. Crassmor and Willow looked up to see the King, Combard, and gentle old Teerse approach. Crassmor stood to bow, Willow to drop a delicate curtsy. Their faces were all question; the dread of war was in both.

Ironwicca's rare mood was evident, though; he laughed outright, a pleasant, puissant sound. "Didn't I tell you, Sir Crassmor, to be of easy mind? Your father and Lord Teerse agree with me; the lizard riders' threat will end—*has* ended. Ravager held them together, and their First Shaman gave them their navigation. There is no one of the Warlord's stature among them now; they will fall out and feud among themselves there in the Beyonds. The probabilities and chains of events that brought them upon us in the first place will be severed or altered. If their surviving shamans are astute, they will find their way back to their own Reality, though I think that world would be better off if the hordes wandered forever. In any case, the barbarians' inroads to the Home Plane have dissipated."

Crassmor considered the King's certainty of tone and how it was connected to his conference with Combard and Teerse. It had been rumored for generations, ever since the Comullo family had begun their marvelous Tapestry, that the Tapestry had, for its weavers, properties of prediction. Crassmor had always doubted that; it had seemed to the young knight that if House Comullo possessed an object of such value and power, it would not be in decay and disrepair, impoverished, maintaining a mere handful of guards and servants. Willow had simply dismissed the subject by refusing, in her good-natured, stubborn way, so much as to discuss it.

Combard, Crassmor noticed, looked, if not happy, then at least less dispirited than he had been. He would never get over the death of Sandur, but he'd now begun to live with it. Combard had greeted Crassmor with surprising forbearance, an unaccustomed warmth which, however labored, had pleased Crassmor mightily.

Combard came to him now. "This casting-out of the invaders is by his Majesty's hand, true, but the King has pronounced it your deed in some part as well." Ironwicca, coming up behind, seconded that. Son and father traded awkward smiles.

Teerse and his daughter departed to see Ironwicca to the bailey, where his escort of Royal Borderers now awaited him. When they were alone, Combard took from the folds of his sash a golden band, the heir's ring, which Crassmor had last seen on the Outrider's lifeless hand.

The old man held it out. As it was, so often, between them, words came only with great difficulty; gestures must speak. Crassmor accepted the ring and slipped it onto his finger. It was a loose fit, though it had been snug on a lesser finger of Sandur's big hand.

Combard sadly eyed it there for a moment, then squared his stooped shoulders, drawing breath. "All is arranged," he said, "with the Grand Master of the Order of the Circle of Onn. You will join our ranks, as did Sandur. Each Tarrant generation must have its serving member; this is our tradition."

"Thank you, fa—fellow knight." Crassmor caught himself, then made formal acceptance. Combard's answering smile was no less welcome for being slight and mingled with sorrow. Unwilling to let the extraordinary moment slip away, Crassmor blurted, "I'm not Sandur; we know I never will be. Son to House Tarrant, though; *that* I shall be as best I know how."

Combard's lips tightened. He cuffed his heir's cheek lightly, affectionately, about to respond. Just then there came a racket from beyond the seamed and crumbling garden walls. Willow appeared, laughing, calling their names. She shouted as she drew near.

"The scouts are back! The lizard riders are gone!" She reached them by then, panting. "It's as the, as the King said. The barbarians have wandered back into their Reality! Ironwicca has set those fierce Challa horsemen the task of following to make sure, but there seems little doubt!"

She threw her arms around Combard and kissed him for joy. He yielded to it stiffly, but his elation was plain. Crassmor clapped hands, laughing straight up into the sky, back arched. Out in the bailey, men were whooping as if drunk; hounds barked and bayed over their masters' exultations. Ironwicca's victory roar sounded above all. Combard hurried off to hear the reports firsthand.

Left behind, Willow stared at Crassmor and he at her. Rejoicing was replaced by simple astonishment at what they saw in each other's eyes. They leaned closer, no longer hearing the exuberant madness nearby but feeling its joyous release. At a moment they both recognized, they kissed.

Crassmor took Willow into his arms and kissed her again as she responded eagerly. When they parted for a moment, he held her a small distance from him and lost himself in the brown-green eyes. His desires were locked in tormented conflict with his conscience. The things he needed to say to her were those he'd never even have permitted himself to think if Sandur had lived. He fought the hardest battle of his life, to convince himself that this elation was no betrayal of his brother.

"I love you, love you, Willow."

He hadn't thought that her face, transformed with happiness, could become so much more rapt, an enchantment. Begun, the words spilled from him before she could utter the acknowledgment forming on her lips. "I always have loved you for so long that I cannot remember not loving—"

He was gripped from behind with brutal fervor, yanked away from her, thrown headlong across the garden path, as a little scream escaped Willow. They'd been so intent on one another that neither had heard Combard re-enter the garden.

Combard stormed, "Animal!" He spit at his son, then

turned to Willow with a moment's tenderness. "Has he hurt
you?" In shock, she shook her head as she tried to frame a
reply, to explain.

Crassmor heaved himself up off the ground. "Father,
you don't—"

*"Silence!"* Combard's voice made the very air crack. Lips
pulled back from his teeth, he half-drew his longsword with
a grating of metal. "Your brother's only days gone, barely
in his crypt. What manner of creature comes slithering after
his betrothed?"

It was a misrepresentation so horrid that Crassmor had
trouble apprehending it. Combard took a step toward him.
"Out! Get out without another word, or, by the Circle I
wear, I'll sword you!"

Combard seldom swore by the circlet of stone on his
finger. Gasping, Crassmor looked to Willow, about to say
the truth even though his life rode with it. Her eyes held
an entreaty not to.

Combard missed that look between them, glaring at his
son. "She is, not for you, I vow."

Crassmor realized what his father meant. As Lord of the
Elder House of Willow's slain fiancé, it was, if he chose to
exercise it, Combard's right to select her husband. Aroused,
Combard was fully capable of such an act.

Willow was right. The matter must be left as it stood
until Combard's fury had cooled. To pursue it now invited
an unheeding, irrevocable decision from Lord Tarrant.
Crassmor had seen that rage in his father before. Crassmor
lowered his eyes to where the heir's ring gleamed and
mocked him from his own hand. Then he turned for the
bailey. Combard clashed his sword home into his scabbard,
coming after like a jailer. Willow looked on hopelessly.

Crassmor entered Gateshield, the fortress of the Circle of
Onn, as custom demanded that each initiate do, alone and
by the Least Door, which was at the rear of that ages-old,
impenetrable mass of masonry.

He had to stoop to do it; the Least Door was a low affair
just off the scullions' privy behind the kitchens. Pausing
amid the reek, he turned, stooping low to avoid bumping

his bare head on the abrasive stone of the ceiling. He read, in the uncertain light leaking out of the kitchens, the graffito over the entrance of the Least Door. It had been scratched there by some nameless initiate generations before: "All Things Cyclical Imply Futility."

Crassmor passed into the kitchens, between carving blocks, stewing vats, ovens and grease pits and cauldrons, through aromas and steamy heat. The kitchen help would be aware of his impending arrival, knowing the tradition of the Least Door. They were preparing a celebratory dinner for the Knights of Onn, though; they had only a few harassed seconds to spare for an inspection of him as they rushed back and forth in their labors, sweating, remonstrating, straining, yelling, mixing, basting, and striving.

As gestures of humility went, Crassmor supposed, this one was rather modest. At least it made a worthy point; the armored, belted, sword-bearing champions in their lofty hall, surrounded by mementos of the Order and boasting their deeds, were fed by the efforts of other human beings. Something was owed in return.

Beyond the kitchens was the traditional waiting place— a small, dark alcove—of the guide who would take him into Gateshield's Great Hall. This duty was carried out by a squire of servitor, or some other who was not numbered among the Circle's knights. In the alcove, Crassmor found his cousin Bint waiting with a glowing lanthorn. Crassmor was pleased that the boy would participate in the ceremony of investiture. Though silence was the rule, he gave Bint a conspiratorial wink. Bint, wooden-faced, turned from him to lead the way.

As custom demanded, the new knight followed Bint through the darkened halls and galleries, despite the fact that he knew the way well, having played there in the fortress many times as a child. Theoretically, Crassmor was meditating on what he'd seen in the fortress and what was to come. In fact, he spent the time pondering what had already happened.

Many eyes and many ears had taken notice of events in the gardens outside the Jade Dome. Combard's attitude toward Crassmor during the ride home and the days thereafter had made his feelings even more apparent. At his father's curt command, Crassmor had remained at home in the interim. No occasion for an explanation had arisen. Combard had refused to permit any mention of the incident. There'd been a single outburst between them, during one of the few meals they'd taken together. The Lord of House Tarrant had flung down his goblet suddenly, vowing, "No man is worthy of the Outrider's bride, least of all you!"

Crassmor's mother Anthalla, kind but by years of habit submissive to Combard, incapable of defying him, had offered what tenuous comfort she could. The all-encompassing sorrow for Sandur and the rift between Combard and Crassmor consumed her, making her presence difficult for Crassmor to bear for long. He'd picked bouquets and sent them to her. He'd paid her brief, painful visits in the quiet, darkened inner quarters to which she'd retired along with her widowed older sister Byborra and a few servants. Lewan-the-Rake had refused an arranged marriage for his heir; Crassmor wondered if Combard had selected Anthalla, in part, for her frailty of spirit, for her acquiescence. He wondered too if Combard blamed Anthalla in part for the disaster in his life named Crassmor. Usually Crassmor avoided her; mother and son were helpless to aid or even comfort one another.

Crassmor had come to understand that Combard saw Willow as a sort of shrine to Sandur, presuming her to feel the same. The Lord of House Tarrant had sent her lavish gifts in lieu of wedding presents. Along with these he'd dispatched several of Sandur's most treasured possessions, taking it for granted that Willow wished to keep her grief always in mind, as Combard did. That his father would marry Willow to another in order to keep her from Crassmor, the knight didn't doubt for a moment now.

In the main, the groom's lord's right of selection of a successor was a tradition observed only by the great Houses of the Singularity. Any number of different customs and rites had found their way through the Beyonds. More appeared constantly, making tolerance an absolute necessity. The traditions of the Elder Houses, though, were bound up with their assorted powers and heritages as well; any disruption risked disorder in, or even loss of, some of those prehistoric gifts and talents that were the bulwarks of the Singularity. If the choice of a new fiancé for Willow were made by Combard, not even Ironwicca could interfere, under law. Moreover, there were few other forces in the Singularity that could challenge the wealth and might of House Tarrant. Any woodcutter's son was freer to make his own life than was Crassmor. Willow's father Teerse might defy Combard's edict for his daughter's sake, but it would serve no point. Combard had the means to pull down the Jade Dome without effort, all within the traditions.

And if Crassmor were simply to take Willow and spirit her away? They would be exiled from the Singularity; there would never be peace or safety for them there. Combard would certainly throw his total resources into locating them and exacting revenge, calling in every debt and oath of fealty owed him. Every hand would be raised against Crassmor and Willow. Too, there was Willow's affection for her frail, aged father. Crassmor didn't see how he could ask her to leave Teerse kinless by running away; he shrank from the thought of presenting her with such a decision, and feared what her decision might be.

The Tarrant heir's ring was still on his finger. Once given, it couldn't be retracted short of death or exile, and Combard hadn't invoked those. The Tarrant lord, stubborn and diligent in observing tradition, had apparently come to peace with his son's possession of the ring. It was Crassmor's sustaining hope; the day might come when Combard would be swayed to allow a match between his remaining son and Willow. Or, failing that, Crassmor would be free to marry her when the Tarrant lordship passed to him on Combard's death. He preferred not to reflect on it, but Sir Crassmor had decided that he could wait until then if no other opportunity arose.

So he followed Bint to the investiture. Combard expected Crassmor to take the vows of the Order of the Circle of Onn since he, Combard, had already posted sponsorship.

To withdraw it would have brought shame on House Tarrant.

Crassmor and Bint entered the Great Hall of Gateshield through its rear door, then paused. Bint went on ahead, according to form, to announce the initiate's arrival to the Grand Master of the Order. As Crassmor waited, he glanced around to find his prospective comrades-in-arms eyeing him, at least those who stood in the rear of the hall, each man leaning on his sword. Because of the lizard riders' threat, nearly the entire Order was present tonight.

Those in the rear were members of lesser prestige, remittance men and ne-er-do-wells. Most of them had been given the dangerous, arduous job of patrolling in the Beyonds and along the borders, dispensing what justice they could—or were inclined to—and keeping vigil for any threat to the Singularity that might materialize there. Among these was a particular group, the Lost Boys, some of whom Crassmor recognized.

Knaves and scoundrels all, to hear the stories, Crassmor reflected. They were said to care considerably more for their skins than for glory or reputation. Among them was lanky Berrin-Gar, whose nickname was Crane, who looked like a gawky youth, all elbows and buckteeth and cowlick, but was, by all accounts, a murderous swordsman. Next to Crane was his constant companion, stout little Pullen of Lai, also called Pony-Keg, his squat body, heavy with fat and muscle, even stronger than it looked. With them was the best gambler in the Order, Tarafon Quickhand, turned out like a peacock, reeking of expensive scent. The gorgeous sword on which Tarafon's gloved hands rested had been in hock to usurers on any number of occasions.

There was Griffin, clean-shaven, handsome as a sculptor's model, more of a student's turn of mind than a warrior's. He'd authored a variety of tracts and monographs on his own and others' experiences in the Beyonds. Griffin was sole survivor of a vendetta that had extinguished another family and left him the only member of his own. By Griffin was old Hoowar Roisterer, fat and pouch-eyed, cheeks dotted with broken red blood vessels, nose forever swollen. Hoowar was a second son, like Crass-

mor; he'd once held promise of becoming Grand Master
of the Order, but had drunk and reveled himself out of the
chance for reasons Crassmor had never heard. Hoowar
caroused still. There was the moody Bosrow Feng, perhaps
the finest rider and horse trainer in the Order. Standing beside him was Bram Lydris, who went two-sworded and
never bore a shield, outcast. Crassmor recalled that, for
some reason, Sandur had liked the Lost Boys.

Bint had announced Crassmor. The Grand Master summoned the initiate to the altar. The gathered Knights of the
Order of the Circle of Onn broke into the Hymn of the
Order. The Lost Boys sang too, with a good deal of hesita-
tion and misremembered words. Crassmor walked that
timeworn stone aisle under banners and blazonry draped in
profusion from the rafters overhead.

Weapons and trophies hung on the smooth brown stone
walls or were suspended by wires from the rafters. Crassmor had never particularly cared for those last, things like
the head of the monster Alixxi, struck off by the knight
Corro long ago, now staring out over the room from its
mounting board like a bulge-eyed fish. No more appetizing
was the desiccated and dusty body of a thing half woman
and half bird, whose wings were deployed by rods. There
was a trophy flag captured by Jaan-Marl, the Grand Master
himself, from the midst of a hundred of Temuchin's men,
and the dirty, chipped, broken jawbone of an ass, clamped
to a plaque commemorating its victory over thousands.

Crassmor reached the altar, central point of the fortress
and focal point of the Order of the Circle itself. Under a
hemisphere of clear skylight which showed the last of the
dusk lay a grassy little hillock, as green and placid as it
had been uncounted years before when the Circle had first
appeared on it. The Circle of Onn rested on it still, like the
finger ring on Combard's hand grown to something five
times the height of a man, standing upright on its rim.
Around it ran carvings whose meanings were lost to the
dwellers of the Singularity. The only real knowledge left
about the Circle was that the Charmed Realm's original
settlers had used it to get there. When, how, whence they'd
come, or why were matters lost to antiquity. Etched into

the stone wall that ran waist-high around the little hillock were the words that had inspired the graffiti over the Least Door: "All Things Cyclical Sustain Hope."

Before the hillock was the plain onyx altar of the Order. On it stood Jaan-Marl, Grand Master of the Order, white-haired and white-bearded, still fit and shrewd, although he was the oldest man present. He sang the hymn in a surprisingly high, tremulous voice, not well but determinedly. As Crassmor joined him on the altar, the hymn ended.

Off to one side were the highest-ranking knights, Combard among them. The initiate was surprised to see that Ironwicca had exercised the royal prerogative in attending, even though the King was no member of the Order.

Jaan-Marl asked who sought admission to the Order; Crassmor answered his name. The Grand Master filled the hall with the questions, "Who vouches for this knight? Who sponsors him to our ranks?"

An uneasy silence grew where Combard should have spoken up at once. As it drew on, the Grand Master's eyes left Crassmor's and sought his father's. Crassmor dared look aside and saw that Combard was staring straight at the Circle of Onn, his face a mask.

Whispers passed among the ranked and waiting champions. The ceremony had never departed from form; all were on new ground. The King put a sinewy hand on Combard's mailed arm. The old man stirred as if emerging from a dream. He handed his sword aside to Ironwicca, stepping out onto the altar as if his legs threatened to fail him.

Crassmor had turned back to face the Grand Master, who waited in glacial calm. Combard came up behind and Jaan-Marl gestured. Crassmor went down on one knee. He felt rather than saw his father's iron-gloved hands hovering over either shoulder. Then they came down, hard. The son dared hope for a moment that it was an affirmation.

Departing from ritual again, Combard announced, "I, Combard, of House Tarrant its Lord, now sponsor in the stead of my slain son Sandur his brother, Sir Crassmor."

Crassmor nearly looked around at that. Certainly it violated nothing for Combard to phrase the thing so, but it made the old man's bitterness clear, Crassmor was only a substitute.

Jaan-Marl resumed. "Where is any man among us who would speak against this initiate? This is the occasion to object; there will be no other, henceforth and forever."

Crassmor thought for a moment that his father might speak. There would then have been only two options: Crassmor's withdrawal from the hall forever, or single combat to decide the issue. Crassmor glanced up at the Circle, gleaming as if it had been polished, though no hand had touched it in generations. He studied the ages-old carvings and resigned himself never to see it again; he felt that the moment was near when he would walk from that hall and not return.

Instead, another silence descended, this one more in keeping with ceremony. The Grand Master let it linger slightly longer than was usual. "There is none," he judged at last. Taking Crassmor's hands, he brought him to his feet. Combard's hands fell away; he resumed his place and took his sword back from Ironwicca. Jaan-Marl drew Crassmor around to face the assembled knights. He boomed, "Welcome, Sir Crassmor, newest of our brothers in the Order of the Circle of Onn."

Swords went aloft in a glittering field. Men cheered, perhaps a little reservedly, but heartily enough to suit Crassmor. When the cheers died away—not a long time—the Grand Master completed his part in the ceremony by saying, "Go forth now, Knight of Onn, in service to this Order and all those things for which it stands. I assign you to go over our borders into the Beyonds. Keep watch against any dangers that may threaten our home and right such wrongs as you may encounter."

Crassmor nearly reeled. *Into the Beyonds!* The only ones to react at once were the Lost Boys, who broke into unseemly hoots. They'd all received that same charge from Jaan-Marl; Crassmor was now one of them. A few seconds later the assembled knights cheered again, without great enthusiasm.

Stunned, Crassmor considered his new predicament. He'd taken it for granted that, as heir to a great House, he'd be assigned duties within the Singularity, to learn jurisprudence, politics, administration, and leadership. Instead, he'd been commissioned to the most perilous and lonely duty, chancing out among the Beyonds, a deep scout. He looked to his father, who met his gaze, and knew that Combard had arranged this with his lifelong friend Jaan-Marl.

It was time for the sponsor to end the ritual. Combard spoke loudly the traditional injunction. "Go forth, Knight of the Circle. Prove yourself worthy." The formula took on new and sobering meaning.

Crassmor threw his head back and howled the prescribed response at the rafters, *"At your command!"*

He descended from the altar in a trance, striding back the way he'd come because he didn't know what else to do. There was no other sound but his footsteps. The other knights began to hail him then with raised blades, but their thoughts, he knew, were more with the feast to come than with their new comrade in arms. Crassmor had no appetite, thirst, or desire for revelry. At the end of the hard gray aisle the Lost Boys were slapping one another on the back and howling. There seemed to be more good humor to it than derision. Crassmor felt a sudden envy of their beleaguered fellowship.

Hoowar Roisterer, bleary-eyed from preparatory celebration, tucked his sword under one arm and cupped his hands to his mouth. "Welcome, Sir Crassmor, to the Beyonds, *where we'd rather rest than quest!*"

Preparations for his departure were carried out by retainers who knew far more about them than Crassmor. He refused use of either Kort or Bordhall when the stablemaster mentioned them; the horses summoned too-vivid memories of Sandur. Crassmor's armor was burnished, his weapons edged, and rations and equipment readied by a household of servitors who preferred not to meet his gaze or address him if they could avoid it. Most of them saw this tacit exile as nothing less than a death sentence. Crassmor had been assigned to the Beyonds; he would be there until such time as the Grand Master should change his commission, but unless Jaan-Marl died and was replaced by someone ill-disposed toward Combard, that change wouldn't come until and unless Combard willed it so.

Barring the rare circumstance of a general recall, for an emergency like the invasion of the lizard riders, there was only one eventuality that would end Crassmor's sojourn, aside from Combard's forgiveness—the death of the Lord of House Tarrant and Crassmor's ascendency. The new knight didn't dwell on that, afraid that longing for Willow might somehow lead him to wish for his father's death. Reconciliation was what Crassmor hoped for, however long he might have to wait; survival was his chosen course.

And he would be alone. He'd thought of taking a squire, but Bint would no longer speak to him beyond what formality demanded, blaming him for Sandur's death, following Combard's lead. In the end, Crassmor decided against asking anyone to share his peril, not wanting the responsibility for another life.

One man had been happy with the turn of events— Crassmor's uncle Furd, abbot of the Klybesians. Couched in pious clichés as it had been, Furd's reaction had shown his delight nevertheless. Should Crassmor fail to survive in the Beyonds, Combard would die without heir. The Tarrant holdings would pass into the guardianship of Furd, a stupendous increase in the wealth of the Klybesians.

The day after his calamitous initiation into the Order, Crassmor came across his father and uncle as they sat together in the solarium of House Tarrant. They were sipping the demitasse Combard so loved and smoking the twisted, ropelike little cigars favored by Furd. In wing-backed chairs, basking in the sunlight, both seemed at ease and harmless. Crassmor, watching unnoticed from the doorway, felt an unexpected pulse of sympathy for them, recalling the tribulations of their upbringing as described by Ironwicca. In a third chair, sharing the cigars and demitasse, was Mooncollar, well known among the Klybesian monks and marked, it was said, for greater things. Mooncollar was small and nearly bald, a thin-boned, older man who walked with a limp from some childhood malady.

Crassmor drew back and listened unashamedly; his presence only interrupted conversations in House Tarrant nowadays, never enhanced them.

Furd eased himself in the chair, his blue velvet cassock whispering against his corpulence. "But, brother, have you forgotten mercy?" The word came to him so easily that he cheapened it, making it sound utilitarian.

"The Beyonds will decide," Combard shot back unhappily. "The decision has passed from my hand." He raised his little cup, then lowered it and turned to Furd in sudden heat as Mooncollar looked on silently. "He is a Knight of Onn now; he wears the heir's ring, both of those by my doing. Would you have me go back on my word?"

The tone of his voice said that he and his brother were on the edge of an irredeemable exchange. Crassmor knew with shock that he was, in a way, in Combard's unbending fashion, being defended. The new knight's mouth compressed; affection dueled with resentment within him.

"Not in a thousand lifetimes," Furd said. Crassmor was surprised to detect no dishonesty in that.

Mooncollar, staring down into his dark coffee, put in, "His Reverence perhaps only meant that you have put a loved one in peril."

Combard had faced him angrily, but Mooncollar's quiet comment had given him no provocation. Now Furd put his fingertips together and added, "How often has this sort of thing happened before? We all look to Sir Crassmor's return."

*With no joy, in your case,* thought the subject of the conversation from where he listened.

Mooncollar had gotten an opening that he seemed to have been working for. "What, then, of problems of succession, of inheritance? This involves a man who will be in the Beyonds, always a difficult state of affairs."

"Setting some sort of limit doesn't seem unreasonable, brother," Furd added. "If you should—if House Tarrant should be left lordless—gods forbid it!—and Crassmor should fail to return after an adequate, *stipulated* time, someone must see to the affairs of this place."

"Legal provisions would not be out of order," Mooncollar suggested with a meaningful glance at Furd.

Crassmor was surprised at the conviction in his father's words. "I send him out into danger; that he deserves." Then he added solemnly, "But I'll set no death sentence on him. *That* he has not earned; I decided that in Blue Dell."

Furd frowned. "Harm may come to House Tarrant by your failure to make the proper provisions."

Combard shouted, "Then harm will!"

Moments passed. "I neither raised nor sentenced him," Furd pointed out.

Combard put down his cup, dropped his cigar, and knelt with a moan at his brother's side. Crassmor understood then how close they'd become under their mother's tutelage. "You did not," Combard acknowledged. "I don't know him, don't understand or trust him. I hope I haven't damned myself for the times I've wished Sandur were alive and—Furd! Don't ask me to abandon him altogether!"

Furd put a hand to Combard's cheek, nodding. Crassmor was somewhere in between an emotional breakdown and outright violence, fingering *Shhing*'s hilt and watching his uncle. "It will all come out right, Combard," the abbot promised.

*For you, you think,* Crassmor finished. He eased back out of the entranceway of the solarium with a particular eagerness to stay alive.

There was only one high point in the days between the ceremony before the Circle of Onn and his departure. A flustered door warder summoned Crassmor to the courtyard of House Tarrant, saying that men were there to see him. Crassmor went, puzzling, to find the place in an uproar.

The Lost Boys had come calling.

The rare occurrence of their all being together in the Singularity—those who'd managed to live through the Beyonds and the war with the lizard riders—had necessitated a momentous, days-long celebration, shadowed by the awareness that they must all go forth again soon, but fueled by it as well. They'd arrived in vehicles borrowed from the extensive collection of otherworldly transport maintained at Gateshield. One of these oddities was a long, brightly painted beer wagon drawn by eight magnificent Clydesdales. Crassmor thought how unlikely it was that any beer remained in the kegs. The other transport was a small flatbed wagon pulled by a team of twelve giant, long-legged, flightless birds. The flatbed rode rather low on its suspension; Crassmor concluded it had come from some Reality with a lighter gravity.

Just now, Hoowar Roisterer was arguing with the Tarrant stablemaster, both men purple-faced, the stablemaster taking issue with the notion of permitting the birds into his province. Crane, seated astride one of the Clydesdales, gave Crassmor a quick, bucktoothed grin and slipped him a wink. Squat little Pullen of Lai—Pony-Keg—had caught another Lost Boy, Tribben the Shriek, who, firmly under the influence, had fallen off the beer wagon.

Griffin was even then engaged in deep conversation with Crassmor's aunt Byborra's new handmaiden; the scholar-knight's hand had already settled on the girl's hip, raising a blush in her cheeks. There seemed to be an altercation taking place over a dice game on the flatbed. The giant birds were giving nasty looks to one and all and calling among themselves in a queer, chirping sort of yodel. Several of the Lost Boys were entreating a startled guardsman to tell them where the nearest latrine was.

Tarafon Quickhand was carrying a plain sword, meaning that his best was in hock yet once more. He was in the process of applying a generous spoonful of mustard to a sandwich. Under his arm was a bottle of that strange beverage he so loved, ginger ale. Tarafon smiled at Crassmor when he saw him. "We have come for your shivaree, lucky lad, moved by good fellowship to welcome a new chum."

"Moved by penury as well," Hoowar Roisterer admitted in a split-second aside, and instantly resumed his remonstrance with the stablemaster.

"And we wore out our welcome just about everywhere else," Pony-Keg put in, and dropped Tribben the Shriek, who scarcely noticed.

House Tarrant was still in mourning for the Outrider's death, but when Combard appeared at the doors—silencing the madness in his courtyard—he simply looked at them for a moment, said, "Make you welcome," and departed. Knights of the Order of the Circle of Onn usually welcomed a new initiate with festival and shivaree, but the more respectable and staid knights, aware of the situation at House Tarrant, had forgone celebration. The Lost Boys, having a new member added to their ignoble group, regarded that as intolerable. In addition, they were never inclined to permit an occasion for carousal to elude them.

Those among the Lost Boys who still had family in the Singularity were out of favor and none of them had much money; the Beyonds were rarely the setting for the acquisition of riches. Crassmor's feeble protests were brushed aside, and the drunken, amiable wastrels invaded the main hall of House Tarrant. Crassmor remembered then that no Knight of Onn could refuse another his hospitality; the Lost Boys began their good-naturedly exploitative wassail.

They stayed for two nights and the day in between, dancing, singing, forcing Crassmor to play the zither and the lap harp, seriously depleting the food and drink of House Tarrant, and making immoral overtures to the scullery maids and female servitors. Crassmor found himself having a good time.

He stopped trying to keep up with their imbibing early in the game, though, not being much of a tippler. They regaled him with stories of their adventures in the Beyonds, each more improbable than the last, nearly all bearing a pointed moral; rules of chivalry and valor and aspirations to glory were fine in Dreambourn, but had a knack of getting a man killed in the Beyonds. It was seldom the case that when a man died among the fluxes of the infinite Realities, word of the circumstances became known. Usually he just failed to show up at one of the periodic rendezvous and couldn't be located. Thus, whether he'd died bravely, foolishly, or in some cowardly manner made little difference. He was simply and finally missing and presumed dead.

All of that made Crassmor even less at ease with the idea of going into the Beyonds, but it bolstered his determination to survive them, mind his own affairs, and stay out of the way of trouble.

And so the gambling—mostly for markers—and skirt chasing and flagon emptying and carousing went on. It gradually dawned on Crassmor that one or another of the Lost Boys was often absent from the group. He came to realize that, one by one, they'd been slipping off to present themselves to Combard, who was shut away in his private chambers, to offer their condolences. Sandur had been friend to these incorrigibles and had enjoyed their company more than that of many reputable knights. Each of these rascals had some memory of a moment shared with the Outrider, or of a deed he'd done. Each presented it to Combard as a sign that he, too, revered Sandur.

None spoke of it. Crassmor assumed that Combard received them with his usual reserve, but knew that those visits would have tremendous meaning to the old man. Crassmor found himself happy that they'd come; in the end, he felt a little less awful about his exile.

The Lost Boys' next and final stop was scheduled to be House Comullo. Teerse had always extended them all the hospitality he could, and Willow delighted in their buffoonish company, while they regarded her as a kindred spirit. Hearing that they were bound that way, Crassmor cast about for some way to get a message to her; he'd had no doubt that his father would quickly know of any visit he might make to her, and trusted no one in House Tarrant to keep silent in the matter of delivering a note. But by the time he was aware of their destination the Lost Boys were collecting themselves and such of their number as were no longer ambulatory and calling for their wagons. Lacking writing materials, Crassmor debated taking one of them aside and imploring his help in contacting Willow. But Combard had come down to see the Lost Boys off; it seemed hopeless.

Tarafon Quickhand stepped over to bid Crassmor farewell with a handclasp. "You depart into the Beyonds tomorrow?" he asked. Between one word and the next, the heir's ring disappeared from Crassmor's finger.

Before Crassmor could overcome his surprise, old Hoowar Roisterer added, "Alone and with no honor guard, eh? Ummmph, 'tis best; gives a man leeway." He belched. "Going by the main routes, are you, then?"

Crassmor spared a quick look to where Combard was trading arm-clasps with Pony-Keg. "No, the high roads for me, up through Blue Dell and a last look from Star Scarp." Tarafon and Hoowar nodded, making no other point about it. Very shortly, the Lost Boys were prepared for leave-taking.

Crassmor pulled on his gauntlets to conceal the absence of the heir's ring. Combard never even noticed, watching the Lost Boys wave and holler farewell as they left. Then the Lord of House Tarrant returned to his chambers.

When Crassmor had finished his own leave-taking with the rest of the household the next day, Combard reappeared. Crassmor still had the feel of his mother's sad kiss on his cheek; she had dissolved into racking sobs when he'd gone out the door. There was a last rite to which Crassmor had claim. He presented himself before his father and comrade in the Order of the Circle of Onn. Combard didn't flinch from the ritual embrace, though Crassmor felt the conflict in the old man's body as stern reserve yielded to a warmer clasp.

Combard held Crassmor out at arm's length and repeated, "Go forth, Knight of the Circle. Prove yourself worthy."

Crassmor stepped out of his father's grip, burdening what should have been a standard reply with the hurt and resentment he felt.

"At your command."

He turned away as quickly as he could from the pain in Combard's face, which always seemed so ready to change to anger.

It was a relief to be out of House Tarrant, to be on the move, even if that move was into the Beyonds. Crassmor let the war horse find his own pace and considered his lot in life.

This was the beginning of something new, at any rate. More importantly, it was an end to the supreme pain of those last days with Combard in House Tarrant. Riding alone from the bitter memories of the mists of Blue Dell, he turned and found his way up onto Star Scarp. He belabored himself for not having tried once more for reconciliation with his father before leaving, but another, even more vital matter was on his mind. He tried not to think about it and risk too great a disappointment if Willow did not appear.

Star Scarp, a small claimancy of soil between the Singularity and approaches to the Beyonds, lay amid peaks and crags that reared to break the fabulous night sky. The place was carpeted with low, soft moss, golden yellow in the daylight, which by some peculiar property thrived at this extreme elevation. There were small pavilions of tightly joined granite and trellises with twisted vines. There were cooking pits and long slab tables flanked by smooth benches, all cut from single pieces of marble. It had been a place of Tarrant celebration in times gone by, though any excursion out onto Star Scarp risked unkind weather.

The weather tonight was benign and, except for a few tenuous clouds at lower altitudes, clear. Crassmor felt himself suspended under the canopy of the blazing night sky of the Singularity. That sky, influenced by the many Realities, hosting numerous visitors from them, was always brilliant. He gazed up at a rich star broth of radiant planets, chains of multicolored moons, wandering comets, and brief, spectacular meteor showers. The night sky held nebulae, clouds of muted incandescence whose names had never been spoken, and shifting constellations.

He pulled the chilly air into his lungs, finding that, gregarious as he was by nature, recent events had made it more pleasant to be alone.

No—not quite alone. He saw a horse with a sidesaddle tethered near one of the pavilions. His heart banged in his chest; one hand felt the finger where the heir's ring had been.

A figure stepped out of the shadows. Winds played around Willow. Her gown and robes were fashioned from the plumage of uncounted birds, a bewildering blend of gleaming colors and intricate, shining markings under the night sky.

He was before her in a moment, unsure what to do or say next, letting fall the rein of his horse. The fear of all fears was that she'd come to say good-bye forever.

Willow smiled the smile he could picture by simply shutting his eyes. His fear was unmade. She held out a golden model of the Circle of Onn, the heir's ring of House Tarrant. His fingers enclosed it.

"How is it that a Knight of Onn rides out without a favor?" Willow asked.

He blinked. Bearing proof of some lady's affection had never even occurred to him. She took her scarf, a trailing band of crimson silk, from her throat and passed it once around his neck. The act should have been accompanied by an exhortation that he do brave deeds, bring honor to himself and his lady, and uphold the ideals of his Order.

Instead, she bade him, "Come back to me, Crassmor." He took her into his arms and kissed her, no chaste chivalrous kiss, even at first. It was a lover's kiss before it was over.

"My single ambition!" he proclaimed when they'd parted for a moment.

She laughed in the way he so adored. Willow brushed the backs of her fingers across his cheek. "My father advised me that there is no thing that cannot change with time, even Combard's blighted heart."

He moved to his war horse, worked knots, and took down his thick bedroll. They tethered their horses where they couldn't be seen from the road, then shared the bedroll under the fantastic night sky of the Singularity.

# — PART II —

# "BY WHAT ETERNAL STREAMS . . ."

# Chapter 9

# RECRUITED

**Sir Crassmor would** not have become involved in the tavern altercation—which proved far less casual than he'd assumed —and would thus have been spared the acquaintance of the giant of John's Winch, if he'd been sober. However, he'd had something more than his usually modest evening's ration of cups, so engrossed was he in chatting with the new barkeep, who was a god.

He wasn't a true deity, of course, or at any rate, not any longer. Yet the barkeep boasted a handsome, flashing metallic sheen to his golden skin and was possessed of a head more elephantine than human. He'd been worshiped in his own Reality, but fluxes and anomalous events had deposited him, as they had so many others, here in the Beyonds.

The erstwhile all-powerful was, Crassmor noticed, reverting to a more mundane sort of fellow. The metamorphosis was attributable, the knight supposed, to the nearness of the Singularity. The unique laws that applied there tended, among other things, to dampen the power and efficacy of outside mystical forces, magical energies, and the like. The god, who'd given up the unmanageable appellation "Tsoora-Rin-Voor" in favor of the far more convenient "Bill," had lost all of his divine powers with the exception of some every passable sleight of hand he'd demonstrated in the course of the evening. Bill's plummet to mere mortality was graphically pointed up by the fact that the ornate settings on his stubby tusks had been stripped of their gems for subsistence funds.

The two being the only ones in the tiny, drafty, rancid-smelling tavern in the storm-racked mountain village of

Toe Hold that night, Crassmor stood a few extra rounds. He was repaid with a tale of ecclesiastical unheaval and religious revisionism. They whiled away the evening, happily leaning on elbows, surrounded by rows of crudely thrown mugs, gouged planks of bar, walls, tables, and benches, deep accumulations of burned grease layering the rafters, and whistling avenues of chilly wind racing through the chinks. Then the trouble started.

This was not to say that Sir Crassmor, who'd come to be known in certain circles as the Reluctant Knight, was any wooer of Dame Combat. He'd tried seeking the heroic rôle and all he'd gotten was being cast out into the Beyonds. Now he'd resolved to pursue peace and pleasure. His resolution had drawn him to Toe Hold. High in the weather-punished mountains, it was off normal routes and its people practiced the exemplary habit of minding their own business. Even a Knight of Onn could take his ease with little fear of having some risky job of errantry thrust upon him.

As extra insurance, Crassmor still had his right wrist laced into a leather brace to feign disability, though it had in point of fact healed since his previous misadventure. He'd arrived with a not-inconsiderable clutch of money, sufficient to see him through the bitterest of the local storm season if he were prudent. Toe Hold, a precarious jutting of stone buildings joined to steep crags in a marriage of expediency, was no Singularity pleasure city, but neither in all fairness could it be called cheerless. It listed an adequate inn, a well-stocked grog shop, a tolerant religion, and weekly dances. In addition, there were impromptu gatherings of amateur musicians from the village and the general area, a pleasant little public bathhouse, decent food, and cooks who knew how to prepare it. Perhaps as a reaction to their environment, Toe Hold's residents liked to dress in bright colors and were more gregarious than Crassmor had expected.

He'd taken an ample room at the inn, wangling long-term rates. Ironically, the room cost less because it was high up in the building and at the back of it, rather than overlooking the village's diminutive marketplace. Thus, he was treated to a spectacular view of vertical cliffs and twisting gorges, lightning-lit peaks and wind-scoured canyons. When the frequent downpours came, runoff created a flume of waterfall which exited the town just under his window to join a score more spouts in the roiling torrent hundreds of feet below. It was a damp place, but the moss and lichen growing throughout the inn and the smell of mildew all around bothered him not at all. To Crassmor they only spoke of life going about its business unpestered.

When the weather broke, there were the walkways, escarpment paths, and low towers of Toe Hold, where he would pace and think homesick thoughts. When it was inclement, there was his journal to write in and such books, folios, and scrolls as he could buy or borrow in the village. At times he tried to capture land- and skyscapes with a woefully limited collection of pastels. He also renewed his determined plectrum-assaults on his old nemesis, the thirty-stringed zither.

The mountaineers, who knew well the importance of privacy and mutual consideration, hadn't bothered him with questions and seemed capable of settling all their own problems themselves. He assumed that they knew that he was one of the Lost Boys, but his respite had been undisturbed. He'd spent many hours daydreaming of Willow, and of his homecoming.

The talk between Crassmor and Bill had turned to the nature of the Singularity. The barkeep was curious about the changes that had overtaken him as he'd drawn closer to it in his wanderings. "My worshippers had weapons of great efficacy; had they but entered your Singularity, they'd soon have ruled it," he said a bit wistfully.

Sir Crassmor burped. "That's no less than the whole point, don't you see? The very substance of the Singularity resists changes like that."

Bill drew them both another round of the authoritative local stout. The knight went on. "Strange weapons, foreign magics, and the like have found their way into the Charmed Realm from time to time. Events tend to work against them—but not always. Ironwicca's scholars suggest that it's some fundamental counterforce that staves off complete chaos, which nature abhors even more than it does a vacuum. That's no hard and fast rule, though; changes there have been, and radical, at times." He pulled the mug to him and drank.

Bill's trunk was now too short for him to imbibe in the traditional pachydermic manner. Instead, he lifted it out of his way and sucked up his stout through a copper tube. Then he said, "And if an army with superior weapons invaded? Would you there in Dreamborn stick to your swords and be slaughtered?"

Crassmor thought of the broken-cross soldiers, annihilated by the darts and lances of the lizard riders. "Events might still work against them. Again, not all the weapons of the Singularity are sword or bow, or even firearms. Enemy weapons have been used, enemy techniques copied in time of need, but people drift back to the things they know and are used to afterward. Reliance on unfamiliar artifacts or alien usages is a rather common way to meet a bad end where I come from."

Bill belched, rather more impressively than had the knight, so that Crassmor leaned away. "I should think that ideas and inventions and trade would be saner currencies in your Singularity than violence, in any case," Bill added.

"You'll get no argument from me," Crassmor replied. "Yet an invention that functions in one Reality is often totally useless in another. Ideas, philosophies, and religions have themselves a habit of canceling one another out. Trade routes which would lead through the Beyonds are risky business indeed. Roving and a taste for profit or booty go with the sort of folk who are not disinclined to do battle. Also, trade routes have a pesky habit of disappearing or changing. Thinkers and traders and explorers and teachers are for the most part welcome in the Singularity, but it seems to attract a good deal more of the rough-hewn sort."

The woman entered the room just then, tiredly, shaking rainwater from her long, sheepskin cloak and hanging it in the inglenook. She wore a floor-sweeping gown of thick-patterned amber velvet, its sack sleeves following her hands' movements gracefully. She took a seat at one of the small tables at the opposite side of the room and asked demurely for a meal. With a majestic jiggling reminiscent, the knight had no doubt, of his former and happier station, the barkeep bustled off to prepare the food, calling for the place's single servant boy to see to her horse.

Crassmor, stroking the thin red mustache he'd cultivated in the Beyonds, considered. *Here, what's this? Such a tender morsel alone in these wicked mountains?*

He tried to catch her eye; she spared him no glance. He saw at once that her teeth were prominent and her twisty hair had a will of its own which defied coifing. She was slender, hips and bosom not much wider than waist. Her face held wit, a knowing sort of humor. He was attracted, though he took her for a late bloomer harboring resentments.

Now she met his eye for a moment, inclining her head amicably, bestowing upon him a broad, bright-eyed smile. He upgraded his opinion of her at once; she was by every indication a discerning, desirable lady. The inner Crassmor licked his chops.

At that moment the outer door sprang open with a muffled crash. There were coughs, laughter and spitting, and the tramping of feet in the hall. The inner door swung on creaking hinges and two men in carter's attire entered, cracking their rain capes and bellowing coarsely for the hospitality of the place. They wore brown homespun, black pigskin vests, and heavy, calf-high boots. Crassmor's lingering inspection of the lady, and hers of him, were rudely curtailed. One carter spied her, slapped his stomach, and proclaimed, "Ten days now have I been in these cursed mountains without roof or love. Here I find both!" He rolled his eyes and elbowed his partner, who sniggered.

"Ludicrous oaf," Crassmor murmured into his drink. Loath to start any trouble, he did no more than that. The carters helped themselves to seats at the lady's table without so much as the courtesy of a bow. She refrained from comment. A popping hearth log suddenly sounded louder. One of the men edged over the table toward her.

She made her rebuff firm but polite. "I shall decline your

company, gentles, thanking you to leave me in peace." The two laughed at that, hitting each other's arms.

"Oh, churls," Crassmor muttered, hoping the barkeep would return. Bill was not forthcoming; her pleading look found the knight; it seemed to hold great promise. He felt his blood warm up, only in part the work of the stout. Passion beckoned; Crassmor fell prey.

One carter's paw had fallen on her shoulder and refused to be dislodged. Crassmor sighed and pushed away his mug, considering various ploys by which he might handle the situation and yet leave *Shhing* in its scabbard.

He reminded himself as he stopped at the disputed table that he presented a fairly impressive appearance. He'd gained a trifle more weight during his long sojourn in the Beyond and had filled out a bit. The appeal of his mustache and goatee was more the product of diligent grooming and tending than of luxuriance, but it was undeniable. His red hair had thinned a little, and he now wore it at collar length, brushed back meticulously from a high forehead. His pale skin and easy carriage suggested no familiarity with menial labor. His elegantly embroidered pourpoint jacket and silken tights, one leg in green and the other in red, set him apart from the local mountaineers. And there was *Shhing* poking over his left shoulder.

Left hand resting arrogantly on hip, he cuffed the overly familiar carter's shoulder confidently but lightly— the question of proper impact being important here. Both newcomers were short, fleshy men, balding, with salt-and-pepper beards. They were rather older, the knight thought, than most men in their trade. It seemed to him a good omen.

The man and his companion looked up angrily. "What would you of me? Away with you!"

Crassmor, eyebrow cocked haughtily, glared down his long, slender nose. "Unless I am mistaken, fellow, this gentle lady would happily forgo your ah, society." And to her he added, "Am I correct?"

Her face showed obvious gratitude and a certain invitation. "Oh, Sir Knight, yes," she said in a shy whisper that touched him. Crassmor, basking in her approval, not unaware of what his reward might be, touched up his mustache with a knuckle and stroked his meticulous goatee.

But the carters were not cooperating with his scenario. "Who are you, to order free men about?" the one Crassmor had addressed snarled. The man's eyes bulged. Both carters pulled their feet up, coming around on their bench and slamming muddy clodhoppers down, making the floorboards shake. Elderly for their trade they might be, but not mellowed by the years.

Crassmor backed off an alarmed step. *Damn me for a brainless intervener!* He held his blasé sneer, though, a favorite instrument. An elaborately casual glance aside told him that Bill still hadn't returned.

"Answer me, sirrah!" the carter barked; daggers appeared in the hands of the two. They held them with no great skill, and their postures indicated only modest ability, but it was a given in the knight's philosophy that any foe was dangerous. It was another that any fight that could be avoided should be.

The two moved promptly, standing. "Defend yourself, O Knight!" the lady implored.

Her petition hadn't been necessary; years of merciless drill took over. Ungiven to brawling Crassmor might be, but he had used up uncounted weary hours in the training required of a knight.

The leather brace on his wrist was loosely laced for zither playing and didn't hamper him. His right hand flashed up, its outer edge swiveling his back-scabbarded sword, so that when his fingers clamped on its hilt and executed the combat draw, *Shhing* sprang forth in a flat arc at neck level, putting its name in the air. His left forearm Crassmor kept close across his chest, safe from the glittering sword sweep.

The carters stopped short. Crassmor made no move to close, holding that a tavern fight was reason neither to behead a man like a nosegay nor take a chance on being gutted. The two stared at him agog, then at each other. The one whom Crassmor had addressed reached up unconsciously to thumb his Adam's apple, plainly reflecting on what the knight's unscabbarding stroke could have done to it.

Though they were irresolute, the duo still gripped their daggers. Seeing that he'd half-daunted them, Crassmor thought he might end things with one more harmless demonstration. Spying a pewter goblet on a nearby table, he took another step back.

He assumed a two-handed grip, close behind his sword's cup hilt. Appraising himself of his center of gravity, he surrendered to learned motions. Crassmor half-pivoted and took a long step; his blade became a silver afterimage on their eyes. *Shhing* hissed through the air and there was shearing impact. The goblet fell away in two tidy pieces, bisected from lip to base.

Crassmor had already recovered, yanking his blade from the wood. He resumed a ready stance with *Shhing* poised before him. The drovers stood frozen in place. The halves of the cloven goblet rocked gently on the table as rain beat at the roof and gusts of wind made the windows tremble and the lamp flames waver.

"That will suffice."

The lady's command cut through the knight's anxious concentration. When the aged carters gathered their rain capes and departed in a rush, suspicion came to Crassmor belatedly. The woman patted the bench next to her. "Won't you join me, praiseworthy knight? Sir Crassmor, is it not?"

He reached up and rescabbarded *Shhing* carefully; it was easy enough to slice a finger or three when one's hands were shaking. Snatching up his mug, he tossed down a mouthful of stout, an uncharacteristic gesture which nearly made him choke.

She shook her head. The tight curls danced as amusement lit those deceitful eyes. "It does you no good to scowl at me as if I were something unpleasant that's gotten smeared on your shoe. Come; that one trick did you no lasting harm. I have no other to play, I pledge."

He sniffed disdainfully to mask his confusion. "And, pray, just what good is your word, madam? You've misused womanhood and played falsely upon one who only sought to help. I am wounded in my heart."

"Pricked in your vanity, more likely," she countered. "It seems by far the larger target. I was informed that I would find here a knight of the Circle of Onn who is not as incapacitated as he'd have people think."

He seated himself, but at the extreme end of the bench from her. "That decided you to come here and unleash those aging bullyboys upon me? Shabby sport, madam."

Her eyes laughed still. "You mean poor old Roode and Dimble? No bullies, nor carters either; only household servants of mine, far more frightened of you than you of them." She ignored his muttered protest. She went on. "They helped me only to prove that, in fact, your sword wrist is not disabled."

The knight stared down guiltily and rubbed the joint in question in its brace. This smarty-girl had caught him cold. Worst of all was Crassmor's conviction that he knew which way this conversation was leading. Before he could rally his wits and forestall her, telling himself, *This is all so unfair!* she spoke the words he dreaded.

"Sir Crassmor, by your station and the vows of errantry of the Order of the Circle of Onn that you serve, I charge you to hear my plaint. I am wronged and helpless and seek redress." A note of real desperation had crept into the formalized petition.

*Trapped!* He hurled his empty mug against the wall, where it shattered into a shower of coarse fragments. Then he crossed one knee over the other, bidding her sweetly, "Pray continue."

She ignored the display, seeing that it was more theater than anger. "I am Alanna of the farmhold of Meere, a place of some bounty but scant military rigor. As places go in the Beyonds, it is stable, like most of this region. My father holds title through fealty, but his overlord rules a large and rough-handed domain and concerns himself little with us. My father scarcely stirs himself, being infirm. My two sisters and I have managed things until now—"

"Alanna," he broke in with syrupy menace, "I'm under some compulsion to aid the oppressed, but none to perish from boredom."

She frowned and made hurrying motions with her hands to quicken herself. "Three months gone, my younger sister Arananth and my elder, Oorda, set out to pay a family visit on the other side of these mountains. Arananth was taken ill. They were delayed in coming home until the storm season; they contracted to come home by river, a more perilous route, but quicker. On the way they were stopped and taken captive by John of John's Winch. You know of him?"

Crassmor lowered his head slowly until his high brow met the table with a despondent clunk. "Vaguely; some rural lout who's set himself up as a petty river pirate. Found himself a cave to live in, is that not so?"

She inclined her head, still frowning. "The place lies on the boundaries of wilderness lands that are nominally ours, though my father exerts no control there. The overlord says it is too far from his purview. He can spare no men or means to help."

Crassmor sighed. "You . . . you're going to make me try to rescue your sisters, aren't you?" He asked it so dolefully that she hesitated.

His head came up again. *"Aren't you?"* he yelled, for the unfairness of it all, so that she jumped a little from her seat. She met his gaze with jaw set and brows meeting, and nodded. Considering the deep gorge out behind the inn, he mused, *Defenestration might be just the solution here.*

"Father's old," she was continuing, "and we're not a warrior folk, I was on my way to see what aid I could solicit in Dreambourn when I heard that there was a Knight of Onn here in Toe Hold who was disinclined to errantry but otherwise unoccupied."

"I am occupied in a good many things," he riposted, "all of them preferable to being harried or killed."

She looked pugnacious. "Are you refusing my entreaty?"

He was quick to contradict her. "Perish the thought. My, ah, injury seems to have healed; I'll undertake to be of what help I can." The last thing he wanted was for her to swear formal complaint against him before Jaan-Marl. The Grand Master would have no recourse but to revoke his membership in the Order and strip him of his knighthood.

Drummed out of the Order, he'd be forced by Tarrant

tradition—and by force of arms, if it came to that—to atone by taking vows of the Klybesians. Celibacy, sobriety, and, no doubt, the cold silence of a praying cell—he began to sweat just thinking about it.

Best to find out a little more about this predicament. Aid and assistance, for example, might improve matters. "Those two servants of yours—I assume they're part of a larger retinue?" Perhaps he could settle a comfortable siege on this river pirate's lair until the fellow saw reason.

"No; we've few servants. Sharecroppers and free yeomen work for us for the most part, and we've little money for help of the mercenary stripe. Threadbare nobility, that's us."

"But a small disbursement's better than risking harm. To your sisters, I meant, of course. Why not run along home like a good girl and talk dear poppa into ransoming them?"

"John's not after ransom. He's taken a fancy to Arananth and means to wed her so that he and his heirs will have claim to the land."

Logical enough, from the pirate's point of view. The area around his cave was peripheral to the overlord's domain. A marriage, along with oaths of fealty and some tribute, would all but insure the bandit's safety from punitive action. Of course, John of John's Winch might have accomplished this without kidnapping, but again perhaps not. Married to Arananth, the pirate would have every hope that the girl's father would cede him the stretch of river he now controlled *de facto* and legitimatize his grip on the area.

*Worse and worse,* Crassmor reflected as he stroked his goatee. "Now, then, how well set out is this John? How many men? What are his defenses?" It just might be possible to enter the place, tell a lie or two, and be off with the darling daughters. The knight was distracted by this thought as Alanna answered his question. He was considering smuggling disguises into the cave and the women out when it dawned on him what she'd just said.

"Eh? He's got a *what?*"

"A giant," Alanna repeated frankly. "John of John's Winch is very much the social climber. Since a guardian dragon's beyond his means, he's come up with a giant. Not a terribly large one, from what I'm told; a wanderer-in, no doubt. John's seer, Fanarion—did I mention him? Something of a lesser magician—recruited the brute, but I—what's wrong?"

He'd buried his head in his hands. "I don't suppose you'd consider leaving your sisters there, would you? Who can say? John might make a good provider and a fine brother-in-law. Arananth might do worse."

Her lower lip had shot out in a manner not denoting acquiescence. He hastened to add, "Just a thought. But if John's set on Arananth, why does he hang on to Oorda?"

"Oorda is, well—" She paused; he raised an aristocratic eyebrow. She went on in a rush. "My older sister has what the harpers call a fiery temper. She is absolutely infernal at times. But she's devoted to Arananth, and Arananth to her. I wager that John had more than enough of Oorda by now, because she can be positively vile when she wishes. Oorda wouldn't hear of leaving John's Winch without Arananth, though."

Crassmor toyed with his glossy beard again. Or course; this John person couldn't simply shove his betrothed's sister into the river. Too unpolitic. Which suggested something.

"I shall do what I may," he said, his mood brightening a bit. "But bear in mind that violence is always a last resort. It carries the great risk that innocent parties will be hurt." *Specifically, me.* She showed her clever smile again. He told himself, *She really would look better with a black eye.*

"There is another thing," she added. Before he could thrust fingers into his ears, she said, "One knight of the Singularity has already attempted rescue, only to be captured and held. I think John plans ransom."

"His name?" Crassmor demanded, wondering which of the Lost Boys had been so foolhardy.

"Sir Bint," Alanna answered. She was surprised when all reserve and reluctance fell away from him. The bench nearly toppled over as he leaped to his feet.

"I'll gather my things," he called to her as he strode off. "We go at once."

# Chapter 10

# REUNITED

**Dusk was pending** as Roode and Dimble paddled the dugout canoe through tall reeds. John's Winch came into view in the distance, a high cliff undercut by the river.

Alanna turned to Crassmor, who, when not worrying about his cousin Bint, divided his time between unhappiness at going into danger and disgruntlement with his own failure to seduce Alanna. She'd rebuffed his advances with good-humored barbs throughout the journey from Toe Hold. Although Willow still held his heart without qualification, he saw no reason to lead the life of a Klybesian, given a willing companion. *In Alanna's case, however,* he decided, *I am not so given.*

Still, between them they'd crafted a plan that seemed as if it might work. As they drew closer to their destination, Crassmor regretted for the thousandth time that the area lay outside any effective authority except that of a knight-errant. He'd had little time to do more than dispatch word and hope that others of the Lost Boys would hear. Perhaps one or more of them would arrive in time to give aid or rescue Bint if Crassmor failed.

"I see no giant," he remarked, scanning the cliff in which the cave lair was situated.

"He's seldom in evidence during the day, I'm told," she replied, "being so gruesome-looking that his appearance alone has stilled many brave hearts."

"Bad for business," Crassmor reasoned. And the giant supposedly operated somewhat like a roving watchdog, patrolling the countryside on both sides of the river against attack or encroachment. "Now, tell me once more about this seer or magician," Crassmor bade her.

She dragged one fair hand in the green river, staring thoughtfully at the ripples it set up. She was dressed, as were Roode and Dimple, in old clothing suitably soiled, so as to invite no close inspection from John's men.

"Fanarion is well along in age, by reports," she said, "weaker now than in his prime, and no shaker of mountains even then. He is more advisor than mage. Nevertheless, the giant is under his spell."

They were closer to John's Winch now, coming into its shadow. The river's pace slowed as it widened. The cave was a flattened oval opening halfway up the face of the cliff, bracketed by the winch's two sturdy shear legs, which hung out over the water. The hoisting line was lowered, the trading platform at river level.

Alanna pulled her veil tightly around her face. To be recognized now, even by her sisters, would mean disaster. Crassmor slung his zither over his shoulder, preparing to disembark as the canoe glided toward the trading platform.

"Remember," Alanna cautioned, "we'll return upriver every night and await you just out of sight downstream." John's pet giant, she'd found out, did not molest anyone encamped on the river unless so instructed.

"And if I don't appear?" he growled softly, his frustration that he and his cousin might lose their lives over the problems of strangers not having abated. "How long before you go off to ensnare some other ill-starred boob in this madness?"

"It's not my fault that you're a knight-errant!" she said, evading his question.

"Nor mine!" he snarled back.

She hushed him emphatically. The dugout's bow bumped the trading platform. Crassmor grunted and made his way clumsily out of his seat among the bundles and bedrolls. He wore no armor and hoped that his green doublet, scarlet hose, and yellow, silver-buckled shoes would lend themselves to his masquerade. He had a long dirk on his belt, since it would have been unusual for any river traveler to be unarmed, but *Shhing* lay wrapped beneath the bundles. A white-plumed, blue-peaked cap sat on his head at a jaunty angle. He wore an elegant cape.

This stretch of the river was rather deep; he could make out nothing of its bottom. The pirates' trading platform was about five paces on a side, built of adzed logs, and had thick ropes rising from each corner to connect the hoisting line in a pyramid overhead. On it were piled casks, crates, and bags and baskets of various kinds. The day's take, the knight supposed, plus whatever the bandits had purchased. The platform rested on piles set in the riverbed. Soiled, makeshift banners, executed with a childish lack of skill, moved sluggishly on short poles. They displayed John's newly adopted heraldry of crossed quarterstaff and long-bow, in grimy white on a field of black.

Two bowmen stood among the trade goods and cargo piled there. Others were stationed on the opposite bank, while more waited at the vantage point of the cave's mouth. Their weapons were long, made of yew wood; the archers carried great goose-feathered shafts in their quivers. One of the platform archers took possession of a coin proffered by Roode from the dugout's bow. Roode made a great show of resentment of this toll for the use of John's part of the river. Then the canoe pushed off, and Crassmor watched it move downriver with a forlorn feeling.

*I wish I were a tavernkeep. I wish I were a hermit. I wish I were a fishwife. I wish—*

"You have business with us?" The toll collector broke into Crassmor's fruitless regrets.

"*If,*" Crassmor replied with a grandiose flourish, assuming the role he must play, "your lord is of sufficient note to require a harper and poet. Surely no court, even here on the river, can be significant without its balladeer, its chronicler. And I, Morodo, offer my services to John of John's Winch."

"*Lord* John, is what you call him, strummer," the archer corrected harshly. He and his mates were a disreputable-looking bunch, attired in frayed clothes of dark green and brown. Crassmor suspected that the man had known no recent concourse with soap and water. The guards' single effort at military uniformity was the wearing of similar iron caps.

"Lord John, of course," the knight amended promptly.

The honor of John's Winch having been satisfied, the bowman admitted, "You're barely in time; we're taking 'er up for the night." Which was just how Crassmor had wanted things.

The bowman blew on a bone whistle. The archers on the opposite bank began dragging a little cockleshell to the water; Alanna's information that no guards were left outside at night was apparently correct. The other bowman on the platform gave his weapon a practice pull before unstringing it. He used a technique of draw that Crassmor had never seen before, holding the string by his jaw as if nocked, then pushing away the horns of the bow.

A moment later the platform began to rise slowly to the sound of creaking lines, lifting clear of the pilings. Crassmor shuffled for balance as it swung free, and had to lurch for a handhold among the mound of goods lashed to the platform. The guards chortled.

The knight ignored them, hoping that the thick hoisting line was sound and that the shear legs' frapping was tightly lashed. The platform, rotating gently, began the ascent of fifty or so feet that would bring it level with the entrance to John's cave. On the second leisurely rotation, Crassmor noted that a steep path in the cliff's face, formed by a split in the rock, had recently been hammered and chiseled away, exposing unweathered stone. John was manifestly a character who valued his security, a matter of no reassurance.

When the platform had been winched level with the cave's mouth, men waiting there secured its edge with ropes passed through gaps in its timbers. It still felt precarious to the knight, though. Crassmor made preliminary contact with his baggage, hoping that the chief archer or one of his mates would lend a hand. The bowmen only smirked and enjoyed his discommodity as he was obliged to serve himself.

During that operation, though, he took note of details of the place for future reference. The two shear legs—fair sized tree trunks—were firmly set in hand-drilled holes in the cave floor, the hawserlike guys fastened to heavy spikes deep-driven into rock walls. The hoisting line passed through a simple pulley at the apex of the shears and ran overhead, back toward the rear of the cave. There, at a wider spot, was the windlass for which the place was named. It was set high, so that the hoisting line wouldn't hamper loading and unloading, and well anchored, harnessed to its crankshaft by elaborate wooden gearing.

People gathered in the gloom of the cave's farther reaches for this daily ritual. There were a few women of the place, drab and worn from drudgery and care; haggard men who'd left some task to help unload and to hear what news there might be; and a few children eager to see who the outsider was. The general populace was even more disreputable-looking than the archers; John's predations on the river hadn't made his people sleek or fat. The cargo was unloaded and the platform was freed for a final descent, to return with the last of the guards and their cockleshell.

Crassmor failed to spy anybody who answered the description of either of Alanna's sisters. The crowd, elbowing one another, parted deferentially. The man who stepped by them had Crassmor's instant attention; the badly embroidered quarterstaff and longbow on his breast proclaimed him lord of this sad little fief.

He was tall, with long, loose-dangling simian arms. His big, knobby hands showed a variety of scars and lumps, confirming that he was a quarter-staff man, as his adopted heraldry implied. He was just beginning to slump with middle age; his curl-kinked brown hair, gray strands corkscrewing through it, looked as if it would defy any comb, but was in retreat from his crown. It could be seen through his bushy beard that John of John's Winch had a prominent overbite. His close-set eyes were ringed with the creases of a habitual squint and held a hard-won shrewdness more the product, the knight guessed, of experience than of native intellect.

Crassmor made a deep bow with casual grace, taking off his cap and nearly sweeping his shoes with it, making an elegant swirl with his fur-trimmed cape.

"Lord John, for so I see you to be, may I present myself? Morodo, harper and poet to nobility! Having heard of the glory of your, er, emergent realm, I am come to offer my humble talents. I would set forth and send abroad songs of the deeds and splendor of my Lord John of John's Winch."

John heard him out with boorishly unconcealed skepticism, but Crassmor didn't miss the man't grudging satisfaction at hearing himself styled a noble. The knight, nose filled with the stenches of animals and people—domesticated and otherwise—making their protracted encampment in the cave, had new respect for his own powers of persuasion.

John dug at one nostril with a thumbnail, still squinting at Crassmor suspiciously. "Harper? Your type's more partial to fancy tables and soft beds, eh? What draws you here?"

The knight smiled engratiatingly. "Now, that is, m'lord— I was intemperate enough, while in my cups, to compose a rather unflattering ditty about the Duke of Ashtar, who rules somewhat farther upriver. The tune, and more to the point, the lyrics, were repeated. Just about the time the duke's men began inquiring after me, I found myself with the undeniable impulse to go a-traveling."

Some of the locals had gathered closer, studying Crassmor's city clothes and urbane mannerisms. He permitted himself to preen just a little.

"Oh, yuh?" John said. "Let's hear that song."

"Aha-ha, m'lord," Crassmor parried a little embarrassedly, "I fear that my journeying has taken its toll on my strength."

John nodded slyly. "You want a free feed to start with, hey? Well, bargain hard for what you're after; that's only right. You can play during dinner. As long as the songs are good, you eat. Fair enough? Done!"

He'd scarcely finished when two women worked their way through the crowd, followed by an elderly gentleman who was in a state of some agitation. The women could only be Arananth and Oorda, Crassmor concluded. Arananth, the younger, was the very image of the damsel in distress, a conformity to stereotype that was rather unusual in Crassmor's experience. She was a pale-skinned girl with a youthful blush high on her cheeks and a heart-shaped face framed by waves of light hair topped by a delicate circlet of pearl-encrusted gold. Her petite figure was nicely set off by the tightly corseted damask gown she wore; her wide, hazel eyes darted here and there with charming innocence.

The older sister, Oorda, was another case entirely. She was overendowed for Crassmor's taste, the look in her eye putting him in mind of a horse that was best watched closely. Her ruddy face was probably pleasant enough in a round-cheeked way when she wasn't glowering. Oorda's brittle-looking hair, brushed back tightly against her skull, had been confined with near-violent severity. She wore a straight-lined, unflattering robe, sleeves pushed up to display respectable forearms and hands that had seen work.

"John!" Oorda said, expelling the name as she might a worm encountered in an apple. The river pirate's face worked irritably as she came to confront him, hands on hips as if she were about to barter for charcoal. "Those idiot lackeys of yours just up and took most of the clothes we have! You lowborn, thieving rat-bastard!" She indicated two men who'd just come up from the depths of the cave. One's jaw was beginning to turn red, promising a variety of colors, while the other's face bore the parallel scratches of a vigorous clawing. John, waving his arms, interrupted with some lack of spirit.

"Oorda . . . *Lady* Oorda, half my people are in rags, and little good cloth comes our way. What choice do I have?"

"Villain!" she shrieked, and kicked his shin. He hopped back, holding it and cursing and, Crassmor noticed, moving very adroitly for such a gangly man.

"You had but to ask politely!" she ranted on. "D'you think my poor sister and I enjoy seeing naked brats and tattered scarecrows all around us? But you show not a particle of consideration!"

She pursued him. He avoided her second kick and caught the fist she swung at his chin. The two men she'd pointed out jumped forward, eluding her blows with caution born of experience, to rescue their leader. As they dragged off the kicking, battling Oorda, her yells echoed back to them.

"You're lower than troll-flops, the whole bunch! Let me go! John, you *mother-jinker!*"

Rubbing his abused shin, the Lord of John's Winch turned to the old man who'd arrived with the sisters. "Fanarion, didn't I tell you to keep that shrew away from me?" Fanarion, John's seer-mage, shuffled nervously, head downcast to study a big toe that was working its way through one of his worn purple velvet carpet slippers. He wore long, symbol-worked red robes, but they were soiled and threadbare. His pink skull gleamed through a few remaining strands of white hair. His nose bore a pair of spectacles, their lenses nearly as thick as Crassmor's least finger.

At length, Fanarion looked up, blinking through his glasses like a woebegone owl. "N-now, Jackie," he stammered, "I must say! I tried, but there's just no deterring that one once she's reared up on her hind legs! Just absolutely!"

"Next time cast a spell over her!" John roared. "Even your down-at-the-heels magic ought to suffice for that!" Fanarion winced, wounded.

"Why, John, *shame!*" Arananth chided. The pirate was suddenly and completely distracted, his pique forgotten, with no eye for anyone else. He gave her the look of a lapdog; she shook a slender white finger at him in a charming fit of displeasure.

"That's insufferably wicked! The way you treat poor Fanarion and my dear sister, really! Nor should you be putting such ideas in this enchanter's sweet old head. A spell on Oorda, *indeed!*"

Crassmor noted the look of profound gratitude that crossed Fanarion's face and reflected that the magician himself was somewhat ensorcelled. John was contrition itself, fawning over her, towering ridiculously above her while slouching with awkward casualness to make less of his height.

"Uh, dearest Arananth, it was the moment's anger. Forgive your, your servant; I have so much on my mind. I'll replace your clothes later, I vow. Once we've wed, I'll smother you in gowns and, um, scarves—combs—" He seemed at the limits of his knowledge of female attire.

"Never," she pledged, turning up her adorable nose and facing away from him. She wore the hint of a smile, though, which, Crassmor saw contemptuously, John missed completely. *Gods, this dullard doesn't even know how the game's played!*

Arananth went off after her sister with Fanarion fussing along behind, leaving John devastated. Seeing his chance, Crassmor slid up to him and half-sang to the wretched outlaw, "M'lord, it's sometimes an evening of merry music that gives wings to a young lady's heart. Singing, dancing; these would raise a swain in a lass' estimation!"

John brightened visibly. "Think you so?" He pressed Crassmor's hand. "Whoa, that's it! The very thing! Poor little darling, she deserves a bit o' gaiety."

He turned to the archer who'd spoken to Crassmor and had been of so little assistance in the matter of luggage transferral. "Hey, Borra; get your crap out of your quarters. My harper's going to be using them. Then fetch Morodo's stuff down there."

He turned back to Crassmor-Morodo. "Harper, if you soften her heart toward me, anything I can give is yours." He sniffled a bit; Crassmor told himself, *If my sense of pity weren't completely dormant . . .*

John and crew fell into an exacting scrutiny of the day's acquisitions. Permitting the resentful Borra to precede him, Crassmor went deeper into the cave, the luggage left behind in a conspicuous pile for now. All the while he wondered how a bold pirate chieftain could be such an unutterable mooncalf.

# Chapter 11

# REGALED

**From the winch** area, the cave's main trunk descended at a considerable incline. The place was sooty and stuffy, lit here and there by candles, torches, and fish-oil lamps. Crassmor concluded that the air was circulating, albeit slowly. Whether this was by virtue of the layout of the place or some hidden apparatus, he had no idea.

The warren was only in part a natural formation, having been expanded by extensive labor, Crassmor saw, at a time he judged to have been generations earlier. The walls were gray, moist rock with occasional lichenous blotches on them. The floors, which had been carefully smoothed, were slick from ages of traffic. The knight wondered idly who the place's original occupants had been.

Crassmor and his escort passed a pungent kitchen chamber reeking of garlic and onions. Through its entrance the knight saw an unwashed male, his back to them, ladling grease off the surface of a soup and emptying it into a barrel. A thick gyve was clamped around his ankle, chaining him to a hefty staple hammered into a crack in the center of the floor. Borra paused to yell, "You there, Bint!"

Crassmor instantly stepped to one side of the doorway so that his cousin wouldn't see him and betray recognition. Borra didn't notice, nor did he see the knight's hand poised coincidentally by his dirk. Were Bint to give the game away somehow, Crassmor resolved, Borra would die and he and his cousin would make the best they could of their dilemma.

"We got a couple more casks of fish oil. John wants you to refill all the lamps in the place before dinner," Borra finished.

The chain rattled abruptly, then stopped, as if Bint had been about to react violently, then reconsidered. The show of restraint made Crassmor wonder how much of Bint's youthful temper had cooled in captivity. He heard his cousin mutter something unintelligible. It apparently satisfied Borra; the archer led the way on.

"The river traffic is light right now," Crassmor remarked, "and your company numerous. Doesn't that make slave keeping impractical?"

"No slave," Borra replied, "but a bothersome fool of a knight from this Singularity we keep hearing about. He tried to steal back yon girlies from us and wounded two or three of our men before John broke a stool over his helm. I was all for giving him to the fish in pieces, but Jo—*Lord* John wants no trouble with this Ironwicca they talk about." Borra shot a sidelong glance at him. "You're no friend to this Singularity, are you, now?"

"I have scant cause to be," Crassmor answered, with such force that it convinced the bowman.

"Any-road, John is content to keep the lad until the wedding's over, then ransom him if he can or turn him loose if not, reckoning that it'll be too late then for him to make trouble."

They clomped downward, coming to a large chamber that had been a grand dining hall in times past. The table was hewn from a single piece of stone, half as wide again as Crassmor's height, long enough to seat fifty people, wonderfully engraved with all manner of arabesques and etched with gylphs. The chairs were high-backed monoliths. Two of the crude fish-oil lamps and a few candles, guttering in their sconces, gave dim light. From there, five tributary tunnels led in various directions. Into one of these, Borra preceded the knight.

The quarters of the dispossessed archer turned out to be a tiny nook at the bottom of a side tunnel, partitioned off by a stiff leather curtain. Its primary claim to opulence was a short bed of woven saplings. There were wall niches for storage and a single lamp on an outcropping of wall. As the former occupant gathered his few belongings, Crassmor entertained himself by trying to analyze the assorted odors contributing to the general rankness of the place. He brought forth a pomander ball and held it to his nose. Borra noticed and gave a snort of derision at the effeteness of that, a reaction Crassmor welcomed.

When Borra had departed, the knight began to give some thought to the love song that would be required of him at dinner. Borra was some time returning with his luggage, as Crassmor had assumed he would be. The disgruntled outlaw, setting down the zither case, shoulder duffel, and bedroll, gave the knight a peculiar look, then left. The leather curtain rustled a little as Crassmor peered after, a moment later, to make certain that the oaf had gone.

Inspection of his belongings revealed that they had, as he'd hoped, been closely examined. Opening the zither case, he saw that the flecks of soot he'd dusted in one corner showed that its false wall had been disturbed. It was a piece of concealment that any pirate or highwayman might be expected to detect. Crassmor drew out the letter that had been carefully replaced there by whoever had done the searching.

> Dearest Friend Crassmor,
> Plans have been made for the rescue of your beloved, my sister Oorda. Word has been sent her that she is to betray no sign of knowing you when you arrive. That you may rescue only one of my sisters, and that your choice would be Oorda, I well understand, for she is your betrothed. I have drawn a map on the back of this letter, detailing the region around John's Winch and the river routes. Bear it with you. I am even now planning the rescue of Arananth in such time, with the help of the gods, that the marriage will not take place. Fair fortune to you, brave knight.
> > Your sister-to-be,
> > Alanna of Meere

John was certainly appraised of the letter's contents by now; everything hinged on his believing them. Having encountered the fierce Oorda, Crassmor refused to think that pirate chieftain wouldn't want the woman out of his cave and out of his life. This, it was to be hoped, would give the knight a certain freedom to operate.

He was considering ways of speaking to or otherwise making contact with his cousin, but was forestalled. The curtain rippled and a figure slipped into the room. Crassmor's hand, at his dirk, checked. It was Bint.

He was rancid with sweat and scullery grease, worn and thinner, with a forefinger to his lips, urging quiet. He bore a stone bottle. Crassmor, catching a whiff of him, plied his pomander with a will.

"What's happened to your leash?" he asked mildly. He hadn't forgotten Bint's silent indictment of him in Gateshield and thereafter.

Bint made a sour face. "They remove it once the winch is up; there are guards there at the cave mouth. But in truth, no leg iron's needed; I've given John my parole, pledging to raise neither hand nor edge to anyone as long as I am here."

Crassmor made no comment. Bint bridled anyway, thinking there was an unspoken insult in the air. "I attempted rescue when word reached me that two women were being held against their will. I'd have died fighting, given the chance—I'd have let them gut me before wearing a chain. But the Lady Arananth begged John to spare me and pleaded with me to give my pledge. She said she wished no more blood spilled on her account."

*She grows more to my liking,* Crassmor thought. He said, "You lost no face with me, cousin. A dead man, even a dead knight, can do nothing for Arananth."

The observation appeared to go over well with Bint; his animosity subsided. He uncorked the stone bottle and poured a careful measure of fish oil into the lamp, making the floating wick quiver and shadows flicker. Though he obviously hadn't been harmed, it was plain that captivity and servitude had been a bitter draught for him to swallow. Crassmor was grateful and a little surprised that John had been so unsanguine about the matter, thinking, *There may be more to that lout than meets the eye.* Aloud, he asked, "How did you know I was here?"

"I overheard John and Borra and the others discussing a

most peculiar letter they found in your baggage. It took several of them to get it read; none here ciphers well but Fanarion, and he's near-blind. I'm on this fueling errand and must be back in the kitchen ere long."

"What of this giant?" Crassmor wanted to know.

Bint shrugged. "Fanarion has put a compulsion on him. He stays in the area, patrolling, and John's people feed him. He comes when Fanarion summons him. They say the sight of him has stilled—"

"—many brave hearts." Crassmor anticipated his words. "Which means that I, for one, have nothing to fear." He only hoped that the creature had observed his injunction to harm no one camped on the riverbank. Crassmor instructed Bint, "Stay ready, but do nothing until we've orchestrated some plan, Bint. All depends on role playing now." He pointed a finger at his cousin. "No whispered messages of encouragement to the sisters, no veiled defiance to John."

Bint pushed back a lock of blond hair from where it had plastered itself to his forehead and nodded. "They will watch me more closely now that they know that there are two knights in John's Winch. But it's ten days since I was captured; I have learned patience. Know this, though: Arananth's people observe the dictates of the stars, and John is aware of that. It's a common religion in this part of the Beyonds. No marriage sealed in this season will be recognized, but that obstacle will be invalid after another five days. John has the nuptials scheduled for then."

He moved back to the curtain while Crassmor considered the changes in his cousin, relieved that Bint expected no prodigious feats of derring-do. At the curtain, Bint paused to say, "I am glad to find you sound of mind, cousin." To Crassmor's quizzical look, he responded, "The letter had you affianced to Oorda, which would not have spoken well of your sanity."

Crassmor chuckled as Bint eased back out of the alcove.

A formal dinner at John's Winch turned out to be an even madder affair than Crassmor had envisioned.

Fanarion came to fetch him without benefit of armed

escort, proof that John was confident of the security of
his realm. Crassmor was inclined to concede it too, particularly with that giant on the prowl. The mage tried to be
pleasant and treat the new harper as a friend rather than
a rival. Crassmor noticed he was blinking behind his
glasses and tended to step back for a better look at things.

"Oh, this place shows great promise, great promise,"
Fanarion was saying as they stepped along. "It is the first
time most of these people have ever had a spot to call
their own."

"My songs will make of them a palace filled with
heroes," the knight assured him blithely.

Though he stepped back to do it, Fanarion fixed Crassmor with a look of surprising acuity. "They'd be grateful
to be freemen in a home of their own," the mage corrected.
Crassmor forgot his next gibe, gesturing to show that he
understood.

Though some of John's followers were making merry
in the lower caverns, the majority of the cave's inhabitants,
some three dozen and more, were seated in the oversized
stone chairs at the lengthy slab of the dining table. Torches
had been set in sockets in the wall, and additional fish-oil
lamps brought in, making the place almost festive, though
they had little effect on the dankness of the chamber. The
viands, platters of trout and carp, small cauldrons of goat
stew, hot breads, bowls of steaming crawfish, and racks
of lamb were surprisingly edible.

John sat at the head of the table, with Arananth to his
right and Fanarion next. Crassmor and Oorda were at the
pirate's left. The knight had the feeling of being a child
once again as he slid into the huge, cold chair which, being immovably heavy, compelled him to lean forward in
order to eat.

The tattered crew had attempted to make themselves
presentable. Most of their clothing seemed at least to have
been washed. The fate of the sisters' wardrobe was evident
in the rich colors of the many patches there. John's band
made little pretense at conversation or table manners, but
fell to what was probably their best feed in some time.

Their chieftain did his best to ply his intended with winning small talk.

Thus John, with an excess of suavity, began, "Lady Arananth, you do honor to this humble table—"

"*And* the dripping ceilings," Oorda broke in spitefully, *and* the corners where the children and dogs piddle, *and* the—" At length John became more glum, refilling his flagon at shorter intervals.

Oorda was chief performer at that zany travesty. She found occasion to revile or threaten nearly everyone present, throwing bones at the dogs that sniffed after table scraps and mocking John in such graphic terms that Crassmor decided, *She holds great promise as a muleteer.* Crassmor began to fear that John would lose patience and simply set the knight and his "fiancée" adrift on the river.

But the knight thought, too, that he detected an underlying note, suspiciously resembling compassion, in the affronts Oorda dispensed so lavishly. In deriding John's little band, she betrayed a keen awareness of their hardships. This, however, didn't keep her from dumping a fistful of spice from one of the bowls into John's food when he wasn't looking. The river pirate's first bite sent him into a fit of sneezing, his eyes watering from some allergy the vindictive Oorda had discovered. Crassmor, for his part, did his best to fill the gaps in John's stumbling sallies to Arananth and duck both Oorda's vitriol and her table scraps.

Arananth, a complete contradiction to her sister, ate quietly, spoke civilly to one and all, and was one of the few to escape Oorda's wrath. She even seemed to listen seriously to some of John's nonsense, possibly out of pity.

The blinking Fanarion did some minor magic—parlor tricks—pleasing most of those present, eliciting bursts of smoke and tongues of fire in diverse colors from the table lamps. Crassmor, familiar with this kind of prestidigitation, concluded after careful observation that Fanarion kept bags of fire granules in his billowing sleeves. It was plain, though, that Fanarion was adept; Crassmor was certain that the old man had real magic and potencies in reserve.

Oorda's outbursts kept the subject of the love song from

arising until Fanarion, flushed with pleasure at his ovation from John's followers, called: "An ode celebrating your host, harper!"

Crassmor took his zither up with some misgiving. He pointed out, "I scarcely know enough about Lord John yet for a proper ballad." It rather broke the unspoken rules of minstrelsy, making public the process of poetic refurbishment, as it were. But no one seemed to object to the prospect of hearing the truth and then having it prettied up before him. John's flagging morale actually appeared to lift at the suggestion.

Crassmor settled his zither and struck a somewhat melodramatic chord. "The tale, then?"

John, brow working furiously, managed, "The king was off to the war; his brother ground us down. We banded together to help one another and ended up battling for our lives, hiding in the forest. Finally, the king came home."

Frowning at the paucity of detail, Crassmor set up an irritated thrumming. This would be more difficult than the simple cobbling together of hyperbole. "So, now, let me see. You rallied the people around you, eh, John? Led the resistance, struck a blow for—"

"The lummox was merely the second-in-command," Oorda sneered. John nodded and shrugged apologetically to Arananth. Crassmor wondered how Oorda had come by that information.

"But was loyal to his king," the knight interposed, "who no doubt gave great praise and was thankful for such good faith."

"The king went right back to squabbling and whoring, mostly overseas," a woman's gravelly voice testified from somewhere down the table.

"And got himself killed with an arrow at that bloody stupid siege at Chaluz," a man added.

"And so his brother took over again," John admitted. "He went straightway to mistreating us all, just as before. This time even the barons couldn't stomach him. They upped and cornered him at Runnymede and forced a pact. He had to go easier on them, but things didn't get much better for us. A few of us from the old days, and some new ones, we threw in together and went looking for a new start."

Crassmor, interested now aside from the song, inquired, "And your former leader?"

"Had his lands and title back," a one-eyed man answered, his black patch rimmed by burn-scar tissue. "What did Robin care for us?"

John's head came up, anger lighting his face like a signal flare. "He had a wife and children and liegemen to think about!" The big man caught his temper; he finished more calmly. "It wouldn't have been right for him to go outlaw again, so we never asked him. We just struck off into the forest and kept going. We met Fanarion wandering there and finally came upon this place."

The old mage, leaning back for focusing distance, squinting through his thick spectacles, agreed. Crassmor wondered if this lot knew or cared that they were no longer in their home Reality.

John went on. "There were brigands here in those days, real ones who robbed and slew without mercy, not toll takers like us."

Oorda said, "Fah!" but he ignored her.

"We took over and chased off the ones we didn't kill in battle. Our toll is small, and we pay or trade for everything else we get. Now you can travel for a day in any direction and never fear. A toll's not a lot to pay for that, is my thought on it."

"And is a kidnapping toll taker any better than a murdering robber?" Oorda queried.

John made his answer to Arananth. "Maybe not. But we could be cast out of this place any time some noble took a fancy to it; that's the way things have always gone for us. At least this way I shall have some legal claim, however slight."

"Little good that will do you when you get what's coming to you—and *you will*," Oorda mocked.

John shot her a look that made even Oorda recoil for a moment. "What does that mean?" he asked quietly.

"I—nothing."

Crassmor cursed the woman's constant sniping; with a

meaningless, goading phrase, she'd aroused all John's suspicions. Now some of her spirit came back. "Are you afraid of mere words? Of a woman's words?"

"Of anything that threatens us here," he answered. "Fanarion! Place upon her your spell of veracity!"

The mage was adjusting his glasses nervously. With an indignant squawk, Oorda tried to bolt. John was there first, out of his seat and around Crassmor's with remarkable agility, reaching with his long arms to clamp her into her seat. Crassmor shrank to one side to avoid the action.

Fanarion was quick to obey John's order. Hand moving through mystical passes, he chanted in his high, rasping voice. The tips of his fingers had begun to glow. The other diners were silent, watching, even Arananth. Crassmor noticed that he himself was being watched, and more than one hand moved closer to a hilt.

The knight's estimate of Fanarion's abilities rose, as did his fear. The mage might have been extraordinarily fortunate in being able to call up the spell at once, or had come to the table prepared with it, or was a much better magician than he looked. Whatever the case, Crassmor had no desire to intervene and stayed still to avoid attracting attention.

Arananth made a little objection then, but was ignored. The Lord of John's Winch was no lovelorn buffoon when it came to his people's safety. The elder sister, for all her resentment and vigor, could do nothing to free herself. Her lurid invective stopped in mid-word as Fanarion leveled his splayed, shining fingers at her. "Let go of me, John, you sorry sack of horse—"

She was blank-eyed, enthralled. Crassmor hunched even farther away from her to stay clear of that invisible lane of enchantment crossing the table. John released Oorda, stepping away. Oorda sat silently. *An aspect of the spell not without its appeal,* Crassmor judged.

John moved around to stand next to Fanarion so that he could watch both Oorda and Crassmor. "What did you mean just now?" he asked the woman, with a distrustful glance for the knight. "What will I get that's coming to me? What danger is there?"

"I know of none," she responded, as in a dream. Fanarion, without taking his hand down, shrugged; it could only be truth. John's confused glare went back to the pale, fretful Crassmor, who'd long since begun thinking about bolting for the door.

John sought Oorda's testimony, still believing she knew of some threat. "What, then, of him whom you love?"

Her brows knitted as if in troubled sleep. "What of him?"

John's voice rumbled throughout the hall. "He is here! Admit his name!"

The somniloquent answer came: "John of John's Winch."

# Chapter 12

# RESOURCEFUL

**In the profound** silence following Oorda's admission, Crassmor heard several of his tablemates choking on their dinner. John was at a loss for words. Running a large hand through his unruly hair, he muttered, "But how . . . how—"

Since it wasn't a proper question, Oorda was unresponsive. Arananth supplied, "She loves you, you ninny; no one can say how."

"Why?" he asked, nonplussed. That was a question, right enough.

Oorda answered, "Because you look after your people and you care for them. You are kind of heart; that is a thing that does not come easily to me. To me, you are heroic."

*She's good at concealing these things,* Crassmor commented to himself as he eyed the door.

John's gaze went back to the knight. "And what of him, Morodo—or shall I say Sir Crassmor? Is he not your betrothed?"

"I have never seen him before today," Oorda answered.

John's eyes narrowed. "I'll have the facts of this yet. Fanarion, here's another one for your truth spell to— 'ware! Catch him!"

Crassmor had leaped from his seat, but the folks of John's Winch rose from theirs to apprehend him. Seeing the odds, he reversed direction and slipped back into the big stone chair, then dropped under the table as cries of alarm went up. He could hear Oorda, released from the spell, beginning a torrent of her choicer invectives.

There was much racing, shuffling, and scuffling around the table. The knight considered his course of action, telling himself, *Prayer might be just the thing right now.*

Just then Fanarion scrunched down in his seat across the way, fingers still splayed, seeking to bring his spell to bear. Before he could, the knight duck-walked and scrambled over to snatch the spectacles off Fanarion's face. The old magician squeaked and began blinking blindly, the lights on his fingers dying as his concentration broke. He groped and bleated.

Crassmor heard others edging down under the table cautiously, and swords being drawn as well. He was reappraising the notion of surrender when inspiration hit him. Tucking the spectacles away in his doublet to forestall any more spell casting, he grabbed Fanarion's right arm, quickly located the bags of fire granules sewn into the sleeve, and ripped out those he could reach.

John and several others were now behind Fanarion, struggling to help the old man and get at Crassmor. Sliding away from them a bit, the knight opened the bags' drawstrings, leaned out from beneath the table, and hurled them up at a torch. The contents were dispersed as the bags flew; a fireball laced with bright, variegated sparks erupted outward from the torch to roll and spread along the ceiling, filling the hall with smells ·and dense, multicolored smoke which curled to engulf the room. There was screaming, along with coughing, gagging, and cries of "Fire!" "Help!" and "Murder!" Many weapons were dropped.

Dinner being effectively over, the participants began stumbling and aiding one another out of the hall by the nearest exits, avoiding the main tunnel's entrance at the head of the table where the smoke was the thickest. John was holding both sisters there by their wrists, however, trying between gasping breaths and hacking coughs to rally his forces.

In Crassmor's tactical assessment, getting past John would be the linchpin of the affair. The knight found a sword abandoned by its owner and took it up as his own eyes began to water. There seemed no alternative to a duel with the alarmingly large and agile John.

Just then Crassmor saw, through the drifting smoke, the delicate Arananth raise a pewter beer pitcher she'd snatched from the table with her free hand and, standing on tiptoe, bring it down on the pirate's head. It made a sound like a town clock Crassmor had once heard. John, rocked, released the women. Arananth took the pitcher with a two-handed grip and dealt him another blow before Oorda, with a cry, grabbed her. The bandit half-collapsed, holding himself up by leaning on his chair, one hand clamped to his scalp.

Crassmor, ever attentive to the moment's advantage, was already on the move. Tucking the sword through his belt and skirting the dazed John, he caught up one sister's hand in each of his and churned toward the exit, ending their difference of opinion.

"But—" Arananth panted.

"What—" Oorda protested.

*"Run!"* Crassmor hollered, shoving them on their way. This they did. He paused and whirled, hearing faltering footsteps behind him. Fanarion staggered out of the swirling smoke, eyes watering, wheezing. He must have known the knight by his voice; the old mage raised a finger and aimed it in his direction. Perhaps it was a brief resurgence of old power, or the emotion of the moment, but green sparks crackled along the digit.

However, Fanarion could apparently bring to mind no truly puissant curse, and so he began spewing maledictions. "May misfortune pursue you! May you never know peace!" The pronouncements didn't frighten the knight particularly, under the circumstances. He did not wish to be the target of some stronger wording, though; he took up a wine goblet and dashed its contents into the mage's face, ending the ranting and dousing the green sparks. Then he raced away. Within seconds, he'd caught up with the sisters.

Crassmor could hear John, who must have shaken off the effects of Arananth's blows, yelling for his men. As the knight ran along the main tunnel, he heard the pack take up the chase, gaining, and still had no idea how to find Bint or deal with the guards on duty at the windlass. He regretted the wasted effort and self-deception of carefully planned rescues. *Grossly unfair,* he reflected, *the scheme of things.*

As they drew up on the kitchen chamber, they saw Bint in the tunnel before them, shouldering a cask. Calling for them to get out of the way, he held it high. They dodged past him. Bint hurled the cask down the tunnel, breaking it on the stone. Fish oil washed down the steep, smoky tunnel, lapping the side walls. Bint had three more casks by his side, their heads already broached. He emptied one with a wide swing, then drew the others down the tunnel, where they shattered.

The younger knight was gasping for breath as they gathered around him, babbling questions. Glancing back down the tunnel, Crassmor could barely make out madly thrashing figures sliding on a quick return trip toward the dining chamber, caroming off one another with yells of distress, thumping off the walls. *Indicators,* Crassmor realized, *of a significant setback in pursuit.*

Bint explained, "I heard the hubbub. It occurred to me that slippery footing might work to our advantage." He grinned proudly through layers of ash and grease.

"Admirable. Resourceful," Crassmor congratulated, catching his breath. "Straight on and around the bend to the winch, is it not? And the guards—"

"Came running when they heard that hoopla," Bint anticipated. "They turned their backs on me when I pretended I was still shackled." He pointed; Crassmor saw two unconscious men lying against a nearby wall. A heavy iron skillet testified to the fact that Bint hadn't violated his word not to raise hand or edge against anyone. He'd been fortunate in that the men hadn't been wearing their steel caps. *This boy holds real promise,* Crassmor decided.

Arananth was eyeing Bint, not without some interest. Oorda gazed back down the tunnel, evincing concern. Bint added, "Best we were off, before Fanarion can whistle up his giant or—"

A clank of metal had come from below. They saw a man working his laborious way up the tunnel, scaling sideways along its wall, avoiding the grease chute of a floor by swinging from hold to chancy hold like an ungainly gibbon. John, of course; the clank had been the sword thrust through his belt. He advanced quickly.

They couldn't simply run, Crassmor knew; John would overtake them before they could reach the cave's mouth. He shoved his cousin at the women. "Get them away however you can. Go downstream; their sister Alanna should be there, not far. Tell her that if she fails to wait for me, I'll come back to haunt her."

Oorda grew stubborn, unsure that she wanted to leave now that she'd spoken her devotion to John. Crassmor bellowed, "Arananth's your responsibility too!"

She sneered at him, but went off with Bint and her sister. Oorda warned Crassmor over her shoulder, "Keep John at bay only! If you hurt him, I shall rip out your liver!"

*Me hurt him?* Crassmor marveled. He turned to watch the pirate laboring toward him. Reasonable to the last, he called out, "I say, John! That's quite far enough, my dear fellow; you mustn't come any closer."

John paused in his difficult ascent. "And if I do?"

Crassmor *tsk*ed. "I haven't taken my sword out yet, you'll notice. I only wish to be on my way."

John resumed, giving no sign of having heard. Since the bandit needed both hands and feet to climb, the knight judged that he could keep John from surer footing with a little judicious pinking.

But, as Crassmor should have understood by then, John was a man of great competence. From just beyond Crassmor's poking range, he stopped and let fly with a knife seized from the dinner table.

Crassmor dropped; the knife passed over him. He hit the floor, then rolled furiously as he saw John draw back with a second blade. The second knife struck a note from the stone. John, having gathered himself, sprang, to land beyond the oil slick as the knight bounced to his feet.

Both had their swords out. "Fanarion will summon the giant," John promised. "You cannot get far from here."

"Far enough, I think. The others are probably down the winch rope already." Crassmor wished he hadn't forgotten his dirk at the table.

The bandit took a resolute step forward; both men went *en garde*. "I have fifty people to think of!" John grated.

Crassmor, shaking his head, answered earnestly, "Each of us has only one life to consider here, my friend. Let us *both* live out the night, what say?"

John attacked; their edges met. John wasn't as skillful as his opponent, but his longer reach and longer sword made the match damnably even. The knight might have inflicted damage by shortening their fencing distance, but wasn't inclined to put himself any further within the other's reach. And he found he had no wish to kill this man who'd spared Bint and taken this band of unfortunates under his protection—not if he could help it.

Plangent stroke and counterstroke sounded in the tunnel. John pressed hard, exploiting his advantages in what Crassmor felt to be an unsportsmanlike fashion.

The knight went on a desperate offensive, calling experience and speed into play, driving the bigger man back across the terrain he'd won. Before Crassmor could quite force John's heel onto the treacherous footing of the slick, the pirate counterattacked and half-turned their positions. In another moment Crassmor found himself with his back to the kitchen doorway.

*Kitchen?* his brain echoed. He backed off from the exchange then and plunged into the kitchen, searching frantically. John poised in the tunnel for a moment, wary of a trap. Then, seeing Crassmor waiting with his back against a heavy butcher's block, he came on.

As his antagonist approached, lifting his sword in both

hands, the knight brought his own left hand into view in a blur. Tumeric flew at John in a spray, halting him in surprise. Crassmor followed up with other spices flung from bowls at random: paprika and nutmeg, gren and brokt and curry, pepper and ginger and soulant.

One, at least, was the specific spice that Oorda had used to touch off John's allergy at the dinner table. He grunted, sneezed, drew a great breath, and sneezed again. His eyes brimmed over; his nose opened like a spigot. More sneezes racked him. He stumbled back in dismay, unable to defend himself.

Crassmor sidled after. John, eyes puffed nearly shut, reeled in the tunnel. "Behind you, John!" the knight called. The Lord of John's Winch began to twist around, realized it was a trick, and spun back frantically, his feet nearly tangling. Crassmor reached to poke him once, lightly, trying not to feel a certain malicious amusement. John flinched away from the sword point, as intended, onto the oil slick. With a howl of fury and gyration of arms and legs, he tobogganed back down the tunnel.

Crassmor turned and raced on, delirious with the joy of being alive. He was speculating on how far downriver he'd have to go to rendezvous with Alanna and the others —and regretting that he'd have to abandon his doublet— when, rounding the corner, he slid to a halt.

Oorda stood by the windlass, aghast, staring off toward the mouth of the cave in a paralysis of fright. Beside her stood Bint, in a similar condition. In front of them, likewise, stood Arananth. From beyond Crassmor's line of vision, its source at the cave's mouth, came a moist, bestial, gargling laugh and a primitive stench that cut through even the pungent odors of John's Winch.

"Look; look!" boomed a voice that sent currents of fear up Crassmor's spine. "Gaze upon me, upon death! The sight of me has stilled many a mortal heart with terror!"

Crassmor's hackles stood straight up and he heard his own teeth chattering. Plainly, the giant had answered Fanarion's summons without delay, intercepting the others. And it sounded as if the creature didn't understand that it was only to capture, not to kill.

It didn't seem just to have come so close only to fail, but, wiping a sweating palm on his doublet, Crassmor concluded that he had. Then his fingers felt Fanarion's spectacles, still tucked away there, summoning a brief image of the squinting magician. A plan burst into the knight's desperate head.

He settled the glasses over his nose, twisting the arms and frames a bit to make them stay on. The blinding distortions of the thick lenses nearly made him ill, but he squared his shoulders and, knowing his life was at stake, stepped around the bend.

He heard the giant's grunt of surprise and knew that the monster had seen him, yet the knight could see nothing clearly in the blurred world of the lenses. All he could discern was a huge, squat form filling the cave before him; that was more than enough.

The giant hooted gleefully, its voice in a bass register so deep that Crassmor had to strain to understand it.

"Another! Another one come forth to die, eh? Cast your eyes upon me, O mortal! See the most terrifying sight in the world!" The form moved indistinctly, the giant's wild gesticulations and threatening motions registering only as shifting blotches of color. Crassmor made an elaborate show of squinting at the creature.

"Can't seem to see you," the knight admitted truthfully.

*"What?"* the giant howled, the blast of his breath stirring the knight's hair. Crassmor's knees began to feel weak. He tapped the spectacles and essayed an embarrassed smile.

"I say, cannot quite make you out, you know. You're too close."

"Another like cursed Fanarion," the giant yowled, "wearing glazen eyes and blind despite those?"

"Oh, there are a good many of us," Crassmor confessed timidly.

The giant roared like a scalded bear and his image wavered. The rock drummed to blows of immense power as he struck it in anger. Even though he couldn't see it, Crassmor was awed by the tantrum.

"Drop that sword!" the giant bellowed, and Crassmor did. "Since you cannot appreciate my magnificent horrendousness, I will slay you first!" He was quite plainly annoyed at having been deprived of a favorite sport, scaring victims, preferably to death.

Crassmor hastened to say solicitously, "A thousand pardons, Terrible One; would that I could look upon your utter frightfulness once before I die! The giant of John's Winch is accounted a wonder to behold. But you are too near to make out clearly."

The huge shape shifted again in the lenses. "*Now* look upon me, little one, and shudder in amazement!" The creature, obviously familiar with Fanarion's need to put distance between himself and the object on which he wished to focus, had presumed that the same was true for Crassmor. The giant had taken a step backward.

"My most craven apologies," Crassmor sniveled. "Though I perceive something of your horrific aspect now, still are you indistinct."

The giant screamed so loudly that Crassmor clapped hands to ears; then the monster took another step back. "Regard now my terrible mien," the monster bade, "and fall to your knees in astonishment!"

"To my knees I go!" Crassmor wailed, suiting action to words. "But gaze upon you in all your monstrousness I cannot. You are yet the slightest distance too close to me yet, though I'll die knowing that the sight of you would have made my heart leap into my throat like a red fish, I'm sure!"

"And so it shall!" the giant expostulated in a voice that must, Crassmor thought, have knocked the birds out of the trees. The creature moved back again, and the knight heard the sound he'd been waiting for, the creak of wood and hawser. The giant had stepped back onto the winch platform.

Crassmor tore off the spectacles, snatched up his sword, and leaped up all in a moment. But though he'd braced himself to sever the hoisting line without a sidewards glance, a snarl from the monster, or perhaps some undeniable drawing power of its horrible appearance, a compulsive aura, made him look that way involuntarily.

Crassmor froze. It was, in fact, an arresting sight, a being that not even a nightmare might endure, but would wake the sleeper from shattered dreams. The giant was stooped over on the platform, a creature perhaps a dozen feet tall, wearing the untanned skins of animals. He was enormously broad, seeming squat for all his height, fully a third of which was a long-jawed, almost lupine head. The mouth was guarded by crooked, yellowed fangs and held a red tongue. But it was the tiny, deep-set, gleaming red eyes that caught and held the knight with something akin to Fanarion's spell, a hypnotic insanity.

Seeing Crassmor's stark, immobilized terror, the giant reared back in a seizure of maniacal laughter; the hawser creaked as the platform shook it. Crassmor was still unable to move.

Without warning, the sword was wrenched from his limp grasp. Like some berserk woodchopper, Bint swung the blade. It struck the hoisting line where it met the windlass. The line, taut with the giant's weight, parted cleanly. One side of the platform was secured at the cave's mouth, and so the platform dropped away from beneath the monster like a trapdoor.

The giant gasped in mid-laugh and doubled over. He made a clumsy grab for one of the shear legs, missed, and plummeted from sight with a shriek of outrage that made the humans cringe. The sound ended with a concussive splash.

Crassmor and the others went to the cave's mouth, and the Tarrant son held a torch out over the water. They could make out nothing of the giant, only dark water flowing around the pilings.

"When you blocked the sight of him from me, I began to throw off the fascination of him," Bint told his cousin. "And then he turned his eyes away in laughter."

Crassmor was already removing his shoes and pushing

them into his belt, pulling off his doublet, and realizing gloomily that it, like his hat and cape, which were still back in Borra's alcove, would soon be outlaw's attire. "Yes, yes, now let's all move quickly," he prompted. "And mind that you throw yourselves well out into the river, or you'll have no better luck than our departed friend." There was no time, he knew, to pay out more hoisting line from the slow-moving windlass.

Bint went first, with a running start, casting the sword aside. He raced in a dive between the shear legs, landing well out in the river. Arananth, stepping out of her layers of clothing, clad only in a charming underslip, followed after with surprising athleticism. Just then there came to Crassmor's ears the furor of renewed pursuit. John and his men had found some method of conquering the fish-oil slick.

Crassmor leaned out over the river. He saw a twisted rope of rawhide hanging nearby and realized that the giant had let himself down from the cliff above when he'd arrived. Crassmor called down, "See if you can locate a cockleshell or canoe-WOOOOOOOOOOOOO!"

He was falling, gasping for air, kicking empty space, having been violently propelled off the cave's brink by Oorda. She must have taken a good start; he flew clear of the shallows to hit the water gracelessly.

Murky water pulled at and chilled him; he eventually surfaced, blowing spray and shaking strands of hair from his eyes. He'd lost his shoes.

Arananth and Bint were not too far away, watching. Crassmor called to them urgently to start off; they swam downriver together. People were gathered at the mouth of the cave, waving torches and yelling a good deal. Above all there rose the voice of the redoubtable Oorda, addressing, Crassmor quickly concluded, John. The knight listened, to determine whether further pursuit was to be feared.

"How dare you talk of going after them when I have poured out my love for you, you *toadsucker!* Have I not proclaimed the tenderest feelings of my heart, no matter how they were elicited? And you would humiliate me, reject me? You'll be a castrato first! My blood's every bit as good as hers!"

Oorda's volume grew and she gained force, overpowering John's feeble objections. Suddenly a stupendous groan and profuse sputtering and splashing made Crassmor scan the far bank. He saw the giant drag himself onto dry land, gasping hoarsely, shedding water in rivulets.

Crassmor, treading water, sank lower and speculated on how long he could hold his breath. But Oorda's attention had been attracted as well; she paused in her tirade. Seeing the monster in the moonlight, she cupped hands to her mouth and called down, "As for *you*, you worthless lump, I want a word with you as well! Your terrorizing days are over, fat clot! From now on, you work for your keep just like everyone else! Now, then, get your big ass back up here this instant!"

She resumed speaking to John and his cowed band. "This wallow is going to see some changes, or there's going to be *real* trouble! What kind of people go around looking like beggars and smelling like sheep dip? *Well?*"

The knight noticed that the giant was still gaping up at her raving silhouette. After a moment the giant of John's Winch turned to slink away upstream into the night, one fearsome guardian yielding his post to another.

Crassmor, breast-stroking away downstream quietly, meditated, not without pity, on the rough-handed civilizing that was about to transform John and John's Winch.

Alanna was as good as her word. A low whistle signaled him, not far downriver. The dugout rested on the bank. "Are you being chased, good Sir Crassmor?" her voice came as he waded tiredly ashore.

"No," he replied. "Your sister has John's heart and mind well in hand, I believe, and more vulnerable components of his anatomy as well." He sneezed.

"Bless," she said automatically. "Come, take a blanket."

He sat on the dugout's gunwale, rubbing his tired arms and a knot in his calf. Alanna lit a lanthorn; in its glow, Bint and Arananth could be seen wrapped in cloaks, gazing blissfully into each other's eyes, fingers intertwined. The swim had, in removing grit and grease, revealed Bint's blond good-looks.

Crassmor snorted. Arananth noticed him then. She asked, "And Oorda remains with John?"

Crassmor sneezed again. "Inseparably."

"Good," Arananth declared promptly. "I was beginning to think she would never confess her feelings. In truth, I wanted to see her happy, but I did not know how much longer I could bear to linger in that cave and put up with John's fumbling courtship."

"*Linger?*" Crassmor screamed, what little satisfaction he had evaporating.

But Arananth was going on kindly. "And though your actions were rather precipitous, I thank you, Sir Knight, for helping Bint save me. Wasn't he splendid?"

Crassmor was composing his reply when Alanna broke in. "Best we were on our way, dears."

Roode and Dimble had appeared, to drag the canoe into the water. When they'd all boarded and shoved off, Alanna, seated behind Crassmor, dropped a flask into his lap. He took a sip of the nectar wine of Luur; his mood improved only marginally.

Arananth was asking, "Alanna, dear, couldn't father find something for Bint to do around the place? He's ever so handy, and we owe him so much."

Bint sighed. "I am a Knight of Onn, sweetest Arananth, and have other obligations."

Crassmor, staring sourly at the stars and listening to the dip of paddles, heard amusement in Alanna's voice. "There are . . . alternatives; we shall have time to explore those. After all, I have to stay on for a while with poor Sir Crassmor to insure that he gets proper attention."

That satisfied Arananth and Bint. Crassmor whispered, "Attention?"

Alanna chuckled. "Taken a chill, have you not? And gone through tribulations without number? You need to recuperate and, no doubt, your sword arm has been strained. A sling would be in order."

Twisting around, he studied her in the moonlight. Her humor and kindness brought up an ache that was Willow.

Alanna promised, "And when some pest shows up with a mission for a knight-errant, there I shall be to vouch that you've already rendered good service." There was mischief to it.

Crassmor, considering that, liked it more each moment. He allowed himself one more modest sip of the nectar wine as the river took him far from John's Winch.

## — PART III —

# AS FATE
# WOULD HAVE IT . . .

# Chapter 13

# UNEXPECTEDLY FORTUNATE

"He calls himself the Count di Cagliostro," Bint said while Crassmor refilled his goblet for him. "When I left, he was about to take up residence in House Tarrant. He has shown great powers of healing, by force of his will and not by medication. He has charmed your father, as he has so many others in Dreambourn since he wandered in from the Beyonds. He's made enemies as well."

That troubled Crassmor. Few other wanderers-in had known the hospitality of House Tarrant and fewer still had won Combard's favor, which was hard enough to win, as Crassmor could attest.

The subject of di Cagliostro wasn't the only thing disturbing the knight's peace of mind. There was also the original mission that had brought Bint into the Beyonds, a general summoning-home of all the Knights of the Order. The Grand Master had simply issued the command, directing Bint, among others, to carry it into the Beyonds.

Crassmor reclined once more on his plush lounging couch, which was carved from cedar in the form of a sphinx. Alanna, Bint, and Arananth occupied, respectively, couches shaped like a dragon, roc, and unicorn. All were positioned, head-inward, around a low table of some blond wood unknown to the knight, set with bands of agate-studded copper. They wore new clothes, the women in satin robes and the men in loose trousers and blouses of bright samite. The town was a fairly peaceful place, but Crassmor had *Shhing* beneath his couch, and Bint's replacement blade was under his.

Dappled shade from an aged elm covered them, but the weather was mild and the breeze held no chill. Only a few paces away, the wide river bore all forms of traffic: a gilt pleasure barge with two banks of oars to a side, laughter and the music of many instruments drifting from it; intricately painted dories with good-fortune totems fastened to their bows; a keelboat being poled by straining men in buckskins and homespun; a graceful junk; and an old dahabeah.

The four had stopped in this river city not far from the borders of the Singularity to rest from their adventures in John's Winch and arrange transport home. It should have been a pleasant interlude for Crassmor, what with the hospitality of the famous Kalleck Inn to enjoy and the company of Alanna. However, word of the general recall and news of this di Cagliostro had disquieted him. Thoughts of homecoming had put Willow's face before him all his waking moments, and his dreams were troubled. He was beginning to suspect that the final curse flung at him by Fanarion, that he never know peace, had taken.

"It's a thing that has worried many of us," Bint continued, "for di Cagliostro's reputation is that of a seer and sorcerer and a necromancer as well, though he claims as his purest interest the art of healing. He has engratiated himself with the Grand Master and won over friends in many of the Elder Houses. He is free-spending with gold and gems, though no one seems to know whence comes his wealth."

Crassmor rubbed the heir's ring. "Perhaps my father supplies him with those?"

Bint shook his head. "It's rumored that di Cagliostro *makes* them, by his thaumaturgy. And his advice is sure profit to any gambler, though he gives it sparingly. The Lady Willow likes him not."

At this, Alanna shot a quick glance at Crassmor, somewhat amused but a little arch as well. Crassmor, avoiding Alanna's gaze, couldn't resist asking Bint, "What of Willow?"

"Di Cagliostro showed interest in visiting her. But when he did, he seemed filled with a great unease. I think he was afraid of those rickety old guardsmen of hers." Bint chuckled. "Can you imagine? And Willow was cold to him,

unlike her usual self altogether, and he was stiff and un-
friendly to her behind his veneer of smooth manners. The
visit was short."

Bint's face had taken on a look of sober earnestness, as
it did for such subjects, but when Arananth smiled at him
prettily and held up her goblet, his mouth turned up in a
grin. He refilled it for her and she scrunched her nose at
him. Bint blushed to the hairline.

Crassmor had just another sip of the wine himself and
tried to thrust aside his misgivings, telling himself to enjoy
life while he could. Alanna regarded him now with less
affection and a certain acerbity. They both knew that the
end of their interlude together was near. She had her
father's farmhold to administer and, as Alanna knew,
Crassmor had his duty to the Order, and Willow.

Crassmor reared up on one elbow to signal with a lazy
forefinger. Across the lawn, by the entrance to the Kalleck
Inn, a servant in a blindingly white tunic caught the gesture
and hurried to fetch another decanter from the cavernous,
whitewashed stucco inn.

Bint added, "This order to get us back to Gateshield
comes directly by the command of the King, but Ironwicca
has told no man his reason." He gave Arananth a guilty
look; the thought of parting came with difficulty to both
young people.

Arananth pushed herself up so that she knelt with knees
deep-sunk in the unicorn's plush. "Fie! Are you so eager to
be shut of me, then? Get you gone! Boor! Kitchen knave!
If you care so little for me, then I care nothing for you!"

She sprang up and flounced away, to stand at the inn's
dock, watching the floating traffic, in a monumental pout.
Bint spilled his wine in his haste to run after her, all apologies. Crassmor and Alanna both laughed softly as Arananth
stamped a slender foot and kept her back to him. Bint's
voice cracked several times as he strove to make amends.

Alanna came and sat at the foot of Crassmor's couch.
"He feels duty-bound to be on his way back to your Singularity," she said.

"Let him learn to savor life while he can," Crassmor
returned. "He'd be duty-bound to the scullery in John's

Winch right now, or dead, if things had gone just a little differently."

Her look was enigmatic. "All would be much different," she said, "if that little lame fellow hadn't found me and told me where I might enlist a Knight of Onn."

He was sitting up in an instant, his tone taking her by surprise. "What fellow?"

She blinked, then shrugged. "Small, old, frail, balding. He walked with a limp. His clothes gave him no distinction, but he spoke well. He came to me in a way station as I waited with Roode and Dimble to resume our journey to Dreambourn, saying he'd heard of my plight from the coachman. He directed me to you in Toe Hold and cautioned that I would have to play a trick upon you, for you were feigning injury. I was not unwary of him, but the time left to me was very short; John wanted to marry Arananth as soon as he could. I decided to try it—"

"A limp, you said," Crassmor interjected. "And what hair was left was white, over a well-freckled pate?"

She nodded. He slapped his forehead and sank back on the couch with eyes tight-shut, to groan, "Mooncollar!"

He reopened them to find her gazing at him oddly. "A Klybesian," he elaborated. "And not in the vicinity by chance, or he wouldn't have been in layman's clothes."

"Perhaps it wasn't the same man," Alanna suggested.

"It was, it was. Klybesians are bound not to take life themselves, and their powers and endeavors are tied up with that vow in some arcane way. But they are geniuses at finding themselves roundabout ways of doing people in. Oh, yes, it was Mooncollar who sent you after me. I'd wager that word of Arananth's plight didn't reach Bint by accident either. Mooncollar came upon an ideal opportunity: your sisters' captivity. He lured Bint in, then used Bint to draw me. Chances were excellent that neither of us would come out."

Alanna was puzzled. "But why a war against you two?"

"Not Bint; me. With me out of the way, a Klybesian would control House Tarrant. I find it hard to believe that Uncle Furd is involved in this, though. Perhaps it is the doing of Mooncollar alone. We may have eluded him when we left John's Winch, but we shall have to be on our guard."

"This is all the more reason for you to return home," she said, a fact she'd accepted. She leaned down upon him, half-lying across his chest on the broad couch. The few diners at the other tables scattered over the broad lawn took little notice; public deportment was a personal matter in most of the Beyonds, as in the Singularity.

He smelled her perfume, and her eyes held his. "Last night in your sleep," she told him, "you said Willow's name." She touched the inner pocket of his blouse, where he carried Willow's red scarf. "And we both know what is here." Her smile was fond and knowing and sad. "It just may be that you are needed back there."

Bint was returning with Arananth, still pressing his apologies and explanations on her. Crassmor said, "And they must part too."

"It is a misfortune," she admitted softly. "This is Bint's first affair of the heart, I think. I know it is Arananth's." Crassmor thought of the poems Bint had composed for the girl, the flowers picked and carefully arranged, the songs sung to her with such feeling.

Alanna spoke up as the younger couple returned. "Bint, I think the time has come for Knights of Onn to heed the command of their Grand Master." Bint was no less taken off guard by that than Crassmor himself.

Arananth, beginning to well over with tears, said, "So Sir Bint rides away and leaves broken the heart of Arananth, nor does he care! Why should he not forget her, there among the pleasures of Dreambourn?"

Alanna suggested, "Why not go with him, silly goose?"

They all turned to her, brows raised. Alanna went on. "Surely the guarantee of two knights is assurance enough for your well-being and safekeeping. You always wished to see the Singularity, sister; now do."

Crassmor listened to Bint's stuttered thanks and Arananth's breathless agreement with amusement, but admired Alanna for her effort to make them happy. "She is welcome at House Tarrant," he offered, adding dryly, "And no one will question the quality of my father's chaperonage." That put a moment's doubt on the faces of the young couple and almost made Crassmor laugh out loud.

"Off with you, Bint," he ordered, "and make preparations for travel. Buy us horses and supplies, but quietly, quietly. And ask about—Lonar, the tavernkeep, would be a good place to start—if anyone resembling Mooncollar has been seen in town. I'll explain later."

Bint set off with Arananth by his side. Alanna took Crassmor's hand and drew him off the couch. "And for us, farewell," she anticipated, "or at least until and unless you wish to see me again. But this I promise," she finished, raising him up and leading him off by the hand toward the rooms they shared. "You will not forget Alanna easily."

They'd come across a series of precipitous tors by means of a trail that switched back and forth on itself. Both knights now bore light lances with glittering, foot-long heads, their reddish, hardwood shafts wound with blue hemp cord. They also bore long oval shields covered with zebra skin. In addition, Bint had a cased bow and quiver hanging from his saddle. The two knights wore hip-length coats of mascled armor. Arananth had on sturdy boots and leggings, swathings of green cloak, and a deep-shadowed hood. Crassmor, having parted company with Alanna, now wore Willow's red scarf attached to *Shhing*'s baldric for reasons he had trouble identifying; it made him feel wretched about the parting, but eager to be home. He wore another scarf, a white one, at his throat.

A forest of blue pines swallowed them up for half a day, the sun penetrating the canopy of needles only now and again with milky rays that seemed to pick out every dust mote in the air. Crassmor and Bint knew with a marrow-deep certainty that they were close to the Singularity.

Time and again Crassmor or Bint would turn to look behind or drop back, to try to see if they were being followed. No scout's trick or wilderness tactic known to either of them gave any confirmation of it. That couldn't dissuade Crassmor from the conviction that Mooncollar was somewhere behind, a scheming shadow. The monk,

Crassmor knew, had a natural gift for stealth, a talent for spying. Again, Mooncollar might have provided himself with some supernatural means of keeping track of the trio's movements. Crassmor had spent enough time in the Beyonds not to discount his own instincts, whether they were borne out by immediate proof or not.

After a stop among the pines, he rode listening with only half an ear to the flirtations of Arananth and Bint as he worked on idea after idea. He could think of no reliable way to draw out Mooncollar without betraying the fact that he knew of the monk's machinations; Crassmor hesitated to yield that slight advantage. He glanced sourly behind, before, to either side, and overhead from habit. He knew by now that the Klybesian would be a prudent distance away, beyond perception.

There had passed through the knight's mind the idea of soliciting help from another Lost Boy, but any meeting with another member of the Order would be sheer luck, and the trio had encountered no one else whom Crassmor had felt he could trust. He'd thought of enlisting magical aid, but had been at a loss as to how to go about it. Robin Goodfellow might cooperate for a lark, or Puck, though the sprites were more inclined to play tricks. And getting in touch with any supernatural entity was an entirely different problem from meeting one at random. Methods of invocation or summoning varied, and the knight was no magician.

The three came out of the forest and through some low hills. They found themselves riding the shore of a broad, rolling sea of grass, which brushed above their horses' fetlocks. They rode warily, keeping near the tree line. It was not the openness of the vast plain that made them cautious; it was what the plain held.

"By all that is worshipped," Arananth breathed. Bint was wordless, and even Crassmor had nothing to add.

It was as if the plain had been covered with a vast throw rug of shaggy brown, eaten through in places so that some patches of yellow-brown grass could be seen. The carpet was alive, composed of individual creatures that moved along slowly, grazing and snorting, shaking

weighty, horned, thick-maned heads and flicking thick
tails at clouds of flies. They raised dust that obscured vision.
The herd stretched away across the plain as far as the eye
could see. Sandur had told Crassmor vivid tales of these
creatures and had himself hunted them here in the Beyonds.

"Bison," Crassmor said with certainty, though he'd
never seen any before. "Buffalo."

The Outrider had chased these beasts in the hard-won
companionship of the unexcelled warrior-hunters who
lived almost exclusively off the enormous herds and who
ruled these plains as horseback lords. Sandur had told a
wide-eyed Crassmor how it was done, as the two brothers
had sat before the hearth at House Tarrant.

The knight looked now at the buffalo that were nearest.
Bearded, humpbacked, with brown, nappy pelts and curling
horns, they lazed along. Calves bleated; tails swished end-
lessly. Crassmor wondered at the power implicit in the
massive forequarters. Sandur had told him how the things
were hunted, and told him something else about them.
Something else . . .

*The meat I love best,* had said the Trickster, Saynday,
whom Crassmor had seen wearing the shape of Coyote.
Crassmor's concept of a good idea was one that averted
danger or hardship, not one that exposed him to it. Still, an
idea had came to him in stark simplicity; he could see no
means of amending it to accommodate his personal prefer-
ences. Here was a way in which he might be able to summon the sort of help he needed.

They had all three drawn up, taking in the remarkable
view. Bint was caught off guard when Crassmor suddenly
turned and held out his shield. The younger man took it,
and his cousin's lance as well.

"Wait here, both," Crassmor instructed as he drew off
his armor. "Keep sharp watch. Don't venture out onto the
plain; the herd will stay away from the trees—or so Sandur
told me."

Arananth watched, amazed, understanding what the
knight intended, thrilling to it. Bint sputtered protests.
"We've enough food, surely, and the Singularity is not so

far." In bewilderment, he added, "Meseems 'tis dangerous, Sir Cousin."

Crassmor's mouth twisted in half amusement. Bint still had trouble ascribing any risk-taking ability to him. Naked from the waist up, he threw his gambeson and armor coat across Arananth's saddle. He thought about leaving *Shhing* behind. *Those men ride lightly, unencumbered,* Sandur had said. A reflex that was virtually an instinct made him put the baldric back on, though.

"It's not for provisions," Crassmor explained as he loosened the ties of his baggage and water skin. His uncaparisoned horse pranced nervously, smelling the strange scents of the buffalo and the plains, sensing a coming test. Crassmor passed his things over to the others. He was perspiring, trying to recall all that his brother had recounted over cups of mulled wine of the hunting techniques of the painted red men. Crassmor recalled leaping orange flames from the hearth illuminating Sandur's handsome face.

"I need . . . an offering," he finished. Bint was dubious, but the word slienced him, speaking as it did of some esoteric purpose. Crassmor lofted his steel cap and liner to Arananth, who caught them with a certain excitement. He knotted Willow's scarf through his belt for luck. The white one, which he'd been wearing at his throat, he tied around his forehead to keep his long red hair out of his eyes. Then he accepted his lance back from Bint. His horse crossstepped a little, unsure of what it was to be called upon to do.

Crassmor took up the reins. Leaving the other two, he eased down the hill at a gentle walk, aware from Sandur's tales that these mighty plains engines, the buffalo, were usually hunted at dawn. A single blessing was that the wind was coming up the slope toward him, off the herd. They seemed to be moving along, grazing without concern, contrary to what Sandur had said about their quickness to stampede at the first sign of danger.

He took his horse down through a fold in a ridge in order to draw closer to the herd without being seen or scented. He was guided only by imperfect memories of stories heard long ago. He knew the herd was moving slowly away to his right and came out of the ridge fold traveling in that direction. If the beasts behind him panicked, it wouldn't matter, he hoped; he would still have some chance of bearing down on the ones that were ahead. He crossed the rise.

Sandur had said that those horse lords, particularly those among them that were young and vainglorious, competed to slay the biggest of the herds' bulls. Crassmor studied the ominous forward curve of the bulls' horns; the largest among them weighed twice what he and his horse did together. He immediately began casting about for a sick cow or a wandering calf, or perhaps an elder citizen of the community who might oblige him by keeling over from heart failure. He spied none.

Lower lip between his teeth, hemp-wound lance held resolutely in his right hand, he eased his skittish horse down into the never-settling dust cloud raised by the boundless herd. He'd started out on this mad venture on impulse, with little forethought. According to Sandur's account, these creatures should have bolted by now, leaving him, since a horse could outrun buffalo, to follow and do as best he could. But they seemed not to register his presence. Then he recalled Sandur's flame-lit face as a backdrop to the phrase, *You can never tell what they'll do.*

Perhaps this wouldn't be as difficult as he'd feared. A simple thrust of the lance, a scattering of any bystanders, a slice of his parrying dagger, and it would all be over. So Sir Crassmor thought, just as the ground began to vibrate so that the dust was shaken loose from the blades of parched grass.

He saw with crawling skin that every animal around him understood what it meant—stampede. It seemed in an instant that he was inside a drum upon which the hooves of the world beat. His horse's eyes rolled to show their whites.

He hadn't entered the herd far behind its leaders. He saw at once that the creatures didn't move by column or flanking maneuvers in this sort of turnabout. Instead, each beast came around—a confused milling. A ridge crowned with massed, frightened, colliding bison hid from his view whatever had scared them.

Huge bulls came end-for-end and cows whirled as best they could, heads hung over some other animal's flanks in the close quarters, to turn back. Calves shifted for themselves; some were trodden under, squealing pitifully. Crassmor's horse whinnied and dodged sideways, avoiding a murderous pair of horns. Then the mount went with the flood of bison, sensible and adaptable as any good Beyonds horse should be. In seconds, Crassmor was being borne along at breakneck speed in the herd, his lance forgotten.

Cursing all inspirations, he concentrated on staying alive. *I can see now as much buffalo meat as I could wish,* he told himself. *Unfortunately, it is all attached to a living flash flood.*

The animals shook the ground, hemming him in, heads down. Even in the grip of the stampede panic, the huge bulls sought to interpose themselves between the horseman and the cows and calves. The bulls' tongues lolled and their heads were lowered, increasing the danger from the horns. Their nostrils dripped and their eyes bulged red; their hooves flung up a cloud that threatened to choke the knight. He lacked the time and the extra hand to pull the white scarf from his forehead and down over his mouth.

The buffalo were not as fast as his horse, though, and he was still galloping somewhat parallel to the tree line. He began to edge over that way, thinking about a kill once more. *You come in close on their left side, you see,* Sandur had told him, *and strike deep for the heart.* The Outrider had owned a buffalo-tail quirt to prove that he'd done it.

The small bull at whom Crassmor aimed somehow sensed his approach and veered away sharply. Crassmor swore and let the beast keep his life, unwilling to cut deeper into the herd. From the right an elderly bull, his hide all matted and layered with brambles and caked soil, raced at horse and rider. The knight might have avoided the horn tips by reining up sharply, but had more faith in speed. He roweled; the horse was more than willing to run all-out. He looked down once more and saw a calf bawling and running awkwardly along a short distance ahead. Crassmor brought the lance into line with a crisp, practiced motion, addressing his target. The calf began to cut back deeper into the herd toward a lumbering, somehow plaintive creature who could only be its mother. By reminding himself of the increased risk and telling himself that immature meat would be of no use to him, he found an excuse for lifting his lance head. He watched the two creatures, battle carrack and tender ship, vanish into the yellow, dusty twilight.

The herd was well aware of him now. Before he knew it, they'd found room to dodge away to all sides. In seconds, members of the rearguard were swinging away to avoid him, traveling quickly because they'd been the herd's leaders and were among the strongest. Crassmor was able to slow up as he considered his options. *Hasty-thought, hasty-gone-wrong,* he chided himself. He coughed, and spit yellow saliva. Then he headed for the nearest rise to find out how far he'd come and try to locate his companions. From there he saw that one kill, at least, had been made that day. He also knew what had caused the stampede.

The hunter had somehow sensed his approach before Crassmor had topped the rise, though the thunder of the stampede must, he thought, surely have masked his trembling horse's hoofbeats. Too, Crassmor was riding crosswind through the remaining dust cloud. Nevertheless, the hunter was staring up at the spot when the knight got there.

The man was the red-brown color Saynday had been, his entire body inured to the touch of sun, wind, and weather. He was tall, holding a posture at once graceful and relaxed, yet tense as a wound spring. Well-defined muscle and sinew broadened a lean, limber body. The hunter wore only moccasins and a soft-tanned breechclout trimmed with metallic beads and human hair, tucked through a narrow belt of braided hide.

On his wrist was an archer's brace; a leather band held a quiver-bowcase, skillfully crafted from a white wolf's pelt, at his back. His face was high-cheekboned, fine-featured, reserved, and full-lipped. Bands of black paint circled his eyes; his gleaming, sable hair was drawn back tightly against his head and gathered in a long scalp lock decked with a raven's feather. He watched Crassmor emotionlessly, unblinking. In his hand glittered a skinning knife.

At the hunter's feet lay his prey, a behemoth bull of the herd, losing the last of its life, kicking in minute spasms which came to a halt even as the knight rode downslope. Nearby, a lithe, glossy pony, the color of its rider's hair, waited, trailing reins that must have been twenty feet long. It bore no saddle, no cincture. There was a single rawhide loop braided into its mane; Crassmor, seeing that, thought what a fearless and skillful rider this man must be.

As the knight approached, the hunter sheathed his knife at his belt. A quirt hanging from his wrist made a snaking motion in response. He turned aside to his pony, showing a profile any artist might have admired. "Quietly, Night," he told the pony, and it became still.

Crassmor leaned his unbloodied lance against his shoulder as he drew close, keeping it at a conspicuously casual cant. He hoped he'd made no trespass on forbidden hunting ground. He stopped well away from the hunter, who gave him silent attention. Crassmor set the lance in its rest and slid from his saddle carefully. Dozens of times before, he'd met people in the Beyonds in this unknown-quantity fashion. It was easy to offend someone else's protocols in the Beyonds. He kept his hands well in sight, away from his body, but in such a manner that his right one was only a split second from *Shhing*'s waiting hilt. He brought his left hand up to indicate himself. "Crassmor."

The other relaxed a little. The knight did then, too. "Wanderer," the hunter responded, fingertips gesturing to his heart.

"A hero's kill, Wanderer," Crassmor complimented, and meant it. They both looked for a moment to the mountainous buffalo and the red-banded arrow sticking out of its side. "I was not so—" He'd almost said "lucky," which might or might not have been an insult. "Skillful," the knight finished truthfully.

Wanderer waited.

"Would you sell, would you trade some of your kill?" Crassmor asked. The hunter tilted his head slightly, a tacit inquiry. Crassmor was making an inventory of his possessions and trappings at that point, wondering what he might offer. Then he saw Wanderer's eyes gauging the hilt of his sword. Their eyes met. Crassmor gave his head the barest shake, vowing, "I'd rather take up the hunt once more." The herd was no more than a distant dust cloud now; Wanderer very nearly smiled at the comment. Tension left them both.

The knight whipped off the white scarf from his forehead. Risking the few steps between them, he held it out. It was a lovely piece of work, with threads of gold woven in and raised embroidery. "The meat is for a friend," Crassmor explained. "It's the meat he loves best."

Wanderer looked from the scarf to Crassmor, then turned and bent to the carcass. His skinning knife was in his hand as quickly as ever *Shhing* had found Crassmor's. When Wanderer straightened again, he held the thick, meaty tongue of the buffalo high for inspection, droplets of blood and saliva streaming from it.

"I believe I know who your . . . *friend* is," Wanderer declared with a hint of amusement. "This is the best part of the meat he loves best." He held forth the tongue.

Crassmor accepted it with his left hand and bowed low. Something in him made him wish to make a more personal payment. He took a step back; his right hand darted and *Shhing,* held high, threw back the dusty light. Wanderer hadn't reacted; he waited. The knights' respect for the hunter grew. Wanderer's eyes followed the reflections along the sword's blade, then sought Crassmor's once more. Crassmor took the blade through a meticulous salute, then sheathed it at his back one-handedly. Wanderer raised his hand in acknowledgment, smiling fully now.

Crassmor told him, "In the place they call the Singularity, Wanderer, you have friendship and a home, always."

Wanderer drew the silken scarf over his fingertips, delighting in its texture and delicate patterning. Then there was the sound of other riders, coming from the distance. The knight saw several horsewomen, dressed in fringed, beaded buckskins, singing and waving, calling out to Wanderer. "It's best I go," the knight said. He remounted, the bloody tongue in hand.

The hunter told him, "You have friendship and a fire among the Comanche." Crassmor grinned, and reined his horse around. He quickly topped the rise once more. Wanderer stroked Night's gleaming neck and watched Crassmor until he'd gone from sight.

The tongue now rested before Crassmor's pommel, wafting a pleasant pungency back to him. Crassmor kept the flies from it with flicks of a horsehair whisk. He was once more attired in armor; the group had swung away from the stretch of plains and was quite close now to the Singularity. Bint and Arananth rode behind; Crassmor was content to go alone before, to let them ride stirrup to stirrup. He wondered if he should pause long enough to smoke the tongue in order to preserve it, or to cut it into strips.

Now he threw his head back, watching light slant across leaves, picking out green murals in the canopy of trees over the trail. "You're not going to sing that dreadful song *again,* are you?" Arananth teased from the rearguard.

Crassmor turned in the saddle in high indignation. "Mark well my every rendition, my beauty; your children will undoubtedly want to hear each detail."

She blushed at the reference to offspring, but gave a grudging snicker. Bint let forth a brief laugh until Arananth back-knuckled his arm in pretended anger. Crassmor closed his eyes and sang, as well as he could remember it, the chant taught him so long ago by Sandur, the chant he'd been singing since he'd been given the tongue by Wanderer. He started out with a yelp.

> Hey!
> Shape-shifter, Prankster!
> Here is the meat you love best!
> Not long ago it ran the plains,
> under the sun that you threw into the sky!
> Hey! Saynday!
> Here is the meat you discovered
> and gave to the people,

the buffalo you brought up
from under the earth!
Here is the meat you love best!

They were leaving the Beyonds behind in subtle, rapid gradations that only Bint and Crassmor perceived, her insensitivity to them vexing Arananth. Now they were passing along comfortably worn tracks, not terribly far from Tarrant lands and House Tarrant itself. Crassmor still had the feeling that Mooncollar lurked somewhere behind. The trio had met few other travelers, and no Tarrant wardens or Royal Borderers, or anyone else who might agree to trace their trail back to search out anyone who followed it.

Crassmor sang his last note downheartedly, wondering if he should abandon the effort. *All I'm doing,* he chastised himself, *is scaring the birds out of the trees.*

Save for one, he saw; a noisy raven perched on an oak limb that overhung the way. Crassmor took a closer look at the bird, then reined up sharply. Bint and Arananth, nearly ramming him from the rear, began their questioning. The raven examined Crassmor first with one eye, then the other.

"Careless Saynday!" the knight mock-scolded. "You still haven't learned!"

The raven guiltily eyed the limp mustache adorning its beak, then gave a ludicrous shrug of its black wings. Arananth's questions turned to a little gasp of surprise as the bird began changing, the lines of its shape running off in different directions, its black plummage turning red-brown. In another moment, the Trickster sat on the tree branch.

"Well, that buffalo tongue smells pretty good," Saynday admitted in his nasal, cracking voice. "It got me to hungerin' and forgettin' to be careful."

"I brought it for a friend of mine," Crassmor said in a mannered dismissal.

Skinny, balloon-muscled Saynday licked his lips and mustache. Eyeing the tongue, he failed to repress his curiosity. "I wouldn't mind knowin' who your friend is," he confessed.

"The one who's going to do me a favor," the knight answered.

"Which favor?" Saynday ventured.

"The one my friend will do me."

Somehow, Bint was managing to stifle Arananth's questions, outcries, and protests.

"Which friend?" the Trickster countered slyly.

"The one who gets this buffalo tongue," the knight replied, and it was his turn to shrug.

"Well, that might be me," Saynday allowed.

"Then you'd have yourself this fine buffalo tongue," Crassmor confided.

Saynday, arms folded across his chest, and without appearing to move a single muscle, slipped off the tree limb to stand before them. No further answer was needed. Crassmor stopped himself before he threw the tongue down; he dismounted and handed it over politely. Saynday registered a certain surprise at the civility.

Crassmor explained, "There is one who follows me. Elderly, small, bald, and walking with a limp is he, freckled across here." With that the knight passed a hand over the top of his head. "And the little thatch that's left is white, strands of white. He's a Klybesian monk, but—"

Saynday, who'd been turning the tongue over in his hands but listening, now held up a palm. "I'll know him; that tribe smells different."

Crassmor made note of that for future inquiry, but kept to the subject at hand. "I shall be at House Tarrant, or thereabouts. I should like to know where Mooncollar goes and to whom he talks."

"Well, you will," Saynday declared. They both knew that, in the Singularity, a promise like that, made under such circumstances, was far better lived up to than reneged on.

# Chapter 14

# GRATEFUL

**"And you're sure,"** Crassmor was saying at the junction in the road that led in one direction to House Tarrant, in the other to Dreambourn, "that you remember no more about this di Cagliostro?"

"Certain, cousin," Bint replied. "He simply wandered in from the Beyonds, as so many do."

Arananth sighed prettily. "Have you two not nattered enough about this fellow and your household goings-on?"

As Bint fell all over himself to assuage her displeasure, Crassmor reflected that if this truly were Arananth's first affair of the heart, she'd done some forestudying. At one point on the trip, Bint had asked him privately if he, Crassmor, thought Arananth was showing true affection. Crassmor, indicating Arananth's coiffure, which had been restyled during their stay at the Kalleck Inn, had suggested, "Muss her hair."

"What?"

"Close your mouth. I said, muss the girl's hair—at the appropriately romantic moment, of course. If she loves you, she won't mind; might even like it. If she becomes testy, you might wish to rethink things."

Later, her hair had been in some disarray. Arananth and Bint had held hands as they rode. Crassmor had thought that Arananth would go far in Dreambourn.

Now she was patting Bint's cheek. "Arananth forgives you! So let us get on to the capital; I am eager to see it."

"No," Crassmor pronounced. She opened her mouth to object, then realized that she lacked any purchase on the older knight. Arananth smiled diplomatically.

Not so Bint. "We are ordered to report to the fortress of

Onn. We should notify the Grand Master of our return, at the least."

"The Charmed Realm is not holding its collective breath against our appearance," Crassmor assured him. They'd seen no hint of war or other trouble in the Singularity. "Doubtless most of the Order has reported already; two of us won't matter for today." Bint yielded the point.

Arananth quite forgot her reserve, gasping and exclaiming aloud when she saw House Tarrant and the vastness of the land it enclosed. The family stronghold was arguably the best-fortified place in the Singularity, with its many turrets and towers, looming bastions and hornworks, built from green-gray stone. Some sections of the place were roofed with slate, some with weighty maroon tiles, and some with copper long gone verdigris green. There were gables all of stained glass and sally gates with old bloodstains still upon them. A weathervane wrought in gold in the shape of a phoenix felt the wind.

Crassmor was recognized and admitted without delay. The trio crossed an already lowered drawbridge, under a barbican that was itself no small keep. As their horses' hooves raised dull echoes from the thick planks, Crassmor saw that all was in good order. Scarp and counterscarp and palisade were all well maintained, as were the other defensive appointments.

The stables had been enlarged, some of the outbuildings extensively repaired, the paved area of the courtyard expanded, and the roof of the central keep replaced, but by and large the place was as he recalled it. Word of the party's arrival had been passed. Combard was awaiting them, hands clasped behind his back, when they were shown into his study. He'd changed even less than had House Tarrant; he was a bit more gaunt, a trifle less erect, no less severe.

Crassmor had noticed that, while the Tarrant lands and the Singularity itself still prospered, they were not as lush as they'd been. The knight saw that his father was tired and thought that that weariness might have passed, through Combard's special ties, to the soil and substance of the Home Plane.

As was his practice, the Lord of House Tarrant was arrayed in the robes of the head of an Elder House, wearing beneath them a gleaming cuirass and a belted sword. The room itself held no martial trophies. Instead, there were maps of the Singularity, specifying cultivated areas and details of their crops, forests, and the amounts and kinds of lumber and wildlife there. They also set forth the features of lakes and other bodies of water, mining and milling operations, pasturage, and the current sizes of herds and flocks.

"Greetings, father," Crassmor said. He went to Combard, while Arananth and Bint stopped a half-dozen paces back.

"Welcome home, fellow knight." Combard gave the standard reply. The old man couldn't keep his eyes from going to the heir's ring; Crassmor thought that it was with regret. It was also custom for father and son to embrace after such a long separation. Combard, ever obedient to tradition, didn't shirk. He opened his arms, the long tippets of his sleeves hanging down, observing the ritual without wavering, whatever reluctance he might feel. Crassmor made no move to cut the embrace short, although Combard was plainly less than comfortable. After that Combard opened his arms to Bint, who'd been watching with a certain reserve. Bint and his uncle embraced heartily, but when they'd parted, Bint gave Crassmor a look that held embarrassment.

The old man's eyes lit sternly on Arananth; he obviously thought his son had brought home a wife or mistress.

"The Lady Arananth of Meere, in the Beyonds," Crassmor made the presentation with a half-grin and a formal bow, "may I present Lord Combard of Tarrant." She dropped the most engaging of curtsies with a radiant smile. Combard cleared his throat and made a stiff, shallow bow, murmuring an uneasy greeting. "Lady Arananth is under the protection of Sir Bint here," Crassmor elaborated, "rescued by him and come hither to pay her respects at the court of Ironwicca."

Combard's features softened; Crassmor hid his smirk. The old man went to her and kissed her hand as she blushed, loving it. A moment later, the lord of the house was calling for servants, instructing them to ready the best guest suite in House Tarrant. Arananth was as happy as a child, dazzled by the wealth and size of the place, eyeing the maidservants' fashions closely. Bint, proud and grave, excused himself and set off to show her the more interesting features of the Tarrant stronghold.

Hearing that his mother had once more shut herself away with melancholia, Crassmor elected to wait before seeing her. He asked Combard, "What may be this trouble that calls together the Order of the Circle of Onn?" He hoped to hear that it was a threat that had been settled, posing no further danger, that the dire recall would be turned into a holiday.

He was disappointed. "The day after tomorrow at Gateshield," Combard told him, "the Grand Master will speak on that. Rumors have the king and Jaan-Marl in frequent consulation, with grim words."

Crassmor's heart sank a bit. The news made him all the more wary of bringing up another subject. He decided to come to it in a roundabout fashion. "And you're well, father? Good. Ah, and Uncle Furd?"

"Furd is himself, as ever," Combard answered, and for a change there was fondness in his voice.

*Which is to say, vindictive as a poison toad,* was Crassmor's opinion. He kept that to himself and pressed on cautiously. "And the Lady Willow?"

Combard's mouth lengthened; tension moved the beard that had lost more of its red and acquired much more gray and some white. "She is hale, though to this day she mourns your brother. Has Bint told you of Teerse's passing? A mercy, in truth; he was long abed, slow in the dying, no kind way to leave this life. Now Willow looks after the Jade Dome and the Tapestry all by herself."

Crassmor felt old, cruel pain at the mention of Sandur. He had been overjoyed, though, to hear from Bint that Willow was unmarried. That left the problem of seeing her; Combard's total opposition to a union between Crassmor and Willow hadn't changed, that much was plain.

A door opened, giving access from one of the chambers off the study. A voice exulted, "Ah, the young cavalier, back from his tour of errantry!" It was a voice of great force, well modulated, not overloud, even though it caught and held the attention at once. The speaker stood framed in the doorway.

He was small and stocky, but his posture and the cant of his head spoke of great animation, as did his eyes. Those eyes held Crassmor's immediately. They were bright and astute, somewhat protruding, penetrant and yet easy to meet—indeed, difficult to look away from. They spoke of a formidable intellect. The man was perhaps fifty years of age, with a fleshy face but a long, well-sculpted nose. His hair, once all jet black, had become mixed with gray and receded a good deal. The weight of middle age had thickened his neck.

He wore long vestments with symbols sewn to them, designs of an esoteric type that Crassmor had never seen before, the vestments themselves being blue and white. There was a winged wand bearing serpents, squares and levels of the mason's trade, what looked to be a compass, and another serpent—this one transfixed in an S-shape by an arrow and bearing in its mouth some globe or fruit. He wore a gorgeous ring with the characters INRI, highly decorated, upon it.

The man's smile automatically elicited a like response from Crassmor, without the knight's will. Then Crassmor noticed the side chamber just as the newcomer pulled the connecting door shut. Combard's things had been moved out of it and all the draperies drawn. Candles burned there and incense. There was a table, and on it a crystal globe; the play of light across the globe made Crassmor think that it was filled with water. On the floor, a pentagram held some elements identifiable to the knight. They shocked him; they were concerned with necromancy.

The man approached jauntily for an introduction. Crassmor saw that Combard was upset by the chance glimpse into the side chamber permitted by the opening of the door, and found himself wondering if it had been all that accidental. Combard said, "My son, Sir Crassmor of the Order of the Circle of Onn, I present to you a friend and guest and worker for good, the Count di Cagliostro."

Di Cagliostro bowed with a flourish and Crassmor did the same, with rather less panache, knuckling his mustache and looking the man over. "A very treasure house of learning," Combard continued, "whose word and aid I have come to value highly." Di Cagliostro's hand swept through a gesture of deprecation.

"It is a pleasure and a meaning in life," the count said, "to be of some worth, particularly to Combard of Tarrant, who is interested in the furtherance of knowledge and the general weal."

Crassmor was surprised to find himself believing that the count meant what he was saying. Inclining his head toward the closed door, Crassmor asked, "And is the craft sinister for the general—"

"You forget yourself, sir!" Combard snapped, furious. Then he regained his composure, aware that he'd overreacted.

Di Cagliostro took up the conversation suavely, "No fact or procedure, even necromancy, is good or bad in itself. That lies in matters of application."

"Just so, Alessandro," Combard agreed more calmly. He turned back to his son. "This good man came initially to House Tarrant to ease your mother's distresses with his healing arts. Since then, he has been of great comfort to me."

Crassmor chose his words carefully. "I meant no slight to a guest of House Tarrant." Di Cagliostro bowed again, with a benign motion of his hand. But the knight's mind had closed on the obvious: there was only one spirit among the dead whom Combard would so wish to contact. For di Cagliostro as for anyone else, the way to Combard's favor lay with the Outrider.

The count was studying Crassmor closely. "If my craft does not deceive me, you yourself wear the aura of some spell or enchantment, do you not, Sir Knight?"

That confirmed it; Fanarion's parting curse, that Crassmor know no peace, had taken. "A minor malediction," the knight admitted.

Di Cagliostro was elaborately sympathetic. "It would be no great task to free you of it," he offered.

*You'll never get the Reluctant Knight into your penta-gram!* was what Crassmor was resolving as he said, "All my gratitude to you. But it is a thing of no consequence whatever." There were others in the Singularity who could help him, whom he trusted.

Combard resumed briskly. "The count and I have some . . . matters of our own to conclude. That is, research. Go, rest, and we'll speak over the dining board tonight."

Crassmor was on guard, certain that this intruder in House Tarrant was interested in much more than simply Combard's gratitude. "Is it some endeavor in which I can be of assistance?" he asked with weighted innocence. Both Combard's and di Cagliostro's faces betrayed the awkward-ness of the inquiry, confirming the knight's suspicions. "After all, father, I've learned a thing or two in the Be-yonds, and have spent no time with you for—it is close on two years now, is it not?"

Combard's brow furrowed, because his son was right. If Crassmor, a Knight of the Order newly returned from the Beyonds, wished to spend time with him, then it would be small of Combard to refuse.

Di Cagliostro, features untroubled once more, put in, "But there is another who anticipates your return. The Lady Willow, that poor, dear girl! She asked to be notified as soon as you answered the recall. Why not pay her a quick visit this afternoon and relieve her tedium?"

Combard's face grew dark; an explosion of temper wasn't far off. Crassmor was taken off balance at the sug-gestion, the intimate knowledge of affairs at House Tarrant that it implied. The clever count had correctly judged that it was just the diversion to keep Crassmor from further meddling.

Di Cagliostro laid a coaxing hand on Combard's arm and employed that persuasive voice to good advantage. "She is so lonely there; how can you deny her a visit from the Outrider's brother? For surely she thinks of little but her lost love? And why bore this fellow here with our aca-demic pastimes, eh?"

*Sly argument,* Crassmor conceded. It assured Combard that Willow was too dedicated to Sandur's memory to be tempted and pointed out that Crassmor's departure could thus be accomplished. It showed shrewd awareness on di Cagliostro's part of how inclined Combard was to assume that others shared his single-minded grief. Too, it indicated a wily appreciation of Crassmor's feelings for Willow; the count knew that nothing, even the worrisome doings in the adjoining room, would keep him from leaping at the chance to be with her again.

*Damn him!* the knight fumed, seeing the count's self-satisfied smile. But Crassmor knew too that Combard might still be stubborn about the visit. The knight compelled himself to play against the obvious. "Actually, sir, I have cultivated an interest in the occult arts. The opportunity to observe your operations would be most welcome, if you've no objection. Or you, father?" He saw from the count's face that di Cagliostro understood that tactic and was impressed.

Combard found himself between two unattractive alternatives. As always, his thoughts were with Sandur. "Our guest is right; our putterings hold no interest for you." Then his brows knitted. "But mind: a quick greeting, then straight home."

Crassmor couldn't resist a last dig. "Are you certain, then, that I can be of no—"

*"Go!"* Combard shouted, with an impatient, shooing motion. "And look to your manners! And be back inside these walls by nightfall!"

"A word first," di Cagliostro put in. He indicated the golden band on Crassmor's hand. "I wonder if I might presume to borrow that? It would be safe with me, on my life I swear it, and soon returned."

*Of course,* Crassmor thought. The heir's ring would have strong ties to Sandur and might help the necromancer succeed. Even Combard was surprised by the request; it was almost an insult to ask such a thing. The old man made no comment, however; he was that committed to the enterprise. Crassmor saw from di Cagliostro's face that the count considered this a part of the tacit bargain that had been struck over and around Combard. The choice didn't take long.

Crassmor compromised by slipping the ring off his finger —removing it with some effort—and pressing it into Combard's palm. Di Cagliostro, pretending not to notice the implied slur, bowed his thanks. Combard regarded his son uncertainly.

*Not five minutes in his presence, and he's gotten the heir's ring off my hand already,* Crassmor mulled, off to order up a fresh mount. He reflected on what an altogether keen and dangerous fellow was this wanderer-in from the Beyonds, this beguiler, this necromancer and opportunist, this di Cagliostro.

Crassmor washed and changed at a dead run, leaving his armor but bearing *Shhing*. He found on his arrival that House Comullo had seen more change than had House Tarrant—the change of disrepair, decay and neglect.

The Jade Dome itself was unaffected by time, a green hemisphere like a gem in its setting, surrounded by the more conventional architecture and fortifications of the place. Crassmor saw that the financial circumstances of House Comullo had fallen even lower than they'd been before the death of Teerse. There were only two guards at that little bailey, and only one to be seen walking the ramparts. These were all aging, decrepit retainers, not young, vigorous armsmen. Crassmor wondered how, as Bint had told him, di Cagliostro could have been so intimidated by them.

Fat old Fordall Urth himself, commander of Willow's tiny force, took Crassmor's reins and wheezily bade him enter. There were even fewer servants than there had been on the knight's last visit.

An elderly, spindle-legged man unknown to Crassmor greeted him within, showing a certain irritability in introducing himself as Racklee. Crassmor dismissed the offer of an escort when he heard that Willow was under the Jade Dome. The fellow seemed glad, in a grumpy way, to have one less duty to perform.

"How long have you served House Comullo?" Crassmor asked, curious that a new face should have appeared there.

Racklee gave an annoyed wave of his hand. "Some two months and more now, lord. I work for my keep and precious little more; these are hard times, and this is no wealthy House."

Crassmor made his way through the place alone, being as familiar with it as a family member and well educated in its various spells of misdirection and glamours of concealment, which would have confused a stranger or intruder.

Dust and thick soot were everywhere in the place. Many of the halls and chambers were sealed off, unused, and the paintings, and furniture, and sculpture covered. The garden, from the glimpse he caught of it, had grown into a jungle. Roof tiles were cracked or missing, water damage from unrepaired leaks was everywhere, and the place smelled of mold and mildew. The carpets were threadbare and, with none of the fireplaces lit, the air was chilly.

Crassmor threaded his way through the maze of corridors and rooms, coming at last to the door of the Jade Dome. It was a remarkable door, not for its height or width, which were prodigious, or even for its substance, the same green jade as the Dome. It had two identical latch handles, one on either side of it, cast in bright brass in the shape of great, outstretched eagle's talons. Only a very few knew how to tell the handles apart. A Sight, bestowed only on those whom House Comullo trusted, was needed. Selecting the wrong one would open the door, not to the Jade Dome, but to the Guardian of that place, and a grisly, horrific death. Also, the ensorcellment of the door was such that the two handles might exchange places at any time without warning.

Seeing the correct handle with the Sight given him so long ago by Teerse, Crassmor opened the door, which swung easily despite its colossal mass. He passed under a portal hewn from a single piece of ivory and stepped into the verdant world of the Dome. It curved over him, a lustrous green gem bowl all of a single piece, smooth and polished. The very air seemed to have taken on that hue, to have become some thicker medium. Under the Dome was a perpetual emerald late afternoon.

In the middle of the Dome, Willow was at work on the Tapestry. The treasure of House Comullo was suspended, flat and nearly motionless, in the center of the Dome, rippling only slightly to Willow's touch as she wove new strands into the Pattern. It hung unsupported, standing free in the air without falling or moving from its place, its lowermost point at about Crassmor's eye level. So it had hung since Willow's ancestors had started it centuries before, slowly weaving its Pattern, employing the strange talent that was the gift of that family, reflecting in its resplendent weft events of importance in the Singularity. It had been begun in the center, unlike any other tapestry, and woven outward in fibers of pure light. Now, generations later, it stretched upwards to many times Crassmor's height.

Willow was at work on a portion of the Tapestry near its upper edge. Holding her aloft patiently, her feet steady on the hard palms of his hands, was a special servant of House Comullo, Pysthesis. He was a man-shaped creature ten times the height of a man, his hands disproportionately large for his size. Pysthesis had been serving the weavers of the Tapestry in this manner for generations now, without fail and without complaint—without any word whatsoever, as far as Crassmor knew.

The knight pulled the door closed. Without looking around, the Tapestry undulating gently under her flying fingers, Willow called over her shoulder, "Welcome back! I shall be through in a moment more."

Crassmor crossed the Dome unhurriedly; he always felt a celestial calm here and loved the peace and quiet of it. No noise or disturbance from the outer world ever penetrated the Jade Dome. Looking up when he neared Pysthesis' feet, he could see nothing at all of Willow; he saw the huge creature himself foreshortened, and the backs of Pysthesis' enormous hands, with curly hairs as thick as yarn. Where Willow's fingers danced, though, expanding the Pattern, light interplayed, spreading out, threads coming to life, giving off radiance. No one but the Comullos knew how they obtained those remarkable threads. For the hundredth time, Crassmor squinted, puzzled, and failed to get any coherent idea of the Pattern's scheme, or of the meanings that Willow and her ancestors had perceived and augmented over the years; that Sight was restricted to her family alone.

Her one personal indulgence was the variety of her clothing, worn for morale's sake and to give diversity to the long sessions under the Jade Dome. Today Willow was wearing a jingling suit of fine, delicate silver mesh, belted at the hip with a broad band of black pearls, trimmed with much braid at each shoulder. Crassmor almost laughed aloud; Willow liked fun from her wardrobe.

"Finished," she said a moment later. "Down, please, Pysthesis."

The gargantuan man-creature obediently knelt and gently lowered his hands so that she could step off his palms. Remembering the savagery of the giant of John's Winch, Crassmor took a closer look at Pysthesis.

The creature had a wild mane of tangled black hair and thick, almost furry body hair covering his grainy white skin. His bulging muscles enabled him to hold a weaver aloft for hours without moving. In form, he was very like a man except for his single huge eye, set in the middle of his brow. He wore loose garments of wool and went unshod. He smelled strongly of homemade soap.

The single eye lit now on Crassmor, then turned back to Willow. "Thank you, Pysthesis," she said, and reached up to stroke the low, proffered brow.

The cyclops rose to his full height, bowed once more, and shambled off toward the door, bound for the oversized outbuilding where he spent virtually all of his time when he wasn't under the Dome. For all the door's height and width, the placid cyclops had to crouch down on hands and knees to leave. According to Willow, Pysthesis spent the bulk of his time either sleeping or in a kind of meditative trance, perhaps thinking back over his long life. Crassmor wondered how much the feeding of the cyclops had added to the impoverishment of House Comullo.

Pysthesis had been brought to the Singularity by a rather crafty mariner who had claimed he had quieted the cyclops' natural savagery forever with potions, certain magics, and an application of guile, and was using the cyclops as a slave to row his ship. Willow's great-grandfather had taken pity on the cowed and mind-clouded brute. He'd purchased the cyclops out of slavery—and brought him to the Jade Dome. Pysthesis had never spoken, but seemed to accept his altered life; free to leave, he'd chosen to stay. Crassmor wondered what thoughts and memories passed through the cyclops' head.

Willow threw her arms around Crassmor's neck and kissed him a welcome that made him forget his troubles, trials, and dangers. When she was done, he kissed her back with every bit as much fervor.

"If you'd come two days past, you'd have found your Lost Boys here." She laughed. "I feted them and missed you terribly. I think they did too; none of them even chased me."

He guffawed. Then he became serious. "I was grieved to hear of Teerse's death," he let himself say, right moment or no. He'd liked the old man. His death added to their misfortunes because it left Willow without kin and thus reinforced Combard's authority to select her husband.

She nodded sadly. "He lived a long life and was happy, right to the end, with what had been given him. I don't think he regretted anything. Not a bad life."

*Would that I were so fortunate!* the knight wished, but only answered, "I would put my oath to that; it's high achievement."

He looked up at the Tapestry again. Iridescent lights of diverse colors flickered along its threads from time to time in brief bursts, tracing lines in the Pattern, branching out across it then vanishing, only to be followed by new light flashes.

Crassmor wondered again if there was any truth to the rumors that the Tapestry gave its weavers some degree of prescience or predictive powers. He'd never managed to get Teerse to talk about that, and Willow had let him see that she was offended by his attempts to learn more; in time, Crassmor had given it up.

"It's grown since I've been gone," he observed, "but it grows slowly."

"There have been many things for the Pattern to record, events to integrate," she answered. She looked up at it and murmured, "And how much longer will it endure? It's a time of great peril, I fear, my love. An end to us all is not beyond the possibilities, a day that may see no more Singularity. The future has the seeds of our destruction, Crassmor; will they blossom, I wonder?"

For a moment it had been on his lips to press her again for information about the Tapestry. He caught himself, wishing to bring no unpleasantness into this most joyous aspect of his homecoming. He belabored himself with logic: *Look around you, fool; the place is crumbling and Willow must be near poverty. Is this the setting for an object of such power?*

"As may be," he said in an attempt at lightness. "We are together once more; I find it a good day in every particular."

She threw her arms around his neck. "Crassmor's home! We have so much to talk about! What of life in the Beyonds? Brave deeds? Heroic feats of arms?"

"Considerable shirking and ducking," he replied, "and the avoidance of all trouble whenever possible. And if I was no paragon of valor, what of you? A model of virtue?"

She poked his belly. "Be you not so curious. I am still here in the Jade Dome, awaiting you; that should suffice."

He drew forth her red scarf. "It does." She took it and knotted it at his throat.

"Come away with me," he begged; her breath caught. "Today. Now. We'll go into the Beyonds and be together always. There are places where we can make a life for ourselves."

She stopped him from embracing her again. "I cannot; I'm bound by tradition and promises and—by other things. Will you accept that?"

He bit back arguments and protests; he could see it in her face that she loved him. "I accept. At least we have this moment."

"We have."

He took her hand and led her from the Jade Dome. In the corridor, he turned them toward the bedchambers of the Lady Willow.

# Chapter 15

# SPELLBOUND

**His shadow was** long when Crassmor crossed the last gentle hills riding toward House Tarrant in late afternoon, half-dreaming in the saddle, his thoughts entirely on Willow.

It had taken her completely serious threat to summon her guardsmen and have him forcibly evicted to convince Crassmor to return home in observance of his father's curfew. The hours he'd spent at House Comullo had only served to make him hungrier for her. When passion had been spent, love and desire had remained unchanged in its wake.

The sun's slanting rays showed a rider approaching. It took an extra second or two for the usually wary knight to break off his reverie and see that the Klybesian monk Mooncollar was riding at him. Crassmor's hand started for his sword; then, recalling that Mooncollar would be unaware that he knew of his plottings, he changed the move to a wave to conceal his original intent. A moment later, he stopped before the monk.

"I trust that this day finds you well, holy sir." Crassmor resisted the impulse to look around for Saynday.

The Klybesian made a sign of benediction. "And upon you, gentle knight, a blessing. May I ride with you a way?"

"An honor." *At my side, but not at my back!* Crassmor nonchalantly scanned the surrounding countryside for sign of ambush; he saw nothing in that open, rolling landscape to alarm him.

As their horses plodded along, Mooncollar said, "I come to you at the behest of others, certain parties whose best interests lie aligned with your own."

Crassmor let show his genuine surprise and disbelief.

Mooncollar went on. "Your plight is known in some quarters, yes, and looked upon with sympathy. There are matters that may be of mutual profit to you and these others of whom I speak."

"I'm always receptive to endeavors of self-improvement," the knight admitted.

"Such is your reputation," the Klybesian commented with what Crassmor suspected to be a note of sarcasm. "But these are not subjects to be discussed openly on the road, or so casually. I know that there is, out in the hills above House Tarrant, a hunting lodge tended by one old retainer. Could we perhaps confer there tomorrow night, at the tenth hour?"

"I see no reason why not," Crassmor lied; he could, in fact, think of several. There would always be time to back out of the meeting later, or simply not show up.

They'd come to the turnoff to House Tarrant. "Until then," the Klybesian said, "may all that is good go with you." Crassmor thanked him, and watched the monk ride away toward Dreambourn.

Crassmor rode on, looking every which way. He came by a hole burrowed at the side of the road. A prairie dog popped out of it, sniffing, attentive. Although it had no mustache, Crassmor stopped and watched it, smiling. There had been no prairie dog hole at the roadside when he'd ridden by earlier.

"How was that tongue?" the knight inquired.

The prairie dog looked at him, erect in its hole, forepaws folded complacently on its stomach. "Well, real good," the prairie dog admitted.

It scampered from its burrow; it elongated in different directions. The Trickster sat cross-legged by the side of the road to House Tarrant. "Mighty good; better than any chicken," Saynday proclaimed. He grinned guiltily. "I should have saved some for pemmican. Couldn't."

Crassmor laughed aloud.

"I followed that fella, though," Saynday went on. "I was comin' along . . ."

The knight stopped laughing. The Trickster told his story. Mooncollar had indeed shown up, an hour or so after Crassmor, Arananth, and Bint had gone by. Instead of going on to Dreambourn, the monk had turned off in the direction of House Tarrant. Saynday had trailed the Kly-besian to a small pavilion on a stream's bank some distance from the stronghold itself. There the monk had waited, and the Trickster as well.

"I was Raven," Saynday admitted. "No mustache this time." They both chuckled.

In time, a man had come down to the stream side to meet Mooncollar. Saynday described symbol-sewn robes; Crassmor was angry and not surprised. The Count di Cag-liostro had strolled down, as if out for a walk at random.

Crassmor stroked his goatee. "He must just have finished with his necromancies. Did you hear, Prankster, what tran-spired?"

Saynday answered, "Well, they sat at the foot of that runnel that feeds into the stream, the spot where the bench is cut from the fallen tree."

Crassmor nodded absently; it had been a childhood play place.

"I was on a branch then," Saynday continued. "This count figures you're either a help or a problem to some plan he's fixin'. Didn't say nothin' about the plan. He gave Mooncollar a job: to meet you and get on a meetin' for tomorrow night."

"This Mooncollar has already done," Crassmor re-sponded. "But to what purpose?"

"Life or death," Saynday answered. "Yours."

"Then I know which outcome I prefer." Saynday rocked over backward with laughter at the reply, holding his toes. Crassmor was sniggering too. "Say on," the knight invited at length.

"Mooncollar's supposed to get you mixed into whatever plans they're hatching. But if you refuse, he's supposed to make sure you don't get through the night. They've cooked up something awful for you." The Trickster shuddered; Crassmor involuntarily followed suit.

Saynday went on. "This di Cagliostro's got strong medi-cine. If Mooncollar can't talk you in, he'll drop it and act like it's nothin'. He'll turn the talk to drinkin' and singin' long before midnight."

"An ominous moment," Crassmor observed, doing his best to say it lightly. "And to what purpose?"

"That di Cagliostro wanted to know if your Mooncollar knew somethin' he called a catch-song. Somethin' named 'The Farm Wife's Jolly Boy.' The monk said he did."

Saynday's eyes almost crossed as he went into a precise repetition. "The count said, 'Contrive to be singing it at just the midnight instant. There is a clock in the lodge, always accurate; attend it closely. Take you the first part and leave Crassmor the second. At midnight, Crassmor is to be singing the lines of his part that run:

> " ' "He chased her up and chased her down,
> pursued her round and round the town
> and in good time did bed her down,
> just as he did intend—O!
> Her temper did amend—O!" ' "

Crassmor gnawed a knuckle, commenting offhandedly, "Your voice isn't bad; you must mind those high notes, though." Saynday giggled shrilly. "Yet what of it, this cater-wauling?"

"The count promised," the Trickster answered, "that at midnight there'd be a summoned spirit near that lodge, eavesdropping, bound and ordered with the best magic there is. What you call a demon. It's gonna grab up the singer of those words and do terrible murder or worse."

Crassmor was already perspiring. "They sort of thought that you're always the one for a drink and a song," Saynday finished sadly.

*My false fame precedes me.* It occurred to Crassmor why di Cagliostro hadn't resorted to something more direct: poisons or assassins. But of course, whether Crassmor was out of favor or no, his murder would send Combard into a vengeful fury that the entire Singularity could scarcely contain—strange to realize that. Crassmor's demise through trafficking with demons, on the other hand, would smack of some occult tampering of Crassmor's own gone against him.

Saynday stirred, nearly done. "Di Cagliostro rushed off to. get everything ready for tonight."

Crassmor considered. The idea of denouncing di Cagliostro was the first that occurred to him, the first to be discarded. The man was firmly entrenched at House Tarrant, and Crassmor could hardly invoke Saynday's testimony. It might only come to some sort of draw. In addition, there was the fact that Crassmor wished to know more about these unspecified plotters, what their scheme was, how it had to do with him. For—who knew?—it might even prove desirable, or acceptable.

Saynday removed the beaded bag from the braided belt of his breechclout. "Carry this. My medicine's a pretty strong thing, even here in your Charmed Realm." Balloon-armed, ludicrous Saynday was in that moment the most honorable man Crassmor had ever met. The offer implied incalculable trust.

The knight, humbled as he looked down at the Indian from his high saddle, shook his head. "It would not work for me, my friend. When the clock—*yi!*"

Saynday jumped a little at the yelp. Then he took pleasure in the malicious smile that spread itself over Crassmor's face. The Trickster replaced the now-unneeded bag at his waist.

Combard, a servitor told Crassmor when he returned to House Tarrant, was with the Lady Arananth, showing off the place to her in the company of the Lady Tarrant and Sir Bint. Crassmor took himself off for a look at the room adjoining the study, where necromancies were taking place.

The effort was for nothing; when he got to the study, Crassmor found the count waiting as if he'd expected the knight. Di Cagliostro was puffing on one of Combard's prized old meerschaums, clouding the room with an aroma that made Crassmor think of his father. Candles and lamps glowed, filling the place with light that didn't warm the knight. Di Cagliostro had unburdened himself of his elab-

orate vestments. He now wore a green velvet doublet,
yellow knee breeches, and white hose with mauve shoes
whose buckles were studded with lapis lazuli. He put down
a book he'd been reading, one of Crassmor's favorites,
Cuthbert J. Twilly's immortal *The Art of Arising the
Morning After.*

Di Cagliostro showed his smile. The dark eyes flashed,
and again Crassmor felt the compulsion that resided in
them. The voice was seductive, but it too was an instrument
of its owner's will, used to steer and sway the listener.

The count asked genially, "You found the Lady Willow
in good health?"

"Very much so," the knight answered cautiously.

The register of that entrancing voice lowered a little.
Though he knew it was a device, Crassmor couldn't help
feeling the sincerity, the weight of the thoughts behind it.
"I understand something of your dilemma from your
father and from other, less biased sources as well. I am in
sympathy with you and Willow." The intense eyes held
such conviction that Crassmor found himself prepared to
believe it.

Di Cagliostro told him, "You find me about to award
myself a modest compensation for the day's labors. To
wit: a small drink." The count moved to a glass tuning fork
which stood on a mahogany pedestal. "Will you join me?"

His appeal was such that Crassmor had nearly mouthed
assent before he knew what he was saying. The knight
hastily changed it to, "You are kind, but no."

Di Cagliostro struck the tuning fork with a slender por-
celain rod which was attached to the fork's base by a chain.
The curtains hanging before an alcove of the study parted.
Out came one of Combard's most prized possessions, an
enormous clockwork tortoise all of brass, responding to the
tuning fork's vibrations.

The tortoise ground along, its burnished body throwing
back all the light in the room. Its articulated legs churned
slowly across the carpet to the pinging and rasping of its
works; its head swung rhythmically from side to side, the
stylized beak opening and closing as the tongue lolled in

and out and its ruby eyes rolled, while the enameled tail wagged. The top of its shell stood nearly as high as Crassmor's waist; the machine was executed in superb detail, elaborately embellished. It reached the end of its preset path and stopped for a moment; then the top half of its shell popped open like a lid.

Di Cagliostro drew out a half-empty bottle of the finest Tarrant vintage and a goblet of polished shell. That the count should feel so free to use the tortoise said a great deal about his status at House Tarrant. He continued speaking as he poured.

"I would that things were different, Sir Crassmor. Hard feelings among family members are a grievous thing. I have put it to your father that he's been harsh with you, but he is difficult to approach on that subject. Yet I mean to devote what modest influence I have to bettering your situation."

Where he'd ordinarily have demanded what business it was of an outsider, Crassmor found himself extending wary thanks. Then he saw that the count was already making inroads and went on the offensive. Pointing to the necromancy chamber, he asked, "Has my father spoken to Sandur yet?"

Di Cagliostro stopped with goblet half raised. He took only the slightest sip, replaced the bottle, and closed the shell lid with a click. "He has not. My arts do not function here quite as they did where I come from. Control is proving difficult in some operations, less so in others."

That didn't surprise Crassmor; it was often the case with the enchantments or machinery of a wanderer-in.

"But I am making progress," the count added, "and I have high hopes." Then, more sharply, "It would give your father great comfort to commune with the spirit of the Outrider. Moreover, anything Sandur would say about you would be in your favor, and you know that. Do you, then, disapprove?"

Crassmor answered carefully, only beginning to see how winning this man could be. "As long as no harm comes of it, no."

Di Cagliostro struck the tuning fork again. The tortoise began a slow reverse crawl to its alcove. "I desire to harm no one," he intoned, so that each syllable penetrated Crassmor's brain with a pulse of conviction.

Then di Cagliostro sighed as the tortoise disappeared backward into its alcove. The ratcheting of its escapements stopped. "I seek only to do good, though that has brought me into disaster more than once. I am said to have some gift for winning friends, but confess to a talent for the making of enemies and rivals as well, though no man wants them less. I would hope that we can be friends."

He trained his eyes on Crassmor, who found himself wishing the same. The knight caught himself again, replying, "You see before you a man with no desire whatsoever to cultivate enemies of any kind."

Di Cagliostro beamed at the answer. He went to the knight, arms outstretched. Crassmor avoided him, pacing around his father's desk, which was all of a piece of ebony and fashioned after the likenesses of titans bearing up a flat slab. Even though this man was prepared to loose some sending on the knight, that voice and that gaze were too persuasive; di Cagliostro's touch was to be shunned. Crassmor temporized. "Has my father made plans to go to the court, or Gateshield?"

"Your father takes Sir Bint and the Lady A
ananth with him to the court of Ironwicca tomorrow evening, to see the King and meet with the Grand Master, who is returning from an inspection tour. There will be festivities; Arananth is eager to see them. Certain of the Knights of Onn will be there: Myles of Roudel, Cyrus Scattersword, and the brothers Granville and Bors of the House Morkor. Your father wished your company there."

Crassmor's brain burned. *My brother's closest friends! No!*

"I, however, made a case for the contrary," di Cagliostro finished. "Lord Combard reconsidered. At last he had no objection to your absence, as long as you forbore to visit the Jade Dome. I said I would have your word on it. Was I mistaken?"

"In no particular," Crassmor confessed, struck again by the count's acuity. Not only did this turn leave Crassmor free to attend the meeting with Mooncollar, but it put Crassmor in di Cagliostro's debt. An evening spent across the table from Sandur's oldest comrades would have been trial indeed. *Almost,* the knight thought, *I could be grateful.*

Di Cagliostro was convivial, encouraging. "Your word, then? Against visiting the Jade Dome?"

Crassmor saw that di Cagliostro was impressed with the adherence of Knights of the Order to their sworn word, a death matter for most of them. But Crassmor betrayed no cynicism; it was some small advantage if the count thought that he was of the same stuff as those heroes. *With a liar, lie!*

"Done," the knight proclaimed. Honesty made him add, "And thank you."

It wasn't the first time Hamdor the elderly caretaker of the hunting lodge, had received similar treatment from Crassmor: a handful of coins to cover the cost of the old fellow's cups and those of his friends besides; the evening off; and instructions not to return until noon. Hamdor grinned crookedly, tugging his forelock, recalling the fair and charming game Crassmor had been wont to pursue and capture as a youth, all without leaving the lodge.

Hamdor gone, Crassmor made his preparations. First he set *Shhing* and his parrying dagger in a wooden rack built under the head of the big dinner table. The rack had been put there at Combard's command; meetings of many sorts had taken place in the lodge over the years, and the Lord of House Tarrant was not one to rely on the good intentions or peaceful demeanor of those with whom he negotiated. There was room in the middle of the rack; there, Crassmor set a crank-wound crossbow, its stock carved of walnut, a broadhead bolt in it, aligned toward the opposite end of the table.

Those things were secondary. Crassmor doubted that a Klybesian monk would be inclined to straghtforward violence. Mooncollar would expect the knight to take precautions and would rely on di Cagliostro's demon. And the knight didn't expect any assassins to be lurking about the place for the simple reason that the demon would be doing so.

This matter of a demon was particularly disturbing in that di Cagliostro was confident of his ability to summon it within the confines of the Charmed Realm. It implied rare talent for the arcane arts. For that reason, Crassmor concealed on his person certain fetishes and amulets intended to ward off infernal entities. He didn't have complete faith in those devices; sorcery was made to be countered. The effects of the actions of warring spells were unpredictable and imprecise. Therefore he made his major preparation, which was to turn the tall, glittering water clock in the lodge's main hall ten minutes slow.

At the tenth hour and a little more, Mooncollar appeared. Crassmor greeted him from the open doorway with no light behind him, acting as cautiously as he would be expected to, while Mooncollar dismounted and tethered his horse in the rippling glare of a ring of burning cressets. As the trees and undergrowth had been cleared back around the lodge for a distance of close to an arrow's flight, Crassmor was assured that there was no one with the monk, at least for the moment.

The knight thought about the Klybesians, that resolute army of scholar-monks, indefatigable cataloguers of every belief system that had been heard of in the Singularity, who claimed to have boiled the hodgepodge down to a virtuous simplicity that Crassmor had always found rather confusing and boring. The Klybesians were a powerful force in the Charmed Realm; many sons of Elder Houses were, like Furd, important clerics. The holdings and influence of the Klybesians gave them vast leverage; they maintained monasteries, schools, libraries, charity centers, and hospitals. They were secretive about the inner workings of their organization, loyal by dint of indoctrination and hidden ceremonies, diligent—some called them fanatical—in supporting and advancing Klybesianism. They numbered among them no women.

"Good evening, Sir Knight," Mooncollar greeted, bowing low, singing another benediction in which Crassmor held no faith whatsoever. The monk presented two earthenware bottles. "I have taken the liberty of fetching a little refreshment for us."

Crassmor put the bottles aside after cursory thanks, no surprise to Mooncollar. They would eat and drink only what the lodge provided. The knight made no search of Mooncollar's person; Klybesians were not warriors. Then the Tarrant son turned up the lamps, relit the candelabras, and threw back the screens on the massive fireplace. He'd already set out an assortment of food and beverage. Mooncollar helped himself to a beaker of ale, which Crassmor graciously mulled with a poker from the fireplace. The monk also lit a rum-soaked cigar from a candle, and Crassmor a *Durango Negro*. Then they found seats at opposite ends of the dining table, where Crassmor has set out places, each of them harboring a reason not to sit too close to the other—the same reason.

Crassmor drank from a flagon of wine he'd prudently and liberally thinned; strong drink was his weak suit. There was a toast to Crassmor's safe return to the Home Plane, but none to Mooncollar's, since Crassmor was theoretically ignorant of that. There followed a round to Mooncollar's health, and one each to the Circle of Onn and the Klybesians. During this, Mooncollar eyed the magnificent water clock more than once.

The talk was general for a time; neither man expected otherwise. But Mooncollar's conversation took on a slant, with frequent allusions to Crassmor's hardships in the Beyonds, the dangers and loneliness there, and the companionship of which he'd been deprived. *The point,* Crassmor reflected, *would not be more conspicuous if whitewashed on the side of a buffalo.*

"It's no short while that I was out there," the knight conceded. "I confess a certain desire for errantry a little closer to home."

Mooncollar liked this drift well. "Under present circumstances, you might despair of the likeliness of that. However, changes in the state of affairs in the Singularity might work changes for Sir Crassmor as well."

Crassmor touched up his mustache, drawing on the *Durango Negro*. "How so?"

Mooncollar's smile wouldn't have been out of place on the snout of a weasel. "Would a new Grand Master of the Order be expected to send *himself* back out into the Beyonds?"

*Me?* Crassmor was jolted. This game was for the highest stakes, he knew then; it might involve the downfall of Ironwicca himself. "The proposal holds great appeal; life in the Beyonds can be unpleasant."

"You are far from the most discontented man in the Singularity tonight, Sir Crassmor."

Crassmor took a sparing sip of his wine and shoved the flagon away from him. "The bargain, then?"

"You can be of great use to us, and we can be of cardinal profit to you."

Crassmor was trying not to think too hard about what an answered prayer Grand Mastery would be, or of how Combard and Willow would feel toward him if he fell in with conspirators in rebellion and treason. "What service can I do you that is so valuable?"

Mooncollar selected a candied fruit from a silver bowl. "You have access to the Jade Dome. You know the layout of the place and have the Sight that will not be confused by its protective glamours. You know how to select the right handle for safe passage through that final door."

Crassmor had forgotten all wiles. "Is this a plot against the Lady Willow?" The smooth walnut of the crossbow stock was under his hand, his finger near the release, the weapon aligned directly with the opposite end of the table. Mooncollar's life was no longer his own.

But the monk was chuckling. "Am I fool enough to approach *you* with a plan to work her harm? No. We know your feelings for her. You two shall be free to be together, and that I'll swear to."

Unseen beneath the table, Crassmor's hand fell away from the crossbow. "I would hear more."

"You've heard a great deal already, Tarrant son. You could work much damage with what I've told you. To say on, I must have your answer. Have we your loyalty in return for the Grand Mastery and Willow?"

Mooncollar drew from his cassock a document limned on fine silk so sheer that the light passed through it easily. Crassmor knew that his signature on it would be difficult to explain away later, whatever might happen. More, this was an instrument of the Klybesians, and Mooncollar, like most of them, was something of a practitioner of magics. There might be a compulsion involved in being a party to this document.

"I shall need time to consider," Crassmor answered carefully. "You will have my decision soon."

Mooncollar regarded Crassmor for a moment, the silken page held in the air. Then he relaxed, whisking it back into his cassock with elaborate indifference. "To be sure; what hurry, eh? We are willing to be patient."

"Does 'we' include my uncle Furd?"

Mooncollar waggled a finger. "That you'll find out when we have your pledge."

The monk turned the talk to other things, drawing Crassmor into it. The knight went along with a show of comradery, gulping down his much-weakened wine. They laughed and gossiped and made faces over the telling of risqué stories.

After one such, Mooncollar said, "By the way, is that clock quite on time? I must leave not long after midnight, to arrive at my priory in time for matins."

The clock was a famous furnishing of the lodge, well known for its accuracy, a much-prized precision piece of Combard's. Crassmor assured the monk that it was on time, and knew that, here in the forest, no temple bell or town crier could prove otherwise.

"That leaves us time for a song or two," Mooncollar declared. "What say?"

Crassmor was all in favor of it. He took up a lyre that rested on a shelf, one he'd often used in the lodge before as he'd pursued the world's oldest, gentlest, friendliest sport.

Hamdor kept the lyre tuned; Crassmor made a great show of tuning it anyway, refamiliarizing himself with it. It was after the eleventh hour by the water clock that Mooncollar joined his rather shaky alto with Crassmor's solid voice. They had a good go at "More's the Pity" and derived enough confidence for an assault on "The Tale of the Slower Hare." At Mooncollar's instigation, Crassmor sang the long, sad "Ballad of Amelia Earhart."

This so dampened the mood of manly good times that Mooncollar had the sudden inspiration to collaborate on "Knights of the Horizontal Persuasion," a fast, ribald piece referring to no others but the Lost Boys, involving a deep drink every time one singer or another missed a phrase in the alliterative verses. Both singers did a fair amount of missing; even with his wine thinned, Crassmor's head began to swim. Mooncollar decreased the ale stock considerably. As the clock hands approached midnight, Mooncollar suggested that they test their talents on "The Farm Wife's Jolly Boy," as a sort of sobriety trial.

"Excellent idea!" Crassmor declared, and struck a chord. "I'll take the first part, and you the second."

"Nay! Never!" the monk hiccuped a trifle too quickly. He amended, "I mean, that is, that I am far better acquainted with the first part. Therefore, pray take you the second." Mooncollar belched.

Crassmor frowned. "It is even the same for me; I know the first role far better than the second. Perhaps it were best to forgo—"

Mooncollar waved his hand as though batting flies. "There's nothing to it! But the second's the role for a younger voice, not my old croaker. I shall teach it to you."

"Princely fellow!" Crassmor proclaimed, voice choked with affection as he struck another chord. He let the Klybesian lead him through the song, though he knew it by heart. He pretended to remember the chords after long disuse, forcing the monk to repeat. Mooncollar grew more exasperated and glared frequently at the clock.

Crassmor stopped as they came to the last verse of the run-through, the one of which Saynday had warned him. "I'm unforgivably stupid, dear Mooncollar, not to have learned this song long since," Crassmor slobbered. The clock hands were approaching ten minutes of midnight. "It may be that we should try some less formidable ditty."

"You're doing fine, you're all right," Mooncollar slurred. "That is, um, I'm fond of this song."

"Then we shall sing it, good and close friend." Crassmor practically wept.

Eye to the clock, the Klybesian said, "Er, you're sure that the timepiece is accurate? Matins, you know."

Crassmor waved grandly. "As accurate as you are pious, good cleric. The lodgekeeper maintains it meticulously, by the great sundial on the archery range, and measures it against my father's hourglass."

Mooncollar grunted, adding, "Let us finish the song, then, dear boy."

Crassmor said, "I do believe that the final verse has at last come to mind:

> " 'And after long and short travail
> She came around, not coy, not frail,
> and jousted 'gainst his lance so hale
> that—' "

"No, no, ye loon!" Mooncollar barked, thumping the table with his fist. Crassmor gave the monk his best wounded look. The Klybesian gathered his temper with visible effort, gritting his teeth in a smile. More calmly, he said, "That is, you have confused the verse with some other, my son."

Crassmor smote his forehead with the palm of his hand. "Forgive me! It must, then, be the one that goes:

> " 'And so they set their clothes aside
> and mounted up to have a ride.
> He plumbed that glo-ri-ous divide
> which—' "

"*Honored host.*" Mooncollar grated the words, holding together the shards of his self-restraint, hand clutching what was left of his hair. "Neither is that it."

Crassmor, lip trembling with his unhappiness, bade, "Then I beg you, reveal it to me. I shall be shamed if you depart before we have sung this tune which so delights you." He hit another chord. The monk shot a quick glance at the clock and saw ten minutes remaining. He sang.

> "He chased her up and chased her down,
> pursued her round and round the town
> and in good time did bed her down,
> just as she did intend—ohhhhhhhh!"

This last was because the shutters of the window nearest the monk burst in, crumpling before strength that was not to be denied by mere iron. Crassmor had debated locking those shutters but entrusted to his own plan instead of locks to save himself. It turned out to be unimportant; the shutters were sprung from their hinges, landing to either side with a clatter.

A cataract of sinuous, scaly body poured from the night into the lodge, oynx coils twice as thick as Crassmor's torso, looped and tensed in tremendous power.

The monster snake's very breath blew brimstone and madness into the room; a hellish inner radiance shone forth from its eyes, and its labial scales seemed white-hot. Its tongue, steaming and glowing, flickered and quested. More of its length heaved into view through the window, spilling in weighty, muscular curves in the lamplight. Crassmor gulped and gasped for breath, remembering the serpent imagery on di Cagliostro's vestments.

Mooncollar was out of his seat, chair overturned, staring with paralyzed disbelief. The demon gathered its coils under it and reared up, higher than their heads, swaying hypnotically. More horribly still, it laughed, hissing, hateful sound born of unreasoning malice. The snake had the monk fixed with its incandescent stare, moving toward him slowly, like a black river.

Mooncollar, immobilized, made a number of silent, mouthing attempts before he finally produced words. "Not me! Him, 'tis the knight! You were not to be here until—"

The monster struck, an avalanche of shadow, weaving before Mooncollar one moment and holding him helpless as a field mouse, lifting him clear of the floor the next. Its breath, in the closeness of the room, had Crassmor near to fainting, but he dared not move.

It held the monk up and gazed into his pasty face with insane amusement, its smoking tongue nearly touching his face, the mouth open so wide that it promised to swallow Mooncollar at a gulp.

And then its voice came. That was the worst of all. Filled with shrewd madness, it told the Klybesian, "I *know* what you expected, manling! You sang the words at the appointed time; by the compulsion of the cursed di Cagliostro, you are my meat!"

Crassmor sat motionless; he saw that the crossbow and *Shhing* would be useless. He wondered if he, too, would meet an unspeakable death. The demon seemed capable of anything.

It gave a squeeze of its looped strength; Mooncollar screamed feebly as the breath was nearly chased from his body and his bones ground together. Squirming and clawing, the Klybesian groped for the script that hung from his corded belt, but was unable to hold on to it once he'd torn it loose. It fell to the floor. Then Mooncollar hung, struggling ineffectually.

The monster serpent looked to the knight now, silencing the monk with another coil thrown around his head. Mooncollar's struggles all but ceased. The thing started to glide around the table, carrying the Klybesian along effortlessly. Fear gave Crassmor the strength to move.

He jumped up and thrust his hand into his doublet, clutching an amulet of preservation that lay within.

But the monster paused and spoke. "You are a fortunate little mortal this evening. Let go your foolish charm, human."

Crassmor backed away a step, but obeyed. "Fortunate?"

The demon laughed again, a sound from evil dreams. "Oh, what a chance you have given me to spite di Cagliostro! No matter that your trick was mere technicality; I hold to the exact wording of the compulsion he set upon me. And so I pay di Cagliostro back, wrong for wrong."

Crassmor was swaying a little as he stood; the air was thick with the thing's breath. The snake went on. "Life for you is death for this one!" The monk's body was shaken like a doll. "And it is woe to di Cagliostro! Live on for now, Sir Crassmor, and di Cagliostro, the Unknown Superior, the Noble Voyager, will think twice before he summons me again!"

The whole of the serpent's body still hadn't entered the room. Now it flowed backward, coil after bunched coil, bearing with it the motionless Klybesian. With a last flick of its smoking tongue and a glance of those furious, forever hate-filled eyes, it was gone into the night. Crassmor heard a last hair-raising laugh from outside as it retreated. "A jest to repeat around the fires of hell for eternity!"

Crassmor leaned on the table so that his knees wouldn't give out and choked on the stench that the thing had left behind it. He was occupied with the horrible realization that, had things gone only slightly askew, Mooncollar might have been the survivor. *It could have been my own tender person tucked in those coils.*

He bent shakily and picked up the monk's fallen script. One side of him saw a practical advantage to the outcome of the evening. *At least I won't have to worry about disposing of a body.* That, he knew, would be done very well indeed.

# Chapter 16

# ABSENT

**Combard had gone** aside with Jaan-Marl and other members of the Order. Arananth stepped out into the vastness of Ironwicca's palace and gasped.

Her scented hand closed on Bint's and she gave a little outcry of delight and astonishment. Overhead were row upon row of giant chandeliers, glass megalopolises so high and wide that each was an island of delightful glitter, held aloft by thick chains. The light they threw was pleasant and yet reached every corner of the place. It was like a golden liquid; in it, Arananth saw, fantastic creatures swam. Bint smiled, pleased that she was impressed. Together, they moved out into the throne room.

They were not announced; throngs crowded the enormous chamber, with visitors arriving or departing constantly, so that announcements would have been impossible. High up on his throne sat Ironwicca, speaking to a few well-chosen advisors. Above and to one side, in a balcony, an orchestra played for the milling crowd. It made music that filled the air with gentle string notes and sharp brasses, a proud processional. In various alcoves around the room were other musicians, alone or in small groups. The notes of a sitar could be heard, and those of melodeon, slide whistle, lyre, jingles, slit drum, and balalaika.

Bint led Arananth through the crowd wending toward the throne. She wore a gown all of flashing sequins, looking like some deep-sea goddess, her hair held up by winding chains of diamonds and interwoven with the rarest blossoms from the gardens of House Tarrant. Her evening pumps had been lent her by Crassmor's mother. Even Combard had been surprised by his wife's fragile, bittersweet smile as she'd looked on Bint and Arananth; moments later, the Lady of House Tarrant had returned to her dim rooms.

Now Bint marched erect, handsome. All manner of people were gathered there. They passed a group of red-bearded men wearing claymores and the dark tartan of the Black Watch—the Ladies from Hell, as Bint had heard the kilted warriors called. Nearby were several men and women, nearly naked but for shellfish necklaces, head-dresses, and other sea jewelry, their bodies covered with fantastic tattoos. Both sexes had braces of long, serviceable whalebone knives strapped to their forearms. Arananth gazed at them with concealed curiosity; she was bright enough, Bint saw, to mimic the tolerant, blasé attitude required of the Singularity's inhabitants.

The two passed other individuals and clusters of people. Arananth took in the bewildering assortment of types. A trousered Parthian rider in a conical cap shared some private joke with a woman in an elegant kimono who made vivacious use of her fan and long lashes, her face reminding Arananth of a white doll. Next along was a rather amazed-looking young man in armor like none Bint had ever seen. It was ingeniously segmented, covering the entire body; its helmet was thrown back to reveal a sober, yellow-brown face. The armor boasted elaborate chest and back packs incorporating air tanks, and an intimidating assortment of weapons of the shooting kind, their emission tubes and muzzles pitted and scarred from much firing. A stencil over an instrumented readout on the young man's chest read: RICO. Bint concluded that he was one of the star-wanderers who ended up in the Singularity so rarely and almost never stayed.

Bint paused now and again to acknowledge greetings from members of other of the Elder Houses and to introduce Arananth. She immediately drew compliments and invitations to upcoming social events. Arananth grew flushed with social success; she hugged Bint's arm excitedly. He was aglow with her unspoken praise. They detoured around a laughing, boisterous knot of men in blue linen pantaloons and the short carmagnole jackets and red caps of the Jaco-

bins. All had the soft hands of aristocrats, successful es-
capees from the Reign of Terror.

Bint and Arananth strolled. A fine-featured woman in a
translucent flaxen dress failed to distract the young knight
from Arananth, who was enthralled by all she saw. Servants
circulated with an apparently inexhaustible supply of re-
freshments. The young couple made their way toward the
throne. Ironwicca chanced to glance down on them just
as Bint was pointing out the King. Ironwicca beckoned.
Bint obediently took Arananth's hand and led her up the
steps as her breath caught with delight.

To reach the throne required climbing several flights of
stairs, switching back and forth on broad landings which
overlooked the crowd. People were waiting there to set
forth various matters, disputes, or proposals before the
King.

The first landing was carved of blocks of tantalum shot
through with wires of gold. Fragrant blue blossoms hung
languidly from convoluted trellises of gleaming teak. There
were gathered some two dozen men and women and children in severe dress, the men tightly coated in black and
collared in white, wearing hats with wide, circular brims
and buckles. The women were rigidly corseted, covered to
the wrists, their hems brushing the floor, hair concealed by
unbecoming bonnets. The children were miniature replicas
of their elders. The women were keeping their eyes downcast, plainly scandalized by what they'd seen around them,
making sure their children stayed close. The men were
speaking to one another uncomfortably, glancing up every
now and then at Ironwicca, awaiting their summons. Several of them wore metal cuirasses, and all bore swords.
Many had short, bell-mouthed rifles. Bint thought that
these people had the look of refugees about to petition for
permission to remain in the Singularity. If they received
it, they would have to learn tolerance, the young knight
knew.

He and Arananth climbed the next staircase, its surface
a painstaking mosaic of gods and demons locked in combat. She asked, "Why does the King allow so many

weapons in his court? They are so diverse here. There could be angry words; there could be death."

Bint smiled. "The presence of Ironwicca is enough, almost always, to prevent that. But he has other means of imposing his will. No life can be taken under this roof unless Ironwicca wishes it so."

The next landing was quartz, snow-flecked and veined with silver. Two groups waited there, representing two separate matters. Five people stood to one side, two males and three females. Their skins were a deep carmine; they were attired in the briefest windings of gauzy white film fastened with delicate brooches of beaten copper leaf. Their scalps were shaven except for topknots of hair resembling gathered chrome fibers. Their eyes had an exotic obliqueness. Their speech was melodic, a high-pitched interchange; they sipped gracefully from long, thin drinking vessels. Arananth thought them the most beautiful things she'd yet seen in the Singularity.

The other group was composed of two separate elements, gathered at the far end of the landing, awaiting the King's pleasure. In the center were four men and two women, all dressed in short jackets of black leather and worn-through, filthy denim. The jackets and denim overvests were adorned with a senseless assortment of insignia, no two alike, and decorated with chains and metal studs. All in that gang were long-haired, the men unbarbered. From them an unpleasant odor wafted, making Arananth wrinkle her nose. On the back of the denim overvest of one of them, Bint saw a winged death's-head. All six wore wraparound sunglasses.

They were plainly the subject of some complaint; ranged around them were four of Oishi Kuranosuke's matchless *ronin*. As Bint looked on, one of the gang members seemed to lose patience. He whirled on a guard, fist raised, with a bellow like some animal's. He found at his throat a glittering sword that had been in its rose-lacquered wooden scabbard a split instant before. The samurai met the outlaw's gaze and gave a guttural warning, softer and far more frightening than the roar had been. The *ronin*'s gaze was colder and more ominous than the dark glasses could ward.

The other samurai looked on without unsheathing their own *katana*. The death's-head man backed off the sword point with ludicrous haste, falling back among his fellows. A thin trickle of blood found its way down from his hairy throat.

A servitor appeared to show Bint and Arananth to the throne. The last flight of steps was made from the blood-thirsty stellae of the Mayans, set down crosswise.

Ironwicca sat with his huge drinking horn set aside in its rest. By the side of his throne was a man who seemed to the two young people to give off a chilly mist. The man was wrapped in a long black cape, an individual of lean height and extreme pallor, though his lips were a fresh, healthy red. His dark brows met in the middle, and a full mustache didn't hide pointed, predatory teeth. One hand gestured as he conversed with the King; Bint saw that its nails were long and honed fine, to daggers. The stranger's ears reached to long points; his eyes shone.

The black-cape realized that others were approaching, because Ironwicca's eyes fixed on Arananth. The King wore his crown tonight, a simple, hard circle of blue steel pressed down on the dense curls of his head. The King rose—a rare courtesy for which Bint was grateful beyond words. Arananth blushed at first, flustered and happy. Bint was about to begin a formal presentation, but then both he and Arananth saw the look the stranger had turned upon them.

Suddenly the King's attention was all for his other visitor. Ironwicca hadn't missed the abrupt, almost ungovernable hunger that had come into those bloodshot eyes, and the barely controlled urge to reach out for her. Bint's hand reflexively found his sword's hilt.

"Count!" Ironwicca said, low; but the tone of it brought the stranger around as if he'd been slapped. Bint and Arananth had seen animal ferocity well up in this count; now they saw him put it down again just as quickly, as he feigned courtliness.

The King went on. "I have just made my decision. You are denied haven here in the Singularity. Get you back on board your hellship, that *Demeter,* and begone. Not to-morrow; this moment."

Bint swallowed hard, squeezing Arananth's hand when she looked to him for explanation. He'd never seen the King so stern. It would be to risk punishment to speak or otherwise distract Ironwicca now.

The count had drawn himself up, a count unlike di Cagliostro, a stranger who gathered his cape around him in a black swirl as he might have wings. Bint and Arananth were reminded of the changes Saynday had performed for them. No shape-shifting took place, though, and for a moment the count looked shocked.

"Not here," the King decreed, shaking his head. His brow looked as if lightning might burst forth from it. "Get you gone. I know what sort of a creature you are now. Mark you: work none of your harm in my realm. *None!* You will taste no drop of blood of any subject of Iron-wicca's! I have the means of dealing with you."

This time that feral impatience prevailed. The count reached out, dagger-nailed. The King's great brown fist closed around the pale hand instantly, containing it. White fingers struggled and wormed around the dark hand. The men's gazes tightened, and their hands. Wills and strengths seemed at first an even match. The count's fingers sought to exert power; the King's loose, green satin sleeve fell back as thick bundles of muscle swelled in his forearm. The pale man's eyes bulged with exertion and hatred and dis-belief.

"And if it comes to that," Ironwicca promised with no sign of strain, "we shall see how we match, fang for fang, claw for claw, you and I." His eyes were lustrous, furious gemstones.

The count yielded his grip, and the King let the hands part. The count backed away a step or two, nursing his cold, white hand. Then he pivoted and fled down the dais past Bint and Arananth, opera cape snapping, leaving behind him a smell so foul that she coughed and the knight blinked. They'd seen fear mixed with the wrath and blood-lust on the pale face. The count raced out a side door, eager to leave the Singularity behind.

Ironwicca came a few steps down the dais to meet them, lithe and proud. Arananth dropped into a flustered curtsy once more; Bint bowed and presented her. The King drew her up and led them both back toward the throne. "I am sorry for that scene; I needed to know what the count's reaction would be to a beautiful woman." He smiled at Arananth. "Will you forgive me?"

She managed a nod. "He is a loathsome thing."

"He is something worse than that," the King answered, "but he is gone now." Ironwicca turned to Bint. "And I do want to hear what happened in the Beyonds when you went out. There are strange reports coming to me."

He glanced aside and spoke an order. One of his trusted advisors appeared, a friendly-faced man in a toga, in his middle years. "Would you be good enough to show this lady about my court and make introductions? I have Sir Bint's counsel to take."

The man took Arananth's hand with delight. Ironwicca grinned. "She is a little too perfect in her beauty for you, is she not?" He winked at Bint. "Ovid dislikes perfect beauty and thinks everything needs a flaw."

Arananth shot Bint a quick, warm smile, but her hand stayed where it was. Ovid led her away, speaking fair words. Bint remembered his duty after some difficulty and turned back to his King. He noticed that the King's new Cup Bearer, the man who'd been selected to replace Sandur, was not present tonight. The new Outrider was Singularity-born, of course, and a member of one of the Elder Houses, as was usually the case. Bint knew him slightly, Dickon of Rotha, a likable and able fighter, though not a member of the Order. Still, since the death of Sandur, Ironwicca had done little ceremonial drinking, and Dickon had had no occasion to act as champion in combat.

The King commanded, "Tell me the things that have happened to you lately, Sir Bint. Mind you, leave out none of the things you know about that other count, di Cagliostro."

# Chapter 17

# FALLEN

**The gathering of** the Knights of the Order of the Circle of Onn found Crassmor morose. He wasn't in the spirit of the coming-together, where at another time he'd have been making jubilee over simply having come into that hall once more.

Every man there knew that some new threat to the Singularity was to be detailed to them by their Grand Master, but the chance to enjoy their rare assembly could not be wasted. Danger and evil signs were nothing new to Knights of the Circle.

One of the ancient treasures of the Singularity had been brought to Gateshield for the occasion by its custodian, Leonidas of House Bannor. It was the famed cornucopia, a wickerwork horn of plenty so large that three men had been required to lift it into its place on a trestle table near the altar of the Circle. From the cornucopia there issued a profusion of fruits, meats, breads, and other provender, a slow glacier of food that moved only as fast as it was consumed. The cornucopia was, like the great torch of House Lyle or the Storm Priestess' cauldron of the winds, an object that had come into the Singularity by means of the Circle itself, along with the original settlers. It had sustained them at first, but that need had diminished in time. Now it was used only ceremonially, since the sustenance pouring from it might mean privation in some Reality.

The Grand Master, Jaan-Marl, let his men vent their spirits and kick up their heels a bit. Many of them, particularly the Lost Boys, had been in no position to do so in this style for a long time. Crassmor sat quietly among the ne'er-do-wells now. He was a conspicuous figure in that, as wearer of the heir's ring of House Tarrant—which Combard had returned to him—he'd fallen farthest of any of the Lost Boys. Across the hall and down the long dining board sat Combard, with a number of the other senior knights, nearly all of them lords of the Elder Houses. Some of these shot occasional reproving glances at the madcap Lost Boys. Among the lords sat the abbot Furd, who was something of a chaplain to the Order.

Bint wasn't too far away, lost in thought, looking no less gloomy than his cousin. He'd given a single humorless twist of the mouth when, before the gathering had begun, Crassmor had whispered Mooncollar's fate to him. Crassmor thought that Bint's mood could only have to do with Arananth, but was too preoccupied with his own problems to inquire. Besides, Bint didn't appear to want either conversation or commiseration.

Crassmor was nursing a horn of very thin beer when Crane and Pony-Keg happened by, bearing opposite ends of a platter laden with most of a side of beef. The servitors were overworked tonight, as on any occasion when all the Order was together, and so the two had pitched in with a will. The more staid and respected knights might consider it beneath them to do so, but the Lost Boys were known to go to extreme lengths to keep a party going.

Off in the corner that had been appropriated by the scoundrels for their own, Hoowar Roisterer did a surprisingly nimble dance to the music of a tin whistle, while most of the others diced, condemning or exalting each toss. Handsome Griffin was singing the song to which Hoowar was dancing, his voice deep and clear. The most notable absence was that of Tarafon Quickhand, who hadn't appeared at the rendezvous, and whom no one had been able to locate in the Beyonds.

Crassmor had little heart to share the merrymaking; he was worried over a number of things, but primarily for Willow. He'd cleared up what damage he could at the hunting lodge and left the rest for Hamdor, sure that the old man would maintain silence, then had turned Mooncollar's horse loose to find its own way home. Examination of the script dropped by the Klybesian had yielded only two items of interest. One was a medallion, heavily cast from a strange alloy, bearing the symbol of an eye in a pyramid. The other was a note:

Mooncollar,
For surety's sake, it were best you obtain the services of some several more bravoes and have them at the crossroads beyond Cronequarters at dawn of the second day from this. Be certain that each wears the eye so that his guide will know him; you know what sort of man we need. Too, they will be convoying our very special agent and his cargo; choose well.

The note bore the signet-seal of the abbot Furd.

But the Klybesian's name did not appear in his own hand. It was an instrument typical of the abbot; too vague to be incriminating in any way. It might even be alleged to be forgery; Furd had powerful protection, not the least of which was Combard's, and no one, not even Crassmor, could accuse him lightly. *And accuse him of what?* the knight asked himself over and over. The date of the note meant that the rendezvous beyond Cronequarters would take place tomorrow. And Cronequarters was not far from House Comullo.

Directly from the lodge, Crassmor had ridden for the Jade Dome, pushing his horse mercilessly. Arriving there to warn Willow of some nebulous plot against her home, he'd found himself barred from House Comullo. He'd considered forcing his way past her guards, but thought better of it when they'd blocked his way with weapons whose blades had glittered under the night sky and with light of their own as well.

Strange, but there had been many more guards around the place than he'd recalled House Comullo's having. Also, the guardsmen were bigger, more alert, and better armed and armored than he'd remembered, with an eager, ferocious aspect. None had been the elderly retainers he'd thought them to be, though he knew them to be the same men—or some of them, at any rate. He'd felt that he was seeing their true nature for the first time. Crassmor had found himself thinking about what Bint had said, that di Cagliostro had shown fear of Willow's guardsmen. The count's powers, it seemed, included seeing certain things in their true aspect.

The guardsmen had left no doubt that Crassmor was not to be admitted. The guard commander, Fordall Urth, still soft-spoken but massive and daunting to look upon now, had handed Crassmor another message.

> Dearest Crassmor,
> I have always loved you, only you, and nothing of that has changed. But there is only danger for you if you are near me now; do not ask how I know, but believe this. We cannot share our love or be together again until I send you word. Guard yourself. Do not doubt that you are forever in the heart of
> Willow

He'd been torn by indecision, but had seen in the end that he had little choice. Too, given Mooncollar's attempts to draw him into the plot, Willow was probably safe for the immediate present, or why would Crassmor be needed? The knight had compromised on a hastily scratched message of his own, detailing what little he knew, and had entrusted it to Fordall Urth. The guard commander, no longer stout or sleepy, had vowed to see it delivered at once. Something unswerving in his tone had convinced Crassmor that he would.

Then Crassmor had returned to House Tarrant. The Count di Cagliostro had been nowhere in evidence. Combard had returned the heir's ring without comment, but Crassmor had seen no sign of success in contacting Sandur in the old man's demeanor. Crassmor had retired for much-needed rest, against the convocation of the Order.

Now a horn was winded through the hall. The knight looked up from his brooding, giving over both the pondering of the danger to House Comullo—he had his suspicions about that—and whether or not he should mention it to Combard or the Grand Master. He hesitated to tell about the things he knew, if only because his own credibility was low, while di Cagliostro's rode high, and the Klybesians' was practically unassailable. The knight's only real witness had been carried off by the monster serpent.

Game and song and banter melted away, even among the Lost Boys. Knights cleared from the middle of the hall, booting from their way the hounds that sprawled there and finding seats. The Grand Master had been lenient, knowing that his men served hard and deserved their diversions. Still, it was never wise to provoke Jaan-Marl by moving too slowly.

The Grand Master was in the middle of the hall, armored, as they all were, his sword belted on. His hands were on his hips, and his brows beetled as he awaited complete silence. When he had it, he said, "We are not in our saddles tonight. Our swords are scabbarded; no lance point is aloft." His voice reached to all corners of the place as he paced down the middle of the room. "But henceforth we are on alert, by direction of the King."

The knights looked at one another; the Order had just been put on a wartime footing. "Each of you knows what is expected of him, and has lived up to it before," Jaan-Marl went on. "Two of every three of us will sleep here in Gateshield tonight, next to our weapons. The rest may go and attend whatever affairs they must. That roster changes tomorrow, and the next day, for each man will have those things to which he must see. Thereafter, all will remain at Gateshield except by my command."

Hard-eyed, he looked them over. "The details of this alarum I cannot disclose. But there is this: there loom before the Singularity great threats. An end to us all is not beyond the possibilities. The future holds seeds of destruction; it may well fall to the Knights of the Order to keep them from blossoming."

Crassmor was upright in his seat now, though the Grand Master had finished, turning to leave. Murmurs rose among the men. Crassmor, stunned, was thinking, *Words from Jaan-Marl so similar to Willow's!* From her, and the Tapestry, Crassmor suddenly knew, had come the warning that had prompted the King and the Grand Master to act. So intent was Crassmor on that realization that he almost missed the recitation of the names of those selected to go off duty first. His own wasn't among them.

But Hoowar Roisterer's was. The portly knight, belly tightening the chain mail around his middle, was back to hoisting cups now that Jaan-Marl had exited. Crassmor vaulted the table and raced for him, nearly bowling over a servitor and scattering a pair of wolfhounds who'd been snoozing, well stuffed, near the dining board.

Hoowar looked up, bleary-eyed, as Crassmor elbowed through to him. "Hoowar, good friend, you must change places with me on the roster!" Crassmor tapped a knuckle against the rotund knight's flagon. "You have business which keeps you here, while I have that which calls me away most urgently."

"Ha, humph," Roisterer commenced, wiping foam from his drooping mustache with the back of his hand. "Crassmor, m'boy, you ask much. What is it? Romance? I like ye well, understand, but—" He gave the other a cagey look, rubbing thumb and forefinger together. "Perhaps for some appropriate compensation."

"What of the time I got you out of that Alhambra?" Crassmor demanded. "And the occasion when I rescued you from the guild of collectors? Not to mention the night I spirited you from that trial-by-combat paternity suit?"

His voice had risen in desperation to a near-yell. He reached out and seized Hoowar's arm. Roisterer looked up, eyes focusing, angered. Crassmor let go at once; aroused, the old walrus was quite capable of breaking him in two.

Hoowar saw Crassmor's hard breathing, though, and the pleading on his face. "Mind you, let the duty officers know ere you leave," Hoowar relented, settling back into his chair and gulping at his flagon.

Crassmor, feet flying, was already halfway to the door. All at once a high stridence filled his ears. Every man's eyes went to the hall's main doors; Crassmor halted in mid-dash.

A bizarre procession filed into the hall, two columns of small, chubby creatures that, though rather human in shape, were furred in gray, black, and brown, reminding Crassmor of rodents. Their teeth were protuberant and their pointy snouts whiskered. They wore armlets, collars, and belts of flower garlands. Both files trudged under the burden of a litter woven of saplings and piled with fresh flowers of many kinds. On it lay the corpse of Tarafon Quickhand.

His armor was rent in several places but polished; his notched sword—a plain one, Tarafon's best being in the keeping of a usurer somewhere—was locked in dead hands. Crassmor wondered absently what method these creatures had used to preserve the body; they'd plainly brought it a long way, from somewhere in the Beyonds. The creatures continued their shrill dirge as Jaan-Marl reappeared to stand before them.

Then they halted, and one of them stepped forward. The height of the Grand Master's waist, it stopped before him and bowed, then chirped, "We seek the home of the hero we bear."

Jaan-Marl nodded stoically. Everyone there knew how he agonized over the loss of any Knight of the Order. "You have found it; we are his brothers-in-arms."

Crassmor saw Hoowar Roisterer, suddenly sober, and Griffin and other Lost Boys coming forward slowly.

The creature went on. "This sword-kinsman of yours answered our plea when we begged his aid. He slew a Thing, a Being that preyed on us and devoured our young, against which we had no defense. But Ta-ra-fon was himself wounded in the battle and died. So now we bring him home in honor, to sing his praise and do him homage." It bowed once more.

Swords came out now. Lost Boys fell in on either side of the little pallbearers without awaiting Jaan-Marl's selection; the Grand Master didn't question their right to serve as honor guard. He pointed to the altar and the Circle of Onn. The procession moved forward, the Lost Boys holding their pace down to that of the little creatures with awkwardly slow steps.

Crassmor remembered how Tarafon's nimble fingers had snatched the heir's ring from his hand and passed it to Willow. He started to join his friends, then remembered the urgency of his mission to the Jade Dome. The Tapestry was far more important than he'd thought; danger could find its way into House Comullo at any time, whether Crassmor had been recruited or not.

Turning once more for the doors, he met Combard's gaze. Both had been reminded how dangerous service in the Beyonds could be. But now, when Crassmor might have spoken to his father, who might even have relented and been receptive to a plea that his son's duty be changed, Crassmor rushed past him, fearful for Willow's safety.

The Lord of House Tarrant stared after him a moment, then fell in with the other Knights of the Order for the death rites.

It all made so much sense, Crassmor thought as he galloped toward House Comullo, that he'd been a fool not to have seen it before. When he considered it in retrospect, he saw that the main thing that had kept him from believing rumors of the Tapestry's foretelling powers had been the fact that neither Willow nor Sandur had ever admitted them to him.

For Crassmor was sure that his brother had known as well, as betrothed to Willow, and Combard, too, as Teerse's best friend. It was clear why Teerse had been one of Ironwicca's most valued advisors. Crassmor was certain, too, that he knew now how Sandur had made the seemingly miraculously lucky capture of the peace envoys from the broken-cross army to the lizard riders: the Pattern had given Sandur his instructions.

Crassmor saw now why House Comullo had been allowed to sink into supposed neglect and poverty even though it was, as he'd been permitted to understand on his last visit, formidably guarded. The Tapestry was one of the Singularity's greatest treasures; easier to safeguard it, then, if no one suspected its worth. These facts also added meaning to Combard's insistence that Crassmor should not have Willow. He would certainly consider Crassmor an unworthy party to such a secret, an unsatisfactory mate for the weaver of the Pattern, and no one to father the next weaver.

The scintillating night sky shone above; the road flew by under his horse's hooves.

He again hoped that he hadn't made a dreadful error by not consulting his father or the Grand Master. At the very least, that would have meant delay, and it had been entirely possible that Combard would have forbidden him to go to the Jade Dome. Before all else, Crassmor meant to be at Willow's side while this danger threatened. He didn't know how di Cagliostro and the Klybesians had discovered the Tapestry's secret, but it was plain that they meant to take control of it. But why, why, he kept asking himself, had *Willow* kept the secret from him?

He was about to demand even more speed from his lathered mount when the horse's hooves were suddenly yanked from under it.

Crassmor hurtled forward, yelling in surprise, as the animal went down. He was ripped from the saddle and stirrups by his own momentum, up and over his saddle, as the horse pitched over with a piercing whinny of pain and fear. Reflexes learned so well under exacting drill-masters, for the purpose of escaping death or injury beneath a falling horse, took over. Crassmor gathered himself as he fell, rolling, breaking the force of the fall without shattering arms or legs, landing by blind good luck in a bed of pine needles at the roadside.

Nevertheless, the ground smashed against him with tremendous force, stretching him out and threatening to separate his shoulder and snap his ribs. He bounced once like a stone skipped across water and plowed to a stop feet-first, toes up. All breath was gone from him, the spurs ripped from his boots. *Shhing* was a hard lump under him.

By great fortune, his horse hadn't landed on top of him. He could hear the poor beast's agonized complaints as it flailed to rise. The night sky whirled above him.

Horses' hooves sounded, approaching. Wrenching fear brought him back to his senses. "Is he dead, then?" a vibrant, eloquent voice asked, and Crassmor knew why di Cagliostro hadn't been at House Tarrant, and what he'd been off arranging. The count obviously wasn't one to hesitate when moving from subtle ploys to straightforward ones. What Crassmor couldn't figure out was how di Cagliostro had known where and when to stage the ambush. Then the knight remembered that Furd had been at Gateshield and had seen him leave; the rest wouldn't be too hard for the abbot to conjecture.

Riders gathered around Crassmor's supine body, a half dozen or so of them, he thought. "So it appears, lord," a rider replied. It was all the knight could do to try to hold his breathing to a careful heaving, but the darkness was his ally. "The trip line has downed his horse."

Di Cagliostro's tone held irritation, the impatience of a man doing that which he considered shameful. "Well, have a look at him! And if he is not dead, you must . . . you are to set things aright with your blade." From the sound of his voice, he had turned aside to address another. "You! Silence that damnable horse!"

There were sounds of weapons sliding free and mounts maneuvering closer to Crassmor's fallen one. Men dismounted. The meaty chop of a sword stroke brought a brief thrashing from the horse and ended its suffering. At the same time Crassmor heard the creak of stirrup straps and saddle, another man dismounting near him.

The knight lay very still, rehearsing in his mind the moves he must make, fighting to keep his breathing shallow after having had the wind slammed out of him. Boots stopped next to him, and a sword point was put at his throat.

"Don't sword him unless he still lives!" di Cagliostro ordered. "This thing may yet be reported as an accident. We can find a suitable passerby to report it, and to claim he put the horse out of its anguish."

Crassmor's heart had stopped for a moment as he'd thought the point would slide through his throat. During this reprieve, he readied himself. The point moved back; he heard the man grunt in effort as he sank to one knee under the weight of armor.

Battered and in pain, Crassmor sprang into furious action, determined not to die. One hand went to the man's sword hand, yanking him down. The other went to his own parrying dagger. They grappled; Crassmor plunged the dagger into the man's chest; there was an outrushing of blood. The man groaned, not with anger or even pain, but with only the shocked, dumb animal recognition that he'd been killed.

Crassmor shoved the dying body off him and rolled clear just in time to keep from being trampled by a horse's hooves. He had *Shhing* from its scabbard and swung as the horse came at him again. The animal made the same sort of sound his own had as flesh and bone parted; it dropped, its rider crying out. Crassmor disregarded agony and heavy armor. Two more horsemen rode at him around their fallen comrade.

Then it was all ducking and dodging and the two-handed use of the cavalry rapier—virtually all defense. He fought as he'd been taught, with sudden whirls and split-second drops to one knee to confuse the enemies who crowded after him. One assassin was dead or dying, a second unhorsed and now scrambling to his feet, while a third stayed back charily from the action.

*Di Cagliostro*, the knight knew. That left only two mounted men against him.

They were not knights, or they'd have ridden him down by now. He parried and ducked, then took a cut on one arm that bit into his mail, registering it. He launched a chop at the rider who'd delivered the cut, working *Shhing* one-handedly now. *Shhing* found flesh, and the horseman drew back with a smothered groan.

"Di Cagliostro!" Crassmor railed at the figure who'd dropped back. "Come, face me yourself! Wounded man on foot against a whole one ahorse; surely even you have the stomach for that match!" The other two waited to see what the reply would be, not opposed to having help. Crassmor watched, peering in the darkness, trying to spot the man he'd unhorsed.

"I have no love of killing," that wonderful voice said. The count was silhouetted against the night sky. "And I take no joy in murder." To his men, his tone carried the flick of a whip. "Finish him!"

Crassmor heard a creak of leather and the jingle of metal behind him. He waited an extra instant, calculating. Crassmor pivoted and brought *Shhing* up through a whistling curve, aiming by sound alone. The sword caught one horseman beneath an arm that held a blade aloft, fortune riding *Shhing*'s point. The man toppled from his saddle. The knight saw a chance to survive. He seized the pommel of the vacant saddle with his left hand and vaulted desperately. He yelled in pain and felt the blood run more quickly from his wound, flesh giving at the strain. Then he was astride a horse once more.

He was still a Knight of the Order of the Circle of Onn, a dangerous man when dismounted and more so in a saddle. Fortunately, his legs were uninjured. Crassmor clamped his knees hard to the beast's barrel, turned it with pressure, and rode at the remaining assassin. The man swung a determined cut that the knight, dazed by wounds and injuries as he was, still contrived to duck. His return stroke was quick; it occurred to him that he was, in this desperate encounter where his own life and Willow's were at stake, fighting better than he ever had fought in his life.

The slash opened the man's chest through the resistance of mail. The assassin drew back, guard faltering. Abruptly, all the energy that Crassmor had felt began to ebb. He tried to count his enemies and remember whom else he should be looking out for. Di Cagliostro? Yes, but the count had backed off. *There was something else . . .* he warned himself dizzily, his thoughts coming sluggishly now.

Sudden, terrible shock took him in the side; metal grated across bone and tore through organ and muscle. It sent Crassmor smashing against his pommel, trying to draw breath that would not come. His eyes started in the unspeakable awareness that a sword now pierced up through his side and chest—a death wound, dealt by the man he'd unhorsed earlier.

The blade was roughly yanked from him. He lost his grip and nearly fell from the saddle. Somehow the learned response of a knight, to keep his seat with knees clamped tight, remained. Crassmor dug in his heels, letting fall his sword. The animal sprang away like an arrow from a bow before a second stroke could be delivered. He got one arm around the pommel and clung to it. Each stride shot waves of torment through his chest.

His horse pulled up. Through blasts of pain he saw di

Cagliostro blocking his way, calling to the wounded assassin and the unhorsed one. "Quickly! We cannot let him—" The count broke off as he grabbed for Crassmor's reins, but missed as the skittish beast sidestepped. "We must see this thing through now!" The count maneuvered to grab for the reins again.

Crassmor was so tired, so near the utter darkness he'd always feared, that he found himself resigned. He knew vaguely that he'd fought well. *Sandur! I wish you'd seen me!*

He toppled from the saddle and lay there, waiting for the finish. A new noise rose quickly in his ears. He couldn't understand why the approach of death should sound like a cavalry charge; surely that ultimate threshold would not involve something so worldly? Far off, it seemed, di Cagliostro pleaded, "No! Do not leave me! Come back!"

Time passed. There were ground-shaking chargers all around, racing by him; one nearly trampled him. He waited for spirit-mounted messengers to pluck him up and bear him away to whatever waited in the afterlife. His body was afire with the wound, and yet he felt cold.

He was surprised to hear a horse stop next to him. A basso voice said, "He is here! Strike a light!" He drifted in a brief delirium, then found himself staring up into the face of Fordall Urth. Other guardsmen of the Jade Dome had gathered around. Fordall was saying, "I shall mount; you men pass him up to me."

Crassmor wanted to tell him not to bother; this was no wound that could be survived. But before he could do so, darkness was all around him.

# Chapter 18

# RISEN

**His half-dreams,** hallucinations, the dark images, and the drifting were put aside rudely by sudden, surging awareness.

Crassmor was in a place that he knew but couldn't identify yet, nor could he tell how he knew it. The blackness and pain had been thrust away; forces he wasn't able to identify coursed within him, arcane energies. He took it for another illusion, but when he drew a deep, experimental breath, no agony came in response.

Resigned to seeing what the afterlife was like, preparing himself for the worst because he'd always suspected that being dead offered little diversity, he instructed himself to open his eyes. He hesitated. Then, remembering that Sandur had preceded him, he snapped his eyes open, his brother's name leaping to his lips.

Green. A sky full of such pleasant green light, restful, serene. He felt at once a great calm. It looked so much like something—he saw it all at once—the Jade Dome.

"Rest, dearest, rest," a voice he adored crooned. It added, "Down, please, Pysthesis."

Crassmor sat up, though that unsettled his balance a little, then slumped back on one elbow on the thick carpeting of the Dome. Nearby, the cyclops set Willow down with his customary gentleness. Willow hurried to the knight. She was dressed in a crimson skin-suit of such cut and sheen that she might have been a garnet sculpture.

The Tarrant son was examining himself. The wounds were still open in his side and arm, but no blood flowed from them and no ache came when he touched them. His hair stood on end as he felt the bits of ring-mail that lay imbedded in his flesh, broken and driven in by the sword.

Willow knelt by him, her face not the most perfect but the most beautiful in the world. She gently tugged his fingers from the gruesome inspection. "Leave them be; they need not concern you."

"You'll have to admit that they're unsightly," he declared, shaken. She did not smile. "If this is past-death," he went on, "it suits me well. But if it isn't, then how—" He made an unresolved motion with his free hand. "How do I come to be—"

She covered his lips; he was content to be silent. Tears weren't far from her eyes. Chin up, she repulsed the urge. "The Tapestry is more than you'd guessed, my love. There is that in the Pattern which shows the weaver something of the future, yes." She smoothed a strand of his hair back from the white brow. "But at times, too, it illuminates the present, or near-present.

"Tonight as I wove, it burst forth to me from the Pattern with terrible clarity that you were in danger nearby. I dispatched Fordall Urth and the others. They brought you back here because—because you were beyond any worldly treatment."

His skin raised in goosebumps at that word—*worldly*. His hand almost went back to the death wound; he took her hand instead. "I should be dead!"

Willow's face was a study in varied emotions. She pointed to the Tapestry. "If not for that, you would be."

Radiant sparks raced intermittently at great speeds along individual strands of the great Pattern. She went behind him, kneeling, helping him sit up, holding him so with hands on his shoulders. For a moment their pose reminded him of his initiation into the Knights of the Circle.

"The Pattern can do more than record what has gone before, more than show what is or predict what is to come," she whispered into his ear. "Its most powerful office is to alter what already *is*. Thus, you are not dead because I have reworked that in the Pattern which is Crassmor. I have managed to keep you within the Tapestry. For now, your death is in abeyance."

Willow moved around to kneel before him once more, as Psythesis watched the two with his one huge eye. The enormity of it all swung Crassmor between disbelief and awe, fear and amazement.

"But that will not last for long," she warned. "To prolong your life, I shall have to alter the Pattern. Then you will be set on a new course, one you dare not defy. It isn't without its cost; your thread could be tied in—"

"But I would live?" he interrupted. The slightest tilt of her head flooded him with relief. He laughed. "Weave away! *You* should be wearing *my* favor, not I yours!"

Willow held his head in her hands, searching his eyes as she searched meanings from the Pattern. After the briefest indecision, she kissed him, then crossed back to the Tapestry. The cyclops lifted her up to hold her before the coursing lights. Willow went back to her work.

Crassmor stared up as her, watching from the side as her hands flew over the glowing weft. The entire Tapestry rippled with brilliancies, individual streaks shooting back and forth along the threads. Willow's weaving changed the Pattern with shifts and new implications. Crassmor couldn't quite see how she accomplished it. Her fingers blurred; effulgences jumped around them. The threads were filaments that blazed in changing colors, curling and intertwining like living things moving, it seemed to the knight, more by their own will than by her manipulations. The effect was mesmerizing. Before long, Crassmor found himself unable to look away from Willow. The light-dance emanated from her, out across the Pattern.

The knight no longer had any feeling, unable to sense the carpet under him or the weight of his mail. He could see nothing but Willow and the cyclops in reflected glare and the blindingly bright Tapestry. Crassmor had a sense of changes taking place within and all around him, though. How long it went on, he couldn't tell with any perceptivity at his command.

The Pattern became a pane of resplendence, pure and terrible. It filled his universe. Time stood still, but some inner part of Crassmor was waiting.

Then the brilliance went away, between one second and the next. The knight lay on the carpet, blinking, mouthing like a fish out of water. No afterimages remained on his eyes; he knew instinctively that he'd seen no normal light. Pysthesis was lowering Willow to the floor again. The Pattern had reverted to its muted flickering. Crassmor rose and went to join her as she stepped from the cyclops' palms.

Then the knight remembered that he'd been dying. He groped for his wounds. He was whole, and could find no scar or seam in his flesh where the fatal wound had been, or where he'd suffered any lesser cut that night. His mail was closed up once more, bearing old repairs but no new ones.

He threw himself at Willow with a whoop of joy and hugged her to him; she suffered herself to be embraced but didn't return it. He queried her with a look.

She was both sad and elated. "There is a cost; I told you there would be." She put her head on his chest. "The Tapestry is unyielding in that; each change has its new, inescapable result. The Pattern moves you toward a confrontation with the Klybesians."

He strove to make his reaction lighthearted. "Well-a-day! They have enmity for me already; they were bound to plague me again in any event. What of it?"

Her face was creased, tight-strung with emphasis. "They're your enemies! And you theirs! The confrontation comes now!"

"So be it," he got out at last. "Er, nothing hasty, of course."

"Yes, yes, *haste!*" she shot back. "If you do not move at once, you will be denying the dictates of the Pattern. My new configuration will slip away; the old one will apply once more." Her hand touched his side, where the wound had been. "Former conditions will prevail. Your life will be forfeit."

He drew her down to the carpet. They sat, he cross-legged and she in his lap. "You must go among them," she said. "That is the mandate of the Tapestry. Learn their plots; fight them. Do otherwise and you die."

He saw the absurdity of it and laughed. He told her of the meeting with Mooncollar and of di Cagliostro's machinations, all revolving around the Tapestry somehow. "In giving me back my life," he snorted, "your Tapestry has purchased itself an agent and ally."

"Those enemies move against me too," she reminded him. "Remember that old free servant, Racklee? He's disappeared; I fear for his safety. When I instructed the guards to keep you away, it was because the Pattern showed great peril for you when you were near me. It was all too true."

Crassmor showed his teeth to the Tapestry. "Danger to you is one more reason for me to serve that—that *thing!* And how many other lives has your precious Tapestry—"

He stopped in mid-breath. He rose, spilling her from his lap, then pulling her up. He shouted, *"Sandur!* Willow, make that cursed Pattern bring back Sandur!" He shook his fist up at the Tapestry, addressing it. "You want a champion, do you? Then you'll give me back my brother!"

Willow pulled down the fist. "It cannot do that." Crassmor listened against his will. "My love, it cannot! If such a thing were possible, don't you think I would have accomplished it already?"

He spun from her. She put a hand on the armored back. "The Pattern has its limitations," she told him. "*Any* alteration risks diminishing its powers. Its permutability is slight. There are already flaws in the Pattern which can't be corrected. They lessen its influence, because some attempted change did not work in the past. The death of Sandur was locked into the Pattern; there was nothing my father and I could do to bring him back."

He turned back to her. "Did you foresee it?"

"There was always death and peril around the Outrider," she answered in a level tone. Crassmor berated himself for thinking that she might have held back a warning. "But Teerse and I learned of Sandur's death only when the Tapestry showed it. We couldn't alter it; we could only tell Ironwicca of it."

She hushed him from the other questions he would have asked. "No more; you must go and do what you can against the Klybesians. It must be the road for you, and tonight."

That brought something to mind. He fished out the things he'd retrieved from Mooncollar's script, the note and the medallion. Willow agreed that they offered a course of action, however vague. He handed Furd's note to her for safekeeping and for whatever evidence it might be, should he fail to return.

"I'll need other clothes," he decided. "Then we'll see what's about at that crossroads tomorrow."

Whether he'd been summoned in some manner that Crassmor hadn't detected or simply shown up at that moment, Fordall Urth appeared just then, bearing *Shhing*, Crassmor's dagger, and the helm he'd lost when his horse had pitched him. Seen in this light, the guard commander was once more a ponderous oldster.

"We also found these on the bodies of the slain," Fordall Urth explained. He held out two more medallions with the eye-in-pyramid.

"I do not think di Cagliostro will dare come here," Willow judged, "but he will send some other to find out what's become of you." She led Crassmor toward the door. "Deceptions may be worked around deceptions. "You're safer if you're thought dead. Leave that to me."

The knight walked steadily, strength renewed, trying not to think about what would happen if the Tapestry's dictates reverted.

The weaver told her guard, "His horse stays in the bailey. If my weaving has removed the bloodstains from his saddle, mark it with sheep's blood. Drop more on the front steps as well, and a trail in the hall."

Fordall Urth said that a fresh mount and provisions would be ready shortly.

"There can be no companion for you from among my liegemen," she told Crassmor at the doorway of the Jade Dome. "They are bound to these lands by Comullo magic. Nor can Bint or your Lost Boys be told; this part of the Pattern speaks to you and the Klybesians alone, at least for now."

With no talent for good-byes, he caught her up in his

arms. Their kiss was urgent, hard. "You're the woman I'll love forever."

"Who'll love you forever."

A moment later, Willow watched Crassmor go off to face the waiting danger, then turned to Fordall Urth. "Someone will come seeking me soon, on some pretext or other. Tell him that you will escort him into the Jade Dome, but arrange for some hubbub among the guards when you've come near the door, and go to see about it. The door will be left ajar; leave whoever it is near enough so that he'll be able to steal over and peer through. Is this clear?"

Fordall bowed. Willow saw him in his true form, a towering fighting man in war helm and glittering black armor. "And, Fordall, use your arts on Crassmor; disguise him." Fordall Urth went to arrange things. Willow returned to the Tapestry.

Under the barely rippling Tapestry she knelt, searching among the fallen threads that had been cut off short or rejected by determinations of the Pattern itself. The pulsations of light in some of the discards weren't altogether dimmed yet. She drew various of them across the palm of her hand, seeking by her weaver's powers. At last the one she wanted was in her hand.

Patient Pysthesis lifted her up to a spot she selected. As Willow had long since learned, the Jade Dome's design resulted in the light from the single doorway throwing shadows across the room to the base of the wall opposite. Held up close to the Tapestry as she was now, Willow would be unable to see it, as any onlooker would be able to tell. But the cyclops, standing where she'd bade him, could see over the top of the Tapestry.

She craned her head to look up at the solitary eye. "Can you see light from the doorway across the Dome?"

The cyclops nodded solemnly.

"When you see that light blocked by someone peering in," she instructed, "give no other sign, but press your thumb against my leg. Signal me again when that person is gone." There was another inclination of the colossal head.

She set about anchoring the salvaged thread to the

Tapestry, even though she knew it would be rejected the moment she relaxed her control. She wasn't trying to effect a change in the Pattern, but only a temporary fastening-on. Her plan required nothing more. Willow fretted, and even swore a little, at the Pattern's resistance. At last she managed a tenuous attachment. Then she fell to an intent study of the Tapestry, passing time in trying to descry something more of the threat of the Klybesians and the hazards awaiting Crassmor. Over an hour passed.

The cyclops' enormous thumb brushed the side of her leg, then fell back. Willow's hands flew at the Tapestry, her movements frenetic. She clicked her anger, rasped her disappointment. She knew that the exploding colors racing outward from her work would show how much energy she was throwing at the Pattern. At her unspoken command, the play of light was fitful, though, speaking of failure.

Willow let the Pattern flash angrily; she moaned and released her control over the thread. It floated down, and she knelt in the cyclops' palms, watching it, crying aloud. She stared at the thread drifting down leisurely between Pysthesis' legs to the carpet, semaphoring its rejection, going dark even before it landed. She gave a little scream, then wept at some volume.

A moment later, the thumb touched her arm. She had Pysthesis set her down. Searching there, she took up the thread she'd let fall, wiping away tears that had nothing to do with its failure.

A rap sounded at the open door. Willow spun as Fordall Urth came through. "His Eminence, Furd, abbot of the Klybesians, my lady!"

Crassmor's uncle entered, in the sort of waddle that kept his chubby inner thighs from chafing under his billowing robe. Furd had been at Gateshield that night, and both the Klybesians and di Cagliostro had their secret means of communication. No wonder, then, that the ambush had been so well timed.

Willow stammered a greeting. Furd, grinning widely, hooking thumbs through his corded belt, wagged a puffy forefinger at her. "Have we grown so far apart that you no longer greet me as Uncle Furdie? I know it is not an early hour, but I was passing and thought to see if you were still working. How long it's been since we have seen one another, my child! And, knowing the unusual hours you sometimes keep under the Jade Dome . . ."

He shrugged broadly, awaiting her reaction. Willow spoke a welcome haltingly. Furd smiled. "Perhaps I should come back some other time? I noticed a bloodied saddle on a horse in the bailey, and your guardsman told me that there has been a . . . hunting accident." There was sympathy in his voice, but none in his eyes.

Willow gazed down blankly at the darkened thread she held, the last of the temporary energies she'd given it now exhausted. She opened her fingers slowly, watching it float to the carpet once more. She answered, "No, your— Uncle Furd. I've no work left to do here. But you will have to excuse me; I'm very, very tired."

The abbot smiled and splayed his fingers across his belly, permitting himself no more secret joy over the death of a kinsman than was proper in a triumphant Klybesian.

# Chapter 19

# AMONG THE CHOSEN

Crassmor fingered the medallion and peered through the foliage at the band of rogues assembled around a small campfire fifty paces from where he crouched in hiding.

By the side of the crossroads were a young Klybesian monk and four other men. As he watched, they rose to greet a new arrival. They stood in a line, ranged out in case of trouble, with the hint of unease of men who were not yet used to functioning together. Only the monk betrayed none. Crassmor, watching them for nearly an hour, was convinced that the fighting men were recent recruits.

One of these wore a cuirass of horizontal metal hoops and an open-faced helm with hinged cheek flaps. He bore an oblong shield and was armed with shortsword, dagger, and heavy spear. His heavy buskins had seen much use. Crassmor had on occasion seen his kind before, a legionary.

Two more of the men were of a kind with one another, arrayed in jerkins of white fur, leathern breeches, and muddy gaiters over heavy sandals. They carried short, cased bows and short axes. One, as he rose, slipped into his pouch a set of dice or knucklebones with which the group had been passing the time—the monk excepted.

The last was extravagantly dressed, a man in a plate corselet and a plumed, wide-brimmed hat streaming with ribbons of many colors. His clothing was dazzling, with sleeves and breeches vented and slashed, billowed and gathered, and fine hose. He bore a huge, two-handed sword over his shoulder, as long a weapon as the longswords of the lizard riders. He carried a smaller one, with S-shaped quillons, at his waist.

There'd been no sign of Furd or di Cagliostro. The knight had been dithering over whether or not to reveal himself; simply trailing the group from a distance held little promise of yielding useful information except their destination, and he had a feeling he already knew that. Still, going among them, even in the disguise provided by Fordall Urth, went against Crassmor's every inclination.

Not that he could complain about Fordall's work, although it had cost the knight his mustache and goatee and transformed his hair to jet black. There had been something about Fordall's craft—the puckered scar applied with a streak of something resembling tree sap that had drawn the corner of Crassmor's mouth downward in a convincing disfigurement; the strokes of grime that had changed the shape of his cheeks—that had smacked of a master at work. He wondered where Willow's guard commander had learned such things. But then, Fordall Urth's own arts of disguise were of a far more curious nature.

There'd also been no sign of anyone who might recognize Crassmor, and he badly wished to know what rendezvous this was. He blasphemed against the fate that had sent him into this adventure with so little opportunity to plan.

The new arrival came in out of the ground fog hugging the intersection. He was an old man, small and bent, on a piebald pony, leading a pack horse burdened with large, carefully secured boxes. Crassmor had been speculating on who the agent mentioned in the note might be and what his cargo. Now at least one question was answered. The knight gave a start as he recognized Racklee, Willow's missing servitor. Crassmor had begun rising, unconsciously; now he squatted back down slowly.

The old man traded curt greetings with the Klybesian. The others began to gather their things and break camp. Crassmor turned and crept down the little rise behind his hiding place, swearing under his breath. Time was running out; the abeyance won for him by Willow was, as she'd been at pains to have him understand, very limited. This new development underscored the danger to her, to the Tapestry, and to the knight himself. He needed to know more, as quickly as possible, even if it meant going in among his enemies. He pulled up the hood of his borrowed, faded blue cloak, settling it low over his face.

He mounted; when he left the copse of trees in which he'd hidden, he was coming from the direction of a nearby village. The armed men among the waiting group were quick to hear and turned on him. Hands went to weapons, and Crassmor made sure that his own was settled at his shoulder for the draw. He'd left his mail behind at House Comullo, but wore a stiff leather jacket, proofed with metal lozenges, under the short cloak.

The waiting warriors had begun to integrate their actions. A quick exchange of glances, a hand signal from the monk, and they'd deployed themselves both to guard against what Crassmor might do and to keep watch for others appearing. The Klybesian came forward expectantly as the knight approached. Crassmor held up the medallion around his neck, the eye-in-pyramid he'd taken from Moon-collar's script; all the others wore the same.

"I was told to come here with this," he said. If he'd said the wrong thing, there'd be a spear cast and arrows, and he carried no shield.

"Who sends you?" the Klybesian, eyeing him, wanted to know.

"Your fellow monk Mooncollar. I'd met him before; he bespoke me in the marketplace in Dreambourn two days ago."

The armsmen looked to the monk. The young Klybesian demanded, "Why so? Mooncollar is not here to speak for you."

*Nor will he be here to speak against me,* Crassmor knew. He scanned them, knowing that they saw a greasy-haired, sunken-cheeked swordsman down on his luck. He shrugged. "The cleric promised good pay, gave me this token to wear, and said to meet him here. My loyalty's for you as well, if you have money."

The monk scratched his chin. "The day ere yesterday, you say?" He thought for a moment; Crassmor hoped that logic would allay his suspicions. If the plot and this meeting had been compromised, why should one man show up instead of Royal Borderers and Knights of Onn, who would have no need of any deception?

The Klybesian apparently saw it that way, concluding that Mooncollar had recruited Crassmor before meeting his ghastly end. "Very well. If you're of a mind to serve without question or condition, there will be reward for you in abundance."

Crassmor responded, "I say to you as I said to Mooncollar: I've a sword to sell, and nothing else. Not convictions, not reservations, not curiosity."

The others armsmen studied him. Crassmor was relieved to see that there were no hotbloods among them, none who cared to test themselves against every potential rival. These men were veterans, canny and sure of themselves. Not surprisingly, there were no introductions.

Old Racklee was now dismounting stiffly. The Klybesian told him, "No, stay mounted. We should have been on our way already. We are expected."

Racklee, one leg on his pony's croup, frowned. "Then another few moments will not matter. I have come far and spent long labor at my crafting. I am weary."

The Klybesian stepped closer. He looked hardly old enough to have taken his final vows, a handsome boy with soft brown hair, large blue eyes, and downy cheeks. There was something in his face, though, cold and absolutely certain, that endowed him with an air of authority. "You would do well to recall whom you serve, old one."

The sourpuss agent examined the boyish monk with a scowl, not used to being contradicted. At length he drew himself back into the saddle with a grunt and an exhalation, rubbing his tired joints.

The rest were on horses now. Crassmor fell in behind Racklee, with the bowmen trailing him and the long-swordsman bringing up the rear. Ahead of the artisan was the legionary and at the head of things the monk. The Klybesian called over his shoulder, "We will stop when we have made some headway. By tonight you shall be well hosted."

Which, for Crassmor, confirmed the destination. Klybesians were rarely so glad-sounding as when they were going home.

The headquarters of the Klybesian sect, its stronghold and generations-old seat, the monastery of Virtuary, opened before them by degrees. The place pointed up the monks' penchant for hiding menace behind a benign face.

Virtuary's defenses were subtle and deadly, constructed over long years and carefully concealed. Its grounds were so designed that, as in most things Klybesian, there was no direct path, no straight road. The riders found themselves obliged to wind along through mazes of turns, covered bridges, and ramps engineered to function as defensive traps. The route was bordered with hedgerows, stone walls, fences, and steep slopes, all fashioned to look scenic and innocent.

Crassmor knew better. He'd visited the place with his father and uncle. In the landscaped, parklike valley that gave access to the place, there were even more ways to come to harm, though any Klybesian would have maintained stoutly that the entire intent of the area was aesthetic. In fact, there was rumored to be not one edge or point anywhere in the place. That didn't change the fact that any number of would-be thieves and intruders, and at least one hostile armed force, had met their end without ever reaching the redoubt that guarded Virtuary.

A visitor came indoors by degrees, not by the simple crossing of a threshold. Countryside yielded to small lawns and gazebos, trellises, latticeworks of vines, and aged wisteria at the roadside. There were rain shelters among the paths, and ornamental walls. All these became more common, pressing in on the slope up to the redoubt which presided over all. Crassmor knew too, because Sandur had told him, that most of the slope was undermined and could be sent crashing down with the severing of a single cord within Virtuary.

The watch maintained there was vigilant. No outsider who entered the region, much less the valley, could avoid encountering a Klybesian. That monk would, in casual but pointed conversation, draw the visitor out and inquire after his intentions. Failing to satisfy the monk's curiosity, the outsider would be informed gently that the monastery could not entertain him. Persisting, the outsider would find that the winding way to the redoubt had become an impossible labyrinth, wrought by the engineering genius of the sect. Resorting to more direct or violent methods, the unwelcome visitor would be fortunate to end up in a tastefully adorned pitfall, but was more likely to meet death or injury. Walls might topple, bridges give way, or trees fall.

No one blocked their way or questioned the riders who wore the medallions, however. They rode in under the pavilion that spread out about the skirts of the redoubt, masking the barbican and providing yet another line of protection. Crassmor wondered if it were true that there were enormous underground reservoirs of volatile liquid that could conveniently catch fire, burning and suffocating and poisoning anyone who assaulted the gates there. The riders passed through the enormous gates and across a drawbridge spanning a moat. The murky water down below swirled with large swimming things that preferred to stay beneath the surface. The company passed in under the bailey.

In the spacious courtyard, meticulously clean and well paved, silent monks rushed forward to take their horses, seeming to avert their eyes from the outsiders. The sourpuss Racklee carefully took down his boxes, unwillingly surrendering them to other Klybesians who, Crassmor saw, also wore the medallion. Then the group ascended long staircases, worn with ages of shoe leather and bare feet, into the main structure.

Crassmor tried to keep track of their progress without appearing to, as monks passed wordlessly in both directions. The other four hired rogues gaped without pretense at their surroundings, making the knight's reconnaissance less conspicuous.

They passed galleries of religious relics, vast rooms crowded with manuscripts and books and scrolls smelling of age. The knight wondered what his companions thought of the winged serpent, wrought in brass wire, suspended over an entire length of corridor; or of the door of blue crystal, heavily locked and secured with a gigantic, time-encrusted waxen seal; or of the other enigmatic appointments of the place. None of them asked any questions, he noticed. Every so often, complicated bell-tone signals chimed, meaning what, Crassmor had no idea.

They came to an extensive room, its brown stone walls bare, its floor uncovered, but its high, groined ceiling crammed with elaborate inscriptions and symbols on every surface. A broad row of wide windows on the opposite side gave a view of the long valley protected by Virtuary. It contained neat and carefully tilled fields and terraces, granaries and pastures, workshops and barns, chapels, vineyards, and orchards. Crassmor saw the tiny figures of monks laboring in one of the wealthiest fiefdoms in the Singularity. The room contained only one item of furniture, a mammoth table of beechwood whose legs were fashioned like monks in heroically pious poses. There was only one occupant.

Crassmor's uncle, the abbot Furd, turned to face them.

The knight tilted his head down a bit, the now-black hair dangling over his eyes, and drew back into his hood. He shuffled into the room more slowly than the others, to stand at the back of the group, berating his luck, trying to puzzle out what was going on. He was caught by the heart-squeezing realization that *Shhing* protruded over his shoulder in silent betrayal. He edged his body around to put the hilt as much out of sight as he could. His uncle had never shown much interest in weapons, and there were many who wore their swords as Crassmor did. Nevertheless, he set himself for battle or a try at flight, but held small hope for success at either.

Furd, however, after a brief look at the armed men, had eyes only for the old servitor-impostor Racklee and the boxes he'd fetched. The abbot, too, now wore the eye-in-pyramid. "Worthy Racklee, loyal fellow, welcome!" Furd said heartily. He took the man's arm as the monks set their burdens on the beechwood table with holy care. "How was your journey?"

"Wearying." Racklee frowned, distracted by his precious cargo.

Furd tut-tutted. "I myself was forced to endure the entire night in a jouncing coach and reached here only a short time ago. But great endeavors demand some sacrifice, is that not so?"

Racklee merely grunted. One monk had produced a short pry bar. Before he could put it to use, the old man grabbed it from him and undertook the job of opening the boxes himself, with remarkable delicacy. He muttered, "An intricate and exhaustive assignment, perhaps my finest work."

"You will find us grateful," Furd assured him with a well-fed smile. The abbot spared enough attention to instruct the monk guide. "Show these new men across the hall, where the rest wait."

Crassmor was the first to turn and follow the young monk out. The group crossed the corridor and passed under an archway. In the room beyond waited perhaps a score of heavily armed men in a variety of costumes and armor, some striking the knight as natives of the Singularity, others having the look of wanderers-in. He saw no one he recognized.

He followed his fellow travelers into the room. "You will be summoned," the monk announced for them all to hear; then he went back out into the corridor and took up position as sentry. Crassmor reached up to stroke a beard that was longer there, then chewed at a thumbnail, speculating and worrying as the others in the room gave one another appraising glances. They shared a common aura of outlawry, a desperate hardness of spirit.

It hadn't occurred to Crassmor that his uncle would be there; Furd went seldom to Virtuary, and had been at Gateshield only the night before. Looking around now, he asked himself, *Mercenaries? Why else, but for battle at House Comullo?* Crassmor had seen Willow's guardsmen in their true shapes, though, and judged that the men before him, tough as they looked, would be no match for Fordall Urth's crew of massive grim reapers.

Conversations in the room were low and general, an occasional harsh laugh or obscenity thrown in. Much of it was about when and where various battles had taken place, both in the Beyonds and in diverse Realities. Crassmor kept his shoulders to the wall, arms and legs crossed and head down, to make it plain that he wished no fellowship. Once or twice, he heard the monk pacing the corridor.

He wondered why this company was gathered in Virtuary. Surely some other place would have been more convenient, particularly one closer to the Jade Dome. Recalling the Klybesians' frequent dabblings in the supernatural, he concluded that the monks would want to insure that their hired champions would fight to the fullest and that there would be no wagging of tongues afterward. He shuddered as he thought how desperate these wolves' heads with their swords-for-hire must be, to agree to undergo a compulsion. His fear grew that he might be trapped.

Voices in the corridor distracted him. Positioned near the door, he heard Furd's heavy steps and Racklee's shuffling ones. The abbot said, "Most admirable! Racklee, you are a master craftsman in truth! Please go down to my suite and await me; you know the way."

At the same moment a man in the room, decked out in a costume of turban, baggy trousers and tunic, pointed-toed boots, and scimitar, muttered, "By the holy! It's hours now that we've been here waiting. Is there no food or drink in the whole of this rock pile?" Others grumbled concordance.

The situation inspired Crassmor. Hooking a thumb toward the corridor, head still lowered, he growled, "Food and drink in plenty, I just heard someone say, for that fat abbot. He doesn't look like the sort to go long in between stuffings."

That was more than enough. The man who'd spoken and a half-dozen more strode into the corridor, spied Furd, and went off after him to press their complaint. Crassmor peeked out a moment later to see his uncle surrounded by irate hirelings, the young monk guide doing his best to shield the abbot. More mercenaries were filtering out to join the group. Racklee, still stiff from his ride, hobbled off in the opposite direction to await Furd. The knight strolled casually across the corridor.

Pieces of the crates lay on the floor. On the table rested what Crassmor thought at first to be some peculiar container or machine. Drawing closer, he saw that it was a model, a precise reconstruction of House Comullo and its grounds. In its midst, like a gem in a setting, was a Jade Dome the size of a large mellon half.

He inspected it closely, keeping an ear cocked for anyone who might discover him there. The model set forth every room and detail precisely, along with the doorway to the Dome. Here and there were arcane symbols which he knew corresponded to the various glamours and spells of confusion located throughout the place. Racklee's willingness to work for Willow without pay made distressing sense now; Crassmor hit a fist on the table, for Willow's insistence on carrying on her pretext of poverty so thoroughly.

The choice of Virtuary for the bringing-together of the hired swords was now even more logical. The compulsion under which they would surely be placed for service to di Cagliostro and the Klybesians could now include exact instructions made possible by the model, glamours or no.

Crassmor cudgeled his brain for an idea. Destroying the model would almost certainly mean his capture and avail nothing; Racklee was present to repair or duplicate it. There seemed no way to steal or otherwise get rid of it. Then a thought came to him and he almost sniggered. Crassmor reached out for the model . . .

He heard steps in the corridor and whirled away from the model in alarm. He could see no place to hide. He had taken several paces toward the door when Furd and the young monk entered. Crassmor saw his uncle's eyes bulge with indignation.

"Out, knave," the abbot barked, adding, "You were to wait across the hall with your comrades. What are you doing in here?"

Crassmor had his head tilted down and drawn back into his hood once more. His inflection gruff and raspy, he improvised. "Someone told us there is food and drink to be had. I'm hungry."

Furd snorted, "You'd do well to think on your job, all you hellions, and less on your bellies! Go back; you will eat after certain aspects of your mission are—are made clear to you."

Crassmor touched a forefinger to the edge of his cowl by way of acknowledgment. "Aye, m'lord." He shuffled toward the door, waving the hand in a gesture of obedience to block his face. "I go."

Swift as a snake, Furd seized the hand and held it, to make sure he'd seen the heir's ring of House Tarrant. Crassmor realized at once the mistake he'd made. The abbot recognized him now; Furd's vehement outpouring was first of shock and surprise at seeing his nephew still alive, then degenerated to strangled, outraged sounds.

Tugging his hand free, Crassmor spun to confront the monk guide, who hadn't yet grasped what was going on. The knight struck him a blow to the side of the head with all the strength he could muster. The Klybesian wobbled for a moment; Crassmor dealt him a second.

As the monk collapsed to the floor, *Shhing* came rasping

from its scabbard. Furd, though no man of action, wasn't slow to save his own skin. He was hurrying around the long table as rapidly as his fleshy frame permitted, bawling for assistance.

Crassmor waved his sword, threatening, "Silence, or I'll give you some of *this!*"

He saw that the threat wouldn't quiet his uncle. All Furd had to do was keep clear of him for a few moments; the alarm would draw help in droves. Bounding over the groaning monk, Crassmor dashed into the corridor. At the far end, Klybesians and some of the hirelings were still arguing over the promised meal. Furd's commotion had begun to attract their attention, though; the monks broke off and came at a run, all of them wearing the medallions. Weapons appeared among the mercenaries.

In that direction lay the route by which the party had come, the one Crassmor had attempted to memorize. But he had no wish to try his luck among the monks and mercenaries. He turned on his heel and raced off in the opposite direction. He could already hear the clang of a distant gong, proof of the monastery's elaborate security arrangements. He rounded a corner and darted through a *locutorium* and the *necessarium* beyond it, into another corridor, and down the first stairway he came to. He fled three steps at a time. Intermittent window slits gave scarcely adequate light for his descent.

So abruptly that he had no chance to slow, he came upon another man on the steep, winding stair. It was Racklee. The old modeler had heard the knight coming; he'd turned with drawn dagger.

Crassmor had an instant's glimpse of Racklee's face, its habitual scowl of bad humor now twisted into surprise and hatred as the old man presumed he was under attack. The knight shifted his sword around in mid-stride, unable to alter course. Largely through luck, he deflected the dagger. Racklee bounced off his shoulder and slammed into the wall.

Crassmor nearly lost his footing. He dropped *Shhing*, clawing at the wall in a frenzied effort to avert a headlong fall. He went down against the outside wall to roll and thrash to a stop, and immediately began pulling himself up again, hearing his sword bouncing and falling down the steps. He was nearly bowled over again as Racklee, his screams punctuated by the brutal thuds of body on stone, tumbled past. The modeler was lost to sight down the curve of the stair.

Crassmor, regaining his balance, started down again, intent on recovering his sword and escaping. He pulled his parrying dagger and ran as fast as he dared, hating the feeling of being without *Shhing*. He didn't hear the ascending footsteps until he was on top of their source.

By wild effort, he jarred to a stop just as a squad of monks appeared around the coiled steps and threw themselves at him. They, too, wore the eye-in-pyramid. He made an off-balance thrust with the dagger, but missed. As he lurched forward, his arm was seized. All went down in a struggling pile, sliding downward to fetch up on a landing.

The knight beat at them and kicked, trying to slash at them. Two monks wrestled his hand around, twisting the weapon from it. The Klybesians grabbed and clutched; once fastened to an arm or leg, they refused to be dislodged despite a broken nose or loosened teeth. *No doubt they're bored with meditation,* Crassmor's brain yammered, *and ready for a spot of excitement.* They were also calling for aid as loudly as they could. He squirmed around for a better grip on two cassocks.

Summoning all his strength in a surprise move, he rammed two heads together. One monk loosened his grip, but the other somehow persevered. Crassmor struck that one square in the face with an almost freed hand. That one, too, lost his hold. The knight, better trained and more experienced than his antagonists, began to batter and writhe his way clear.

His remaining foes tried to redistribute themselves to forestall him. It was a close contest until reinforcements arrived. Crassmor found himself buried under a hill of cassocks. None of the Klybesians purposely struck him; that wasn't their way. Yet somehow, restraining him, they managed to cut off his wind effectively enough. Very shortly, things went black.

# Chapter 20

# BELEAGUERED

**The next thing** he knew was hearing the sound of voices. He looked up as bodies moved aside—though he was kept well pinned—and a light was brought closer to his face.

"Ah, nephew, you are a trial to me."

His vision had cleared sufficiently for Crassmor to see Furd hovering over the tangle of Klybesians and knight. Looking back over his shoulder to someone Crassmor couldn't see, Furd snapped impatiently, "And just where is Brother Tomat, then? *Well?*" The reply satisfied him, though Crassmor didn't catch it. Furd grunted and turned back to his immobilized nephew.

Crassmor heaved once, trying in vain to bridge himself on heels and the rough stone floor that abraded his head. "Weight him steady, blessed lads," Furd encouraged the monks. "See what evidence of evil he carries." Crassmor's pouch was taken from him; a small satisfaction was that he'd left Furd's incriminating letter with Willow.

"Shall we take him up to the mercenaries, Lord Abbot?" ventured one of those not directly involved with the project of holding Crassmor down. "Surely they know how to deal with such a one."

Furd rejected the notion with the slash of a fat hand. "The deed might not lie secret with them; those adventurers are all weak and wicked men. And if Combard were to hear—" It came to Crassmor that there was only debate as to means; killing him seemed to be a foregone conclusion. "No, my son," Furd was saying. "We shall handle this matter in our own manner."

"The garden maze?" another proposed. "We could set him out there."

Furd pulled on his lip. "No; this must be confined strictly to those of us who wear the eye. It shall be the catacombs. I've already sent for Brother Tomat and the key."

There were gasps among the monks. Crassmor redoubled his efforts but accomplished nothing, dreading the catacombs of Virtuary without any clear idea what Furd had in mind. There came footsteps, and a jangling of keys.

"And what of poor Racklee here?" someone asked. "He is dead."

"Two of you take him to my private chambers," Furd said. "We shall make proper disposition of his mortal remains later."

Crassmor felt himself lifted up by many hands. "Sprightly, carefully now!" Furd ordered. "Bear him downstairs, holding him fast. Two of you with those torches, go before; two more come behind. One of you fetch along his sword there. We want no trace of him about." *Shhing*, lifted from where it had come to rest, chimed softly.

The knight was carried down the spiral stairway headfirst, watching the monks who held him and the ceiling overhead. His objections, pleas, and insults were ignored. In time, a hand clamped across his mouth to silence him. At long last there was a halt, as a key grated in a reluctant lock. Hearing the difficulty with which the door was forced, Crassmor knew that many years had passed since its last use.

He was borne through, wondering whether they intended to wall him up, chain him, or simply fling him down a dry cistern. He hoped it would be whichever was quickest. He was carried down into the catacombs of Virtuary, struggling uselessly. Torches threw guttering light onto the patched and blotchy masonry of the groin-vaulted ceiling. Cobwebs and dust had gathered everywhere, and there was a terrible stench of decay and corruption. They passed enormous columns of the foundation of the place and walls of bedrock. Crassmor's hackles were up, but not from the dank chill.

From narrow passageways between the colossal columns, the unusual procession came out at last into an open area beneath a ceiling supported by lesser columns. Passing under a free-standing arch, Crassmor read the inscription: "All Things Cyclical Demand Governance."

They carried him into a circle of heavy stone biers, tombs aligned with their ends pointed at some central spot. The group stopped there and the knight was spread-eagled across stone, some table or altar. He heard the clang of his sword being set aside. There was a complaint of rusty metal and the gritty sound of encrusted chain links. Heavy breathing and the creaking of stubborn hinges indicated effort.

"These manacles are useless," someone commented, "and the leg chains as well. They haven't been used since Grand Abbot Moloko's stewardship, I would wager. I suppose we could bind him well enough with our waist cords."

"No, Tomat," Furd answered absently. "I know a little something that is more reliable. It wouldn't do for all of us to be walking around Virtuary without our belts, or to have him free himself somehow." Crassmor could see Furd staring around in the dark, empty space.

"The summoning spell will work, won't it, Abbot?" one monk asked.

With high indignation, Furd shot back, "Work? Shame on your lack of faith! That just earned you penance. Our revered predecessors have never failed the Klybesians! We have been, er, attending to the ungodly for hundreds of years in just this fashion."

The monk muttered an apology. Furd went on. "Quiet this sinner, and you shall see." He pushed aside two of the monks. The Klybesians were bending to the task of holding the squirming Crassmor. Furd looked into his nephew's face. A hand was removed from the knight's mouth at Furd's gesture.

Another hand slipped the medallion off over Crassmor's head. He began pleading at once. "Uncle, I know we haven't been great favorites of one another, but I have seen the errors of my ways, I swear it. You have always been the forgiving, generous, loving sort—"

"Hush, hush," Furd bade, unheeding. The hand returned, to stop Crassmor's carefully assembled fibs. The abbot began mystic finger passes in the air before Crassmor's eyes, calling Klybesian magic into play. He left little contours of green light in the air.

"Sleep, sleep," Furd chanted. "This spell of somnolence will ease you over. Rest; all will be finished before you know it."

*All what?* the knight tried to shriek; it came out a muffled raving. He found the finger passes strangely restful, his eyelids an insuperable weight. He seemed to drift for a while, as he had in the Jade Dome.

He began to revive after a bit, hearing Furd's voice in the distance in loud incantation. It was discordant, using a language the knight didn't recognize. Crassmor stirred lazily, finding that he was still held. "He wakes, Lord Abbot," one of the monks called.

Furd broke off his chant in irritation. "Only for the moment. I shall renew the spell ere we depart. Now, be silent! I reach the most critical portion of the summoning."

Somehow, Crassmor was unbothered by that. Sleep was all he cared for now. He drifted, warm and comfortable, back toward slumber, vaguely curious about what Furd was summoning. Perhaps he'd ask his uncle, after a little nap . . .

There was the hollow scraping of a heavy stone slab or lid. It penetrated even the somnolence spell, striking to the core of self-preservation in Crassmor, evoking a spasm of effort. He couldn't lift his head; his limbs wouldn't answer his commands, though he was no longer held. He settled for flopping his head in the direction of the sound, a major exertion. He opened his eyes through sheer willpower, spurred by a feeling of dread.

The Klybesians were hurrying back the way they'd come, torches bobbing in the darkness. From a nearby light, he knew they'd left a torch or two behind. Last in line was Furd, herding the rest along. Crassmor thought blurrily that he was glad to see the back of them. He was about to resume his rest when he remembered the sound he'd heard.

Then he noticed the tomb lid's movement.

"Our revered predecessors," Furd had said; that plainly meant Klybesians. *Dead ones!* It came to Crassmor in a flash. Sleep spell or no, he struggled to sit up, gurgling horror he couldn't enunciate, in a hysterical effort to throw off the spell before the dead came fully to life.

Furd caught the choked sound. The abbot looked back from where he stood, fingers flying through the passes again, their green light reinforcing the somnolence. "Sleep, sleep," he chanted, but he was plainly eager to be away. Somewhere, another tomb lid was sliding open.

*And me with no magic of my own,* Crassmor regretted. *It's all so unfair— Ho!* The tripwire in his brain was triggered as simply as that. He tried to speak. There were more scrapings now, tomb lids unmoved in years now loosened by Furd's cantation. When they finally slid aside, the dead would come forth. Already, dry, skeletal rattlings, eager jostlings of creatures resentful of the living, could be heard.

Welling panic gave Crassmor just enough strength to get out the all-important word. "P-peace?"

"Yes, yes," Furd rasped, redoubling the finger passes. "Peace. Know total and eternal peace. Now, *sleep!*"

Crassmor's eyes closed; he never heard Furd's departure or the final sliding aside of tomb covers. But deep within him a turbulence had started, something incompatible with the somnolence spell. A trembling began at the marrow of his bones, spreading outward in shudders of increasing violence. Soon his arms and legs twitched and jumped in convulsive leaps, and his head and torso shook.

"May you never know peace" had been the last curse thrown at him by Fanarion that night in John's Winch. That curse had taken, as he already knew to his own regret and by di Cagliostro's confirmation. Crassmor had gotten his uncle to incorporate the word, setting magic against magic. They weren't particularly powerful spells, but now they were mutually antagonistic.

He felt strange currents flowing through him, his teeth chattering and breath coming unevenly, stretching him tight as a lyre string. Just as he thought that he could bear no more and that his muscles must pull loose of their moorings the terrible tension was gone. He slumped back down, breathing regularly, head clear. The urge to sleep had left him completely.

He was wondering if Fanarion's other spell, that misfortunes pursue him, had been dissipated as well when he felt something grip his arm.

Crassmor unlidded his eyes in utter hysteria. The tombs had opened at Furd's command, letting forth the mummified bodies of Klybesians long since dead. Empty eye sockets glared down at him from skulls that grinned mirthlessly. Clothing and skin flaked away with each movement, dead jaws clicked, and he heard the tread of feet whose shoes were falling away to rot, leaving only bone to plow the dust and drag and clack on the stone.

A dozen of the things closed in around the slab, reaching, grinning. Their finger bones clawed at him as they prepared to perform their office of execution. No living Klybesian was supposed to do murder, at least not directly. That abjuration apparently didn't extend to animated bodies of the dead, a technicality that satisfied the monks.

Crassmor broke his paralysis with a scream, breaking free of the clutching of the Klybesian dead, pounding and beating at them, shaking and twisting. To his surprise, he broke through their ring. Scrambling off the sacrificial slab, he threw himself at one of the nearby pillars, all in blind panic, before they could stop him.

He fought down some of his hysteria, looking around for a weapon, weighing his tactical situation. He wondered if he should simply run, but knew he would have to grab a torch first; he'd like as not knock himself cold against a pillar otherwise.

He became aware of something clinging to his shoulder. It was a bony hand that had maintained its grip when he'd fought free. He beat it off with his fist, yelling at the top of his lungs without realizing it. The dead things were closing in on him, limping and shuffling, reaching.

He looked around frantically for *Shhing*, without success. Then what the frailty of that clinging hand implied occured to him—brittle bones and decayed cartilage.

He understood the meaning of the manacles and leg irons on the sacrificial slab. Until now, victims had always been fastened down and helpless. Crassmor was supposed to have been under Furd's sleep spell. It had been many years since these zombies had been last raised to do a Klybesian murder. Even with the monks' mummification techniques, even with the resurrecting spell, how fragile had the aging corpses become over centuries? *Very, if that broken hand means anything,* he concluded.

Just then a corpse came grasping at him. A total unwillingness to die made him slap the thing's hand away violently. The horrible-smelling corpse was spun around by the force of the blow, sinking to its knees, struggling feebly to rise again. The knight hopped forward a step and kicked with all his might; the thing's skull went flying off its body into the darkness. What remained of the body sprawled in the deep dust, kicking weakly, scrabbling to rise but not appearing likely to do so.

A weight landed on the knight's shoulders. He squirmed, reached, and dragged a second zombie from him. The odor it gave off was appalling, but it struggled with a surprising lack of strength. He raised it up and hurled it against the pillar with all his might. It hit with a cracking of bones and fell to the floor in a heap of dust and ruin.

"You're all falling apart!" he shouted at them in triumph, dancing a little in the wavering torchlight. He advanced at the nearest of the slow-moving things, sticking his tongue out at it and feinting and jabbing, striking too rapidly for it to counter. "You're *crumbling!*"

He ducked, weaved, and cuffed the thing at will. Confused, it batted at him hopelessly. Bobbing under its grasping bony arms, he came up behind it and gave it a hearty shove. It went down on its face, three of its toes breaking off.

Crassmor had already gone on to the next, filled with elation. The creatures had stopped now; it had come to them dimly that things were not as they should be.

The knight began an energetic approach on his next adversary, with exaggerated infighting moves, feinting and crying, "Hah! Stand and deliver, old bag o' bones!"

The corpse made to retreat, but Crassmor got a foot behind its knee and gave it a push. It fell, and he jumped on it with both feet, hearing rib bones cave in and its spine give.

He sprang at another. It managed by chance to strike him with its left hand, a blow of pitifully little power. The blow angered him, though, changing all his fear to fury. He tore the offending arm off, flinging it into the distance with all his might, then punched the corpse as hard as he could. Another skull sailed through the air. He broke apart the remainder of it with his hands and kicked bone from bone with his feet.

Whirling, he found that the corpses were retreating in every direction. *Running for their lives, as it were?* he babbled to himself giddily. He ran to where one was lowering itself back into the only safety it knew, the confines of its tomb, pulling uselessly at the heavy cover.

It saw him coming, and the thing drew back from him, cringing into a corner of its tomb, seeking to get back even farther. Its bones made pitiful scratchings on the stone. Speechless, it still communicated mindless fear.

Crassmor, hands out to drag it forth, suddenly stopped, ashamed. Several mummies were finding their way back to the sanctuary of their resting places. The others, such as could still move, were gone from the circle of torchlight. The knight found that he had no more stomach for terrorizing or destroying these pathetic things; it was bad enough simply to leave them here.

"How do I get out of this place?" he demanded of the one before him. "Come, tell; this Virtuary is a warren to those who know it. There must be underground exits from this valley!"

The thing only persisted in trying to get as far away from him as it possibly could. He bellowed, "Tell me, or I'll smash you to flinders!"

It stopped, shifted. A single fleshless finger was extended, pointing off at a row of pillars. Crassmor went back to the sacrificial slab, searched, and found *Shhing* there. Of his parrying dagger there was no sign. Taking up a torch, he peered along the row of pillars. A faint path had been worn in the stone by centuries of monkish comings and goings. In the distance he saw a small door in a fountain wall, and thought of underground passageways and postern gates.

He went a few more steps. There were deep-etched arrowheads on every third pillar, giving the way to the door. He paused for a last look behind him. The dead Klybesian had pulled its hand back into the tomb.

With dirt and cobwebs from the underground passageways of Virtuary in his hair and on his clothes, Crassmor was at large. He was riding an old nag commandeered— an adjudicator might have called it stolen—from her owner, a gentleman farmer. He'd seen nothing of the Klybesians or their hirelings and didn't know if they were ahead of or behind him. Aware that Willow was alert to trouble, he'd resolved that he must secure help and not simply rush to the Jade Dome. Arriving slightly sooner with one extra sword would be less likely to be of use than coming somewhat later with many.

Thoughts of raising a force at House Tarrant had been dismissed at once. That would bring him into conflict with di Cagliostro, delaying him. For that matter, Crassmor wasn't certain that he wouldn't meet interference from his father. Added to this was the fact that he was away from the Order without permission, having violated his brief leave.

Not knowing whom else he might trust or who, for that matter, would trust him, Crassmor elected to seek the Lost Boys. But contacting them at Gateshield presented another problem, since the fortress was on the alert, all its entrances closely guarded. Being caught outside would amount to disaster, what with the Grand Master's habit of cautiously and slowly sorting out any issue.

As he rode, Crassmor considered the possibilities. Maybe he'd be lucky and some of the Lost Boys would be on guard. If they weren't, on the other hand, they would probably stay clear of the sleeping quarters, where officers of the Order would prevent merrymaking. The kitchens and wine cellars would be off limits to all, but most especially to those scoundrels. The Great Hall would hold no attraction, since no celebration would be permitted there now.

The masters-at-arms and fuglemen would undoubtedly

be looking for all otherwise unoccupied knights to hie them down to the drill fields and lists, which lay outside the fortress, to sharpen their battle skills. There they'd have the opportunity to slip off from the more conscientious knights for some relaxation.

And so, when he arrived at Gateshield, Crassmor rode to the drill field reining up before the deserted reviewing stand. Knights of Onn were dueling and exercising, casting and shooting at targets with assorted weapons, clustering to talk and pass time. Nowhere could Crassmor see his friends until he heard raucous, conspiratorial laughter. He spotted a group of men who were lounging in the gloom under the reviewing stand, with backs against its uprights—the Lost Boys, ignoring their hard-practicing fellows.

There was a dice game in progress. Crassmor saw a number of bottles, jugs, and decanters being passed from hand to hand, lit by the slots of sunlight that penetrated there. He dismounted; his nag, completely done in, stood with head lowered and legs trembling. He bent over to go in under the reviewing stand, pulling back his hood.

Hoowar Roisterer was there, and Crane, along with Pony-Keg. Griffin, sitting in one of the larger pools of light, was penning another of his scholarly monographs. Crassmor was surprised to see an outsider among them, his cousin Bint, looking moody and taking his turn at a drinking jar when it came his way.

Arananth had thrown herself into life at court, unwilling to stay at House Tarrant while Bint was confined to Gateshield. The gifts and poems and flowers he'd had deilvered to her had brought only the briefest, most noncommittal messages in response; she was simply taken with the social whirl of Dreambourn. Bint had found that he didn't hold it against her, but somehow he no longer wished the companionship of the more proper and upright knights.

The Lost Boys inspected the newcomer as he stepped into a shaft of sunlight. "Might be Crassmor," Hoowar hazarded, "save that if the bumpkin has any sense left, he'll stay clear of this place and the Grand Master for good."

" 'Tis as I did always say," Pony-Keg contributed. "That

beard did a great service in concealing an altogether unprepossessing chin."

"Cannot say that I am much taken with the dyed hair either," Crane added, his bucktoothed smirk making him look like a fourteen-year-old. "Have you considered a periwig, good Crassmor?"

"I have need of you all," Crassmor panted in reply.

Hoowar Roisterer cocked an eye at him and rumbled unhappily, then backhanded beer foam from his mustache. "You arrive breathing hard and all in a commotion?" he observed. "Anxious for aid and most intense? Go away, Crassmor; this smacks to me of sword work!"

"It is in poor taste," Crane added.

"Violates all our traditions," sir Logran the Wooer pointed out.

"I wonder if dinner's ready yet?" Pony-Keg asked Griffin, who only shrugged and grinned.

Crassmor hadn't moved; he knew just how they felt. Hoowar snarled, "Begone! This poor little jug's young yet and has no one else but me to care for it!"

*"Harken to me!"* the Tarrant son roared, throwing himself at the stout knight. He stopped when Hoowar raised the drinking vessel, threatening swift reprisal. Crassmor went on. "There is a force of arms on its way even now to the Jade Dome. They mean to raid and to slay."

The Lost Boys looked at one another and shifted uncomfortably at that. "I'll drag by his gorget the man who refuses to come!" Crassmor vowed. They saw that he meant it and traded dubious glances.

"Why not speak to the Grand Master like a good chap?" Bosrow Feng suggested. "Have him round up a number of knights. A multitude of them. I should be happy to ride rearguard."

"A poor idea," Bint put in. "Crassmor is accounted absent without permission. Jaan-Marl is more than moderately displeased."

Crassmor said in a level tone, "By the time explanations are made, Willow will be dead."

That startled all of them. Willow had shown special affection for the Lost Boys and hosted their revelries many times. "And di Cagliostro will control the Jade Dome. No time to go into it now, but it will put the Singularity in his grip. He means to rule here."

They all knew of the count. "There's always been good guesting at House Comullo," Pony-Keg admitted. "I should hate to see us lose a soft touch."

"It's not a bad day for a ride," Crane conceded, scratching his cowlick.

"But no war mounts or saddle horses may leave the stables without the Grand Master's permission," Hoowar reminded them all. "He's set an officer to make certain."

Griffin closed his inkwell and put his materials aside carefully. "If we cannot have chargers, we shall simply have to travel by other means. Or do we let Willow come to harm?"

They immediately began to gather themselves up. Griffin showed his handsome smile. "Hoowar, tell the stablemaster to turn his head the other way for a moment while you take something suitable from the Order's vehicle collection. There shouldn't be any officers watching that or the draft animals. Tell the stablemaster that if he does not comply, we'll let the head kitchener know who's been dancing the horizontal with his wife."

"And what if Jaan-Marl comes after us in hot pursuit?" Pony-Keg demanded.

"So much the better, as long as he doesn't catch us until we get to the Jade Dome," Crassmor was quick to declare.

A change came over them as they prepared, a crispness of action. Crassmor turned to Bint, who was also making ready to come. "You have changed the company you keep."

Bint's face was set. "Arananth has time for many suitors, it seems. Your friends aren't such a bad lot."

*No, they are not,* Crassmor thought, suddenly feeling himself a fortunate man. He clapped his cousin on the shoulder. "She's not the first to fall in love with life in Creambourn; you can't blame her too much." It was only then that he noticed that Bint now wore the beautiful sword of Tarafon Quickhand, purchased out of hock.

Having levered himself up, Hoowar tossed down some more beer. "Mark me: the Grand Master won't like this."

Griffin chuckled. "Yes; Jaan-Marl might even send us out into the Beyonds, eh?" The Lost Boys all found a moment in which to laugh.

## Chapter 21

# ENLIGHTENED

**Aware of the** glittering selection of cutlery available to the jealous kitchener, the stablemaster cooperated. Minutes later, as Crassmor paced and slapped fist to palm in frustration, Hoowar Roisterer returned.

He was at the reins of one of the prizes of the fortress' collection of outland vehicles; its incomprehensible name was Skiver/Newsham Delux. It was a fire-fighting wagon, some seven paces or more in length, all red-painted wood and gleaming brass fittings, high black wheels and long pumping arms. Hoowar drew in sharply where the rest waited. The eight horses in the team stamped and snorted, tossing their heads, eager to run.

"We might conceivably attract attention with that," Pony-Keg conjectured.

"*Board!*" Crassmor hollered. "We've little time!" He was already swarming up to sit next to Hoowar, taking the reins from him. "How'd you get it hitched up so quickly?"

Hoowar stroked his beard proudly. "The stablemaster was more than eager to see me gone. Had his helpers and boys jump to it. I told them all that I'd thrash any one of 'em who didn't agree that the whole deed was mine."

Other knights and officers of the Order were pausing from their drill to see what was going on. Lost Boys climbed aboard the Skiver/Newsham, ducking under pumping arms to find seats on the central benches and setting their feet on the treadles. Others stood on the running boards. Crassmor took the whip from its socket and cracked it; the firewagon started with a jerk, its passengers clinging with both hands.

Crassmor guided it around in a violent turn; a forty-foot high length of greased leather hose went sliding from its well. Then they were banging off toward the Jade Dome while water sloshed in the wagon's cisterns.

In one manner, at least, the vehicle was ideal; all other traffic scattered before it. Hoowar discovered a particular delight in ringing the brass bell mounted behind the driver's bench. The horses, having pulled the wagon before, worked well. The Lost Boys, used to finding what entertainment they could in whatever situation the fates threw their way, took pleasure in Crassmor's utter disregard for courtesies of the road.

Lesser personages were used to getting out of the way of larger or more important vehicles or riders, but aristocrats' carriage drivers, knights and officials of one kind or another, and pious clerics were unaccustomed to yielding the way. They learned quickly, seeing the big wagon bearing down on them at top speed, spending more time in the air than on the road. Sedan chairs, oxcarts, and pedestrians of all stripes were at great pains to get out of the way as promptly as possible. But one rider, a huge, mightily thewed, sun-browned swordsman, apparently considered himself deadly insulted by the Skiver/Newsham's near-collision with him.

He came galloping after, long raven locks flying, waving a broadsword. Crane and Pony-Keg, who knew something of the firewagon's operation, got the men seated on the benches to work the auxiliary pumping treadles. Griffin aimed the brass playpipe. A stream of water gushed forth, straight into the face of their pursuer, also drenching his frightened horse. The man howled his fury as the horse lost its footing. The Lost Boys left the man in a sudden mud puddle in the middle of the road. The swordsman shook a fearsome, scarred fist at them as they bounced off.

Crassmor had taken little note of this or any obstacle before him. He was watching worriedly for the armed band from Virtuary. Had he come upon them on the road, his intention had been simply to ride through their formation, eliminating whom he could, and carry on the fight from the firewagon, since the Skiver/Newsham Delux couldn't outrace horsemen. He saw no sign of them and slowed the horses slightly to save the team for the extended trip to House Comullo.

As he drove, he yelled what few words of explanation he could to Hoowar. When the firewagon came jolting over the top of the last hill, Crassmor saw in the distance a turmoil around the gates of the place. The sight of the gates of House Comullo ajar put a chill in his spine. Men fought there; the knight could make out both the diverse costumes of the hirelings and the colors of Willow's guardsmen.

Hoowar saw too, shouted to the others, and pointed. There was still a considerable distance to cover across the valley. As they watched, the mercenaries fighting before the gates began to pour into the bailey.

"Too late!" the fat knight mourned over the furor of their passage. "They'll be into the Jade Dome before we can get there."

Crassmor shook his head. "We've got just enough time; tell the others to be ready."

Hoowar asked, "How can they not be in the Dome in good time? Did you not say they know it from a model of the place?"

Crassmor nodded without taking his eyes from the road. "Aye. But before I was discovered at Virtuary, I gave its Dome-piece a half-turn within the rest of the model."

The Roisterer exhaled a laugh that rose above the noise of the wind. "They will be fumbling around so badly that they'll have trouble finding their own arses!" He slammed a meaty hand against his thigh, then turned to warn the others to prepare.

Crassmor had to stand, one foot braced on the driver's footrest, one on the brake, and haul with all his might to bring the team in and gradually halt the Skiver/Newsham Delux. Before it had stopped, he sprang down with *Shhing* in his hand and ran for the still-open gates. At his back came the Lost Boys, blades out, no longer merry.

In the bailey was Fordall Urth, prone, moving feebly. Around him were others of Willow's guardsmen; all bore wounds, and several were almost certainly dead. They were no longer the fierce, hulking sentinels Crassmor had been permitted to glimpse, but aging, out-of-condition pensioners. That would be di Cagliostro's doing. In some magus fashion, he'd used the disguising magic of the guards against them, making them in fact what they'd only appeared to be, forcing substance to conform to illusion. To be sure, the count had had ample time and resources to ready such an enchantment during his stay at House Tarrant. But the guardsmen had given what battle they could; Klybesian hirelings, wounded and dead, were on the scene too.

Crassmor took in and thought all of this as he charged across the bailey without pause. Through the main doors of the keep he dashed, into the gloom of ill-kept, ill-lit corridors. Then he slid to a stop. The Lost Boys caught up with him as he tried to think.

"Which way?" Griffin pressed him.

"They'll think the entrance lies that way, to the left," Crassmor answered, "when in fact it's to the right." *If Furd didn't notice the discrepancy,* Crassmor added to himself. He could only hope it was so. Furd had never been one to occupy himself with details; there was a good chance that the abbot had taken only a cursory look at the model. Racklee had joined his ancestors, and there had been no one else in Virtuary who could have spotted the deception.

" 'Twill not take 'em long to find out they've been diddled," Hoowar predicted.

"Then we'll go straight on," Crassmor decided, "as near the Dome as we can get, and cut to the right." Off he sprinted, concentrating on recalling the layout of the place, the others close behind him. The compulsion put upon the mercenaries with the aid of the altered model would make it possible for them to find their way around despite House Comullo's spells of misdirection and glamours of confusion. The best course for the raiders, once they'd discovered their error and found no doorway to the Jade Dome, Crassmor concluded, would be to skirt along the Dome and search for it. If Crassmor and his friends intercepted the hirelings, all well and good; getting to the Dome's doorway first, on the other hand, the Lost Boys would be able to defend it. What clutched at Crassmor's heart was the fear that they might be too late.

He led the way through the hall, across the little laird's garden, and down homecoming walk. Moments later, he was rushing down the grand staircase at the keep's fest-hall, and speculation became reality. He heard, then spied, the company of armed men running in his direction from the left.

The Lost Boys raced down the steps, savage in attack now that they were committed to it. The numbers of the two groups were closely matched.

Crassmor, riding surprise like a charger, threw himself in among the mercenaries with a two-handed swing of his sword. Before him was a hireling decked out in a crude ring-mail hauberk, wearing a helm of boar's tusks, and carrying a round shield and spike-headed mace. Astonishment made the man slow to react. *Shhing* found an unprotected spot under his arm as he threw up his shield; the man fell before he was well aware of what was happening, blood pumping from him rhythmically.

The knight turned just as another mercenary, bearing a greatsword the height of a man, brought it up in defense. This was the fellow who'd ridden to Virtuary with Crassmor, the one who'd termed himself a *landsknecht*. The *landsknecht* held his weapon's leather-bound ricasso to shorten his grip for close fighting. Crassmor had brought his lighter blade around quickly, to his great advantage. He put his shoulders behind it, battering down the heavier greatsword. The place was chaotic with the general mêlée that had ignited all around him.

There was a fleeting moment in which the knight saw in his opponent's eyes the knowledge that no maneuver would save him, a forever-instant. But the *landsknecht* tried, with an upward slash, backstepping at the same time, pulling frantically on the ricasso for that stroke. His ribbons and plumes swirled. Crassmor deflected the stroke blade to blade, the respective leverages favoring him. He was inside the other's guard, rammed hilts aside, and ran him through.

The man let his weapon fall as his knees gave, his hands clutched to his neck.

Crassmor turned to look on the part of hell suddenly let forth in House Comullo. The Lost Boys, for all their storied reluctance, were hardened Knights of Onn; the Klybesians had enlisted veteran, uncaring warriors and motivated them with compulsion. The fest-hall was filled with swirling combat, darting weapons, cries, pealing steel, and death.

Crassmor spied di Cagliostro among the raiders, staying well back, plainly under no compulsion; the count saw him as well. Though the heavyset little mage carried a long, thin blade, he had no intention of putting his life at risk. Instead, he yelled to one of his men, "Teach!"

The knight followed his enemy's glance and saw an enormous man in a red, knee-length coat and high black boots. The hireling had tied slow-burning wax matches in among the plaits of his black beard and set them alight for the raid, tucking others under the wide brim of his hat. The sight made his scarred, hate-mad face doubly intimidating. He bore a bloodied weapon of the sort Crassmor knew to be a cutlass.

Teach, if that was his name rather than a mannered injunction from di Cagliostro, saw whom his master had singled out with a point of the rapier. Some distance separated them; Crassmor expected to see the man come at him. Instead, Teach pulled a bludgeon-sized device of wood and metal from his baldric and pointed its hollow end at the knight.

Firearms weren't unknown in the Singularity, though they were rarities. Crassmor had been around long enough, in both the Singularity and the Beyonds, to duck when a hollow tube was aimed his way. There was the puff of the weapon's primer pan. An instant later the pistol belched flame and black smoke with a roar. Something whizzed past the knight's ear and ricocheted off the marble banister, whining away into the distance. Some of the combatants seemed shocked, but there was only a slight lull in the battle. In an instant it had resumed at full pitch.

Teach hurled the pistol aside, which told Crassmor that it was a single-shot weapon. The man apparently had no other; he rushed at the knight, dodging other fighters, cutlass raised high.

Their swords belled from one another. Crassmor quickly found that his foeman used both edge and point. He was dangerous by dint of his size and brute strength, but not as skilled as Crassmor had feared. Teach was a hacker, very like a berserker, but quick to defend himself from Crassmor's parry-riposte.

The knight ignored the slow-burning matches and ferocious grimacing, pressing his attack. Teach, eyes bulging, roared, cursed, and foamed at the mouth, but he'd come up against the only man in House Comullo at a higher emotional pitch than he. Willow was in danger; Crassmor couldn't have cared less about Teach's histrionics. Crassmor used *Shhing* one-handedly for the most part, but resorted to two hands when Teach's maniacal attacks demanded it.

Teach put him on a determined defensive with an especially furious advance. The knight withdrew slowly, a foot or two at a time, waiting, countering when he could. In time, the cutlass, much the heavier weapon, must tire even this giant.

The attack began to flag. Crassmor threw all his strength into a bind, taking the cutlass around. The bigger man exerted himself to work out of it, as the knight had thought he would. Crassmor reversed the bind, carrying the movement, and found a clear way. *Shhing* flashed. Teach threw himself back, taking the slash across his ruffled shirt and the flesh of his chest instead of his throat. It put him off balance.

Crassmor followed up with a drawing cut, opening the man's forearm to the bone. Teach dropped the cutlass, clapping left hand to forearm to staunch the blood flow. The madness left his face; it looked to Crassmor as if the trauma of the wounds had wiped the compulsion away. The wounds slowed him little, however; Teach turned and ran, high boot tops flopping, the matches and his beard whipping back, abandoning the fight.

There was the sound of a body hitting the floor behind Crassmor. He pivoted, to see another hireling, a man dressed in greaves, breastplate, and horsehair-plumed helmet, stretched out face down. His tower shield had fallen from his arm, and one of Crane's throwing crosses stood out from the hireling's back. Crassmor had no opportunity to thank the gawky knight for saving him from the mercenary's shortsword; Crane was already engaged with another opponent. For all his resemblance to a bucktoothed adolescent at other times, Crane was lethal and self-assured now.

Crassmor scanned the fight, looking for di Cagliostro, but saw him nowhere. Hoowar Roisterer, swinging his broadsword two-handedly, was being backed toward a wall by two adversaries. As he was about to be joined by Logran the Wooer, he needed no help from Crassmor. Another Lost Boy, Kylon of Beck, though wounded, was holding his own against a tall, hawk-faced man who wielded a scimitar and was also losing blood. Griffin was putting on a dazzling display of the fencing style he'd evolved from the many he'd come to know. He was against an equally able foe, a cadaverous fellow in brocade who also knew a great deal about that art.

Nowhere in the confusion could Crassmor see di Cagliostro. He was struck by the sudden conviction that the count had gone on toward the Dome and Willow. The knight started off in that direction, only to have his way blocked by a fox-faced man with a wickedly curled mustache and a darting rapier. There was no getting around him; Crassmor agonized over what the delay might cost.

All at once there was a third man on the scene, back to Crassmor, sword *en garde*—Bint, with Tarafon Quickhand's weapon. Fox-face's eyes opened a little and one eyebrow lifted. He engaged the young knight. Bint answered well. As they ran a quick dialogue of blades, Crassmor found his way clear. He bit his lip, seeing the opportunity to go on, but fearing for his cousin; this opponent was very capable.

"Go on" Bint hollered without looking aside. "I am a Knight of Onn! Go save her!"

Crassmor hesitated no longer. As he sprinted by, he took

a cut at Fox-face. The man ducked without appearing to look aside, after which he bore in hard on Bint.

Noise of the battle fell behind as Crassmor raced along corridors he knew well. He was certain that House Comullo's minor defensive magics would not have deterred the mage for long, since he had Racklee's findings to work from.

Crassmor got to the flambeau-lit door of the Jade Dome, only to find it closed, with no indication that anyone had passed through. It was in his mind to enter; he eyed the eagle talons at either side of the door.

Then it occurred to him that even if di Cagliostro had developed some sorcerous method of divining the secret of the door, it would have demanded time and invocation to bring that spell to bear. The mage hadn't had that much head start on the knight. There was another, more certain way of discovering the correct latch handle: by waiting until Crassmor, Willow, or someone else used it.

The knight stopped well short of the door, peering suspiciously into every shadow, bringing *Shhing* up to the ready. Di Cagliostro stepped from behind the concealment of a decorative pillar.

"I'd thought you would be along soon, young Tarrant," the count said with no rancor. "I have seen that this door might resist my spells, putting me at considerable hazard. It was my hope that you would reveal to me which talon gives entrance, and which death." He moved closer.

Crassmor gazed at him over *Shhing*'s bright length, but di Cagliostro's rapier was sheathed. The count waved at the knight's weapon. "No need; I am more than convinced of your aptitude by now. There is always time to fight, and all too little to talk. Moreover, I am no swordsman."

"Reassuring words on any other occasion," Crassmor scoffed.

"The issue has come to a certain pass," the count continued. "I find it preferable to reason with you. You have much to gain by helping me, as much as I have by succeeding."

"After you and those eye-in-pyramid monks control the Tapestry? After the Klybesians are in charge?"

Di Cagliostro shook his head indulgently. "I have allowed the monks to think that. They've coveted the treasure of House Comullo since they first learned of its powers." The thick lips shaped a smile of surprising appeal; the dark eyes windowed that luminous personality.

"The eye-in-pyramid isn't served by the Klybesians alone, Crassmor. Its influence and power reach through space and time. I was once hierophant to it, but that is behind me. The monks do not know that, or they would never have helped me. My intent is not to control the Tapestry; I mean to destroy it."

Crassmor was astonished. "Destr—surely you knew before I—the Pattern controls the Singularity, at least to some extent. What can be served by destroying it?"

"Its loss would seal off the Beyonds from all Realities," the count answered calmly. Crassmor saw that the man relished the scene, loved the drama for itself, arguing there by the Jade Dome. "And my motive? This area is unique. Sealed off from outside influences, it would be the perfect place in which to achieve true communion with the Eternal. Complete, sublime, and permanent. That has always eluded me."

Crassmor was caught up by the captivating voice, the seductive words, the riveting eyes. Unnoticed, *Shhing's* point lowered. "I cannot underst—"

"A woman," di Cagliostro interrupted. "A situation not altogether unlike your own. My Lorenza!" That beautiful voice truly soared now. "My beloved, my betrayer; still I search for her, still I yearn for her. She is dead. There is no rejoining her save in the Eternal, in perfect union. Simple death would not do; too much of essence is lost."

He was amused at Crassmor's incredulity. "I have escaped spells in my travails, Sir Knight, yes, and graves as well." He rubbed a finger over the letters INRI on his heavy ring. "It is of no use to me to be reborn from death, intact and pure, without Lorenza, although I could be. *I could be!* I am an Unknown Superior, Crassmor, a Noble Voyager. The idea of altering a cosmos is not so much."

Crassmor's brain was aswim in the idea. "But can the Singularity remain with no Beyonds and no Realities to stabilize it? Can the center of a spiderweb remain when its strands are cut? Willow said—"

"Willow is nothing but a country witch!" di Cagliostro snapped, his irritation showing for the first time. He reasserted control. "You could be with her, take up the Tarrant heritage."

Crassmor tossed his head, throwing back a strand of dyed hair. "I'll take Willow's counsel first."

"She has no say in this! Nor would you have, if it weren't more expedient. If I must, I'll resort to spellcraft. Now, which talon?"

Crassmor evaded. "There is still the cyclops; Pysthesis may be within."

Di Cagliostro was more composed. "I know all about the big fellow; he poses no problem to me." The contours of the fleshy face hardened again. "I shan't ask you another time."

Several times in the moments during which they glared at each other then, Crassmor was close to agreeing. An end to his wanderings and perils; Willow and a home; those were nearly more powerful enticements than he could resist.

But the count spoke first, breaking the deadlock. "Very well."

His hand came up, not in the subtle passes of minor magic, but with the stark pointing of a forefinger. The incandescent eyes held Crassmor's and transmitted their owner's will.

"You are numb," the count intoned. "You are leaden."

Crassmor found himself powerless. Arms and legs were suddenly weighted; *Shhing* fell to the stone with a clang.

"Your limbs are becoming stiff," the magus told him in a voice that was at once drone and revelation. The world began to go dark; Crassmor knew that in another moment he would fall. He puzzled briefly over why di Cagliostro didn't simply command him to point out the correct talon. Perhaps the count's arts, here in the Singularity, didn't permit him such precise ordination, or perhaps he didn't trust—

The plan came to Crassmor just that quickly. The knight drew on all his reserves in a simple effort, with no regard for what it might cost. He threw himself at the right-hand talon.

Di Cagliostro yelled with the sudden comprehension that came to him, shocked and horrified. But Crassmor missed it by fingers' widths as the paralysis took complete hold. The floor rose up to smack him.

Di Cagliostro stood over the fallen knight. "And they call *you* coward? You would have opened the door the wrong way to save her!" He stooped and, with unaccustomed effort, dragged Crassmor's body to one side. Between grunts of exertion, he added, "I will not hurt her. I hope that we may still be friends, Crassmor; you understand love."

Still puffing, di Cagliostro was within Crassmor's line of vision as he stepped to the left hand talon and turned it, pulling. The door had no sooner opened a crack than it threw itself wide, of its own accord. A gale blew into the corridor, sulfurous and hot and evil. Crassmor heard di Cagliostro's scream quite clearly.

The Guardian sat in the dark, incomprehensible zone beyond the door, lit as if by searchlights set a half-mile behind it. It sat in a perfect lotus position, fat, naked, slack of lip and empty of eye. It would have looked for all the world like an idiotic baby, but for the giant blood vessels that thrummed across its skull.

It made a foolish, calculated smile. The count squealed like a throat-slit pig. He moved sideways, but an enormous, fat hand blocked him there. Di Cagliostro saw that it was no use to go the other way; the floor of House Comullo had resounded to the descent of another hand. The thing boxed di Cagliostro between its hands; numb as he was and still hating the count, Crassmor felt sorry for him.

Simple as an infant, malign as a psychopath the Guardian reached out for di Cagliostro with its blubbery fists. The count couldn't avoid it; he was pulled toward the yawning doorway as Crassmor lay, stunned, on the floor.

Di Cagliostro's hands caught at the side of the doorframe, holding for a moment against the strength of the Guardian, a ridiculous, doomed contest. The count looked around as smoke tongued all about him as if in anger. Those marvelous eyes met Crassmor's and held them. Crassmor could only stare, knowing that he would never forget the pleading and anguish he saw. Di Cagliostro was yanked into the awful universe where the Guardian resided. His howl echoed and echoed back through infinite space: *"Lorenza!"*

The door then slammed closed, shutting up the winds of space and time. Its lock sounded a muted click.

Di Cagliostro's spell had already begun to wane; now it dissipated completely. Crassmor rose, quivering, and sheathed *Shhing*. He turned to the other talon, the correct one, twisted and pulled it, and looked into the Jade Dome.

It was all silence in there, with the brilliance of the Pattern in the flutter of air from the doorway. Pysthesis sat cross-legged off to the side, his one eye unfocused. Of Willow there was no sign. Radiance crisscrossed the Tapestry.

*Destroy it,* di Cagliostro had said, promising peace and Willow. In a moment Crassmor had hoisted a flambeau from its socket, reckoning that fire would be quickest. Flames lit the inverted bowl of the Dome with unaccustomed vividness as he crossed the carpet. The cyclops made no move to interfere. Crassmor's shadow jumped eerily under him.

He looked up at the Pattern that bound together so many threads. Willow would be somewhere nearby; Crassmor could have her hand in his before the Pattern was consumed. *Then either we'll be safe and together or the world will pull apart. I would prefer either one to this. I shall hold her hand and hope.*

He tilted the flambeau forward, murmuring, "Your reign is done." But he hesitated because it was Willow's treasure. "What good have you done? Not saved Sandur, not softened Combard's heart. And Willow? You have no intention of giving her up, have you?"

Flames leaped, hungry for the Tapestry. Crassmor swayed, exhausted and drained but lucid with decision. "You moved us all to save yourself. How will you save yourself *now?*"

Orange-yellow flickers stretched themselves to taste the Tapestry's edge . . .

The Tapestry heeded the knight, acting to save itself. Blinding glare burst across the Pattern. Crassmor cried out, blinking like a mole, shielding his eyes with one hand, nearly dropping the flambeau. He spilled fire onto the carpet, but the flames didn't take; they merely made the carpet smolder.

Crassmor had the meanings and implications of the Pattern opened to him, searing him like a sunburst. He saw the significance of every part of the Pattern. It was more information than his mind could deal with. A part of it said to him: "Nothing Is Precisely Cyclical." Crassmor saw friends, strangers, influences and effects, strands of the past and inferences of the future. He saw the elements of the Pattern that were himself and Willow.

Combard's touched theirs often, and Teerse's, Jaan-Marl's, and Ironwicca's. Designs sprang from Sandur's persona. Crassmor's mind and eyes were drawn to extrapolation. The Pattern spoke to the knight about danger and hardship and the chaotic influence that was the Beyonds. It told of privation and, worst of all, of separation from Willow. Yet its implications were specific; the element that was Willow and the one that was Crassmor were moving toward a final joining. They would be together, remain together, if they lived; if no new element appeared; if Crassmor weren't killed in the Beyonds.

He put aside misgivings. It might be madness or ruse, this vision, but he couldn't bring himself to destroy it. That part of the Pattern that represented himself and Willow suggested a continuance, offspring. That the vision might be false didn't matter; he couldn't harm the Tapestry. So much was such a future to be desired . . .

Crassmor held the flambeau upright, stamping out the smoldering carpet, coughing in the smoke. When he looked up, his new Sight had left him. The Pattern was only a confused running-together of unfathomable lights.

From where she'd stood and watched, Willow came forth, dressed in the costume of a gaucho. A perplexed Crassmor wondered where she'd been; there were no places of concalment in the Jade Dome. *More work of the Tapestry?*

It came to him that she'd have let him burn it if he'd so decided.

Willow smiled, blinking back tears. "I would have relied on something stronger than the Pattern to hold you to me."

"Willow, I—I *saw*—"

"Nothing like that has ever happened before," she told him. "The Pattern is as you saw it, though you're not of Comullo blood. It carries a hope that we will win ourselves a life together after all."

He remembered suddenly. "Bint!" He'd left the mêlée in full session.

Before he could bolt, she pressed Furd's note into his hand. "Furd came that night to see if you were dead."

Then he was running for the door, pulling at *Shhing*. "Stay here! The battle's not over yet!"

## Chapter 22

# RESIGNED

Sir Crassmor was wrong. The battle for House Comullo was over and won. He wondered whether this undeclared war was finished, though.

In the place where he'd left the fight raging, he found its aftermath. Di Cagliostro's hirelings were all dead or captive, save for the man Teach, who had escaped. Among the Lost Boys there were more than enough wounds to go around and two lost lives: Bosrow Feng, the première rider, and Bram Lydis, the two-sworder. Bosrow had been stabbed in the back while extricating Bint from an uneven combat. Crassmor's cousin, wounded in the duel in which he had slain the fox-faced swordsman, had been pitted against two foemen. A moment too late, Crane had cut down the man who'd killed Bosrow.

Hoowar Roisterer had been wounded a half-dozen times

in degrees between a minor pinking and a slash that had opened his side. Griffin knelt by him now, suturing the cut with a needle and some flax thread borrowed from a servitor. He exhibited the skill of a field surgeon. Pony-Keg, seeing Crassmor, told him, "Those few who were left on their feet keeled over all at once, as if life had left them."

Crassmor absorbed that, willing to wager that it had been the same moment in which di Cagliostro had met his doom at the Jade Dome. Bint was seated by Sir Bosrow Feng's lifeless body, mourning, reflecting, Crassmor didn't doubt, on the odd fact that one life often cost another.

As Crassmor went to him, Bint looked up. "He's—"

"The Lost Boys try not to use that word," Crassmor cautioned. "Bosrow would undoubtedly prefer you to say that he's no longer available for errantry. And only blame yourself if you wouldn't have done the same for him; that is another rule." Bint nodded and got to his feet.

A commotion of many men and the sounds of weapons and armor came to them. Hoowar sighed and groped for his broadsword even as Griffin tied off the last stitch. "Seems there's no end to it," the fat knight grumbled.

"Put aside that sword and hush, you clown," Griffin chided, "else you ruin my fine needlepoint. This is no attack."

He was right. Jaan-Marl appeared at the head of the stairs along with Combard and a throng of Knights of Onn. Combard turned to call back over his shoulder, "Here! They are in the fest-hall!" It occurred to Crassmor that there would probably be some problem in rounding up knights who'd become confused by glamours and defensive enchantments.

Combard descended the steps at a labored run, with the others up close behind. Before he'd reached the bottom step, he was demanding, "What losses? Di Cagliostro was seen coming this way with an armed band." He took in Crassmor's disreputable clothing, blackened hair, and lack of beard and mustache. "Where is he?"

Crassmor gestured to Bosrow Feng and Bram Lydis. "Here are two of us who'll never ride forth again, father."

The rest survive, if with clips and cuts. The Tapestry is safe; the count met the Guardian of the Dome."

A scowling Jaan-Marl was at Combard's elbow. To him, Crassmor said, "We are here without your permission, Master, but all guilt is mine. The Tapestry is undamaged." The Grand Master's face showed that he appreciated the importance of that. "Had it been a matter of a few more minutes, things would have been otherwise. There was no time to obtain your permission."

"I shall pass judgment on that when I have heard all. It lies in your favor that, as I see, the Jade Dome was menaced but saved. I am less angry with you now than when the officers reported the departure of this group from Gateshield, less angry than when your father and I set out on your trail."

"I believe you will find my motive sound, if not my method," Crassmor declared.

Another man came bustling in, the abbot Furd, edging through the crowding knights. He threw both arms around his shocked nephew.

"Thank the Klybesian Holy you're safe, m'boy! I come here with word of vile plotting against this House; I see I am too late, but that all is well. Blessing indeed!"

More likely, Crassmor thought, Furd had somehow found out that the Klybesian dead had failed to carry out his will, and had hastened here to House Comullo either to warn di Cagliostro or to claim his own innocence, depending on which way things went. Seeing the place swarming with Knights of the Order, the abbot had wisely chosen the latter course.

Crassmor pushed his uncle out to arm's length with a bleak smile. "I think there will be right punishment meted out for this, Furd."

Furd smiled back blandly. "There has already been, of a sort. This plot involved some of the members of my own religion, can you imagine? The ringleaders, being found out, confessed all to me, then took their own lives. Most un-Klybesian. Shows how far the wretches—the poor, misguided sinners—had gone astray."

That some of the eye-in-pyramid monks were already

dead, Crassmor didn't doubt in the least. He wondered if they'd sacrificed their lives for their cause—or had that decision been made for them by the abbot? Crassmor took out the note he'd recovered from Willow, the one he'd taken from Mooncollar's script, implicating Furd. He saw that the abbot recognized it. As Crassmor was about to reveal its content, Furd drew out a letter of his own.

"This is yours, I believe, nephew. An epistle of no importance, but I found it in the possession of one of the plotters."

Crassmor stopped, seeing it was the note Willow had written to him when she'd had her guards turn him away. It had been taken from him at Virtuary, he recalled now; events had moved so swiftly that this was the first time he'd realized that.

"No doubt they wished to copy your hand for some purpose of knavery," Furd added.

He'd made himself clear. Any airing of charges and countercharges would see the letter brought to light. The letter would be a terrible wound to Combard, Willow's statement in her own hand that she'd never loved Sandur, but only Crassmor. It would rekindle the old man's rage and resentment.

And what good would be the airing of Furd's note? It was unsigned, in a scribe's handwriting. It held nothing incriminating in and of itself. The knight guessed, too, that there would be no witnesses available at Virtuary; Furd's agents were undoubtedly abroad even now.

Before all else, Crassmor considered the threat to the promise he'd seen in the Pattern. A royal inquiry, with its revelations, stood a good chance of pushing Combard to a public act of fury, giving Willow to some other man. No new element must be introduced to that part of the Pattern.

"Ah, yes, thank you," Crassmor replied smoothly. He looked aside and saw Combard and Jaan-Marl organizing the evacuation of the wounded, ignoring the conversation. Furd watched him expectantly. "And this may be of interest to you; something to do with the plotters, I think." He was already making up lies as to where he'd been and what had happened after he'd left Gateshield that night.

"I shall root the blackguards out to the last man," Furd vowed. He contrived to look casual as he and Crassmor exchanged evidence. Each man assured himself he'd been given what had been agreed.

Hoowar Roisterer clapped the Grand Master on the back as Jaan-Marl, suffering the action without comment, helped him out. There was a somber sense of fellowship among the Lost Boys in which neither the Grand Master nor any other man there, except Bint, could take part. In the bailey, Fordall Urth and the other guardsmen who'd survived were being ministered to. Fordall, who'd seemed at death's door before, now looked merely like an old man who'd taken a less-than-lethal wound. Crassmor assumed that his disguised strength had returned to him with di Cagliostro's demise.

Combard cleared his throat as he and Crassmor watched the Lost Boys resume their places on the Skiver/Newsham Delux. "Well fought," the old man allowed, hands locked behind his back. "You seem determined to be a hero on your own terms."

"My own terms include nothing of being a hero," Crassmor answered.

Combard's face darkened. "That is not a good sentiment. There is also this matter of your failure in discipline. You are still away from Gateshield without permission and have much to answer for, do you realize that?"

"Which is more important—doing, or failing with propriety?"

"Enough!" Combard commanded, brows closing in like a blizzard front.

Just then there was the clatter of iron-shod hooves. The King galloped into the bailey at the head of a troop of Royal Borderers. Men bowed low, even the wounded among the Lost Boys. Ironwicca was helmed and clad for war.

"It seems I am tardy," he declared. "When the Order rides forth, it behooves me to come seek out what the problem is. But matters are well in hand, I see."

Of course, he would have his own sources of information on movements at Gateshield; word of goings-on throughout the Singularity came to the King swiftly, by many hidden channels. Too, Crassmor remembered that he'd seen something in the Pattern, an implied connection between the Knights of Onn and danger to the Tapestry. Small wonder, then, that Ironwicca had commanded Jaan-Marl to issue a general recall and keep his men at Gateshield. There it would be easier to monitor things. Even so, events had eluded the King's control.

In a moment Ironwicca had dismounted, drawing the gist of the situation from Combard, Jaan-Marl, and Crassmor. When the King took Crassmor aside alone, Combard and the Grand Master were surprised, but conspicuous in turning their attention to other matters, obedient and unquestioning. After receiving a warning glance, Furd did the same. The abbot spoke to his brother, and Crassmor could see that they were as warm to each other as ever.

Crassmor explained things to Ironwicca as simply as he could, in a low voice.

"I have seen that eye-in-pyramid before," the King told him at length. "This is not all of them, you know; they are in many Realities. Even some in the Singularity will have the means to evade the crown's justice." He paused for a glance at Furd, who was unaware of it. "Or do you think I should test their power?"

Crassmor hesitated. "Tell me what you think," Ironwicca ordered, not harshly. The knight told him then of the two letters. The King nodded to himself as he listened.

"Scant evidence," the King decided, "and it wouldn't surprise me if Furd has found a way to destroy his own note already. Accusations would only do damage to you and Willow. I'll let Furd be for now. I am content with the outcome today; your uncle and I will contest again. These things that you've told me I shall protect as royal privy testimony. Not even Combard or the Grand Master will be able to question you about what's happened, or how."

Crassmor was quick to thank him. Ironwicca told the knight, "I am aware of many things the Pattern predicts. I think you would make a good father to the next weaver."

He chuckled as, leaving Crassmor dumbfounded, he went off to commend the Lost Boys for their valor.

Then the knight was distracted as milling armsmen made a path for Willow. Bint had been to one side, arranging for a keg of ale for the Skiver/Newsham's return trip. He saw how Crassmor's heart soared when he spied Willow; her own look showed nothing less. Bint abruptly understood; thinking of the failure of his own courtly romance with Arananth, he felt, in the kindliest sense, stirrings of envy.

Willow looked small and fragile among the ironclads. Combard went to her, slipping a fatherly arm around her. It took all of Crassmor's willpower not to dash to her. Combard caught the look passing between the two, though. They both saw his temper rise. "There are gaps in the ranks of those who ride in the Beyonds," he told Willow, but he was glaring at his son. "All the more will each man be needed out there who has experience." Crassmor knew with a sinking heart that his assignment hadn't changed. Another sojourn there awaited.

Bint put in, "That shortage is one man less than you think, uncle." He had his hand on the hilt of the ornate sword of Tarafon Quickhand. "Sir Bosrow Feng fell saving me; I ride out in his place." He grinned at Crassmor's disbelief. "There are worse things to do in life."

*Not any that you could learn from me!* Crassmor mused.

Jaan-Marl had come up. "Time enough for all wounds to heal first, Sir Bint. The Lost Boys will not resist a convalescent leave here at home, eh?" He took Combard's arm. "The King wishes to speak to us both; we must arrange temporary security for House Comullo. The Tapestry's secret is secret no longer, it seems."

The Grand Master said merrily to Willow then, "Bid farewell to peace and quiet; this will become a busy, guarded place." Willow sighed.

Combard had no choice but to let himself be led away, yielding his hold on Willow. Furd kept well up with the two old warriors, an ear cocked to listen. With a last stern glance, Combard told his son, "I shall except you at my side when I ride for House Tarrant."

Knights of Onn were being organized and assigned to posts. Fordall Urth and his men were being borne inside House Comullo. The Lost Boys bounced away on the firewagon; a glorious wake of dust, roars, and song was left behind them. Bint was driving. In moments, Crassmor and Willow were alone.

"He is still adamant," the knight said, watching his father go off with Ironwicca, Furd, and Jaan-Marl.

"Perhaps less so," Willow ventured, taking his hand.

"Another tour in the Beyonds for me," he said bitterly. "Another parting for us. I am filled with fear, Willow, that the Pattern will fail us."

She ran a hand through the black-dyed hair. "It will not, it must not. Fear is only one of the passions, and you are filled with those."

## Epilogue

# HOPEFUL

**Crassmor and the** Cherokee Kid, whose name was actually something else, were seated on a bench near the table where Alanna had sat on another night. Bill, the tavernkeep who had once been Tsoora-Rin-Voor, drew two more drinks behind the bar as Toe Hold winds howled outside. Bill's trunk was now nearly completely a nose, albeit a large one. His tusks were all but gone, but he retained an elephantine look.

The Kid was twirling a loop of white lariat around and around himself and Crassmor, making it look easy. Crassmor took one more sip of his stout and watched the lasso blur.

On the wall was a handbill:

TEXAS JACK'S CIRCUS
the
CHEROKEE KID
the world's
CHAMPION LASSOER

Texas Jack's show had come upon hard times there in the Beyonds, and so the Kid was at liberty. Crassmor was standing the drinks. The Kid was dressed in a cowboy suit of red velvet and gold trim, complete with chaps. Crassmor wore a new pourpoint jacket in purple and white and hose in gleaming russet, with new shoes of soft green leather.

Bill had carried a somewhat groggy Bint upstairs to bed a short time earlier. It had been a delightful evening, and Crassmor was well satisfied with the festivities.

Now the Cherokee Kid grinned and worked his wrist. The rope sang and spun. The Kid could throw three ropes at a time, jump back and forth through a spinning loop, or loft one with the toe of his silver-and-turquoise-tipped cowboy boot. Crassmor suspected that the lariats were sentient.

His stout finished, Crassmor threw his flagon into the air without warning. The rope—"small, light, hard twist," the Kid had called it—went up as the flagon lofted toward the high ceiling. A moment later, the Kid had the flagon in hand. He was a friendly young fellow with a sharp, deadpan, folksy wit. He had a broad, shy grin, a winning manner, and a cowlick much like Crane's. He'd just won a bet.

Crassmor clapped his hands in amusement, laughed, and passed over two brass chips. The Kid in turn threw them through the air to Bill, buying the next round.

"It never even came *close* to the ceiling," Crassmor remarked with admiration. "I've never seen its like."

The Kid laughed modestly, rubbing a sunburned nose with his forefinger. He shrugged. "I only know what I read in the papers," he drawled.

Crassmor had an admonition in mind against too much self-deprecation. Before he could voice it, the first roar sounded from outside.

There were more shouts directly thereafter, coming closer quickly. They were ferocious and issued, so it sounded, by lungs of great power. Crassmor heard the outer door pulled open. All eyes went to the inner door of the place. Crassmor felt a sinking feeling begin in his midsection. Before he could gather his wits sufficiently to absent himself from the premises, the door banged open and the girl rushed in.

"Oh, no!" Crassmor nearly wept.

She was young and gorgeous and terrified, rather tall, with ringlets of auburn hair that fell nearly to her waist. Her eyes were large and impossibly clear-blue; her mobile, subtle, and eloquent mouth was pursed as she panted for breath. She wore a body suit like gunmetal, clinging to her every curve, with a shimmering golden cloak. The body suit was rent in two places; she had minor wounds. On her brow was a headdress carved from coral, a fantastic thing of spikes and swirls.

She spied Sir Crassmor just as ponderous footsteps made the entranceway shake. She cried, "By your station and the vows—"

She got no further, though Crassmor had already wailed and dropped his head onto his folded arms as the Cherokee Kid looked on sympathetically. Into the tavern burst a creature something like a human being.

He wore what looked to be several hundredsweight of armor, forged in a bizarre, rococo style. His helmet left his low-browed, brutish face exposed. His skin was a dead gray, and his yellow fangs protruded several inches from his lip. He was a head and more taller than Crassmor. He saw the girl.

"Save me, Sir Knight!" she screamed, dodging away from the newcomer. The creature hadn't missed seeing to whom the entreaty was addressed. He attacked like a locomotive, raising a weapon that resembled a ball-headed mace armed with twin axe blades. Its shaft was the size of a lamppost.

The Cherokee Kid had the sense to dive off to one side. As the weapon descended, Crassmor made a sound very much like *Eeep!* and dived the other way. The axe blade passed through the thick planks of the bench with little resistance, to bury itself in the floor. The attacker yanked it free with no apparent strain, leaving a two-foot-long cleft in the wood.

Crassmor, arms folded close to his chest, rolled and rolled. The creature, blade held high, came after, ready to cleave. Crassmor gulped and thought of Willow . . .

A circlet of small, light, hard twist settled over the axe-mace's head at the top of its backswing. The Cherokee Kid dug in and hauled at the line. The swing was of such raw power that he was yanked forward, the rowels of his spurs cutting the floor, his chaps rasping as he was dragged along. The Kid had professed never to have met a man he didn't like, but that plainly did not apply to the newcomer. Crassmor just did manage to scramble aside, and the blow missed.

The monstrous attacker turned angrily on the source of his annoyance. The Cherokee Kid demonstrated good judgment yet again, abandoning the lasso and scuttling for safety. The creature turned back to Crassmor, who'd fetched up against a wooden pillar. Crassmor threw himself flat once more; the axe flashed in a horizontal arc, parting the pillar.

But such an enormous weapon demanded a considerable recovery, even from the creature who wielded it now. Crassmor was up, drawing *Shhing,* as he vaulted a table and wondered which exit he should use. The interloper howled angrily.

Crassmor's sword was between the two now; glittering feints and thrusts partitioned the air. The outlandish attacker, for all his size and strength, became more cautious. He seemed to remember the girl just when Crassmor did.

She was cringing against the bar; Bill had ducked behind it, and Crassmor could hear the tavernkeep rummaging around back there. The huge warrior advanced on her, to slay her before finishing with the knight. The floor planks creaked under his weight; the girl shrank back and closed her eyes, preparing to die.

But a hand closed on her forearm. She was pulled up and out of the way as the axe blade split a considerable portion of the bar. Her auburn hair stood out from her as she was whirled, a pirouette of golden cloak and gleaming body suit, behind the man who'd just entered the battle.

Bint held up Tarafon Quickhand's ornate sword. His hair was tousled from sleep; he wore only his midnight-black hose. The monster snarled, his fangs protruding, his hairline meeting the bridge of his nose. The girl cowered behind Bint, her long fingers digging at the muscles of his arm.

Crassmor skipped around a table to stand on the intruder's off side. Taking turns chipping away appeared to be the best plan. The brute still seemed inclined to finish the girl. Crassmor prepared to go for his armpit.

"Here, here! Settle down, now!" It was Bill, who'd once

been a god. He was peering through the sights of a large metal weapon that resembled a length of stovepipe, balancing it on his shoulder. The formerly divine index finger poised on an electric trigger.

The would-be assassin might not have understood exactly what the weapon was, but he didn't miss the absolute certainty in Bill's voice, a habit of command remaining to him from his days as a deity. The creature growled, shook his great axe-mace, and fled, making the building tremble as he pounded back out of the tavern.

Bill lowered the bazooka. "It was left here by a chap who passed through," he explained. "Fortunate it is that the creature did not press me; the weapon is empty."

The Cherokee Kid eased out from behind a table, lowering the stool he'd been about to throw. Bint had the sobbing girl in his arms now. She clung to him, face pressed to his broad, bare chest. Bill looked to Crassmor, as did the Kid. Bint's gaze also sought his cousin.

In a few moments the girl's tears stopped. She glanced up at Bint, then her eyes went to Crassmor.

He lowered himself onto a bench, recognizing the situation. "I wonder if you'd be so kind as to pack us a lunch, Bill?" the Reluctant Knight asked.

# — ABOUT THE AUTHOR —

Brian Daley was born in rural New Jersey in 1947 and currently lives at no fixed address. After an army hitch and the usual odd jobs, he enrolled in college, where he began his first novel. His is the author of *The Doomfarers of Coramonde* and *The Starfollowers of Coramonde,* as well as the Han Solo trilogy. Mr. Daley also scripted the thirteen-episode National Public Radio adaptation of *Star Wars.*